Ex
Libris

Romance
Treasury

Romance Treasury

The Romance Treasury
Association

New York·Toronto·London

These stories were originally published as follows:

THE MOUNTAIN OF STARS

Copyright © 1956 by Catherine Airlie
First published in London by Mills & Boon Limited in 1956

THE EMERALD CUCKOO

Copyright © 1970 by Gwen Westwood
First published in London by Mills & Boon Limited in 1970

A NIGHT FOR POSSUMS

Copyright © 1971 by Dorothy Cork
First published in London by Mills & Boon Limited in 1971

ROMANCE TREASURY is published by:
The Romance Treasury Association, Stratford, Ontario, Canada

Editorial Board: A. W. Boon, Judith Burgess, Ruth Palmour and Janet Humphreys

Dust Jacket Art by Don Besco
Story Illustrations by Gordon Rayner
Book Design by Harold Boyd
Printed by Richardson, Bond & Wright, Limited, Owen Sound, Ontario

ISBN 0-919860-10-9

Printed in Canada   AO11

CONTENTS

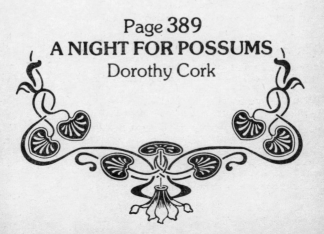

THE MOUNTAIN OF STARS

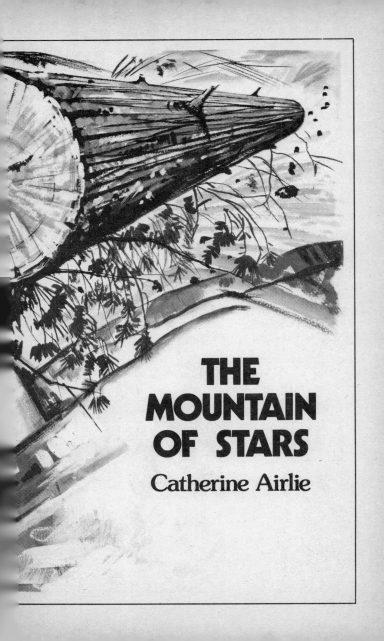

THE
MOUNTAIN
OF STARS

Catherine Airlie

"Does Thor govern your heart too, Meg?"
Eric demanded. "Because if that is so, you will
soon learn what unhappiness means!"

Despite Thor's brooding aloofness, Meg had
to admit he held a strange power over her. He
was the man she wanted — even if it meant
marrying for security instead of love.

Meg only hoped she could make her home in
this land of mountains and fjords and accept
the reality that she could never compete
with a ghost.

CHAPTER ONE

WHEN Margaret Holden sailed for Bergen that bright August afternoon she imagined that she was prepared for Norway.

"Tell me about it!" she had demanded as a child, and her father filled her mind and heart with tales of the land he had loved.

Twice he had gone to Norway to bring back a bride, although his second marriage had lasted no longer than a year.

Turning from the ship's rail, Margaret looked looked down at her stepmother.

"How eager you are, *vesla*!" Eide Holden smiled. "It is as if you could not wait to get there!" She had never lost the soft, lilting Sogne accent which she had brought with her across the North Sea, and if she had known hardship in her adopted country after her husband had died, she had never complained. Faithful to his trust in her, she had carried out his last wish that his daughter by his first marriage should finish her education in England. "It has been a long-promised journey," she added gently, her eyes going wistfully to the distant horizon, "but it will have been worth the waiting once we get there!"

How true that was, Margaret thought.

"It's like something in a dream," she said, her blue eyes going back to the sea. "Something you want to hold on to but which might elude you if you try too hard."

Eide laughed.

"You are one of us!" she smiled. "Norway will claim you as her own."

Margaret looked thoughtful, turning back from the rail.

"It seems—more than generous of your people to accept me," she said.

"You must not worry about that," Eide declared. "It is all arranged. When I wrote to Helmsdal I had

no hesitation about including you, and Thor would
be only too willing to extend the invitation."

She had managed to keep hesitation out of her
voice, but Margaret, quick to respond to every shade
of emotion in the woman she knew so well, saw the
shadow of doubt for a fleeting moment in her stepmother's eyes. In that instant a small harsh fear,
which was to deepen to certainty before a week had
passed, entered her heart.

Thor Revold was no more than a name to her,
but he suggested power and wealth and a certain
ruthlessness, at which Eide had no more than hinted.

"Thor has had a hard life," her stepmother added,
almost in defence of her nephew. "His mother, who
was my sister, died when he was no more than fourteen years of age. Thor was always an impressionable
boy, sensitive to a degree which it might be difficult
to understand unless you knew him."

"What age is he now?" Margaret asked.

"Thirty." Eide made a rapid re-calculation.
"Yes, he must be thirty," she agreed. "How swiftly
the years go past—and he might have been my own
son!"

Surprised, Margaret looked down at her.

"It is a long story," Eide smiled. "An old story
now. Thor's father was my first love, but he married
my sister. I thought that I would never marry at
all." Her smile deepened, edged a little with sadness.
"And then I met your father when he was on a visit
to Norway on business and had one perfect, wonderful year as his wife. It doesn't seem long in a lifetime,
but it held so much."

Margaret knew how true that was. In spite of her
own youth she had recognized the glow of perfect
happiness which had surrounded Eide and her father,
brightening the home they had made for her and
softening the blow of her father's untimely death
when it fell so unexpectedly.

"I'm glad," she told her stepmother. "I'm glad
my father made you happy."

"It is the most important thing," Eide said. "When we can look back on happiness life can never be really empty."

Margaret's thoughts wandered back to Thor Revold and their destination. She knew so little about him, apart from the fact that he was now the head of the family, an important position bound up with the ties of tradition which had passed from father to son through several generations, and never so strong as in the hidden and secret valleys between the silent fjords of the West Country. Thor was the pivot upon which the whole Revold family turned, and Eide was his responsibility because she was his mother's sister.

"Eide," Margaret asked, aware that she had never thought about the possibility, "is Thor Revold married? Has he a family of his own?"

For a split second her stepmother hesitated.

"No," she said at last. "No, he never married."

Her reply had held reserve and it disturbed Margaret, although there was no reason why it should.

"Will he be at Bergen to meet us?" she asked.

"I expect so. At Bergen, to be sure!" There was a deep ring of joy in Eide's pleasant voice and her eyes took on a new light of anticipation to replace the longing which Margaret had so often surprised in them as her stepmother had looked out across the grey North Sea towards the hidden land of her birth. "Bergen is a place of meetings. Your father and I used to think of it as a place of so much happiness— the gateway to our love." Her voice softened, dropping to a whisper. "We planned to return like this— together."

Margaret left her to her memories, turning back to the rail to look out across the grey-blue water to the faint blur of islands on the horizon. For the past hour she had thought of her father as journeying with them, his Viking ship afloat on a wider sea, perhaps, but his spirit beside them, and suddenly Norway became real, vibrant, alive for her also, the land destined to hold so much for her in the future.

Slowly, even as she looked, it took shape, island upon island riding the waves like phantom galleons drawing out of the mist and haze of ages until they formed a definite pattern against the land. They were magic islands dotted with little white wooden chalets flying the Norwegian flag, each with its own boat-house and an air of independence which stirred something deep in her heart. She saw it as a quiet, mediaeval land, unexploited by sophisticated man, remaining very much as it was when its inhabitants worshipped Odin and Thor.

Thor! she thought. Thor! The name had persisted down through the centuries—unchanged.

"Look!" Eide said, coming to stand beside her. "There's Marstein Fyr. I always think when we see the lighthouse we are almost there!"

The ship nosed its way in among the islands. The land was very near, almost near enough to touch, and suddenly it seemed to Margaret that her stepmother wanted to do just that. To set foot on her native land—once more.

A hard, gripping fear seized her by the throat as she looked round at the small figure standing beside her. This past year of illness and intermittent pain had stolen the fresh colour from Eide Holden's cheeks, and at times there was a suggestion of strain and a transparency about her which could not be overlooked. She had made the effort to come on this journey with tremendous zest, however, and the family doctor in England had said that, with care, she might live for years.

Margaret thrust the persistent little worry to the back of her mind, allowing it to be filled by thoughts of the future.

"When we reach Helmsdal I must find something to do," she suggested. "A year is a long time to be idle."

Eide smiled.

"There is always plenty to do in Norway," she said, "if you can be content without the bright lights. A year will soon pass. They have a way of passing swiftly, especially as we grow older, or when we are very happy. Take your year, Margaret. You have earned it. A rest will do you good."

A year, Margaret thought, and then what? She realized that her stepmother was not looking beyond that year. She was prepared to live it, day by day, in peace.

Her eyes sought the Norwegian coastline. They were sailing close between the mainland and a long green island, with the red roofs of Bergen glittering in the sunshine ahead of them. There had been a swift shower of rain as they had turned into the Sound, but it had dispersed as quickly as it had come, leaving a smiling city to greet them.

Eide stood pointing out landmarks to her as the ship edged in towards the quay, but for Margaret there was only the general impression of a lovely old town kneeling beside the sea and ringed about by dark and mysterious mountains which shouldered each other to the distant skyline. Beyond, there were more mountains, range upon range of them, interlaced by still, dark fjords, and somewhere deep in their silent heart lay Helmsdal, which was to be their home for the next twelve months.

"I'll go and see about getting the luggage brought up," she offered almost reluctantly. "Don't bother to come, Eide. People will be milling about all over the place. You'll be better up here on deck."

"Yes," her stepmother agreed with her eyes still on the mountains, "I'll wait here."

Margaret went down to the cabin, giving the luggage a last check over as the ship docked. Everything seemed to be in order, and she turned eagerly to the companionway to go back on deck as the bells from the bridge signalled their mooring instructions to the engineers down below.

Most of the passengers were jamming the entrance to the forward lounge, and she hurried towards the sun-deck with a sense of relief. Then, with a swift intake of breath, she realized that something was wrong. A small group of people had gathered in the corner where she had left her stepmother, and a tall man in a broad-brimmed hat was pressing them back, kindly but firmly. He spoke in Norwegian, so that she could not understand what he was saying, but instinctively she knew that it concerned Eide.

White-faced, she pressed in at the edge of the crowd.

"Will you let me pass, please?" she begged.

The tall stranger turned towards her.

"You are with this lady?" he asked, speaking English with a slight American accent although, somehow, she knew that he was Norwegian. "She is in your charge?"

"Yes, we are together. She is my stepmother." The fear was strong in Margaret's heart again as she pushed through the crowd and stood looking down on Eide's still, blanched face. "How could—anything like this have happened so quickly?" she whispered.

The tall man took her by the arm, steadying her. He had a warm, friendly voice, infinitely soothing in its pity.

"You are not to worry," he told her. "A little too much excitement, that is all. I am a doctor," he added briefly. "She has had a slight stroke. It is nothing more than a warning."

Margaret knelt on the deck and took her stepmother's unresponsive hand between both her own, chafing the cold fingers with a gentle, persuasive movement which seemed to bring a little response, although Eide did not open her eyes.

"You are being met?" the doctor enquired.

"Yes—yes, I think so." Suddenly it seemed imperative that Thor Revold should be there on the quayside to claim them. "We are going on to Helmsdal."

"In Sognefjorden?" He looked surprised, shaking his head after a moment or two's consideration. "That is too great a journey to attempt now. At least, not for a day or two."

Margaret stared at him in bewilderment. She felt completely at a loss; she had left most of the arrangements for this trip to her stepmother, never dreaming that she might have to step into the breach like this.

"I have no idea how far Helmsdal is," she confessed. "It all sounds so terribly remote now," she added, meeting the shrewd blue eyes above her that seemed to have taken in her situation at a glance. "I—don't know what to do."

"You must let me manage this for you, at least till you are met on the quay," the tall man said. "My name is Loren—Paul Loren. I have been in England to a conference, but I am going on holiday now, into the mountains. To fish," he added, and suddenly the irrelevant little detail banished the first paralysing shreds of fear which had held her in their grip.

"You're very kind," Margaret said. She was to say it again, months later, when her heart was numb with pain, a deeper, more searing pain even than the pain of death.

Eide had stirred, her blue eyes opening to the blue of the sky above her head. She sighed a little, and smiled, and tried to move, but Paul Loren bent and pressed her back into the low-slung deck-chair.

"We've moored," he said. "We're alongside." His eyes were full of wisdom and pity. "Soon you will go ashore. You have come on a visit home?"

"Yes," Eide answered. "I've come—home."

The other passengers were beginning to file down the steep gangway on to the quayside, and the ship's doctor came to see what arrangements he could make to take Eide ashore with the minimum of exertion.

For one agonizing moment Margaret thought that Paul Loren was about to leave them, handing them over to his colleague aboard ship, whose responsibility she supposed they really were, but when he had walked to the head of gangway to arrange about his own luggage going ashore he came back along the deck to where they were waiting.

"I'll see about a *drosje*," he offered, "if you will have your luggage collected. I have a reservation at the Hotel Norge, which you can have," he added thoughtfully, "but I feel that your stepmother would be better in hospital for tonight, at least."

Tears stung at the back of Margaret's eyes. Eide's glorious adventure had fallen to pieces, shattered by an old heart complaint, and she felt curiously helpless and inexperienced as she contemplated her own lack of initiative. But for this stranger, she would not have known what to do.

Gratefully she turned towards him, noticing for the first time how tall he was, even in this land of tall, fair men.

"I shall never be able to repay you, Doctor Loren," she confessed awkwardly. "You see, I've never been to Norway before, although both my mother and my stepmother were born here in Bergen. I know only a few words of the language, so that— it might have been a very difficult situation for me."

"Someone would have helped you, never fear!" Paul Loren said kindly. "There is always someone there in an emergency." He looked down at her with a friendly smile. "You said that you expected to be met," he reminded her. "Had we better try to find your friend?"

Thor Revold! Margaret had forgotten him for a moment. Was he waiting down on the quayside, impatiently, perhaps, wondering why they had not filed down the gangway with the other passengers?

"If you give me his name," Loren suggested, "I can have an intimation made over the loud-speakers. The custom sheds are busy and he may have gone there to find you."

"His name is Thor Revold," Margaret explained and saw his fair brows draw together in a swift frown. "Do you know him?"

"I have met him," Paul admitted. "We have been in the same hunting party together. Thor Revold is the richest man in all Helmsdal. I cannot say that he is the happiest."

The stirring in her heart that was almost a premonition of disaster held Margaret silent for a moment.

"It's kind of you to try to find him for me," she said at last, feeling that he had been more than kind to someone who was, after all, a stranger to him.

Five minutes later she heard the voice over the loud-speakers communicating his request from the ship to the quayside, but she could not understand what was said. A word here and there was familiar because she had heard Eide use it, but she had never mastered her mother's tongue to any advantage, a neglect which she deeply regretted now.

Stray passengers were still filing down the gangway, and presently a tall young man in a red knitted cap came to stand at the foot of it, looking up at the ship.

To Margaret, in that moment when responsibility had been thrust heavily upon her shoulders for the first time, he looked the very personification of youth, and as their eyes met she all but smiled. She watched him climb the gangway and disappear when he reached the deck, going swiftly towards the purser's office below.

Almost immediately, however, he reappeared, with the purser and the ship's surgeon in attendance. The little group came swiftly towards her, yet, even in that moment of surprise, Margaret knew that this could not be Thor Revold. He had sent a deputy to meet them.

The young man's eyes were very blue but they were graver now.

"I'm Erik Borge," he introduced himself. "I'm sorry to hear of your trouble. Thor sent me to bring you to the railhead at Voss and through to Helmsdal by car."

Borge? The name meant nothing to her, Margaret realized, and yet she seemed to remember that there was some connection between Thor Revold and the Borges. How foolish she had been not to ask Eide more about their future host and his way of life! She had contented herself with the fact that he was apparently willing enough to have them at Helmsdal because it had once been Eide's home.

"My stepmother was taken ill so suddenly," she explained as the surgeon and the ship's nurse bent over the small huddled figure in the deck-chair.

"It is very unfortunate," Erik Borge commiserated, while he seemed to be thinking of something else. "It is not thought wise to continue our journey at once. Doctor Loren wishes Mrs. Holden to rest in Bergen for a day or two."

Eide was being moved towards the gangway, wrapped in rugs on a narrow stretcher. Her eyes were closed and she looked distressingly pale and thin, so that Margaret's heart caught in pity and a new, strange anguish. How happily and with what carefree pleasure they had discussed this moment less than twenty four hours ago, the moment when they would set foot on Norwegian soil!

Her lips trembled as she followed the little procession down the gangway and unobtrusively, kindly, Paul Loren took her arm.

"You are not to worry," he said again. "Leave everything to me. Erik Borge will take you directly to the Hotel Norge and I will go with your stepmother to the hospital."

Standing on the almost deserted quay, Margaret shook her head.

"Please don't ask me to leave her," she begged. "This is her own country, but when she regains consciousness she will want to have someone she she knows near her. We have never been apart since I left school, and I have nursed her before."

Paul Loren looked down at her, thinking how young she was, how utterly unprepared for life in spite of her grave reassurances to the contrary. He did not tell her that her stepmother might not recover consciousness again for many hours, if indeed she recovered at all, and he found himself wondering, as he signalled for a taxi, what would become of her if his first professional summing-up of the situation should prove correct.

He did not argue against her decision to come to the hospital. When the ambulance he had phoned for came swiftly along the quay he saw his patient settled inside and joined Erik Borge and Margaret in the *drosje*.

They drove swiftly along the quayside, the drumming of the *drosje's* tyres on the uneven stones beating a numbing tattoo in Margaret's brain. She could not think clearly and she did not hear what Paul Loren had to say, except when he spoke about Eide.

When they reached the hospital she was left alone in a waiting-room with Erik Borge. It was a bright room, painted in blues and clear grey, with splashes of yellow here and there, like sunlight, but her mind refused to accept its suggestion of warmth or, in fact, any comfort.

Her companion stood with his back to her, staring out of the window, obviously finding it difficult to offer sympathy and understanding in the right words, yet he had already made her feel that he was genuinely sorry.

"Should we try to get in touch with Helmsdal?" she asked at last.

"I was thinking about that." He turned from the window. "Thor will be expecting us, and now his plans will be upset. Thor does not like his plans to be upset."

Margaret drew in a swift breath.

"But surely," she protested, "it will be all right once he knows. This is an emergency. Nobody could put his own plans before a—a matter of life and death."

"Oh, yes," he agreed instantly, "it will be all right when Thor knows. I was going to say that I must tell him why we have been delayed."

For a moment she was conscious of resentment, swift and fierce and deeply-penetrating. Who was this demi-god who sat up there in his mountain stronghold, "the richest man in all Helmsdal", demanding their servile attention in any emergency? Something leashed and protesting in the tall young giant standing at the other side of the room had communicated itself to her even in their short acquaintance of an hour, and she was seeing Thor Revold through the eyes of a third party who gave his allegiance to the older man with reluctance.

"Do you live in Helmsdal?" she asked.

"Part of the year." Erik shrugged his lean shoulders. "I am forced to do so because Thor is my guardian." He had sought for the correct English word, but Margaret thought that he might just as well have said "captor". "For the other months," he added, "I study in Oslo. I am at the University there."

"You like it?" she asked, seeing him with part of her mind only. The other part was with Eide, wondering why Paul Loren was so long a time in returning to them with the news she was waiting for.

"I like Oslo," Erik answered. "I like being there."

"Is it like Bergen?" she asked, conscious of trying to make conversation lest the lengthening silence in the corridor should crush the hope in her heart.

"Not in the least!" Her companion laughed, white teeth flashing, eyes intensely blue and full of light. "They are two entirely different cities. Bergen is quite dead."

"What I have seen of it looks charming," Margaret told him. "The mountains are lovely."

"You will see enough of the mountains when you reach Helmsdal," he warned. "They will close you in—entomb you."

She looked taken aback. There had been a passionate intensity in his voice which she would not have expected in anyone who looked so carefree as he did. Her first impression of him, she remembered, had been one of exuberant youth. What was it, then, which made him feel incarcerated in Thor Revold's mountains?

There was no hope of an answer to that question, she supposed, until they got there, and perhaps the smouldering resentment in her companion's blue eyes was nothing more than the passing shadow of a fancied injustice.

She looked at him almost for the first time, seeing the height of his loosely-knit frame as something to be expected in this land of fair young giants with the proud heads of ancient gods and the blue eyes of their

Viking forbears which seemed eternally fixed on some distant seascape. Erik Borge was at once handsome and unformed; his youth made him vulnerable and his passionate hatred of Helmsdal burned in him like a fire.

She was not to know until long afterwards that he was scarcely representative of his race. His mother had been a Spanish girl who had fallen in love with a sailor fifteen years her senior and come lightheartedly with him to the land of eternal snow, to regret her impulsive bargain almost as soon as she landed there. She had borne Edvard Borge three children and died at the birth of the third, thwarted and embittered by the fact that her husband had been the son of a small farmer instead of the heir to the large and prosperous estate which she had fondly imagined when he had spoken with such unconscious pride of his home in Norway.

Margaret forgot Thor and Erik immediately, however, when Paul Loren came back into the room. His face was grave.

"You have bad news for me?" she asked in a voice which rose no higher than a whisper.

"We are doing what we can for her," he comforted, putting a steady hand on her arm. "I want you to go now to the hotel. There is nothing you can do here at present. As soon as your stepmother regains consciousness, I will come for you and bring you back. It is not far."

She wanted to protest, to argue against going, but he was leading her gently but firmly towards the door.

"If only I could be with her——"

"You will come back before nightfall," he told her kindly, "I want you to rest, and you could unpack her case and bring a few of her own clothes to the hospital."

She knew that he was merely finding her something to do, and she felt vulnerably young and inadequate of a sudden, although she had nursed her stepmother for the past year with what the local doctor in England had called "exemplary patience".

She had never stopped to wonder if she had been patient, or how much she was missing of the things youth took for granted. She had given her services willingly, as Eide herself had done in the past.

Erik Borge followed them into the foyer.

"You will see that she gets to the hotel?" Loren asked. "I don't know what your plans are," he added briefly, "but I think you should telephone Helmsdal and let Revold know what has happened."

"I must do that right away," Erik agreed, letting Margaret walk on a little way ahead before he asked: "How long would you say we would have to remain here?"

Paul looked him directly in the eyes.

"Not very long," he said.

Margaret turned to Erik. In some strange way his youth was reassuring.

"If there was anything else you wanted to do," she suggested, "I could find my own way to the hotel."

"The only thing I have to do is to phone Thor," he answered. "The only important thing."

The *drosje* which Paul Loren had ordered drew up at the foot of the hospital steps. "I will send for you immediately there is any change," he promised, bending to the window when he had helped her in.

Margaret sat back against the cool leather cushioning, trying to relax, trying to force her mind away from the fear of disaster, but the very fact that she and Eide were now seperated shook her courage as nothing else could have done. They had always been close companions, more like sisters than stepmother and stepdaughter, and now the gulf which divided them seemed very wide indeed.

In spite of all the kindness she had met with, she was still a stranger in a strange land, an inexperienced stranger whose courage had begun to ebb a little because she felt that she could not look into the future with any certainty.

They reached the Hotel Norge and once again Paul Loren had made everything easy for her. The room he had booked for the night was at her disposal and the manager showed her up personally, hoping, in the kindest way, that she would soon hear good news from the hospital.

In spite of their kindness, however, it was all so terribly impersonal. Margaret felt the need for Eide as never before, and she almost wept when she was left alone at last. In the next instant, however, she was forcing herself to activity, unpacking her own hand luggage and laying aside the few personal articles she would take back to the hospital for Eide's greater comfort.

Wondering if she would see Paul Loren again, she felt that she had not yet thanked him sufficiently, and then she remembered that he had promised to send for her as soon as Eide regained consciousness.

There was comfort in the thought, although she could not bring herself to obey him and rest. Sitting down on the edge of the bed, she changed her shoes, gave herself a quick wash, and went downstairs again.

Erik Borge was there, waiting for her in the lounge.

"I have phoned Helmsdal, but Thor had already set out to meet us," he explained. "The only thing I could do after that was to send a message to Sogndalsfjord to try to catch him there before he boarded the ferry. If he had already crossed the fjord, they will contact him at Voss."

"That was as far as he meant to come," Margaret remembered vaguely. "Is it a very long way?"

"Not really," Erik shrugged. "But this is Thor's busiest time. There is much work to be done on the *saetre* with all the winter fodder for the animals to be stocked and the timber to be brought down from the high valleys."

Dismay smote Margaret like a douche of cold water flung in her face. Were they really going to be made welcome in this strange, hidden dale among these alien mountains? Thor Revold's welcome seemed almost half-hearted now, a thing of proxy, yet could she really have expected a busy farmer to drop everything and come rushing across fjord and valley to meet them?

"I wish we had arranged to come at some other time, or at least to complete our journey alone," she said, and then, remembering how ungrateful that must sound, she added warmly: "I shouldn't have said that. You have come a long way to meet us."

"In Norway we do not worry about distances," Erik assured her. "All distances are great and I am always most willing to leave Thor's mountains." He made a rueful face, smiling down at her as he added: "You consider me ungrateful, huh?"

Margaret could not resist an answering smile.

"I'm not in a position to judge," she told him, wondering if he would understand her meaning, but apparently his command of English was quite equal to the occasion.

"Wait till you have met Thor and seen Helmsdal," he advised. "I cannot imagine that there is one place in England to compare with it!"

"Yet Eide loved it," Margaret mused aloud. "She wanted so much to go back."

"Perhaps I am giving you a wrong impression of your future home. I'm sorry. I must let you decide these things for yourself."

Erik had spoken abruptly, and he was steering her towards the *spisestue*, where the tables were already set for dinner, as if that put an end to all argument.

This elastic main meal of the day would have surprised Margaret in other circumstances, but she had lost all track of time during the past few hours. She could not have said whether it was two o'clock or ten. The light in the sky had not faded and it might have been minutes or hours since they had left the ship.

Or years! An age in time seemed to have passed in which her anxious heart had been tortured by the fear and pain of loss, and she could only make a pretence at eating when they sat down. The lavish cold table to which she was to become accustomed held no attraction for her, and Erik seemed to sense her distress at last, suggesting that they might walk slowly through the streets to the hospital.

Bergen seemed to be deserted. Save for a few elderly people sitting on the benches in the square through which they passed, the streets were empty. The sun still shone and the sky was blue, but Margaret knew that it was getting late.

"I shall wait for you out here," Erik said when they reached the hospital steps. He looked tense and uneasy, but he had also been very kind, Margaret remembered. "It is not good to trouble these people too much."

"I hope I'm not doing that," she said unsteadily, and almost immediately she saw Paul Loren coming from the foyer to meet them.

"I had sent to the hotel," he said. "You are just in time."

CHAPTER TWO

THAT night Eide Holden died in the little hospital at the edge of the fjord while Thor Revold sped across the mountains to meet them.

Margaret could never remember in strictest detail her first meeting with Thor. She saw a tall man whose dark face and darker hair made him look strangely alien in his own country; certainly a man alien to city streets. His clothes were of the country, and when he walked he strode. His large, thickly-set body seemed to take up all the space in the little waiting-room where she had been sitting for the past half-hour trying to realize that Eide was dead and she was alone in a strange land. He had none of Paul Loren's gentleness of approach. Of that she was completely sure. He was the man of action, not of words, a man accustomed to be obeyed.

She felt exhausted, beaten down by emotion and the swift tragedy of events, yet she was aware of a power about this man which might amount to ruthlessness but which would get things done. And she leant on that power. Her courage—which had sustained her during the hours when she sat beside Eide watching the peculiar lightening of a sky which had only known a grey twilight throughout the night —ebbed before his obvious assurance, and she waited for him to make her decisions for her.

"You're tired," he said almost brusquely. "You must get some sleep. We will be forced to stay here for some days," he added. "There will be formalities about my aunt's death which I shall have to deal with before I can return to Helmsdal."

His English was faultless, with only the barest trace of hesitation before a word which eluded him for a moment.

Responsibility had crowded in upon Thor Revold at an early age, and the man who stood before her now would accept responsibility as a matter of course.

The knowledge of her own position assailed her with shattering clarity. At least for the next few days she would be completely dependent upon Thor.

She tried not to read impatience in his dark face or the hint of it in his brusque manner as he stood back from the doorway to let her pass.

"Paul Loren mentioned that he has made provision for you at the Norge," he said, leading the way to a *drosje* standing at the foot of the hospital steps. "That seems to be the best arrangement for the present."

"Doctor Loren has been more than kind," Margaret managed to say without her voice quivering. "We met on the *Asta*. He was coming over from England from a medical conference."

Her companion's face seemed to harden and the blue eyes became remote.

"Yes," he agreed. "Loren is a man of much talent. He is a clever surgeon, a recognized authority on the brain. He must have delayed his journey to Oslo in order to look after you."

"I should have been completely at a loss without his help—and Erik's," Margaret confessed uneasily.

It seemed that this man found her presence irksome. He had not been prepared for the present emergency, she admitted, but at least he had agreed to Eide's coming to Norway and bringing her stepdaughter with her.

"Eide's death has changed so much," she went on nervously, plunging directly to the heart of the situation because there seemed no other way of approaching Thor Revold. "I don't think she had made any plans for the future beyond her holiday with you at Helmsdal, but now I—I shall have to think of something to do."

He turned on the seat beside her as the *drosje* moved into the stream of traffic beyond the hospital gates, his blue eyes full and searching on her pale face.

"In Norway?" he queried. "That will not be easy."

"I wasn't thinking of Norway," she said, feeling as if she had thrown down some sort of challenge. "I must return to England as soon as possible after Eide—after your aunt——"

Her voice faltered and the first tears gathered behind her eyes. Swiftly she turned her head away so that he might not see them. She felt that this man would be contemptuous of tears; even a woman's tears. He would see them as a weakness to be condemned.

Surprisingly, his voice was softer as he said:

"That is a decision for the future. Before she left England my aunt wrote to me. She almost seemed to see this sort of emergency." He paused and then he added deliberately: "It was her wish that you should continue your holiday, that you should see and learn something of the land she loved."

The protest Margaret might have made was silenced in her heart. The request was typical of her stepmother. It was the sort of wish Eide would have made because of all those years of longing when they had both seen Norway as their ultimate goal, the green and distant land of heart's desire.

"But it will probably inconvenience you terribly," she began and for the first time Thor Revold smiled.

"Not in the least," he assured her. "Helmsdal is a large and rambling valley and Solstua itself is a house of many rooms."

The remoteness in his voice and the suggestion that it would be easy enough for him to isolate himself in his secret northern dale, if need be, chilled her, crushing out the rush of gratitude which had filled her heart when he had mentioned Eide's last request. His indifference was not assumed. It stood like a wall between him and the outside world, and if she should be foolish enough to bruise herself by hurling herself against it, that would be her own affair.

Watching him covertly in case the fierce blue eyes would turn full upon her, baring her inmost thoughts at a glance, she tried to define the quality in him which drew and yet repelled her. She could be nothing more than an encumbrance to him, yet he had accepted her.

It was days before she knew that he did it as a duty, and weeks before she knew what duty meant to him.

Erik was waiting for them at the Norge. He stood rather uncertainly just inside the revolving glass doors and he did not seem greatly surprised when Thor announced that he was to return to Helmsdal immediately.

"I want you to see Fred Sonsburg about the timber we're bringing down from Drakensval," he said. "I hadn't time to contact him before I left. And tomorrow the men are paid. You know what to do. Nothing should go wrong if Sonsburg has the logs in the river before the end of the week, and by then I should be home."

"That," Erik remarked when Thor had left them, "is typical. Decisions are made by Thor and adhered to as a matter of course. Even decisions that might affect one's whole life." The young voice hardened and the blue eyes were flint-like as Erik continued: "People respect Thor, and so will you. Then one day you will come up against the hard core in him that no one can break. He will not allow you to remain in Helmsdal long enough for you to disrupt his ordered way of life."

Margaret flushed.

"He need not worry!" she announced with some spirit. "But for the fact that he asked me, I would not be going now."

Erik regarded her with complete incredulity.

"He asked you?" he repeated. "Thor invited you of his own free will?"

"Not exactly." Margaret hesitated, wondering how deep this thing really went. "He had a letter from my stepmother before we left England. I think she expressed the wish that I should see Helmsdal. She wanted me to go there."

Erik ordered a Pilsener and a cup of coffee, which he pushed towards her across the yellow pine table.

"Ah!" he said. "A duty? Yes, Thor would invite you to come. I had forgotten for a moment that your stepmother was his aunt."

Margaret felt something tighten in her throat.

"Is he so very difficult to know?" she asked.

Erik drank his beer, pushing the empty glass away from him.

"I doubt if anyone has ever known Thor," he said. "Not even my sister."

"They were—in love?" Margaret asked, wondering why she should feel so sure about it even before Erik answered her.

"Yes."

The brief monosyllable died in the silence between them as his thoughts slid down into the past, unhappy thoughts that were linked too fiercely to the present. When she looked round at him his face was quite grey.

"Don't let's talk about it if it distresses you, Erik," she said. "I won't be staying in Helmsdal long enough to need to know Thor's story."

Suddenly his eyes blazed.

"You couldn't be in Helmsdal five minutes without wondering about it, though," he told her. "The whole dale is full of it, bounded by it, crushed by it! Thor has shut himself up there with the past—with the love he meant to have—and no one else can be free of it."

Margaret found nothing to say. No words of hers seemed adequate to meet the intensity of emotion which her half-halting question had evoked in him, and so she remained silent. Erik had reached the end of their present confidences, and she was glad. She did not want to pry into the secret places of Thor Revold's heart.

When Thor came to the hotel again he had made complete and detailed arrangements for their journey north before the week-end.

"We will travel a day sooner," he intimated. "I think it would have been my aunt's wish to be buried in the valley she knew so well."

Margaret looked at him and almost wept.

"I can't thank you," she said. "I can't thank you enough."

Duty was one thing, but this time it had gone hand-in-hand with understanding.

Paul Loren had offered Erik a lift as far as Voss. He came to the Norge to pick up his passenger and to say goodbye.

"How long do you mean to stay in Helmsdal?" he asked Margaret, holding her outstretched hand in a firm and friendly grip.

"I don't know." She glanced across the hotel lounge to where Thor was standing at the reception desk making arrangements about her luggage. "I don't really know about anything."

Paul gave her a keen, searching look as Erik joined them.

"I think you are too wise a person to judge by first impressions," he said, "and I hope we will meet again one day quite soon."

"I hope so," Margaret answered, but she could not see ahead to such a meeting or think where it might take place unless Paul Loren came to Helmsdal, which seemed unlikely.

"I will see you, Thor," Paul said. "The reindeer are plentiful this year, I am told. We must follow up that big fellow we trailed last autumn. He is sure to be about again."

"I have seen him," Thor answered non-committally.

He had not given Paul a direct invitation, and he stood aside, watching almost impatiently, as Erik and Margaret said goodbye.

Unexpectedly Erik put an arm about Margaret's slim shoulders.

"When Thor brings you to Helmsdal," he said, "I also will be there."

If Thor heard Erik's parting reassurance he made no sign. Long ago, it seemed, he had schooled himself to hide his emotions from a curious world, and for the next two days Margaret saw little of him. She realized, of course, that he had a great deal to do in connection with Eide's sudden death, and he spared her the harrowing details wherever he could.

Time hung heavily on Margaret's hands, even although Thor insisted that she should see something of Bergen while she was there and hired a car to take her to Troldhaugen for the afternoon and to Solstrand the following day. It was kindly meant, but Margaret would have given a great deal if he had offered to accompany her, even on the shorter journey to Edvard Grieg's lovely lakeside home.

A desperate sense of loneliness took possession of her at Solstrand, too, and she stood facing the sea and the future with a desolate heart. There were people everywhere around her: naked little children playing happily in the sand; white-sailed boats skimming across an incredibly blue bay; fair-haired girls and long-limbed youths with smooth, tanned skins lying in the sun, and all of them strangers to her. She thought of Erik and Paul Loren, but it was Erik who would have brought the warmth and gaiety of Solstrand into her heart.

When she returned to the hotel Thor was there, waiting.

"You are tired," he said, giving her one of his swiftly-penetrating looks. "Perhaps it would be better if you went straight to bed. We have a long journey before us in the morning."

"I'm not tired in the way you mean," she told him. "Not physically tired. If there is anything you want me to do, please let me do it," she added impulsively. "I've felt so utterly helpless these past two days—so inadequate."

"There was nothing you could have done," he assured her, "with such a limited knowledge of my country."

"In some ways," Margaret said wistfully, "I should feel that it is my country, too. At least in part."

"Yes," he agreed. "Your mother was Norwegian, wasn't she?"

"It should make me belong a little." She smiled, meeting the remote blue eyes with a tentative friendliness in her own. "Today, at Solstrand, I felt

that I wanted to belong—desperately—only there
was no one I knew, of course. I couldn't even understand what the children called to each other when
they ran laughing along the beach and tumbled into
the sea."

"I'm sorry," he apologized almost frigidly. "I
should have made the effort to go with you."

"No," she objected immediately, "you were
busy," but she wished that he had not said that he
should have "made the effort". It made the other
little kindnesses he had shown her appear very much
like tasks.

"Perhaps I am a little tired," she told him suddenly. "I think I will go to bed."

He made no attempt to persuade her to stay,
rising with what seemed relief to accompany her to
to the lift.

"Tomorrow," he asked, "will you be ready by
eight?".

She nodded, half strangled by a strange constriction in her throat which choked back even
conventional words. A meal together, the promise
that the future at Helmsdal might hold something
of happiness for her, or companionship even for a
short time, a brief handshake—any of these things
would have given her a peculiar sense of comfort in
that moment, but he offered none of them.

Instead, she saw him turn away even before the
lift had whisked her out of sight.

In the early morning, when the eastern mountains
along the Hardangerfjord were flushed with a pale
fire and the sky above them was a deep, translucent
blue, they took the train from Bergen on the first
stage of their journey to distant Helmsdal.

"This is the more direct, overland route," Thor
explained as they settled in their seats facing each
other and the train plunged almost immediately into
a tunnel in the mountainside. "The other way is by
sea along the Sognefjorden. It would take us the best
part of two days."

It was the way she would have liked to have gone
in happier circumstances, Margaret realized, but this,

as Thor had pointed out, was the quicker way. He made no effort at pretence. He wanted to get back to Helmsdal as swiftly as possible because he was needed there and because it gave him all he desired in life.

At times, when they plunged into the dark heart of the mountains, she tried to envisage their journey's end but could not. Each turn in the way, each curve of the upwardwinding track brought her nearer to the vast immensity of these rugged giants, yet she could not explain the strange fascination they held for her. Their strength and remoteness were immeasurable and, she saw, reflected clearly in the men they bred. Thor had that strength, and Paul Loren. If Erik lacked it perhaps it was because his heart had been given to the more gentle south, to the gaiety of a city and a city's way of life.

Yet she thought of Erik Borge with a wistful sort of longing, her mislaid youth holding out eager hands to his.

"Will Erik meet us before we reach Helmsdal?" she asked Thor as the grain emerged on to a high green plateau where the sun shone on soft white seas of cotton grass and the deep pools in the rock-strewn rivers were cool and dark.

"No," he answered immediately. "There is no time for Erik to make unnecessary journeys."

Margaret felt crushed, and sympathetic towards Erik as never before, but it would be useless to try to tell Thor that she thought he was being unjust. She could imagine him smiling at her criticism in the distant way he had, dismissing it without comment, perhaps.

When they left the train at Voss the world of the high mountains came very near, encompassing them, drawing them close. It almost seemed to Margaret as if they had touched her, and instinctively she drew back.

Standing on the narrow platform as the train steamed out, she could almost feel their compelling strength, and when she turned from them Thor was coming towards her. He had collected their luggage, supervising its transfer to the boot of a large American car which waited further along the track, but for a moment everything seemed to pale before the fact that Thor had come into his own. She saw his tall, powerful body silhouetted against a dark range of jagged hills, his hair ruffled by the upland wind, his eyes keen and intent upon the scene before him, and the suggestion of isolation had never been so strong. Isolation and something more.

She wanted to know. In spite of what she had said to Erik two days ago, she wanted to know about Thor.

Almost immediately she was remembering Erik's words. "I doubt if anyone has ever known Thor. Not even my sister."

Thor Revold had been in love, deeply, intensely in love, and that love held him still. It would always hold him.. It was useless to feel that she could have any part in his life, if that was what she had hoped.

Shaken by the force of an unnamed emotion, she turned away, suddenly cold in the warm August sunlight.

"We can have a meal here if you would prefer it," Thor suggested. "There will be no other stopping place till we reach Stalheim. This is bleak country."

"I'd rather go on," she said. "I'm not at all hungry."

What had happened to her since she had come into these mountains. The past had all been swept away, or so it seemed, and there was only the present. The present here with Thor Revold, journeying into the deep silences of his own country.

She could not thrust the conviction of inevitability from her, and as they plunged downwards between the rolling hills, deeper and deeper into their silent heart, she could not speak.

At Stalheim there was only the hotel. It stood a thousand feet up above a dark and terrifying gorge set between mountains which must have risen to another four thousand feet on every side, yet in spite of their isolation—almost because of it—she felt nearer to Thor than ever before.

"A hundred years ago," he told her, looking out across the stupefying panorama of canyon and rugged, shadowed heights, "only men on foot and on the sturdiest of ponies could reach this point. Then an engineer chiselled a roadway out of the Naeroydalen down there and made the road to Voss a commercial possibility."

His admiration for the man of action who might look down on such a scene of his own achievement glittered in his eyes, and Margaret supposed that he had forgotten her for the moment.

"In a way, it is something like that I am trying to do for Helmsdal," he added unexpectedly.

"And you have no one to help you?" she asked.

Thor looked down at her as if he did not understand her meaning for a moment, and then his mouth tightened and his eyes were remote again.

"I can stand alone," he said.

The grim decision raised the old barrier between them, and he retreated behind the stern mask of reserve which he had worn so persistently ever since they had met. If he had permitted her one brief glance beneath it by confessing his ambitions for the future of Helmsdal, it did not mean that she had penetrated to the heart of the man. He had set himself a grim and ruthless task in his native dale, but he was strong enough to complete it alone.

Margaret wondered if Erik had ever had any part in his plans, but did not think so. It was perhaps in that moment that she first realized how little she really knew about either of them, about their way of life, or the past, or what might come of the future.

The meal the hotel provided for them was the usual lavish one, the cold table set out for them to choose from stretching half the length of the room, and Margaret saw Thor's dark face soften to a smile as she sampled one after another of the luscious native dishes.

"The mountain air has given you an appetite," he observed, " and put a new colour into your cheeks."

She realized how pale she had looked during these past few days, but did not think Thor would have noticed.

"I have worried," she admitted truthfully, "but you have made everything so much easier for me."

"Do not thank me," he cautioned. "You must remember that Eide was my mother's sister."

Of course, she thought, there was the family tie. Nothing he had done was really personal. Thor's kindness was a duty.

They got back into the car and plunged down into the canyon by a breathtaking, difficult road until suddenly the sun glinted on a narrow arm of water in the distance and a blue fjord opened out to the north.

Margaret lost track of time after that. They embarked on the waiting fjord steamer, a bell clanged somewhere amidships, and the quay was left behind. It was all done so silently; no shouted instructions, no orders flung from ship to quay, nothing to disturb the utter peace which seeped down out of the surrounding mountains.

Thor found her a place on deck where, from time to time, she could almost have stretched out her hand and touched the close-set hillside. They sailed for three hours into the endless heart of the fjord, close to the precipitate wall of rock which bounded it, feeling the spray from innumerable waterfalls damp on their faces until Thor turned almost abruptly and left her.

They were steaming towards a narrow gorge where the mountains came down sheer on either side and the fjord water came slipping through between dark rocks, deep and ominous-looking even in this day of sunshine.

Looking at it, Margaret held her breath. The water seemed to pour through the gap with a sort of restrained fury, leashed only for the moment, and the cruel black rocks above it offered no hope of sanctuary. On this comparatively windless day all was still, but she could imagine the treacherous ferocity of that ugly passageway when a gale had whipped the fjord water into mounting waves pounding against a too-narrow opening in their mad rush to enter the inner fjord.

Instinctively she turned away from it to look for Thor. In the next instant, however, she wished that she had remained where she was. She found him standing a hundred paces away across the deck, his head flung back, his face upturned to the mountains with an agony of pain and regret pencilled darkly upon it which she knew that she had no right to see. She knew, too, that she would never forget it.

In panic, she turned away, wishing that she had the power to obliterate what she had seen from her mind for the sake of its future peace. But even when the fjord opened out, blue and fair between the green foothills of Helmsdal, and Thor came back to her, she could not thrust its memory aside.

"We are almost there," he told her. "We have only a short journey to make now."

So they were not really at journey's end? Margaret looked back over the way they had come as the steamer eased itself against the miniature white quay with its inevitable warehouse and piles of merchandise waiting to be shipped to Gudvangen across the outer fjord, and all she could see was the dark gap in the mountains where the water poured through, silently and stealthily today, under the sun.

Erik had come to the fjord head to meet them. He strode across the gangway as soon as it was pushed aboard and stood on the deck holding her hand and looking down at her with a smile of welcome in his eyes.

"All has gone well," he told Thor briefly. "Everything is in readiness for tomorrow."

Thor collected the luggage and his own rucksack and they made their way towards the only car standing at the end of the quay.

Beyond it, Margaret saw a group of small wooden houses with gaily-painted shutters thrown back to let in the sunshine, and a white church with a thin wooden spire standing on a knoll above them. The entire population of the village seemed to have turned out to watch the arrival of the steamer, and she noticed that they saluted Thor respectfully.

Amazingly fat sheep and lambs cropped the grass by the roadside and were not disturbed even when the car drove quite close to them. Thor drove swiftly and well over the rutted, uneven road, and Erik sat in the back with Margaret, closer than he need have done, for the car was big and comfortable and roomy. Yet his nearness seemed to welcome her to Helmsdal in a silent way.

Almost at once the valley began to close in, to reach for the hills, where a wealth of timber grew. Fir and pine and larch, all giants of their kind, stood sentinel-like above the green fields where the hay was strung up to dry in the sun, but after they left the fjordside there was no sign of a house for miles.

Could all this land belong to Thor, Margaret wondered, and, if so, surely he had already done much to reclaim his valley? The whole dale looked prosperous and contented, and high on the hills above the tree-line cattle grazed on the summer grass.

The road penetrated right into the heart of the hills, the only way, it seemed, and then, suddenly, it was cut off. They had come to Solstua.

Whoever had named it, Margaret thought, had named it well. It was indeed a house in the sun. Standing high above the valley floor, it looked down across the fields and a broad, swiftly-flowing river to the gleam of distant fjord water far below. It was the typical white frame house of the Norwegian countryside, forming one side of a square and surrounded by outhouses, but suddenly she realized that all of them were new. Even the house had been recently rebuilt, and a swift glance behind it showed her the blackened shell of what had once been the old farm dwelling and the original *stabbur*—the big barn.

Before the car reached the house a girl in a full black skirt and embroidered blouse came to the open door. She stood there with her hands clasped before her, shyly at a loss in the presence of a stranger, but her likeness to Erik was unmistakable.

"This is Ellen, my sister," Erik said.

Margaret's heart seemed to miss a beat. Was this, then, the girl that Thor had loved? Instinct told her that it could not be. That love of Thor's had been darkened by tragedy. No one who had glimpsed his ravaged face out there on the fjord steamer could ever have doubted the fact—and Ellen was no more than a child.

Thor turned towards her.

"Come, *vesla*, and meet our visitor," he said, speaking slowly and in English. "You must show her to the room you have prepared and make her comfortable."

Ellen smiled up at him, all her affection for him shining in her clear blue eyes.

"Yes, Thor," she said obediently. "All is ready."

She looked at Margaret, smiling at her too, but somewhere behind the smile there was a reserve, a suggestion that friendship would not come easily.

Margaret felt chilled, as she had felt chilled by Thor. Were all these mountain people alike, she wondered, silent and withdrawn, needing only a minimum of words or gestures to express themselves and not taking kindly to the stranger in their midst?

It was a disconcerting thought, and she followed Ellen in silence.

Solstua was a two-storey house, built entirely of wood, its corner posts standing straight and proud as they had stood on the mountainside not so long ago. It had been constructed lovingly, with a wealth of detailed carving inside which suggested that native craftsmanship was still very much alive in the dale. Every corner, every piece of substantial furniture spoke of a passionately cherished tradition, and there was no doubt in Margaret's mind that Thor had reproduced his old home in every detail.

The long main room they entered spanned the entire breadth of the house, and it was full of sun. Sunshine poured in through the wide windows with their gay folk-weave curtains, and the illusion of sunlight was reflected from the waxed pine floor and echoed again and again in the tapestries which hung on the walls.

It was a lovely room, and yet it lacked something. It had been dusted and polished till it shone, but it had lost its heart. Everything was in order, but she imagined that it was rarely used.

Ellen led the way to a square hall and began to mount a wide, uncarpeted staircase which ended rather surprisingly in a narrow gallery overlooking the room they had just left.

"This is where the father and mother slept long ago," she explained, adding in her careful English: "One hundred and fifty years ago, or two hundred years."

It was as if time meant nothing, Margaret thought. These mountain people had long memories. The whole valley seemed enfolded in the past, and Thor Revold had been at the greatest pains to preserve it.

She followed Ellen along the gallery, unfurnished now save for the loosely-woven runner on the polished floorboards, and stood behind her when she halted at a half-open door. Most of the bedrooms on this upper floor would lead from the corridor, Margaret supposed, and they would all be light and airy and have a wonderful view.

"This is where you will go," Ellen said quickly, and as quickly disappeared.

Slightly taken aback at the younger girl's abrupt behaviour, Margaret went on into the room. It was delightful, but once again the whole atmosphere was impersonal. She shook off the impression as best she could, washed in ice-cold water which must have been drawn from the heart of the mountains, tidied her hair and stood for a moment in the centre of the polished floor thinking.

There hadn't been much time to think since she had left Bergen with Thor early that morning, but now that she was here the sense of loneliness which had overwhelmed her on the crowded beach at Solstrand flooded back. If only Eide had been here with her! If she could have had her stepmother's companionship and understanding, how different everything would have been! Her lips quivered and she blinked the tears from her eyes. She could not believe that Eide, warm and kind and generous Eide, was dead.

Swiftly, almost blindly, she crossed the room and pulled open the door. The silence, the dreadful isolation she felt when she was alone could only be countered by action.

In the corridor she turned the wrong way, coming to the end of it before she realized her mistake and finding herself facing a small, panelled cul-de-sac out of which two doors led. They were both firmly closed, unlike the others she had just passed, and subconsciously she had the impression of a barrier.

Before she could retreat, however, hurried footsteps sounded along the corridor behind her.

"Not that way!" Ellen's voice, tense and imperative arrested any further progress she might have made. "It is not the way to go."

"Oh, I'm sorry!" Margaret whirled round. "I had no idea that I was—trespassing."

Looking into the flushed, resentful face with which Ellen confronted her, she knew that the other girl did not understand her words, but she knew almost as surely that she had been guilty of trespass.

"Are they Thor's rooms?" she asked.

Ellen shook her head, her blue eyes darkening perceptibly.

"No," she said, "not Thor's. They were my sister's."

The chill which she had known before struck deeply into Margaret's heart. Ellen's sister—Erik's sister—the woman whom Thor had loved! She was alive in this house as surely as if she walked in the flesh along these silent corridors. Kept alive by Thor. Certainly, wherever she was, whatever had happened to her, her memory was evergreen within these four stout walls where she had lived not so long ago.

A thousand questions surged in Margaret's mind, but she could not bring herself to ask one of them. Too soon, she thought, she would hear all about Thor Revold's beloved.

Ellen led the way back down the staircase and into a room leading from the hall where a long refectory table was set for a meal.

"We must wait for Thor," Ellen intimated, moving polished wooden platters of food on to the table from the carved dresser opposite the window. "He will not be long delayed."

Erik came in, and Margaret felt relieved. She had liked Ellen, but the girl's reserve and natural shyness constituted a barrier to easy conversation, and somehow she felt that the little incident in the upstairs corridor had scarcely helped their friendship. She was sorry if Ellen had thought that she was prying, but, after all, she had not gone into the forbidden rooms. It had all been an unfortunate mistake which she would rather not have made.

"Thor asks to be excused," Erik said. "There is some uncertainty about the timber being brought down from the upper valley which he wishes to attend to right away. Seemingly," he added dryly, "I have not been efficient enough."

Margaret glanced at her watch. It was after nine o'clock. Thor and she had travelled over two hundred miles since early morning, by rail and road and fjord steamer, yet he had gone out to work while the light still held. She knew that it would not fade, even at midnight, but surely the work of felling would not be going on at this late hour. And surely Thor himself was human enough to feel tired.

"Thor is a machine!" Erik informed her, almost as if he had read her thoughts. "He is not like any ordinary person. He never lets up, as the Americans say! When you have been in the dale a little time you will recognize that, and much more besides."

He sat down, leaving the heavily-carved chair at the head of the table vacant. It faced the wide stone fireplace, and Margaret supposed that it was always occupied by the head of the family. Thor, of course, would keep such a custom alive.

Almost reluctantly she turned her gaze to the other end of the long table. The space there was empty. Ellen had sat down facing her and Erik took the chair by her side.

"How did you weather the journey?" he asked.

"I would have loved every minute of it—under happier circumstances," Margaret confessed.

"Yes," he admitted, letting his fingers touch hers on the polished board, "I'm sorry about your step-mother."

Ellen sat watching them. If she did not quite understand all they said, at least she had noticed the touching of their hands, and Margaret saw her smile faintly, as if some doubt had been cleared up in her mind.

"Ellen is learning English," Erik said. "It is Thor's wish."

"Perhaps I can help?" Margaret offered eagerly. "It would be something for me to do."

"If you are only to remain for a short time," Ellen said slowly, "there will be much for you to see and do in the dale. Erik will be glad to show you everything."

She was not smiling now and she looked directly across the table into Margaret's eyes. Suddenly she looked older and as sternly determined as Thor. They did not expect her to stay, Margaret realized, conscious of a new, deep hurt which would not be eased even by Erik's stout avowal that nothing would please him more than to show her about the dale.

"Please let me help you to clear away, Ellen," she offered when they rose from the table, but Ellen shook her head.

"You are the guest," Erik explained. "Besides, she will wait for Thor."

"Perhaps we should have waited too?" Margaret suggested.

"Oh, no! Thor often dines in solitary state. More often than not, in fact, and this was an emergency. The log boom across the river gave way, and Thor will work on it with the lumbermen till it is in action again."

There did not seem to be any suggestion that Erik, too, might have gone to work in the emergency, and Margaret wondered if Thor had deputed him to entertain their guest.

The word hurt when she considered it, but after all she supposed that she was not really one of the family, as Eide had been. There was no real relationship between her and Thor. Only the fact that his mother's sister had married her father and had loved her as if she had been her own child.

"Are you tired, Margaret?" Erik asked.

She shook her head. She was not in the least tired, in spite of the long, eventful day behind her.

"Come and I will show you the fjord," he said, holding out his hand. "It is very beautiful at night."

They left the house, following a scarcely-distinguishable pathway up the hillside which led eventually into the trees. Erik paused before they reached them, however, standing on a rocky outcrop to turn her to face the west.

Above the nearer hills the sky was stained a pale lemon streaked with vermilion, and the vibrant flicker of the Aurora lengthened and grew even as they watched. It lit up the hills, setting its own pale glow on the snow-caps of the Jotunheimen, lending the icy barrier of these distant mountains a warmth she had not expected. Then, suddenly, it died, leaving them harsh and cold and remote, flung up against the greying northern skyline like grotesque giants, dark and defiant and withdrawn.

"Is there any way through these mountains, Erik?" she found herself asking.

"There is the Sognfjell road," he told her with a shrug. "It is open for a few short months in the summer, but soon it will be closed."

"And you will be cut off here?"

He shook his head.

"No. There is the way by the fjord."

"The way we came," Margaret said, remembering the dark gap between the rocks which led to the inner fjord. "That, too, could be closed by storm, couldn't it?"

"Oh, yes," he agreed, unperturbed by the possibility. "There is often no way of getting out of the dale in winter. No way of escape."

"Is that how you think of it?" she asked, trying to make her voice sound light. "But you live here, Erik. You were born in Helmsdal, perhaps?"

He shrugged.

"Yes, that is true. My father farmed here in the dale, and his father before him."

"Would you tell me about them?" she asked.

He looked at her as if he would refuse, and then his eyes lit in a smile.

"Why not?" he asked. "You will hear it, sooner or later. Perhaps not from Thor, because he is modest about his part in it, but from someone else. Helmsdal still remembers."

Margaret fixed her eyes on the bright gleam of fjord water which they could see far down the valley, waiting for Erik to continue, and aware that what he would tell her would give her her first real insight into the character of Thor Revold, who owned this land as far as the eye could see.

"It's not a very long story," he said. "It happened during the Occupation when the Nazis were here. Thor's father was one of the leaders of the Resistance and eventually he became known to the Gestapo. Soon they were on the run. My father helped them and they escaped to England. When they came back to Helmsdal at the end of the war, Solstua—the old Solstua—had been razed to the ground and all their land taken. It was restored to Thor, of course, but just as it was. He had to build everything up again."

"And—his father?" Margaret asked.

"Edvard Revold did not survive the war," Erik told her. "He was killed at Narvik."

"What about—your people?"

"They were shot because they had helped the Revolds to escape. My father and his brother and my grandfather."

Margaret drew in a deep breath. This was all she had to know. Like the pieces shaken together in a kaleidoscope, the pattern of Thor Revold's life became suddenly clear. He had made himself responsible for Erik and what remained of the Borge family.

"I was given my chance to go to the University of Oslo when the time came. Thor, who never had that chance, wanted it so," he added.

"And you?" Margaret asked with a strange coldness in her heart.

He shrugged.

"Of course, I am grateful."

But not content. She could not have told where the conviction came from, but she knew that Erik was not entirely happy in his present way of life.

"Ellen has left school now," Erik said as they moved slowly down the hill towards Solstua. "She is happy to serve Thor." Suddenly he turned to face her. "And now you know about us," he said. "About Ellen and Thor and me, but not about Gerda."

Gerda! It had come. Margaret put her hands out in silent protest, as if she would ward off a levelling blow, and Erik caught them, holding them fast. He seemed determined that she should hear the end of his story.

"That, also, is all tragedy," he said. "Gerda was the loveliest creature that ever lived. She was tall and slim and gay, and Thor loved her. She was his Snow Princess, something set high on a mountain of stars. He built a house for her in the high valley, up in Drakensval, but she never lived in it."

"Please, Erik—stop!" Margaret cried. "Thor would not want me to know this."

"Why not? It is known everywhere. Thor worshipped her. Gerda was all he had ever sought in a woman and he had known her all his life. Then, with utter suddenness she died." Erik turned to look down on Solstua and the flash of distant water still faintly gleaming on the valley floor. "She was drowned in the entrance to the fjord two days before their wedding was due to take place in the village *kirke*."

His words ebbed into a long silence stretching to eak infinity of hopeless love and longing, and

Margaret felt herself caught up in it, with no prospect of escape.

"Thor will never let himself forget," Erik said. "He taught Gerda to sail the boat and she took it out alone that day. He is the sort of person who will remember for ever."

They reached the house. It was silent, but a lamp burned in the room where they had dined little more than an hour ago. Thor would be in there, waited upon by Ellen; Thor with everything he wanted in the world except the one passionate love of his life.

I can't go in, Margaret thought. I can't see him again tonight with that tragic story fresh in my mind.

"Will you tell Thor that I have gone to bed?" she asked Erik. "Will you ask him to excuse me? I am very tired."

She reached her room, closing the stout wooden door firmly behind her, but she could not close out the memory of Thor.

CHAPTER THREE

MARGARET realized that she was being accepted in Helmsdal as much for the fact that Eide had been buried in the little church beside the fjord as for her own sake. Eide Holden, who had once been Eide Thorensen and had lived there all her life until she had married the Englishman and gone with him across the North Sea, was still remembered and beloved, and for that reason alone many doors were opened to her stepdaughter which might have remained closed until Thor made some formal effort to enlist their friendship on her behalf.

It did not seem as if Thor would ever have made such an effort. After the funeral he handed her over to Erik as a matter of course, and all she saw of him was an infrequent glimpse at meal times when he was working near enough to come to the house at midday.

Reluctant to admit the attraction he held for her, Margaret turned to Erik, who was only too eager to act as guide and companion.

"You've got to meet people," he said, "and then, when the winter comes, you will not be lonely."

Margaret did not think she would be there in the winter. She had not made any plans, but she felt that she could not go on staying indefinitely as Thor's guest. Apart from Ellen, who was perpetually busy about the house, there was an old woman in the kitchen called Signe, who had a disconcerting habit of appearing from nowhere to gaze dumbly at the stranger and disappear again as silently as she had come. There were three farm hands who slept in a lofty apartment above the *stabbur*, and two young girls who attended the cattle on the summer farm high above the dale itself. They made goat cheese and butter up there and would not return to Helmsdal until the first snow was showing on the mountains above the pass.

It was not very long before Margaret became aware that she was not expected to penetrate very far beyond the summer farm.

"We've never been any farther than the *saetre*," she remarked one day as she climbed beside Erik up the narrow goat track. "Yet the road does go farther, doesn't it?"

"It goes all the way to Drakensval," Erik agreed, "but I would not be popular with Thor if I took you there."

Margaret bit her lip, wishing that she had remembered about Drakensval and the house that Thor Revold had built there for the girl who should have been his bride.

"Is it very lovely?" she asked. "The valley, I mean."

"It is very isolated. Thor and Gerda could only have lived up there during the summer months—if Gerda could have lived there at all."

The last half-dozen words had slipped out almost as an afterthought, an unguarded admission which Erik seemed anxious to recall.

"She would have gone, of course," he said, "if Thor had wished it."

Margaret was silent. Whenever anyone spoke of Gerda she was conscious of a dismal sense of inferiority, of most things at Solstua being measured by Gerda's standard of excellence. The idea of a "Snow Princess" whom Thor had worshipped was never far from her mind, and his almost taciturn rejection of feminine company seemed to bear out Erik's declaration that Thor would never love again.

"Was—Gerda very young?" she asked, so that they need not talk of Drakensval.

"A year younger than Thor." Erik turned to help her up a particularly rough stretch of track. "They were ideal together. She was as fair as Ellen, and Thor——" He laughed, putting an arm about her shoulders. "Well, you know what Thor is like!"

A vision of those two walking up this very path, swam before Margaret's eyes: Thor, tall and lissom, with that easy, swinging stride of his, his dark face happier than she had ever seen it, and the girl beside him almost as tall, with her flawless skin and the glorious Scandinavian colouring of honey-blonde hair and eyes as deeply blue as fjord water on a cloudless day. All their days must have been cloudless until that fateful day when a little boat had set out to cross the fjord and had not been strong enough to reach the other side.

Margaret shivered.

"Not cold?" Erik asked because the sun was shining. "All right! I shall take off my knitted coat and put it over your shoulders, and then you will really belong to the mountains!"

He laughed, and Margaret thought that the thing she liked most about Erik was his laughter. Resolutely she made up her mind not to think about Gerda or even about Thor.

"Where are you taking me, and shouldn't we be doing something more productive than just climbing in the sun?" she asked.

"You must not ask too many questions at once," he said, smiling down into her eyes. "I can only answer one at a time."

"Then you can answer the last one," she decided. "Don't you think we should be helping at the farm?"

"Which means don't I think *I* should be helping at the farm!" he translated without rancour. "I will do that soon, if Thor needs me. Just now he needs me more to look after you, to see that your holiday in Helmsdal is an agreeable one."

Margaret tried not to feel hurt, telling herself that she should have accepted the fact by now that Thor could not spare the time to take her walking for hours into the mountains, even if he had wanted to.

Almost recklessly she laughed the hurt aside.

"I won't worry about Thor, then," she decided. "I thought that you normally worked on the farm when you were on holiday."

"Normally," he agreed, "yes. The summer vacation is a long one, to be filled in somehow. When I am not in Oslo, the time hangs heavily for me. There is no conversation here in Helmsdal save of timber and sheep, and, since my sister's death, there has been little music at Solstua. We are a musical people here in the mountains, but Thor has locked his violin away. I do not think that he will ever use it again," Erik added simply. "To play it would pain him too much."

Margaret turned her head away.

"I am making you sad," Erik said after a moment's reflection in which he had studied the soft contours of her averted cheek, "and that is not at all courteous of me." She knew that his blue eyes would be deeply concerned with a serious effort to please her. "What would you most wish to do?" he asked.

"I'd like to climb to the very top of the valley," she said instantly. "Right to the tree-line."

"Thor should be felling up there," Erik said. "We will go and have some coffee at the lumber camp."

Instantly Margaret was sorry that she had made the request. "I didn't know there was work in progress," she said. "Perhaps it would be as well to wait."

"Thor will not mind if you go to the camp," Erik assured her. "There are many people up there. It is only Drakensval that is forbidden territory."

They began to climb again, up over the rich summer grass where the goats roamed at will to the ridge where the trees began. It was gloriously warm, with the sun beating down on them out of a cloudless sky, and once or twice Margaret paused to draw breath and look in rapturous incredulity at the magic panorama of Helmsdal.

All along the way they had come little waterfalls leapt from the rocks, flinging their silver spray high into the air to be caught in a rainbow arc of true, bright colours, and far below on the valley floor the river which bore them to the waiting fjord wound like a glittering ribbon between dark green trees.

If Thor had been cutting timber over a number of years, as she supposed he must have done, he had certainly worked to a plan which would not denude the hills of their dark girdle of pine and spruce, and even when they eventually came to the edge of the clearing she could see that he had taken thought for the future. Young trees had already been planted where the old had been felled, old sores hidden by new, upsurging growth.

The whine of a saw reached them as they followed a narrow track through the trees.

"I'm not too keen on seeing timber coming down," Erik confessed, walking close beside her. "I suppose that means I'm a perfectionist. I don't like to see beauty spoiled."

"I don't think anyone does," Margaret agreed, "Unless he is a complete barbarian, and then he never thinks about it. There must always be a sense of loss and regret—and—yes, pity—when it does happen."

Erik laughed softly, drawing her to him.

"You have a gentle heart, Meg!" he said. "Why do you say you feel pity for a tree?"

"I wasn't thinking only of trees," Margaret confessed. "I suppose I was thinking about people, too. People who suddenly find themselves—disfigured in some way—cut off from beauty or from love."

She bit her lip, not understanding why she should have spoken to Erik so seriously.

"You will never have to fear that," he assured her softly. "You are very beautiful, Meg. Your English beauty is like a rose, warmer and more gentle than I had thought."

She turned her head, laughing up at him, putting the compliment aside because it had made her uneasy in his company for the first time.

"Now I think you are a poet as well as a perfectionist!" she smiled. "But when Thor has felled his trees they are made into beautiful things, too. All the wood in Norway is lovingly and beautifully carved. The men who work with it must have a feeling for the living tree."

He looked at her sharply.

"Did you know that most of the carvings at Solstua were done by Thor?" he asked almost jealously.

Margaret felt suddenly disconcerted

"You mean—the dragons on the eaves, and the serpents and the troll candle sticks?"

"Most of them," Erik confirmed laconically. "It is Thor's way of expressing himself in his varying moods, perhaps, now that he no longer plays his violin. You should see Drakensval!"

"I don't think that I want to see Drakensval!" Margaret answered sharply.

"Well, come and see the camp instead!" Erik was never depressed for long. "There are no trolls or dragons there!"

She followed him quickly, but the thought of Drakensval went with her. Ellen had said that Thor spent long hours up there in the secret valley above the hills when he did not want to come to Solstua.

Long before they reached the sawmill and the main clearing where the cabins were Margaret saw Thor standing beneath the trees. He was stripped to the waist, wielding a fine axe as expertly as any of his men, but he dropped it and put on his shirt as they came within hailing distance.

As always, she could not decide what he felt about their intrusion.

"You have come in time," he said. "We are just going to have something to drink."

"If we are holding things up," Margaret said, "please go on working. We only came to see the logs being floated into the river."

"You may be disappointed," he warned, swinging the axe to stick it into a tree-stump and, walking beside her towards the cabins. "We haven't got the boom quite in working order yet. You must come again."

They had reached the largest of the cabins and laughter came pouring out through the open doorway. To Margaret's complete surprise, the group inside included girls as well as men.

"Kirsten has come up to do the books," Thor explained to Erik. "You must meet Kirsten Moe," he added, propelling Margaret forward with a firm hand beneath her elbow. "She is our village schoolteacher, but during the long vacation she likes to work up here among the trees."

Margaret, face to face with Kirsten Moe for the first time, felt that she had met a woman whose friendship and understanding, once given, would be a pearl above price.

Kirsten was tall and slim, like most of her compatriots, with a wonderfully regal carriage which was accentuated by a coronet of thick yellow hair plaited and coiled about her head. Her face was too angular, her cheek-bones too high and prominent for actual beauty, but her eyes had a quality which defeated criticism and lent more than beauty to an arresting personality. She stretched out a slim brown hand and shook Margaret's warmly, while those deep blue eyes penetrated through any sham there might have been, seeking for the truth. What she saw she liked.

"Thor has been telling me about you," she said, "and I should have met you before this, but he has made such a muddle of his arithmetic up here in the woods that I have much to do to straighten him out before the Government inspector gets hold of him!"

The blue eyes twinkled as they met Thor's and Kirsten made a place for Margaret on the wooden bench by her side.

"Sit down, Thor," she commanded, "and take some rest. You work too hard. You should be like Erik here," she added as Erik found a seat on Margaret's other side. "You should also learn to play a little."

"When the time comes," Thor said, ordering their coffee, "I shall do that, too."

"Oh, yes, we know!" Kirsten laughed. "You will liberate those dreadful Eskimo dogs of yours and go off to the hunt—preferably alone. For days on end you will beat across the mountains and come back exhausted—to work again! Why do you not go to Oslo more often—or to Bergen?"

"Because there is nothing in Oslo to interest Thor," Erik put in. "He is happier in his mountains."

"He is certainly more free," Kirsten agreed, looking across the table at Thor. "No," she decided, "I cannot imagine you living in Oslo, Thor. But now that you have taken time to sit down, tell me whom you met in Bergen."

Thor smiled.

"Larsen, the timber man, and Ole Dagfin," he told her good-humouredly.

"They are not interesting," Kirsten decided. "They can only talk about wood and fish!"

"There was also Paul Loren."

"Oh?" A deep colour flooded Kirsten's cheeks. "Was he about to start on a journey—to America, perhaps?"

"No, he was coming back."

"He was so kind to me," Margaret told Kirsten. "I shall never be able to repay him. He travelled on the *Asta* with us and helped when my stepmother was taken ill."

"Paul is usually there at the right moment," Kirsten said lightly, but she did not ask if Paul Loren was likely to visit Helmsdal.

They drank their coffee in silence for a minute or two, each busy with their own thoughts, until deep in the clearing a bell rang out and the lumbermen began to drift away from the bar where they had been drinking Pilsener and black coffee.

Thor got to his feet.

"If you would like to see the rest of the camp," he suggested, "we can go down with the jeep."

"I'd love to," Margaret accepted eagerly. "If you are not too busy."

"It will not take long," he answered. "I'll have a word with the foreman to see where they are felling along the road."

Kirsten got up from the table to shake hands.

"I shall see you again quite soon," she said as they strolled towards the door, waiting for Thor. "I come to Solstua to give English lessons to Ellen. She must learn soon to read and write the language, as well as speak it."

"I thought I might have been able to help in that respect," Margaret confessed, "but Ellen is still very shy."

Kirsten gave her a long, direct look.

"You may find Ellen difficult," she said briefly. "She has not been much away from Helmsdal except to go to school, and she is a person of intense allegiances."

"She is very loyal to Thor," Margaret agreed.

"Yes." Kirsten's lips were suddenly compressed. "That was because Thor and her sister were about to be married."

Something in the slightly altered tone of the pleasant voice made Margaret look up with a swift question in her eyes. Was it possible that Kirsten Moe, of all people, had not liked Gerda? Kirsten's expression did not betray her, however. Perhaps it was too early in their acquaintance for confidences; perhaps she had even imagined that quick change in Kirsten's voice, an inflection which could have meant anything—or nothing.

There was no time to wonder. Erik had followed them out of the canteen and Thor drove the jeep up to the door.

"It is not the height of comfort," he apologized, "but it will be easier than walking. The roads are rutted and difficult where we have been hauling."

Erik held the door open for Margaret. He did not seem greatly enthusiastic about their tour of inspection, but he had evidently decided to join it.

"Will you come, also?" Thor asked Kirsten.

"You pay me to work!" Kirsten laughed. "Not today, Thor," she added more seriously. "I must really strike a balance in those accounts of yours sometime."

They drove away, with Kirsten waving to them from the doorway of the tiny office where she worked and where, Margaret supposed, Thor also worked some of the time, although she could not imagine him seated behind a desk for long.

Sitting close beside him in the jeep, she was aware of time running away far too quickly, and she wanted to arrest it, to hold this moment fast against any disappointment which the future might hold.

They circled a clearing where newly-felled trees were being hauled by chains down the hillside, and once or twice Thor stopped the jeep to give an order or to make way for the sturdy horse-teams which worked where the tractors were of little use.

"Most of the camp is mechanized," he explained, "but we work with horses, too. There is often a response from an animal which one can't demand from a machine."

They had been moving slowly downhill and were now in a clearing just above the river. Here, in a wide semi-circle of comparatively still water, men were toiling at the log-boom which had broken the night before.

"The logs are gathered here and made into rafts, which are floated down to the fjord," Thor explained. "This is as far as the present camp goes." He pulled up on the river bank. "There is a timber road through the pines which will take you back to Solstua without going through the camp again," he added.

Margaret wondered if they had been dismissed, and certainly Erik looked eager enough to take the timber road back to Solstua as quickly as possible. Yet she found herself completely fascinated by the work that was going on beneath her.

Thor had gone down to the riverside and was giving instructions to the men wading waist-deep in the water.

"Well," Erik asked almost jealously, "have you seen enough of Thor's kingdom?"

"I feel that I haven't seen one half of it," she answered him truthfully. "It is all so—vast, so un-believably interesting."

"You've seen the conventional part," he answered dryly. "The other part Thor keeps to himself. Like Peer Gynt, he prefers to roam his mountains alone."

Perhaps that was true, Margaret acknowledged, but at least this afternoon Thor had been the perfect host.

She watched him coming up the bank towards them as the waggon-team came down between the trees and the first logs were levered from the carrier with long steel poles, and then, so suddenly that there had been no time to think, in the split second of an emergency, he had reached her and flung her aside.

Dazed and bewildered, she heard the scream of a broken chain, as it whipped past only inches from her unprotected body, and the roar and plunge of the great log as it rolled into the river below. A fountain-like column of water rose into the air in front of her, yet she was only aware of two arms about her that were like steel, of being held, protected against Thor's broad chest while the heart beneath it pounded with sledgehammer intensity against her own.

She quivered and stood still. The moment seemed to last for ever, and then she heard Erik's voice.

"Whew! That was a near thing! Are you all right, Meg?" He gave her a shaken laugh. "I had a horrible vision of you ending in the river without a head!"

Thor did not speak. His grip slackened, but for a moment longer he continued to hold Margaret, supporting her until she was wholly recovered from her shock of surprise.

"It all happened so suddenly," she breathed at last.

Even now, fear had no place in her emotions, yet nothing she could say or do would quieten that insistent throbbing of her heart which had beat in unison with Thor's.

She turned away, aware that he was watching her closely.

"Are you all right?" he asked, seeing the sudden pallor of her face. "It was a most unfortunate experience. When you are ready I will take you back to Solstua in the jeep."

"No, please!" Margaret begged. "I can quite easily walk back. Nothing happened." She tried to smile her assurance. "You were so quick about everything."

Nothing happened, she tried to convince herself. I am no different from the Margaret Holden who walked here to the river ten minutes ago. Because my silly heart is beating like some fluttering wild thing, because Thor Revold has held me in his arms, it does not mean that life has changed for me.

"All the same," Thor said decisively, "we will go back by jeep."

He drove swiftly, and before her heart had stopped its wild, insistent beating, they were at Solstua.

Ellen ran out, as if she sensed that something had gone wrong. Thor rarely returned home in the middle of the afternoon. He spoke to her in Norwegian and Ellen glanced swiftly at Margaret and away again. She turned back towards the house, and when Margaret followed Erik indoors she was already brewing black coffee over the stove.

To Margaret's surprise, Thor came in with them. He did not mention the accident again, but Margaret saw him pour something from an ornate cut-glass decanter into her coffee.

"What is it?" she asked when he passed it to her.

"Drink it up," he commanded without satisfying her curiosity. "It will do you good."

The scalding mixture stung her throat, but within seconds it had sent a tingling warmth through her veins, bringing back the colour into her cheeks.

"That's better!" Thor observed almost kindly. "Now I can leave you without worrying about you."

"You couldn't help an accident," Margaret told him.

Suddenly his eyes were very dark.

"You might have been killed," he said.

Erik turned from the fire as Thor strode out to the jeep.

"That sort of thing isn't supposed to happen to Thor," he observed. "There will be some pointed questions asked when he gets back to the camp."

"But an accident!" Margaret protested. "Surely Thor wouldn't blame anyone for an accident?"

"No, but he'll want to know why every precaution wasn't taken," Erik said. "Thor doesn't leave much to chance. I suppose one accident in a lifetime is enough."

He was referring to Gerda's death, but she could not bring herself to talk about Gerda at that moment.

"You won't mind if I go up and change, will you?" she asked. "I feel completely dishevelled."

He straightened, coming to put his arm about her as she walked towards the hall.

"You never look dishevelled, Meg," he told her. "Always, you look perfect."

"I thought Norwegians never paid compliments!" she called back to him from half-way up the stairs.

"They will to you!" He laughed up at her. "Will you come sailing with me when you have changed, because tomorrow I have to go to Geilo on business for Thor?"

Part of the afternoon and all the evening still lay before them, but she found herself hesitating.

"You will have all day tomorrow to yourself," Erik reminded her, and his eager insistence won her over.

When she came downstairs again he had raided Ellen's carefully prepared *smorbrod* and was piling the open sandwiches one on top of the other to be eaten when they felt hungry out on the fjord.

"Will you come, Ellen?" he asked his sister not very hopefully. "We are going to sail."

Ellen shook her head.

"It is too late now. Thor will be home early tonight."

Erik chose a goat-track over the hills behind the house, and when they had climbed for an hour over the rough scree, he halted, pointing downwards to where a shaft of sunlight lay on blue water.

This unexpected arm of the fjord was almost at Solstua's back door, but there was no way of reaching it except by the narrow track by which they had come. Behind them she could see another track leading inland and marked at intervals with a large letter T. Because the moorland on either side was thick with cotton-grass, she guessed that it must be the way through peat bogs to a hidden upper valley sealed in behind the hills.

"Where does the other path lead?" she asked.

"To Drakensval."

She had half expected his answer.

"Is this—the only way?" she asked.

"There is the mountain road, but Thor has closed it," Erik said. "He is felling timber on the ridge to bring down to the camp."

"I see."

They walked in silence over the short, coarse grass which the cows loved, till they were nearly at the level of the fjord.

"Down there!" Erik pointed. "The boat-house. Can you see it? We have only to walk to it now."

"I don't think I want to go down," Margaret said suddenly, aware that this must have been the boat-house from which Gerda had set sail on that ill-fated day when she had sought to cross the fjord alone.

"You can't stand and admire mountains for ever!" Erik laughed, not seeing her white, pinched expression. "There is more to do in life than 'stand and stare'!"

"Who taught you to speak English, Erik?" she asked when she realized that she could not offer him her real reason for wanting to avoid that particular stretch of fjord.

"Thor."

The answer to everything, she thought, was Thor.

They scrambled down the last few hundred feet to the narrow ledge of turf which was all that supported the inevitable fjord-side jetty and the hut which housed Thor's boat.

They sailed for an hour, penetrating along a narrow tongue of water which went deep into the heart of the mountains till they rose, black and sheer, on either side. Ragged peaks which the sunlight had deserted stabbed the sky, and the icy glint of a glacier shimmered with the coldness of unsheathed steel in the grey north light. Sudden crags sprang into view, carved by nature or some demon of the wilds into fantastic shapes. They reminded Margaret of the carvings at Solstua; the trolls with tortured faces and and a single eye, the dragons and the serpents, and the wonderfully realistic flowers.

"Erik," she asked suddenly, "can we go back into the sun?"

"Anywhere!" he assured her at once. "You have only to command me!"

He had been very gay since they had left Solstua behind, and all the way back along the fjord, with the boat sailing gently before a light breeze, he sang the songs of the countryside which Margaret had been longing to hear. He had a pleasing tenor voice which echoed across the blue water and seemed to re-echo against the hillside as they neared their destination.

Before they reached the boat-house, however, the wind had strengthened and the sky had become over-cast. Clouds obliterated the highest peaks to the north, and Erik ended his impromptu serenade to give his full skill and attention to the boat. He was still completely confident, there was no doubt about that, but he had a respect for these wild waters which kept him from taking unnecessary risks.

On the final tack the wind seemed to drop completely, and looking up, Margaret saw that they had come into the shelter of the hills above Drakensval.

Erik let down the sail and their sturdy little craft drifted inshore towards the jetty.

"Well?" he demanded, leaning forwards across the tiller to where Margaret sat facing him in the tiny cockpit. "Were you afraid?"

"No," she answered quite truthfully. "It was— an adventure."

He laughed, the blue of his eyes deepening as he stretched across and pulled her strongly towards him.

"Meg, you are very sweet!" he told her, and kissed her full on the mouth.

The kiss surprised her. It had been lightly given, but beneath it she sensed warmth and insistence. She drew back a little, her breath coming swiftly between her parted lips. It was a situation she had not expected, but one that she should have been able to meet.

"Don't look so upset!" Erik laughed. "I'm in love with you, Meg! I shall always be in love with you." Then before she could answer him or even protest, he looked beyond her, as if some movement on the hill-side above them had drawn his attention from her.

"Thor," he said, his face flushing. "Up there on the hill, communing with his trolls, no doubt! He has come from Drakensval."

Slowly the boat turned as it took the little pier and Margaret found herself facing the hill. Thor was nowhere to be seen. She could not doubt, however, that Erik had recognized the unmistakable figure of his guardian silhouetted against the skyline.

CHAPTER FOUR

IT WAS fully an hour before Erik had moored the boat and spread his sails to dry on the racks along the boat-house roof. He worked leisurely, as if time meant nothing to him, which was perhaps the only characteristic he had in common with the people of the dale.

Margaret had no idea what time it was. She had forgotten to wear her wrist-watch and, indeed, had hardly used it at all since she had come to Helmsdal. She knew that it must be late, however, because the sun had dropped behind the western mountains, leaving only a pale lemon aftermath with bands of thin grey cloud across it, like a veil.

That glimpse of Thor on the horizon had made her feel strangely uneasy about their return to Sol-stua and more determined than ever to ask if she might do something constructive for her keep during the coming weeks.

There was, of course, the possibility that Thor had no intention of letting her stay.

Thrusting the disconcerting thought to the back of her mind, she climbed beside Erik up the narrow zig-zag path to the top of the cliff. They had eaten Ellen's sandwiches out on the fjord as they sailed along and she was conscious of feeling hungry again.

"We're going to be late," she reminded Erik when he would have lingered at the top of the cliff. "Thor won't want to wait for his meal till midnight."

Erik said: "You worry too much about Thor," but he quickened his pace and soon they were going downhill, with Solstua's red rooftop appearing in the distance as soon as they left the trees behind.

There were lights in the main sitting-room, and when they came nearer Margaret was surprised to hear the sound of a piano. It was being played exquisitely, and she stood beneath the window to listen as the liquid notes sped out into the night air.

"The slow movement from Grieg's piano Concerto," she murmured. "It's lovely, and so right, up here where it belongs!"

"That will be Prost Jorgensen," Erik explained. "No one else in the valley plays quite so well. Thor, apparently, has vistors!"

The music dropped into a deep silence as they moved away from the window towards the side door.

"I can't imagine Thor planning this," Erik remarked. "Though he could have made the arrangement at the camp this afternoon." He turned to smile down at her. "You ought to feel honoured, Meg," he added dryly.

"I feel as if we've let him down," Margaret said regretfully. "We should not have stayed away so long."

"No one would have expected Thor to entertain, even in a modest way," Erik said, "and it is not so very late. The party can only just have begun. Thor himself was up there at Drakensval less than an hour ago," he reminded her.

Ellen was crossing the hall with a tray of food when they went in.

"I told Thor you had gone to the fjord," she said.

"He probably saw us," Erik suggested, hanging up his *anorak*.

"Yes," Ellen agreed, "he did. I heard him telling Prost Jorgensen that you would not be long."

"Who else is there?" Erik asked, warming up to the idea of congenial company.

"Froken Moe, and the foreman from the camp." Ellen moved on ahead of them. "They have been here for one hour."

A tall, dark-coated priest rose from the piano stool when they appeared, crossing the room to shake hands. He was a handsome, broad-shouldered giant of a man, as tall as Thor himself, and looked as if he could wield an axe with as much ease. His grey-blue eyes were warm and friendly as he asked Margaret how she was settling down. They had met before, at her stepmother's funeral, and she had hoped that they might be able to renew their acquaintance like this.

"We were about to send out a search-party!" he smiled. "But Thor said no!"

"We stayed away longer than we intended to," Margaret apologized, turning to greet Kirsten Moe. "When it is never truly dark one loses all sense of time."

Kirsten's friendly gaze went beyond her to Erik. She was smiling, but the blue eyes were questioning, too.

Thor turned slowly from the long, heavily-carved sideboard where he had been mixing drinks. His expression told her nothing. This evening might have been like any other spent at Solstua during the past few weeks.

Fred Sonsberg, the foreman of the timber-felling gang, lumbered across to shake hands. He was like a big, goodnatured bear and blushed as easily as a schoolboy. His English was not good, but he gripped Margaret's fingers in a vice-like handshake which assured her that he was pleased to make her acquaintance. His grandmother, he said, had been a Scotswoman. She had been born in Dundee.

This being the extent of his conversational powers, at least in English, he slipped unobtrusively away to help Ellen with her trays.

The elaborate *aftens* which was being spread out on the table must have taken Ellen and Signe between them hours to prepare. Apart from the usual cold dishes which appeared at every meal, there were salmon and ham and small new potatoes tossed in butter, and bowls of tart little raspberries and bilberry jam.

"A meal fit for the gods!" Olav Jorgensen declared, helping Margaret to a varied selection from the cold table.

"The lusty, Viking gods!" Kirsten laughed. "Margaret may not yet have acquired an appetite for raw fish!"

"She will learn!" the young priest declared passing Margaret her plate. "How long do you mean to stay with us, Miss Holden?"

Margaret knew that she should have been prepared for the question instead of being flung into a
confusion of doubt and uncertainty because Thor
stood facing her across the narrow table and did not
say a word. He would not help her by making her
decision for her. He would not bid her to stay. His
cool, grey-blue gaze held hers, but it told her nothing.

I'm not sure," she faltered. "So much has
changed since I left England."

"Of course you'll stay, Meg!" Erik had come up
behind her and put a proprietorial arm about her
waist. "You've hardly seen anything of Norway yet.
You must see the mountains when the snow comes,
and learn to ski, and come to Oslo when you want to
return to civilization now and then!"

Thor turned away, a small pulse hammering
beneath his temple, his jaw set in an even harder line.

"Erik believes that we are complete barbarians
because we choose to remain here all the year,"
Kirsten said lightly. "But that is not so. We lead a
very full life, and we are content. You, also, will be
content, Margaret, if you decide to stay."

The decision did not rest with her, Margaret
thought unhappily. It must lie with Thor.

"Margaret will have the best of two worlds,"
Thor said, speaking for the first time. "The mountains—and Oslo when the mountains begin to pall."

"Don't think that you will be entirely buried alive
in Helmsdal, Miss Holden," Olav Jorgensen said.
"We may be a small community and the snow may
be an effective barrier between us and the outside
world on occasion, but we have our own methods of
passing the time. We have music, for instance, and
companionship, and work."

Margaret knew that these were the things she
understood, but without warmth, without the welcome she had wanted to feel at Solstua, how could she
accept them, how could she stay, even till winter
came?

Thor's indifference, his almost cynical acceptance
of the compromise which Erik had proposed, had

chilled her, making it difficult for her to feel that she would ever be accepted in her mother's country.

When the meal was over and without having to be asked, Olav Jorgensen went back to the piano, and for the next hour Margaret sat entranced, listening to the Chopin melodies she loved, and Bach and Debussy and Grieg, rendered faultlessly by ear. The young priest was an artist who would have graced any concert platform, but he took his talent for granted. He was a simple man and he saw it as a gift which he must share.

They sat in a semi-circle round the wide stone fireplace in the corner of the room, Thor at one side, with his dark head in the shadows and Ellen seated on a low stool at his feet, and Margaret at the opposite side, with Erik and Kirsten and Fred Sonsburg between them.

The music changed and Olav began to play the folk songs of the countryside. Kirsten and Ellen reached for the two mandolines which stood on either side of the chimneypiece, but although Ellen looked at Thor expectantly, he did not move. Remembering what Erik had said about his violin, Margaret supposed that this impromptu sing-song must be painful to him and she did not look at him as Kirsten drew out her plectrum and ran it gently across the mandoline's strings.

It was enchanting music, soft and beguiling as the blue fjord water under the summer sun, and wild and strange and compelling as the silent mountains beneath their first covering of snow. Margaret felt it running in her veins like a mad ecstasy, her pulses throbbing to its secret beauty, her whole being entranced by it. Some of the songs she had heard before, from Eide, but there were many still to learn.

The young priest's repertoire seemed endless, and even Erik appeared to enjoy it. When a song appealed to him he sang it lustily; when he was silent he looked almost content. Stretched out on the dark bearskin rug at Margaret's feet, he threw back his fair head to look at her, and once, when the music was low and soft and tender, he stretched up his hand and took hers, holding her fingers in a close grip.

In the shadows on the far side of the fireplace Thor moved. It was almost a violent movement, as if he would thrust a memory away from him. The last few bars of the love-song throbbed into silence and he rose to his feet, thrusting another log into the heart of the fire with a savagery which linked his mood with Olav's wilder music and turned the softer tones of love aside.

"Another drink?" he suggested, crossing to the piano. "This must be thirsty work."

He could be the perfect host, Margaret decided, easy and natural with the people he knew and liked.

"It's after midnight," Olav Jorgensen protested. "We ought to go."

"The night is still young," Thor assured him, crossing to the sideboard where the glasses were. "I will run you back to the camp."

He did not seem to consider rest for himself, yet Margaret knew that he would be up before six in the morning, when the pale light which did not die even at midnight would be clear and strong again with the rising sun.

Kirsten took Olav's place on the piano stool, playing little, lively tunes that were as light as air.

"The tunes of the happy trolls!" she told Margaret, who had come to stand at the piano. "For, you see," she added, looking up suddenly, "there is much happiness in the mountains if you care to look for it."

A sudden constriction in her throat made it impossible for Margaret to reply. Already this strange, wild land of blue glaciers and savage mountain peaks and deeply silent vales had taken possession of her heart and she knew that it would never be quite the same again. If she had to leave Norway, she would leave so much of her heart behind.

"Parties never break up unless someone is very firm about it!" Kirsten declared at last, getting up from the piano and closing it with an air of finality.

"It was nice of you, Thor," she added on a more serious note, "to have us."

Thor looked down at her with a smile in his eyes.

"You know that you are always welcome, Kirsten," he assured her.

Margaret turned sharply away. He really meant that about Kirsten. She would always be a welcome guest at Solstua whenever she liked to come.

"Tired?" Erik asked. "Or have you time to look at the stars?"

"I should help Ellen," Margaret protested, but he swept the suggestion aside.

"Signe will do that."

They stood on the top step together while Thor brought round the car.

"Come to the camp again," Kirsten invited. "Any day. When Erik returns to Oslo you must not feel lonely."

Thor let in his clutch and the car slid away.

"I don't know whether Kirsten feels that she might marry Thor or not," Erik observed. "She is often at Solstua these days, but once it was said that she would marry Paul Loren. That was before Loren went away to become famous as a surgeon. Kirsten is a strange person. She never seems to want to leave the mountains, yet she has undoubted talent."

"I think she is a very nice person," Margaret said, remembering the look on Kirsten Moe's face when Thor had mentioned Paul Loren's name. "She seems to be staunch and loyal, and I feel that her friendship would be a worthwhile thing."

Erik smiled, drawing her close.

"How serious you are, Meg!" he teased. "You think such long, long thoughts!"

"Don't you—sometimes?" she queried.

"Quite often," he agreed. "I think, for instance, that I could marry you and be reasonably happy. I think that you are so beautiful that I could always look at you and be glad!"

"You set a great store on beauty, Erik," she said lightly. "But surely there are other things to consider about marriage."

"Only whether you will be happy or not!" He drew her close again, kissing her. "We could be happy, Meg. We could make a wonderful life together!"

"It's—too soon to speak of that sort of thing," she said, drawing her hands away. "There is your career to think about, the year you still have to spend at the University."

He laughed her reminder aside.

"That is not important," he said. "Not so important on a night of stars!" He put his arm about her, drawing her with him out across the shadowed lawn. "Come up the hillside a little way, Meg, and I will show you a whole mountain of stars! It is a night to see a very long way."

The night held a subtle magic and Margaret was far from tired. If Thor had asked her to go to the camp with him, driving through the silent forest for the sheer beauty and pleasure of the journey, she would have known rapture, but he had not asked. He had left it to Erik to show her the stars.

What a fool she was to care. What a romantic, senseless fool! Yet her heart slowed down a pace as she followed Erik up the pathway to the hill.

In the bright gleam of a million stars they could see all the mountains above Helmsdal, set high and clear-cut against the pale opal of the sky. Erik stopped and turned her to face the north.

"There it is," he said. "Your view to remember!"

Above them, and above its surrounding peaks, a giant amongst mountains reared its snow-capped head against the glittering heavens, so high that the stars themselves seemed to be resting on its brow.

"You've seen it before, during the day," Erik reminded her, "but the Skagastöl has an added magic by night. It is the highest peak in the Horung." He laughed down at her. "The Jotunheimen are the home of the Giants, and once you are captured there is no way out!"

He was teasing her and she should have been able to laugh in return, but somehow she could not. Deep down in her was an awareness that his joking words carried their own conviction. Was she already captured? Had she already left her easily-wounded heart in the home of the Giants?

"Why do we see it so plainly now?" she asked unsteadily.

"Because we are on the other side of Drakensval."

Erik turned back towards Solstua, but for a moment Margaret could not follow him. The other side of Drakensval! These steep, tortuous paths along the mountainsides confused and bewildered her, and Drakensval seemed to be everywhere. Wherever she turned she was confronted by it and the thought of the tragic place it held in Thor Revold's memories.

"It's very late," she said. "We must go back."

When they reached the house Thor's car was standing in the shadow of the *stabbur*, but Thor himself was nowhere to be seen. Solstua was in darkness, save for a light high up near the rafters, in Ellen's room, but somehow Margaret knew that Thor was not asleep within those sheltering walls.

"Meg," Erik whispered, drawing her to him, "promise me that you will not leave Solstua till I come back. Promise me that nothing Thor can do will separate us."

He was holding her against him, bending her head back to kiss her as soon as she gave him her promise, and a shiver ran through her that was almost a premonition of disaster. Yet he was to return to the mountains in two days' time; he was to come back to Solstua to lay his careless claim to her heart long before the shadow of Thor ever came between them.

"It is too soon to promise," Margaret said. "You have so much to do yet, Erik."

She felt that she had been playing for time, and she did not sllep well during what still remained of the night. She was conscious of an emptiness about Solstua, of security gone out of it, which kept her awake until the stars had paled, and when she did fall asleep it was only after she had crossed the floor and barred her shutters against the encroaching daylight.

Because of these barred shutters, she slept late and was thoroughly ashamed of herself when she arrived downstairs to discover that both Thor and Erik had gone. An isolated place was set for her at one end of the long refectory table, and Ellen came in as soon as she heard her moving about.

The tray she carried held the usual assortment of cold meats and fish garnished with onion and hard-boiled eggs, but Margaret rejected them in favour of *flatbrod*, coffee and milk, feeling that the wafer-thin breakfast biscuit was as much as she could manage after the generous meal of the night before.

"Are you not tired, Ellen?" she asked, making conversation, and quite sure that Ellen must have been up before six o'clock, milking goats and preparing Thor's breakfast.

"We are never tired in the mountains," Ellen assured her slowly, gathering up the rejected platter to carry it to the kitchen.

Her reserve was more than shyness and not quite hostility, and Margaret found it difficult to meet. The watchful blue eyes were constantly upon her, yet she could not believe that Ellen resented her friendship with Erik.

"Ellen," she tried again, "would you like me to teach you to write and spell in English?"

Ellen gave her a long, considering look, in which the desire for knowledge struggled with a much more primitive emotion.

"Is it long to learn?" she asked guardedly.

"It shouldn't be, since you speak quite well already."

"If Thor says so," Ellen conceded, "it will be all right. You will not be long here, but I will learn as much as I can."

Had Thor said that? "She will not be long here and we will be alone in our isolation again." Suddenly Margaret knew that Ellen's hostility was almost impersonal. She would have resented anyone who might take her dead sister's place in Thor Revold's affections.

She needn't worry, Margaret thought bleakly. Thor has shut up his heart in Drakensval, and his humanity with it.

If the bitter accusation was not entirely justified, she did not stop to think about it. Thor resented her. She had crashed in on his lost love; she had thrust herself between him and his memories. Unwittingly —yes, but as surely as if she had done it with the utmost intention.

Restlessly, she contemplated the day before her, missing Erik's cheerful companionship more than she had expected. She could, of course, go to the lumber camp and seek out Kirsten Moe, but Kirsten would be busy with her book-keeping and she might run into Thor, who would only see her as an encumbrance. Ellen would not accept her offer of tuition till Thor had agreed to it, and there seemed to be nothing else she could do about the house.

She began to wish that it had been possible for her to go with Erik to Geilo, but he was to be away overnight, staying with Thor's business acquaintance and returning on the following day.

The thought of the time they had spent on the fjord the previous afternoon kept recurring to her. It had been cool and pleasant beside the water, but but it was too far to walk to the foot of the valley, to the village and the inner fjord. The way over the hill was quicker and certainly within walking distance.

Ellen said that she could have *middag* whenever she wanted it, and the meal was so satisfying that she did not trouble to ask for sandwiches to tide her over till her return in the evening.

"When will you come back?" Ellen asked. "I will tell Thor."

"I shall be back before Thor comes," Margaret assured her. "I am only going a short distance over the hill. Perhaps as far as the boat-house on the fjord."

Ellen looked surprised, but did not make any comment, as was her way. She supposed that Margaret knew what she was doing.

A sense of exhilaration, compounded of the need for action and the keen mountain air, took Margaret on her way with a light step. Although the track led uphill as soon as she had left Solstua behind, she covered it at a brisk pace, thankful that the sun did not glare down on her so fiercely as it had done the previous afternoon. It was veiled by a thin mist which had not quite dispersed all morning, but it did not obstruct her view and she was more thankful for it than anything else. She would not have believed that Norway could be so warm, even in August.

It was, of course, nearly September now, she remembered, thinking of the passing days with a little catch in her throat. September and October, perhaps, and then the snow would begin to fall.

By that time she would have made up her mind. Long before the snow came, perhaps, she would be back in England, looking for a job and trying to forget all this.

She gazed about her at the crowding mountains which reminded her, always, of Thor. Their strength and remoteness set them apart, isolating them in a world of their own.

When she reached the fjordside she sat on the wooden jetty for an hour, looking out across water that had changed overnight from blue to slate. It was still placid, with the mountains reflected clearly in it, but overhead the sky was a universal grey. If a storm blew up this exposed arm of the fjord would be whipped into a lashing fury of angry waves dashing themselves to pieces against the black rocks beneath her.

Suddenly she was remembering the narrow entrance to the inner fjord, that dark strait of swiftly-flowing water which wind and tide would turn into a swirling fury, bringing destruction to anything which might be caught in it.

Swiftly she rose to her feet. The silence had become oppressive; the beauty of the day had passed.

She began the steep ascent of the cliff, up and up by the narrow, winding track until a suspicious moisture made her pause to look about her. She could see only a yard or two on either side. The water beneath her had disappeared in a grey sea of mist which thickened even as she watched it. Thin columns of it spiralled and dissolved above her head until the path was lost, and she knew a moment of panic groping for it in the obscuring greyness.

There was nothing she could do but go on. To remain trapped there between the cliff-top and the narrow ledge at fjord level would involve a wetting anyway, and to return to the boat-house for shelter seemed equally foolish. She could not handle the boat alone, far less hope to steer it between the ugly crags of the entrance to the inner fjord, and that was the only way that led from the jetty back to Helmsdal and Solstua.

She had to continue her climb, whatever she felt about it.

In places she had almost to go on hands and knees, and it seemed hours before she felt the short, coarse grass of the cliff top beneath her feet. Visibility up here was reduced to less than a yard, and then to inches. The insidious, creeping mist had clamped down on everything about her.

There was no sound, not even the cry of a sea-bird to mock her, and nothing to guide her. Blindly she sought the path, realizing that her feet stayed on solid ground only by a miracle. It was difficult to keep track of time; she seemed to be walking on and on in an infinity of space where only the obscuring grey pall of mist was real.

If I can keep to the path, she thought desperately, I can't go wrong. Soon I should reach the ridge of hills above Solstua. Soon the path should be going down.

The path led on and up. Once she stumbled against something hard and sharp, recognizing it with horror to be one of the red metal T's which marked the peat bogs and veering away from it till she touched solid ground again. This was treacherous. If she stumbled into a bog she would be lost.

Almost uncannily her feet kept to the hard track of the path, and perhaps she had miscalculated the

time it had taken them to reach the ridge above the
dale the afternoon before. Then, suddenly, the path
she was following broadened and dipped and she
almost cried out with joy as her feet began to go
downwards.

Within seconds the thin trails of mist began to
disperse. She could see the path again, a broader path
than she remembered, leading surprisingly into a
valley among unfamiliar hills.

She knew then what must have happened. Somewhere up there on the ridge the path had divided.
Erik had pointed out this way to her as they went
back to Solstua, the way that led to Drakensval.

Standing there while the mist swirled behind her
like the closing of a curtain, she knew that she could
not go back by the way she had come. It was too
dangerous. She must go on and find the timber road
that went through Thor's secret valley.

Aware of the same sense of trespass which she had
experienced in the silent corridor at Solstua, she
forced herself to walk on. There was no other way.

Gradually the valley broadened out to cradle a
narrow lake of glacier-green water, with the glacier
itself lying in a cleft of the surrounding mountains
like a thin, unsheathed sword, thrown down in challenge by the giants of the Jotunheimen. The valley
itself was beautiful. When Margaret turned from her
contemplation of the glacier to look at it the mist had
cleared, and she drew in her breath in silent wonder.
If this indeed was Drakensval, no wonder Thor loved
it and had hoped to make his home there, at least for
half the year. It was green and gentle and kind,
clothed on its northern side by a vast forest of tall,
straight pines whose slender tops looked as if they
touched the sky.

From where she stood she could see almost the
whole length of the lake with its wooden jetty and
the inevitable boat-house which every stretch of
water in Norway seemed to boast. And above the
jetty, standing out against the green hillside, was
what she had come to recognize as a summer farm.

It was larger than most of the others she had seen and was designed in chalet style, with a group of turf-roofed huts at some distance from it, where cattle might be kept, but there was no sign of life about it.

As she came closer she could see that the gables and steps of the heavy roof had been richly carved. The conventional dragons of the high mountains jutted out above the eaves at each of its four corners to keep away the evil spirits that roamed above the hills, and door and lintel bore similar carvings on a smaller scale. Silhouetted against the grey skyline, these strange carved heads were the last thing she had expected to see. They looked fantastic with their bared teeth and raised claws, and their flaring nostrils seemed entirely out of place in the gentle peace of the green vale they were supposed to guard.

Then, suddenly, fantastically, that peace was rent by awful sound. A dozen baying dogs came charging down the hillside towards her, let loose, it seemed, from one of the turf-roofed huts.

In the split second before she turned in ignominious flight, she realized that they were separated from her by a barrier of heavy wire netting, but even then she ran a little way to put distance also between them.

They were evidently a dog-team, used for drawing a sled in the winter and fretted now by inactivity as they threw themselves against the wire. Margaret supposed them to be huskies. She wondered if they belonged to Thor.

Backing discreetly towards the chalet on the hill, she had a peculiar sensation of being watched by unseen eyes. The chalet itself had an empty, un-lived-in appearance, and most of its windows were tightly shuttered, but presently an elderly Lapp with a witch's face put her head round the door and stared.

Margaret supposed that it would be useless to try to explain her predicament to the woman or ask for shelter in the few words of Norwegian she had mastered. Vaguely she signalled to where she thought the timber road might be, and the old crone gave her a toothless smile, pointing in turn towards the trees.

A path led round the side of the house and Margaret followed it because it also went in the direction of the trees. The old woman smiled again, coming out on to the broad wooden step of the chalet to watch her progress.

When she had safely negotiated the gable end of the house Margaret found herself in an orchard where ripe apples were already falling to the ground and sheep strayed beneath the trees. The path led through the orchard to a clearing, set high on a miniature plateau above a curve of the lake, and here the grass, which once must have been verdantly fresh and was still being cropped round the edges by some surprised-looking sheep, had been burned in a wide circle. The dark patch of naked earth was a shock to the senses after so much beauty, and she stood staring down at it for fully a minute before she realized that she was not alone.

Looking up, she found Thor Revold facing her across the breadth of the clearing, his eyes narrowed, the bitter anger in his heart strongly reflected in his tense, drawn face.

"Why have you come here?" he demanded. "What did you hope to find?"

The shock of their meeting, even though she had known that the chalet must be his, stunned Margaret into silence. Thor stood looking at her for a moment longer, and then he strode across the burnt clearing to her side.

"What happened?" he asked briefly. "How did you get here?"

He realized, then, that she had not come out of curiosity, deliberately prying into the past.

"I went to the fjord," she confessed. "I was foolish enough to want to repeat my pleasure of yesterday. After I had been there for an hour I started to climb back up the cliff."

She was almost breathless. It was difficult to explain such an adventure to Thor without making it all sound utterly foolish and child-like.

"And you were caught by the mist?" he suggested grimly. "You realize, of course, that you might not have got here safely? These coastal mists come down in a second and you could have been trapped in a bog or fallen hundreds of feet straight into the fjord."

She had been well aware of her peril for the past half-hour, and his stern reminder almost unnerved her. It was only when she had come into the valley and the mist had cleared that she had fully realized how dangerous her journey had been.

"I'm sorry," she said. "You must think me an utter fool."

Thor took one look at her and turned back towards the chalet, not saying what he thought.

"You've had about enough," he decided grimly. "You're soaking wet, and you must be chilled to the bone."

She could hardly believe the rough kindness of his voice, but she could not let him open the chalet to her because of her momentary need of warmth and shelter.

"If we could go home, Thor—back to Solstua," she suggested. "I will be all right."

He looked at her again and would not change his mind.

"It's seven miles to Solstua and eight to the camp," he told her briefly. "I walked over, so I haven't the car to take you back in. When you have had something warm to drink I will send for it. We are on the telephone here."

He would drive back over the timber road, Margaret supposed, with a thousand demons of regret and bitterness snarling close behind him, awakened by her foolish stumbling upon forbidden ground.

"Please let me try to walk back—now," she begged. "It isn't really far, and perhaps I could wait somewhere along the road if it did prove too much for me."

They had reached the gable end of the chalet and the carved dragon heads seemed to leer down at her mockingly.

"The place is empty," Thor said "There is no reason why you should not go in."

It was true. If the chalet had once been furnished, ready for a bride, there was nothing left of all Thor's loving preparations for the woman he had expected to marry The hollow sound of their footsteps echoed against bare boards to the lofty rafters, and the closely-shuttered windows drove out all the light.

Thor opened one of them, letting the harshness of the grey day stab the deeper gloom within.

"Wait here," he commanded, "and I'll light a fire."

He disappeared, returning in a moment or two bearing the necessary kindling and followed by the Lapp woman. She gave Margaret a long, sideways look and smiled her toothless smile.

"Is she your caretaker?" Margaret asked Thor as he crossed the thinly chopped wood in a lattice pattern in the iron stove which stood in one corner of the room.

"In a way. She looks after me when I come here, but she does not live in the house." He straightened and stood looking down into the leaping flames. "Her home is in one of the summer huts up on the hillside. Her husband attends to the dogs and she makes butter and goat-cheese for the men at the camp."

Margaret could not imagine Thor living in this empty house when he came to Drakensval, with only the Lapp woman to look after him, but it seemed that he needed little comfort. Somewhere, perhaps, there would be a bed and a chair and a table where he could eat his meals, if he bothered much with meals at all.

When the fire was roaring in the stove he motioned her towards it.

"You'd better take off that wet jacket and try to thaw out," he advised. "Your shoes are soaking, too. You must have strayed off the path more than once."

Remembering her plunges into the edge of the bogs, Margaret shivered.

"You always seem to be coming to my rescue, Thor," she said.

He did not answer that, leaving her to take off her shoes and jacket and dry them at the fire. When he came back he was carrying a wooden tray with a jug of steaming coffee on it and two yellow beakers.

"Here you are!" he said. "This should complete the thaw!"

The hot, black liquid stung Margaret's throat, but she was grateful for its warmth. Thor had left the stove doors open and the orange-red flames leapt through, flickering on the carved panelling of the walls and on the ancient rafters overhead. Part of the chalet was old and some of the carvings must have been done hundreds of years ago, yet the motif was much the same as Thor's efforts at Solstua. There were flowers and serpents and small, darting lizards, and trolls with evil faces, and fat, contented trolls, usually with only one eye.

Margaret left the warm circle of firelight to run an exploring finger over the panel behind the stove.

"All this is very old," she said, "yet you have repeated it most faithfully at Solstua."

He came to stand beside her.

"It's a sort of tradition in the valleys," he explained, "and it doesn't change much. When the original Solstua was destroyed some of the panelling was recovered practically unharmed, and I built it in here. Then I copied it at Solstua during the winter months."

"It must have taken many winters and a great deal of work," Margaret observed.

He shrugged.

"Not so very long. We have much time to spend indoors and—I had an incentive to work, which makes any task easy."

He meant the thought of his marriage to Gerda, and she had awakened his memories by her inquisitive questioning. Margaret put her empty beaker down on the tray and turned to the window.

"The sun seems to be coming through," she said unsteadily. "My shoes are quite dry now. I can easily walk back to Solstua if you show me the way."

He closed the stove with a deliberation she had noticed in him before.

"I have sent for the car," he told her briefly. "It will be better if you wait here till it comes."

Margaret did not want to stay in the empty house. The sun had broken through the clouds and lay in a golden shaft across the valley, ringing the mountain-tops in a noose of yellow light, but perhaps Thor did not want her to explore his secret kingdom.

"I would like to wait in the sun," she said. "Perhaps I could sit out on the porch at the front door till the car comes."

He followed her out, closing the heavy door behind them, and Margaret felt the sun on her face with a new warmth. The whole broad valley seemed full of it. Only inside the chalet had there been a sense of chill.

"Would it have been shorter to go back by the cliff path?" she asked, aware that the mist was clearing in that direction, too.

"Shorter, perhaps, but still dangerous," he answered. "I think it would be safer if you avoided the cliff paths while you are here, Margaret," he added.

While she remained there! Was there the hope behind his suggestion that her stay would not be long?

"I wanted to speak to you about that, Thor," she said, standing beside him and gripping the rough wooden balustrade in front of her. "If—if I am to stay, I would like to feel that I am being useful."

"There is no need for you to work," he assured her. "Signe and Ellen run Solstua quite smoothly between them."

"I was thinking of Ellen," Margaret said. "I wondered if I could help with her English."

He gave her a quick, searching scrutiny.

"You might try," he agreed. "She is eager to learn, but I warn you that she can be difficult."

"I shall have to tackle that obstacle when I come to it," Margaret said, feeling happier than she had done for days. "I think Ellen and I might become quite good friends if we understood each other better."

He looked at her with a sudden wry smile.

"Is that your recipe for ultimate happiness between two people, Margaret?" he asked. "Understanding?"

"Isn't it a fairly sure one?" she said quickly.

"Perhaps you are right," he agreed. "I want Ellen to have every opportunity of leading a full and a happy life," he continued thoughtfully. "She does not wish to leave Solstua at the moment, but I don't want anything to be lacking in her education if she does decide to go away. If you will help with her English, I shall be grateful."

It was a formal enough acceptance of her help, but there had been a suggestion of warmth between them for a moment which she longed to preserve.

"I'll do my best," she promised, smiling. "The rest will be up to Ellen."

They walked down the chalet steps and out of the shadow of its overhanging eaves, to be greeted instantly by the huskies on the far side of the wire netting.

"I had visions of being torn to pieces," Margaret laughed, "when I first saw them bounding towards me down the hill! I was never so glad to see a fence in all my life!"

"They are not completely domesticated," he admitted. "They are sleigh dogs, and some of them are used for hunting. It would not do to tame them too much. They would become soft and too easily turned from their main objective, which is to work."

Wondering if that was also Thor's personal philosophy, Margaret followed him up the hill towards the turf-roofed huts where, he told her, the cattle were kept in winter, and not until the car swung into view round a bend in the twisting timber road did she realize that he had assiduously steered her away from the scarred clearing on the other hillside.

CHAPTER FIVE

WHEN Erik returned to Solstua he claimed Margaret's attention with a smiling deliberation which suggested some sort of understanding, at least, between them. He found her a light rod which she could handle easily and taught her to fish in the swift-flowing streams; he arranged long and often arduous treks into the mountains, and he taught her to sail the boat on the fjord.

Occasionally work intervened and he was asked to help Thor, while Margaret gave Ellen the first of her English lessons. Ellen proved an apt pupil, but even at the end of two weeks it could not be said that their friendship had progressed. The almost hostile reserve remained. Ellen was willing to accept her as a teacher, but not as an intimate. Margaret could feel that barrier between them like some tangible thing thrust deliberately in her path, and she could not scale it. Ellen had accepted the gesture she had made because Thor wished her to perfect her English, but that was all.

Baffled and a little hurt by her failure, Margaret found herself spending more and more of her free time in Erik's company. He was the only one at Solstua who seemed to have time to spare for her. Thor was constantly at the lumber camp and it might almost be said that he was avoiding her. Since he had brought her down from Drakensval that afternoon she had scarcely seen him to speak to. He left the house before she was awake in the mornings and returned late to the solitary meal which Ellen prepared for him. Erik shrugged and said that one day Thor would work himself to a standstill.

"I know the timber has to come down before the snow begins to fall," he told Margaret, "but Thor need not really work as if his life depended upon it. Perhaps, of course, it is his way of trying to forget," he mused. "My sister's death has hardened Thor."

Erik had accepted the fact that Thor would never forget Gerda. Everyone accepted it, Margaret thought unhappily. Even Ellen's silent hostility was a reflection of it. Ellen who thought the world of Thor and had worshipped her sister from her earliest childhood. Ellen's grief at Gerda's death would have been almost as great as Thor's.

During those early days of September the lumber camp was a hive of industry, but once in a while the men relaxed to go off in twos and threes on hunting expeditions over the high plateau, or simply to laze and fish under the autumn sun.

On one such occasion Kirsten Moe arranged a picnic.

"You mustn't bring anything with you," she said when she telephoned from the camp to invite Margaret and Erik to join her. "It's entirely my party. You may not survive my cooking, but at least you can try to walk it off! Bring Ellen," she added as an afterthought.

Surprisingly, Ellen agreed to come.

"Thor will be away," she said. "He is going into the mountains."

"Alone?" Margaret asked.

"Yes," Ellen said. "Thor always goes alone."

The car was left at Solstua for their use. Thor set off early in the morning on foot with a gun over his shoulder and a rucksack strapped to his back. Two of the dogs had been brought down from Drakensval the evening before and they followed eagerly at his heels, as well aware as their master that the chase was on.

If Thor had known about Kirsten's picnic, he had not mentioned it. It seemed that he preferred to be alone.

Erik drove them to the camp in the car.

"Hullo, there!" Kirsten greeted them. "We're almost ready. Do you think I'm going to get all this food into the boot?" she added doubtfully, surveying the pile of packages and baskets on the canteen steps.

"I think we're going to have to struggle," Erik laughed. "There's always the jeep, of course!"

"We can't take the whole camp along with us," Kirsten reminded him, "although it looks as if we are trying to!" She had even brought a stove, which she said they would need to brew fresh coffee when they got as far as the glacier. "Olav Jorgensen is coming, and Fred Sonsburg," she added, glancing in Ellen's direction.

Ellen flushed, but did not respond, and Kirsten turned to hail the jeep with the priest and the timber foreman on board.

"It looks as if we're going to be overloaded," she called to them apologetically. "Do you think we ought to take the jeep?"

"I think it would be safer," Olav laughed. "I'm quite sure you'll want to sit beside the stove!"

Erik got back into the car beside Margaret.

"You're going to enjoy this," he said. "Kirsten is famous for her picnics. Something always happens —something she hasn't planned!"

"Erik is being grossly unfair!" Kirsten protested. "I leave absolutely nothing to chance, as a rule."

"Rules are nearly always broken!" Erik observed. "What is the surprise element to be this time, Kirsten?"

"If I told you, it wouldn't be a surprise," Kirsten reminded him. "You must wait and see!"

It was a glorious day, and as they penetrated farther and farther into the mountains Margaret almost forgot that Thor might have been with them. It would have been the most natural thing, and she was sure that Kirsten had asked him, but he had chosen to go off on his own.

High on the Sognfjell Road, with the great snow-crested peaks of the Jotunheimen towering above them, she forgot time and even Thor for a moment. The utter beauty of their surroundings arrested thought, but when they stopped for their first meal on the edge of the glacier she felt that she was beginning to understand the essential Thor. This was somewhere where you had to come alone. Thor had been born and bred here, and no man who loved these mountains and had lived among them all his life could ever love lightly.

The tour which Kirsten had mapped out for them was a circular one, but it seemed inevitable that they should stray from it at least once.

"Let's see this!" "We must show Margaret that!" she would cry, and off they would drive at a tangent, but towards the end of the afternoon she appeared to have a definite object in view. They had been travelling west at a high speed for about an hour, leaving the jagged edge of the Horung behind them, when she signalled the jeep to slow down.

"We are going to leave the cars here and climb up to the hut," she told Erik from the back seat. "It is all arranged."

"Margaret will never do it," Erik objected. "She has walked a score of miles as it is."

"Norwegian miles into the bargain!" Margaret laughed. "But I'd love to go. I'm not in the least tired."

Erik grunted, drawing the car on to the side of the road.

"You've seen a waterfall before," he pointed out.

"But not this one!" Kirsten declared.

It was true. Half-way up the hillside they heard the rush of the falls, the great spate of water as it tumbled from the plateau above them sheer over the face of the mountain to the valley below. The water itself remained hidden, however, until they were almost upon it.

Then, as they rounded a bend in the path, a dog rushed towards them, to be called immediately to heel by a familiar voice.

Thor!

"Thor promised to meet us here," Kirsten explained with a small, half-triumphant smile. "He said that Margaret should see the falls."

Before anyone could reply, Thor had joined them. This must have been his objective of the day, and he had covered the ground on foot, walking the best part of twenty miles.

Margaret felt her heart beating fast as their eyes met.

"Any luck?" Olav Jorgensen asked.

Thor shrugged.

"Not a thing. They say it is unlucky to hunt alone!"

Kirsten laughed.

"You do not believe in luck, Thor!" she reminded him.

"No, that is true," he agreed.

Erik drew Margaret's hand through his arm.

"Come on, Meg," he said, "I'll show you the falls."

"We're having a meal first," Kirsten called after them almost sharply. "It's all arranged "

Erik hesitated, but it was useless to argue against Kirsten Moe when she had made up her mind.

Round another bend in the path they came to a small guest-house which Margaret had come to recognize as typical of these mountain regions. It was tucked into the hillside, with very little ground attached to it, but it commanded a superb view across a valley and this one boasted the added attraction of a waterfall.

Thor had already ordered their meal, and when it was finished he led the way to the falls.

Margaret found herself walking beside him, with the rush and plunge of the water very near. Nature had hidden her masterpiece behind a green curtain of pine, and not until they were almost upon it did the silver waterfall appear in all its full magnificence, falling like a fine white veil from the rock above. Margaret gave a gasp of sheer, awed surprise and stood still.

"It's—wonderful!" she breathed at last. "I've never seen anything quite like it before."

For a moment she was alone with Thor. They stood beside the water looking up to the smooth dark ridge of rock from which it spilled.

"What's its name?" she asked, because the lovely, descriptive Norse words always fascinated her.

"On maps it is called the Nordfoss," Thor said slowly. "The locals call it the Bridal Veil."

He had spoken without looking round, and perhaps she had only imagined that his voice had hardened on the last half-dozen words. The others came up behind them, Erik to take Margaret's arm again and Kirsten to ask:

"Can we go into the cave, Thor? Do you think there is time?"

Thor turned.

"Why not?" he asked. "It is the conventional thing to do."

Margaret went first, with Erik. They went in behind the wide curtain of water to a deep cavern beyond it where the light was a strange, pale green and a thin line of stalactites hung down from the roof like fairy banners encrusted with pearls. The sound of the falling water deafened them so that they walked in silence. Margaret wondered if Thor had come into the cave with them. He had probably seen it all before, and perhaps he had come here often with Gerda.

When her eyes had become accustomed to the strange light she saw that they were penetrating along a sort of passage which went deep into the hillside and here, Erik warned her, the narrow path began to go down.

"We come out at a lower level," he explained, "but still under the falls."

In this narrow cleft between the rocks the roar of the water was reduced and Margaret could recognize the voices behind her. Kirsten's ready laughter and Olav Jorgensen's pleasant banter floated down to them, with now and then Ellen's voice, speaking to the timber foreman in their own language, but if Thor were there, he must be bringing up the rear alone and in silence.

The rush and roar of the water met them again as the light strengthened and a fine mist of spray came drifting back into their faces.

"We may have to run for it here," Erik shouted,

grasping her hand. "There isn't such a wide clearance between the cave and the drop."

They ran out into the sunshine, dazzled after the dimness of the cave and, one by one, the others followed. Kirsten had misjudged her swift dash behind the waterfall and emerged with a wetting, and Margaret had a halo of dewy drops on the fringe of dark hair above her brow. She did not think to brush them away as Thor followed Ellen and Fred Sonsburg from the cave.

It was minutes before she was aware of Ellen's concentrated stare, and fully another second before the younger girl spoke.

"The waterfall!" she said. "You have it on your hair!"

"Yes." Margaret brushed her hand across her brow. "I felt it when I came through. It is nothing much."

Ellen continued to stare at her.

"How can you say it is nothing?" she demanded. "It is what we all know up here in the Helmsdal." She paused, drawing in a deep breath. "When the Bridal Veil clings to you it means that you will be married before the year is out!"

There could be no doubt about Ellen's belief in the ancient superstition.

"That isn't entirely beyond the bounds of possibility!" Erik declared, putting an arm about Margaret's shoulders. "Don't try to brush it away, Meg. The Bridal Veil suits you!"

"What about me?" Kirsten's voice seemed to crash into an awkward silence. "I'm positively drowned in it!"

"It must mean that I am going to be a very busy man before the end of the year!" Olav Jorgensen said with a twinkle in his eyes. "Ellen, you are too young for a bridal veil yet, but you can wear the bridesmaid's wreath of Christmas roses!"

They laughed, forming themselves into a little procession to go down towards the waiting cars, and only Margaret seemed to notice that Thor had not spoken nor joined in their laughter.

It was late when they reached Solstua, but it was taken for granted that Kirsten and the two men would stay for the elaborate *aftens* which Signe had prepared. This late supper was the most companionable meal of the day in the average Norwegian household, and especially in the mountain farm, for then the men were home, their work completed and honest rest a thing to be enjoyed.

Thor sat at the head of the long table, with Kirsten and Margaret on either side. He was the perfect host, but Margaret could not keep her eyes from straying to the far end of the lavishly-spread board where there was an empty space. There was no mistress at Solstua and she wondered if there ever would be.

With coffee on a tray before them, they sat afterwards round a crackling wood fire discussing their day and planning another before winter should clamp down on the dale, but it seemed to Margaret that they all avoided mention of the Nordfoss, the magic waterfall which Thor had called the Bridal Veil.

Thor saw his guests safely back to the camp. It was well after midnight when they left, but Margaret did not sleep for over an hour when she finally went to bed. All the impressions of that golden day kept crowding in upon her to keep her awake, but even when she heard two o'clock strike on the big clock in the hall she had not heard Thor return. She wondered then if he had gone to Drakensval.

The following week Erik began work at the lumber camp in earnest, but whether by Thor's edict or from his own personal inclination Margaret could not be sure. Certainly he had not worked particularly hard before.

"It won't be for long," he assured her when he returned late one evening, but earlier than Thor. "There's a lot of wood still to come down and I suppose I owe it to Thor to help, but I wasn't cut out for a lumberman."

"What do you mean to do, Erik?" Margaret

asked. "When you are through the University, I mean."

"I've a notion I could write," he said. "You know—plays and that sort of thing—but I shall have to find a job first, I suppose. I can't go on sponging on Thor for ever."

"I don't think Thor considers your education 'sponging', you know," Margaret said. "Have you told him what you really want to do?"

"Good heavens, no!" Erik laughed. "Can you imagine what Thor would say?"

"You could hope that he would understand," she tried to point out, not quite knowing what to think herself about this unexpected confession of Erik's. They were exactly the same age, but at times she felt a great deal older than Erik. "Thor might be quite willing to help."

Erik shook his head.

"Thor doesn't understand anything but honest, hard work, preferably in the mountains," he said acidly. "He goes to Oslo as rarely as he can, and always on business. When he is there, the theatre is the last thing he thinks about. Thor, shall we say, is a man of action, never so happy as when he is in the great out-of-doors! It is probably more in keeping with our national character, of course, but it can be crippling from an artist's point of view."

"What would he like you to do?" Margaret asked.

"Come back to Helmsdale and teach."

"And you feel that you might have to—disappoint him?"

He gave her a lazy, considering smile.

"I'm not so sure, now," he said. "Thor's vision of higher education in Helmsdal might have its compensations. He would like to see a larger school built in the village so that the older children need not leave home and travel miles to one of the older established boarding-schools farther down the fjord. It has always been a dream of Thor's to make the dale independent and completely self-supporting. Kirsten, of course, is all for it," he added. "Has she never suggested you might also apply for a job? Officially, I mean."

Margaret considered him in bewilderment.

"Here?" she asked. "In Helmsdal?"

"Why not?" He came over to sit beside her, imprisoning her hand in his. "We don't want to lose you, Meg," he told her. "We've grown very fond of you."

Margaret's heart seemed to miss a beat.

"But—there's Thor," she said.

Erik laughed.

"Why do you say that—like that?" he asked. "Thor will not really care what you do, but I dare say if you could get a reasonable grasp of Norwegian and were to offer your services to the dale as an English teacher he would be at least grateful."

The warmth with which he had made his own personal plea cancelled out much of his guardian's indifference, and she found herself saying lightly:

"My Norwegian is coming on! I even had the courage to ask Signe if I might make myself some English toast this morning, although I'm sure she thought afterwards that I was quite mad to try to burn her wonderful bread!"

Erik laughed.

"Ellen could help you, you know," he said after a moment. "If she liked."

Margaret drew in a deep breath.

"I wish I got on a little better with Ellen," she confessed.

Erik frowned.

"She will change," he predicted. "She hasn't quite got Gerda out of her system yet. It's strange about Ellen," he went on musingly. "Gerda was her ideal, of course, but she's never really spoken much about her since—that day. She has guarded Thor instead. It seems that she cannot bear the thought of anyone ever taking Gerda's place."

Margaret had not been prepared for such insight on Erik's part, but he had just put all her own troubled feelings about Ellen into words. The reluctance to accept friendship even when it was repeatedly offered; the scarcely-veiled hostility; the acceptance of her only as a teacher; all added up to an almost fanatical love of Gerda which was all the more pitiful because Ellen was determined to preserve it in utter loneliness.

"One can't help wondering why such things happen," she said unsteadily. "Thor must have felt that his whole world had crumbled when your sister died. Was it—long ago?"

"More than two years. It was in April, when the snows were melting, and the fjord was treacherous and wild. Sometimes it can be like that—an avenging fury of water intent on destruction. Gerda took the boat to sail across the fjord. No one quite knows why. It was a foolish thing to do on such a day of storm, and it is not the sort of thing one wants to think about—afterwards."

"I'm sorry, Erik," Margaret apologized. "I shouldn't have asked."

"Death and destruction depress me," he confessed, getting up from the fire and drawing her gently to her feet. "I suppose that's the artist in me, the part bequeathed by my Spanish mother, perhaps. Let us talk about something more pleasant. You, for instance. Make up your mind to stay in Helmsdal, Meg, and I shall promise to come back. That way, everyone will be pleased—including Thor!"

Including Thor!

"We shall see," Margaret said in a small, thin voice. "So many things can happen in so short a time, and you have still a year to study in Oslo."

"I could take my degree in the next six months," he told her. "Now that there is something to come back for."

Margaret flushed, turning rather abruptly towards the window where the curtains had not yet been drawn.

"Why not make the effort anyway?" she suggested. "It would be a sort of gesture to Thor."

Erik crossed the room in two swift strides.

"Thor! Thor!" he mocked. "Does he govern your heart, too, Meg? Because, if that is so, you will soon come to learn what unhappiness means!"

Savagely he kissed her, his whole slim body registering his protest and jealousy of the older man. Thor, it seemed, had dominated his life for too long. In the next instant, however, being Erik, he was sorry.

"Forget about that," he begged. "But I do want you to stay, Meg. I'm in love with you. You are the most beautiful thing that has ever happened to me."

Margaret drew herself away from his encircling arms. In this mood Erik was like quicksilver, capable of sweeping her off her feet, capable of anything. I'm far older than he is, she thought again. I can see that we must wait.

"Tomorrow," he said, "I'm going to take you to Laerdal. I have friends there—people you will meet in Oslo when you come. Thor is felling right down at the river now and the road might be closed, but we'll get away early. I'll work in the morning, and as soon as the logs are in the water we'll set out. You can walk over to the camp and I'll ask Thor to let me have the car."

The following morning was dry and sunny, with all the harlequin glory of an early autumn staining the hillsides where the green of pine and spruce was interspersed with the gold of larch and the tawny brown of chestnut and oak. Margaret walked leisurely, wondering about their visit to Laerdal. They were to go by car for part of the way and afterwards by fjord steamer, and she was eagerly looking forward to the trip. Anything which enriched her knowledge of Norway was exciting to her, and it would also be interesting to meet Erik's friends from Oslo.

It was more the surprising, therefore, when Kirsten Moe seemed rather doubtful about the whole thing.

"Does Thor know you are going?" she asked when they were seated in the camp canteen drinking the nevitable black coffee which seemed to sustain even the hard-working lumberjacks for hours on end.

"I expect so." Margaret frowned. "Would he be likely to object, do you think?"

Kirsten flushed.

"I've spoken out of turn," she apologized. "No, I don't think Thor would raise any definite objection to your going. I only wondered why Erik had chosen Laerdal, of all unlikely places."

"Some friends of his from Oslo are there," Margaret explained none too happily. "They are up after reindeer or elk or something."

"Most likely elk," Kirsten decided as if it interested her.

"Well, I hope you have a happy trip. Is Erik going to collect you up here?"

"He said he would. Kirsten," Margaret asked after a moment's reflection, "Erik mentioned yesterday that Thor hoped to have the village school enlarged and that his first concern would be to get sufficient teaching staff. He suggested that I might offer my services as an English mistress, but I thought I would like to ask your opinion first."

Kirsten considered the question, turning her candid blue eyes full in Margaret's direction.

"Did Erik also suggest that he might return to Helmsdal when he has qualified?" she asked frankly.

"Yes," Margaret agreed, colouring a little, "he did."

"Hm-m!" observed Kirsten enigmatically.

"I wish I knew what to do!" Margaret said uneasily.

"Ask Thor if you can be of any use to the dale," Kirsten advised unexpectedly, "but don't let Erik make it a condition of his coming home to teach." She rose, pushing her stool aside. "And now I must get on! This is my last week up here, by the way, but I hope it won't mean that we are not going to see each other. Of course, if you come to the school that will be different. You may even begin to feel that you are seeing too much of me!"

"I don't think I shall ever feel that, Kirsten," Margaret answered truthfully. "If I come."

That was something else that depended upon Thor. She would have to abide by his decision. It was a decision which could change her whole future, for unless he allowed her to be of some use in the dale she knew that she could not go on living there. She could not continue to stay in Helmsdal as Thor's guest.

Outside the canteen she stood in the sunshine waiting for Erik to pick her up. The big clearing was quite deserted and the whole world seemed very still, with only the sun slanting through the boles of the distant trees in dusty bars of light. Even the voice of the saw was silenced today, and the weir below the log-dam was too far down-river for her to catch its constant murmur as it spilled over the wooden sluice.

Erik was a long time in coming, and somehow she knew that when he did turn up he would be angry. Something must have gone wrong at the dam to upset his plans.

Wondering if she should make an attempt to go to meet him, she walked towards the encircling trees, but there were two timber roads leading into the camp now and she did not know which one to take.

As she hesitated the car swung into view, driven recklessly at a furious pace. Erik jammed on his brakes when he saw her, flinging open the off-side door.

"Get in!" he commanded through set teeth. "We're going to catch that steamer if it kills me!"

"What happened?" she managed to ask when he had swung the car round and they were travelling back by the way he had come.

"Everything!" he growled. "Logs stuck, there was a hitch with the leading team, and, to end everything, Thor decided to go on felling on the road section."

"I'm sorry," she said. "Would it help if we didn't go to Laerdal this afternoon?"

"It wouldn't help in the slightest," Erik informed her icily.

Margaret sat in silence. The speed with which Erik drove made the car lurch drunkenly from side to side of the narrow, dusty road so that it would have been difficult to sustain a conversation for any length of time, even if they had wished.

"I'm sorry if you're being shaken up," Erik said when they had been travelling for about half an hour, "but this is quicker than taking the main road through the dale."

They sped on between the trees and through a clearing where the logs had already been hauled to the river bank. Here the road turned uphill a little, breasting a sudden rise. At the top of it a man in a checked lumber jacket stood beside the path, signalling and stepping into their path as soon as he saw the car coming. He shouted something to Erik, which Margaret did not quite catch, something in their own language.

Erik did not pause. He drove straight on, and the man jumped out of his way just in time to avoid an accident.

"Why did he want us to stop?" Margaret shouted. The open top of the car let the wind rush through and for a moment she thought that Erik had not heard. "Why did he signal to you to pull up?" she repeated.

"He wanted us to use the main road to the village." Erik's mouth was set, his eyes narrowed on the track ahead. "We'd never make the steamer in time if we went all that way round," he added, "and Thor has a habit of closing the timber road hours before he's ready to fell. I'm taking a chance."

Margaret's heart quickened but she supposed that Erik knew what he was doing. The car thundered on. They were in among the trees again, and she saw that they were giants of their kind, spiralling upwards towards the hidden sky. Their green tops scarcely moved in the little wind there was, and then, suddenly, one of them seemed to sway, as if it had been disturbed. There was a great shout from somewhere deep in the undergrowth and the car seemed to hesitate and lurch on. For a split second she saw Erik bent over the wheel, his face pale and grim, his mouth tensed, and then there was a rending, tearing sound above them that ended in darkness— and silence.

CHAPTER SIX

THE sky had turned grey and cold and somewhere a voice kept crying, "Erik! Erik!" Margaret wanted to still the voice but could not. It had been calling endlessly, it seemed —as long as she could remember.

"Erik!" it repeated. "Erik!"

It could not be her own voice. It was too feeble and weak and too far away. She opened her eyes and saw that some of the greyness had dispersed. She was in her own room at Solstua and someone was standing before the window, a giant of a man with his hands thrust deep in his trousers' pockets who seemed to take up all the available space and shut out most of the light.

Thor? He turned when she tried to move, coming swiftly towards the bed.

"How does it feel now?" he asked in a deeply-kind voice that was not Thor's voice. "Have you any pain in your head?"

Hazily Margaret completed her recognition.

"Doctor Loren?"

"The same!" Paul Loren assured her with his quick smile. "I told you I would come to Helmsdal one day to see you, but I did not think it would be like this."

He was watching her closely, and Margaret tried to force her mind back into the past.

"What has happened?" she appealed when it became too difficult. "Why am I here, Doctor Loren?"

" 'Paul' might be easier," he suggested, still smiling down at her, although she was now aware of a searching professional scrutiny behind the smile. "There was an accident at the lumber camp. You got in the way of a falling tree." He sat down on the edge of the bed. "How much can you remember?" he asked briefly.

Margaret passed an unsteady hand across her brow, feeling it heavily bandaged.

"I remember the tree," she said shakily. "It swayed and swayed——" Her voice trailed away and a cold horror shook her as memory came flooding back. "We were in the car and—we couldn't stop. Not in time. The car went on and on. We were trying to escape—trying to beat the falling tree—but it caught us."

Her voice trailed away and Paul Loren put a gentle hand over her thin fingers where they lay on the padded *dyne*.

"That's all right," he said. "Don't worry about it any more. Thor got you out. The car was smashed, but thank God! you were still alive."

Margaret lay very still, feeling that there was something else she should ask about, but the effort to remember proved too great. She wanted to sleep.

Paul Loren let her sleep. It was hours before she opened her eyes again to a lamp burning on the table beside her bed. There was still someone in the room.

"Who is it?" she asked. "Kirsten?"

Kirsten Moe, quiet and practical, rose from the shadows on the other side of the bed.

"Yes," she said. "I had been hoping that you would wake up before I went off duty."

"How long have I been here?" Margaret asked, aware that she had completely lost count of time.

"Ten days."

"Ten?" It seemed incredible. The horror of that falling tree was so real, so near. "Have I been—very ill?"

"Enough to impress us," Kirsten conceded.

"But I'm all right now?" Margaret felt that she had to insist about that. "I don't want to be a burden to—to anyone."

"There's no question of burdens," Kirsten said almost harshly. "All that matters is that you should get well."

Margaret turned her head towards the long panel of the window where the curtains had not yet been drawn. The night sky had lost its pale luminosity. It was darker than she had ever seen it.

"Has the snow come?" she asked.

"Not yet. It is only the beginning of October. It has fallen in the mountains, but we are sheltered here."

"How long will it be," Margaret asked painfully, "before I am able to get up?"

There seemed to be too long a pause before Kirsten answered.

"In a week or two, perhaps."

Margaret roused herself.

"I can't just lie here for weeks," she protested. "Ever since I've come, Kirsten, I've made things—difficult for Thor. He must wish that he had never asked me."

Kirsten sat down on the chair beside the bed, leaning forward with the lamplight behind her. Her face was in shadow and Margaret could not see her expression, but she spoke with a kindly conviction.

"We've got to get this straight," she declared. "Thor wanted you to come here because of your stepmother, and he's not the sort of person to go back on a bargain or regret it once it is made. Nobody could have been more concerned about you than Thor has been these past few days," she added. "You must believe that."

The words were meant to be reassuring, yet at the back of Margaret's mind was the suggestion of anger, Thor's anger.

"I've been so useless," she murmured. "Always doing the wrong thing."

Kirsten's generous mouth tightened.

"You could hardly be held responsible for this," she observed dryly. "Get it out of your mind, Margaret, that Thor is angry with you."

Who, then? Suddenly Margaret realized that nobody had spoken about Erik. She remembered the feeble, plaintive voice of those first dim moments of consciousness, her own voice, she recognized now, the voice that had called, "Erik! Erik!" constantly.

"Kirsten," she asked, while a small, cold fear gripped her by the throat, "did Erik—die?"

Kirsten Moe laughed, and the sound was brittle, like shattering glass.

"No," she said, "Erik got off without a scratch. He was shaken, but that was all."

"I'm so glad!" Relief poured over Margaret like a swiftly-flowing tide. "I thought—for a moment I thought that he could not possibly have escaped."

Kirsten wanted to say that the Eriks of this world generally managed to escape, but did not.

"He isn't here, is he?" Margaret asked, although she thought that she already knew the answer.

"No," Kirsten agreed, "he isn't. He went back to Oslo last week."

"I see." Margaret's voice was a little more than a thin thread of weakness, trailing away. "Paul was here," she said after a while. "Paul Loren."

"Yes," Kirsten acknowledged. "Thor sent for him."

Margaret roused herself.

"Why did he do that?"

"Because you were in Paul's department. The local doctor had done all he could."

"Kirsten," Margaret asked, "what is 'Paul's department'?"

"Oh—all sorts of things." There was evasion here. "Spine and head mostly. All the little twiddly bits that keep us knotted into one piece."

"Am I—not going to be—knotted properly?" The question hardly seemed to touch her.

"Of course you are!" Kirsten assured her gallantly, but Margaret knew then that there was doubt.

Regret, as bitter as gall, flooded in on her. Why had she not insisted that Erik should go back on to the main road? The accident need not have happened. If they had obeyed the lumberjack Thor had posted on the hill above the point where he was felling and not tried to beat the tree because Erik thought that Thor always closed the timber roads too soon, they might have missed their connection to Laerdal but she would not be lying here now, a burden to Thor.

She tried to raise herself on the bed, but there was no response from her shattered body. A cold, bleak certainty, which grew and grew as the seconds ticked away into endless minutes, held her by the throat, choking back speech. If this was true, if it meant that she might never walk again—upright, like Thor and Kirsten and Erik—what could she do?

There was a tap on the door and Ellen came in with a tray. She was a curiously subdued Ellen, but she did not appear to be any more friendly.

"I've brought you this," she said, setting the tray down on the *dyne*. "Doctor Loren is coming to see you."

"I must be off!" Kirsten announced, as if the doctor's presence could only embarrass her. "I'll come back again," she promised, "after Paul has seen you."

Margaret drank the milk and supped the thin gruel which Signe had prepared, finding it curiously tasteless. There was a dryness at the back of her throat that was more than fear, and she could not look with any confidence into the future.

When Ellen had taken away the tray Paul came, bringing with him a sharp breath of the out-of-doors. During his examination, as his thin, sensitive fingers probed gently along the length of her spine, he chatted about the ordinary things which made up their lives here in the mountains.

"You've been a perfectly logical excuse for me to spend six days away from Oslo," he told her lightly. "I try to get a week's hunting in the autumn, but sometimes I find it almost impossible to leave my work. It is a busy life," he added after one of several pauses. "An exacting profession, perhaps, but always rewarding. Yes," he added, as if he had come to some conclusion, "it must be rewarding, otherwise we would not find the courage to go on."

Margaret wondered if he would have the courage to tell her the truth when he had come to his final decision. They were friends. Paul had helped her before. Surely he would not find it necessary to lie to her now?

"Thor would like to see you," Paul said. "I have told him he can come."

Margaret knew a desperate panic of indecision. "Oh, please, no! How can I see Thor?"

Paul stood looking down at her, smiling a little. "I think it will be easy," he said.

"Will you stay?" she found herself pleading weakly.

"Why should I stay?" Paul asked. "You do not need me to stay. Thor and you are old friends."

She smiled wanly, letting him go. Some time or other she would have to meet Thor. "Thor and you are old friends," Paul had said. If only that had been true! She lay quite still, waiting.

Thor came in quietly, crossing the room in two swift strides. She had heard him speaking to Paul out in the corridor, the low murmur of their voices rising and falling like the tide against the dark rocks of the hidden fjord. Perhaps they had been discussing her; perhaps Paul had already told Thor that she would not walk again.

Searching his dark face, she read nothing of fear in it. There was not even anger any more, or impatience, only a quiet determination in the eyes which held her own when she would have looked away from that first searching scrutiny which went too deep.

"This is a meagre visit," he told her. "Paul has only allowed me five minutes."

She lay gazing up at him, wondering what she could say to him, and then, quite suddenly, he took the initiative from her. He stood beside the bed, with the shaded lamp striking up into his face, its shadow casting grotesque shapes across the timbered ceiling, and when he spoke his voice was quiet and kind.

"I came because I have something to say to you, Margaret," he began. "Something of importance. I don't want you to make a decision about it right away. I couldn't expect that. I want you to take time to think it over."

He paused, and the whole room seemed deathly still. Margaret knew that he was going to offer her

a home, a permanent shelter here at Solstua, and
something in her heart rebelled. Thor's pity was the
last thing she wanted.

"Margaret," he said, "I want you to marry me."

She closed her eyes, not able to believe what she
had heard. It was all too cruel, too harsh a trick of
her imagination. Thor saying that he loved her.
But he had not said that! "Margaret," he had said,
"I want you to marry me."

She opened her eyes and they were full of tears.

"You can't mean that, Thor," she said. "You
can only be trying to be kind."

He bent over her, his face darkly shadowed as it
came between her and the lamp.

"Why should I try to be kind?" he questioned.
"I have asked you to marry me, to think it over, at
least. If love doesn't come into it for one of us, at
least we will have security. Solstua can offer you a
great deal, Margaret, and I shall not be—demanding."

She turned her head away, not knowing what to
say to him.

"Think it over," he repeated. "I am not pressing
you for an answer now. You will stay at Solstua, of
course. There is nowhere else for you to go. You
have no relations, I understand, in England.'

"No," she agreed. "But when I am well again I
must go back there and try to find something to do."

He straightened, turning his back on her to
stride to the window where there was only the
starless night to look at.

"I think you belong here," he said almost
roughly. "Solstua needs a woman's touch."

After he had gone that final sentence of his
echoed and re-echoed in Margaret's heart. He
needed someone at Solstua, the essential mistress for
his home, and he was offering her the job—without
love.

She tried to laugh, but it was a hollow sound, and
weak tears persisted in seeping through between her
closed lids. Why do I make it so difficult? she thought.
I love him. One love like this should surely be

enough. It might be true that Thor would never love again—not as he had loved—but he could offer her companionship and security.

Was that enough? Security? She tried to examine the word, finding it cold and numbing when it was offered as a substitute for love.

Burying her face in the pillows, she smothered the agonizing question in her heart. Could she, in the end, find happiness and give it to Thor?

"Think it over," he had said, but she had already thought it over. She wanted to marry Thor. Her own love was enough. She could have told him then: "Yes, Thor, I will marry you!"

Even if he had only second best to offer, even if the full vigour of his love was always to remain with Gerda in the past, there would be compensation in other things. In a hundred other ways, she thought, life could still be full.

When Kirsten came to say goodnight, as she had promised, Margaret told her.

"Kirsten," she said, "Thor has asked me to marry him."

The amazing thing was that Kirsten did not seem surprised.

"I thought he would," she said quietly. "It is the best thing that could happen—for both of you."

"You can honestly say that," Margaret asked, "when you know that he does not love me?"

Kirsten smoothed the crumpled *dyne*, staring down at it for a moment before she answered.

"I think what matters most is whether you are in love with Thor," she said.

A small inarticulate sound, half-sigh, half-sob, escaped Margaret's parted lips.

"I've never been in love before," she confessed, "but I know about this, Kirsten. It's everything and all of me. I could marry Thor and give him my love even if he has nothing to offer me in return."

"Which is unlikely," Kirsten said. "Thor can be kind, in spite of his aloofness. When you come to know him better, you will understand what I mean. I never liked Gerda," she added bluntly. "I can't pretend about that, but I know, too, that Thor loved her to distraction and that he is not the sort of man to forget easily. But Gerda is dead. Thor's love for her is in the past, and he has offered you the future."

Margaret lay very still.

"This has helped, Kirsten," she said. "Just talking to you."

In the morning, when Thor came, she told him that she would marry him.

"I'll try to make you happy," she whispered, holding on to the hand he gave her. I'll try to make our marriage real."

A shadow which was almost an agony passed in his grey-blue eyes as he disengaged his fingers from her grasp with the utmost gentleness and went to take up his old position at the window.

"We have a great deal to do together," he said. "First of all, Margaret, we must get you well."

"That should be easy now," she said eagerly. "What has Paul Loren got to say about me? How long must I lie here, Thor? I don't want to be a sort of invalid for ever."

He came back to stand beside the bed, tall and straight, like one of his own trees, and full of vigour, and suddenly her heart caught in a first, agonizing doubt.

"Paul wants a second opinion," he said. "He wants to take you to Oslo."

"Alone?" Her eyes sought his in pathetic alarm.

"No," he said. "I shall go with you."

"How soon?"

"As soon as Paul sees how you shape on your feet, I think."

He had not spoken of their marriage. Probably he had not even considered a time for it, and he had not even kissed her.

Looking at the thin, compressed lips so near to her own as he bent to adjust her head-rest, she felt a swift agony of longing sweep through her, a fire in her veins which scorched her and clouded her vision with sudden tears.

"Thor!" she cried. "Thor!" and held out her arms to him.

He bent down, gathering her gently against his heart.

"Soon," he said, "it will be all right." His voice was no more than comforting. "You have only to wait a little while."

Her face was drenched in tears, but not because she was afraid or in pain. He took out his handkerchief and wiped them away.

"This is upsetting you," he said. "I must go and let you sleep. Tomorrow we will make our plans for the future."

He bent, kissing her gently on the lips. It was the sort of kiss that a brother might have given her. All the pouring out of love which she had offered in that first moment had been turned back within her. She felt drowned in it, this pathetic, rejected love which could only grow and grow no matter what happened.

It was evening before she noticed that all her meals had been brought up by Signe. Ellen had always been the one to bring her tray, whether willingly or unwillingly she did not know.

"Where is Ellen?" she asked Signe in her halting Norwegian. "She has not been all day."

Signe lifted faded blue eyes to her face.

"She is sad in her heart," she answered, laying her work-roughened hands against her own meagre breast where she supposed her heart must be. "She work hard in the *stabbur* with the cows."

The blunt explanation distressed Margaret, but when she asked Thor about Ellen he seemed surprised.

"Hasn't she been to see you?" he asked. "I told her this morning about our plans."

So that was it, Margaret thought. Ellen could not bring herself to congratulate her on her engagement to Thor. It was only natural, perhaps, but it was the first tiny cloud on Margaret's horizon.

After Thor had said goodnight and gone away,

bending over her for a moment to clasp her hand, she thought about Ellen for a long time.

In the morning, however, it was Ellen who came with her breakfast tray.

"*Frokost!*" she announced, opening the bedroom door, but when she drew the curtains her eyes were bleak.

"Ellen," Margaret said gently, "Thor has told me that you know we are going to be married. It—might be quite soon, and it will be a very quiet wedding, but I'd like you to be there. If you would, I should like you to be my bridesmaid."

Ellen could only be said to recoil before the impulsive suggestion.

"How could I?" she cried. "How could I stand there before the altar and see you married to Thor? He does not love you. How could he when he loved my sister so much? Thor is marrying you because of his sorrow, because you are now crippled and unable to walk, and because it was his order that made the tree come down. That is all. Thor will never love you. He is sorry. He is only sorry for you and trying to make amends!"

All the blood in her body seemed to converge on Margaret's heart in a swift, paralysing rush. She could feel it draining from her face and out of her useless limbs, leaving her numb and cold. This had been her secret fear, the agonizing thought which she had been crushing down in her mind for the past forty-eight hours, but she could not let herself believe that it was the truth. The cruelty of Ellen's words stung her to sudden anger.

"That isn't true, Ellen," she said with a strange new dignity. "Thor has—other reasons for asking me to marry him, reasons you would not understand. I am not trying to steal Gerda's love. I couldn't do that, but I am entitled to a love of my own."

"Not Thor's love!" Ellen cried passionately. "You have no right to that. It belonged to Gerda and always will."

"Gerda is dead," Margaret said firmly, and almost immediately realized her mistake.

"You think that matters?" Ellen cried. "It does not matter at all. Gerda is still alive in this house and always will be. Thor has locked himself up with her memory, here and at Drakensval. You will find that is true if you think you are going to be happy as his wife."

Margaret turned her head on the pillow, staring out of the window.

"In spite of what you feel, Ellen," she said, "I still think I can make Thor a good wife. I feel I might even be able to make him happy, in time."

Ellen rushed to the door.

"You will see!" she cried. "You will see!"

The following day Kirsten Moe moved in to Solstua.

"Thor is having some difficulty with Ellen," she explained when she brought up Margaret's tray. "He thinks she may need a holiday."

Margaret twisted round on her pillows, her face quite pale.

"He hasn't—sent her away?"

"Oh, no!" Kirsten answered immediately. "Thor wouldn't do that. He's far too conscious of his obligation to the whole Borge family to ever think of turning any of them adrift, no matter what they do."

"But for their father," Margaret pointed out, "Thor would not be here today, back in Solstua where he belongs.

"I know all that," Kirsten agreed, "but Thor has already repaid much of this debt of his. He will go on repaying it, of course, so long as it is demanded of him." Kirsten sighed. "Debts are odd things, aren't they? Once they are incurred, so many of us tend to over-repay them, and Thor's sort of debt seems to involve a lifetime of repayment because a life was given.

"What can he do about Ellen if she refuses to live here after—after we are married?" Margaret asked, following her own train of thought.

"Thor will think of something," Kirsten declared. "Ellen is so very young, and all young things tend to be over-intense in their loyalties, Meg. Situations are magnified for them out of all proportion when they happen to touch their impressionable hearts. Ellen has never been out into the world. She is little more than a child, with a child's reactions to events." She leaned over the bed. "If she has said anything to distress you, my dear, try to forget about it. Ellen will get over her little jealousies in time."

Margaret wanted to believe that, but after Kirsten had gone she lay, cold and shaken, on the great box bed with the feather *dyne* drawn up close under her chin, wondering how much truth there was in all Ellen had said. She had rejected it proudly in Ellen's presence and Kirsten had said it did not matter, but even a grain of truth had the power to hurt.

The evening shadows fell and darkness inked in the oblong of the window, but Thor remained away. She knew that he was probably busy, but she lay listening for his footsteps with her lamp unlit. When they came, at last, firm and unmistakable, she felt as if her heart must burst. Its beating was like some small and pitiful caged thing struggling to be free.

Breathlessly she lay quite still. The footsteps sounded across the gallery and on into the corridor. Soon they would reach her door. Soon Thor would come!

They did not hesitate. They passed her door and went on. Margaret heard them as if they had trodden across her heart, going on to the end of the corridor, to the two locked doors which led to Gerda's rooms.

Thrusting the edge of the *dyne* between her teeth, she choked back harsh dry sobs which stuck somewhere in her throat. I haven't any tears, she thought. I haven't any tears to spare!

Long afterwards she could remember the sound of Thor walking in the rooms which Gerda had made her own. There was only one wall between them, a thick wall that might have been a prison wall, and Thor was on the other side of it, alone with his memories. What was he thinking? Had he gone there to try to readjust his life, to beg, perhaps, for Gerda's understanding and her forgiveness? "Gerda is still alive in this house, and always will be!" The memory of Ellen's impassioned declaration filled the room. Had she the courage to accept it? Had she the faith she needed in her own love and the patience and perseverance to go on?

In the morning it was Paul Loren who was first to come to her.

"It's time we had you up," he intimated, masking his professional scrutiny with a smile. "Kirsten is coming, and Thor. We must see how you are able to use those legs of yours."

"Paul," she appealed, "could we do without Thor? I'm—horribly nervous."

"Thor will soon cure that!" he said. "He is the most practical person I know." He gave her a quick, direct look. "You must not be afraid."

Margaret wondered if she had only been afraid of meeting Thor because she had lain listening to his footsteps going past her door, hearing them again in the rooms which had once been Gerda's, listening and listening until it was too late to hope that he would come to her.

Kirsten followed Paul in. She was more at ease in his company these days, more confident of carrying off a difficult situation with courage and dignity. Paul Loren had left Helmsdal long ago to conquer the world, but there was no suggestion that Kirsten had stayed behind and worn out her heart. She had found her own niche in the dale, fulfilling the promise of her early youth, as Paul had done, and offering it to the wide green valley among the mountains along with her heart. On her lovely face, unlined and completely free from discontent, Margaret read fulfilment and a strange, calm peace. It was the sort of peace she had seen on the faces of the very old, the people who had lived in these mountains all their lives, and it was no dispirited resignation. It was an acceptance of life which, in its time, brought joy.

She looked up to see Thor standing in the doorway. For a moment he did not speak, and his face was paler and more drawn that she had ever seen it.

"I'm sorry if I've kept you waiting," he apologized to Paul before he crossed to the bed. "Sonsburg came down from the camp to see Ellen off to Laerdal." He stood looking down at Margaret and there could be no doubting the expression in his eyes. They were full of compassion and a deep-rooted pity. "It won't take long," he said. "Paul will spare you all he can."

Paul can spare my stupid body, Margaret thought, but who will spare my heart?

Kirsten folded back the *dyne* and Thor held a pair of fleece-lined slippers for her to put her feet into. The small, helpful gesture caught at her throat, but she crushed back the tears with a determined effort.

"Now," said Paul, "you are to lift your legs over the bed and stand up. Kirsten will help you—but not too much—and Thor will be there if you feel that you might fall." He bent over her, taking both her hands. "You will not fall," he told her decisively. "Now, let me see!"

Margaret twisted on the bed, her feet swinging out, and Kirsten half lifted her into a sitting position. There was no pain; only a terrible weakness. Her heart lifted for very joy.

"Now," said Paul again, "we are going to walk."

Margaret knew before she had taken half a dozen steps, before she collapsed ignominiously into Thor's arms, burying her white and shattered face against his breast, that she would not walk straight and free again. She had dragged her limbs, and her left hip seemed hopelessly twisted. Paul, on the other hand, appeared to be elated.

"Good! Good!" he cried. "This is more than I could have hoped for. A little improvement every day, that is the way. A miracle is so often worked *slowly*!"

Very gently Thor lifted Margaret, laying her back on the bed, and for that one moment, while she remained in his arms, she knew sanctuary and peace.

"You must rest now," he said. "It was a splendid effort. Soon Paul will have you well again."

Was that true? There was fear in Margaret's heart, a twisting, gnawing agony of doubt and uncertainty which would not let her go. If this was all, if this was how she must remain, she could not marry Thor. She could not accept his sacrifice.

Ellen's words taunted her endlessly and it took all of Kirsten's reassuring love and friendship to convince her that she should go on with her marriage.

"Paul says you will walk quite well, in time," Kirsten declared. "I know he was afraid at first that you would be wholly bedridden because of the injury to your spine, but there has been a sort of miracle, Meg. You were able to walk after all."

"It may be—cheating Thor," Margaret said unhappily. "I may never be the sort of wife he needs."

Kirsten smiled.

"Thor isn't easily cheated," she said. "He will know what he wants from his marriage."

That was true, Margaret thought. Thor's demands would be limited. She would look after Solstua and make it a home, and a warmth that was not quite love would grow between them in time.

If her heart quailed at the prospect, she did not examine it too closely. After all, Solstua and Thor's companionship might be enough.

It was Thor who finally told her that she must go to Oslo. He came to sit with her for half an hour or so each evening when his day's work was done and he explained the Oslo journey from Paul Loren's point of view.

"It isn't fair to Paul to expect him to work miracles up here," he said, sitting on the edge of the bed to face her, perhaps even to argue against any indecision on her part. "He needs the facilities of a hospital, and I think he may also want a second opinion. It's quite usual in these cases," he added briefly. "Almost a routine procedure, in fact."

"How soon must I go?"Margaret asked.

"As soon as we are married." He got up and walked to the window, standing with his back to her for a moment. "I don't want you to be difficult about this, Margaret," he told her, coming back to stand beside the bed, his face composed and almost expressionless. "I want our marriage to take place at once. Before we go to Oslo."

"I thought perhaps we could wait." Margaret's lips were trembling and she made a valiant effort to steady them. "It might be better to wait and see if—if——"

He bent and took her hands firmly in his.

"Margaret," he said, "you're panicking. We've made a bargain. Can't you fulfil your side of it?"

She fought desperately to keep tears out of her eyes.

"It's your side I'm thinking about," she whispered. "How unfair it would be if—if Paul's hopes were unfounded."

"Paul doesn't often make mistakes," he said, straightening, "and we can't expect him to wait here in the mountains for ever. He wants you to be in Oslo before the end of the month."

CHAPTER SEVEN

ON her wedding day Margaret woke to a deep stillness.

"The snow has come," Kirsten said, opening her shutters so that she could see out, "but the sun is shining!"

Sun on snow. The whole, still world was dazzling, with a million sparkling diamonds glittering on the orchard where the sun had touched it, and the blue of the distant glacier looking like a patch of fallen sky. It was almost too lovely to look at, Margaret thought, struggling out of bed.

"Here!" Kirsten said, holding out her dressing-gown, "you must not catch cold—not today of all days! It is only eight o'clock," she added, "but I thought you would like to get up. I am glad about the snow. You will go to the *kirke* in a sleigh now, and Thor will meet you at the door!"

Margaret turned her head away.

"Kirsten, I must be the most unconventional bride that ever was," she said, "hobbling to the altar on two sticks and not at all sure of the future."

"No one can be entirely sure of the future," Kirsten reminded her briskly. "All we have is faith, and a blind understanding of God's goodness. We all grope our way ahead, really. You are not alone."

"And not ungrateful." Margaret turned to give her an affectionate smile. "I shall never be able to repay you, Kirsten, for all you have done for me during these past few weeks."

"Now we are making pretty speeches!" Kirsten mocked. "You know I would do anything for you, Meg, and for Thor. I'm not very good at saying these things, but Thor and I have been firm friends for ten years. I want to see him with some chance of happiness in the future."

She was still standing at the window looking out over the snow-clad orchard, and suddenly her expression changed.

"What is it?" Margaret asked.

"Nothing. Just Thor and Paul Loren walking in the orchard with their heads together. You mustn't look!" Kirsten admonished. "Is it not considered unlucky in your country for a girl to see her fiancé on her wedding day before she goes to church?"

But Margaret had already seen Thor. The two men had come close till they were almost underneath her window, and Thor had flung back his dark head and was looking straight up at her. Their eyes met for a fraction of a second before Kirsten whisked her out of sight.

"Thor shouldn't have done that!" she declared with more vigour than Margaret expected. "It is useless to court disaster."

"Thor doesn't believe in luck, good or bad," Margaret said. "Nor in superstition. He would only consider it foolish if he thought we did.

Kirsten left the remark unanswered. She was at the big clothes cupboard at the far end of the room, opening the heavily-carved doors to inspect its contents.

"What are you going to wear?" she asked.

Margaret flushed. She had not had time to order any special wedding dress, and she had not given her meagre wardrobe a great deal of thought until now.

"I told you I wasn't a conventional bride," she tried to say lightly. "It will have to be something I've worn before."

"H'm!" Kirsten observed. "I suppose so. It will also have to be something warm, though we could tuck you well up in the sleigh to keep out the cold."

Margaret was hardly thinking of the journey to the church. She was thinking of the service itself, of that moment when Prost Jorgensen would make them man and wife.

Footsteps sounded along the corridor outside, quick and urgent, to be followed by a muffled tap on the door. Kirsten sprang to open it, ready to defeat any further attempt on Thor's part to see his bride. It was not Thor, however, who stood there, but Signe, almost completely obliterated by a large cardboard box which she carried upright in her arms.

"Whatever is this, Signe?" Kirsten asked.

"For the Froken," Signe announced, wide-eyed with curiosity. "It came by special carrier, and there is another box!"

Thrusting her burden into Kirsten's arms, she disappeared, her heavy footsteps echoing along the corridor and back down the uncarpeted stairs.

"For you, Meg!" Kirsten put the box down on the bed where Margaret had taken refuge, her shabby old dressing-gown wrapped tightly about her. She was trembling, but not with cold. "Hurry," Kirsten urged, "and open it! I'm burned up with curiosity—or should I have said 'consumed'? My English always suffers when I am excited!"

Margaret's fingers trembled as she unfastened the string. The box bore the name of an Oslo fashion house, but how anyone could have sent her a gift from Oslo she could not think.

Erik? He was the only person she knew in the capital, but somehow she could not imagine her gift to be from him. Erik had only written to her once since he had left the dale, a short note, hoping that she would soon get over the accident and apologizing for it as best he could. No, Erik had passed completely out of her life. Or so she thought

"Here!" Kirsten thrust a pair of scissors into her hand. "Don't bother with economy. Cut it!"

"You are far more impatient than I am!" Margaret laughed.

Drifts of tissue paper fell to the floor when the box lid was removed. Like snow, on this day of snow, lying all around her. Her fingers shook as she lifted the final layer.

"Oh!" Kirsten gasped. "How lovely! Meg, how really, really lovely!"

A deceptively simple dress of fine creamy-coloured wool, with a deep yoke embroidered in tiny seed-pearls, lay revealed in the box, the pearls like small drops of dew clinging to the lovely fabric, and suddenly Margaret was remembering the waterfall high above the valley floor, and the superstition that clung to it.

"It's from Thor!" Kirsten announced. She was as excited as a child over the unexpected gift, holding it up for the bride's inspection. "It must be from Thor! He went away two days ago, but I did not know he had gone as far as Oslo."

Margaret took the dress, holding it against her, pressing it close to her heart. There was a card at the bottom of the box, and it said simply: "From Thor."

"I knew it!" Kirsten triumphed. "I knew it! Thor's like that." Then, when she saw the tears in Margaret's eyes, she added brusquely: "For heaven's sake, don't cry! You'll ruin your wedding dress."

Signe was at the door again. This time there was no box. The old servant carried a superb sable coat over her arm, with a small cap to match.

"I knew Thor had bought that," Kirsten confessed almost sheepishly. "I went with him to choose it."

"When," Margaret asked through her tears, "did you ever do any work?"

"It was before the school started," Kirsten pointed out righteously. "When Thor first asked you to marry him."

"These, also," Signe announced from the doorway. "They came with the box from Oslo."

Two round cellophane flower containers were thrust into Kirsten's hands and Margaret saw some of the colour recede from her friend's cheeks as she looked at them.

"How—ridiculous of Paul!" Kirsten laughed unsteadily. "I'm past the age for pretty compliments!"

"But not for pretty flowers!" Margaret said gently. "Kirsten, they're lovely—and it was wonderful of Paul."

"I wonder why they thought that gardenias were right for me and lily of the valley for you?" Kirsten murmured, taking up the flowers.

"Isn't lily of the valley also called the Rose of Sharon?" Margaret asked. "Perhaps it was because

Paul thought I should have a rose of some sort, being English."

"Paul wouldn't send you flowers," Kirsten reminded her. "They, too, will have come from Thor, and—I think he meant them to be lilies of the valley."

Margaret turned sharply away. She could not bear this happiness without tears. It was all too much—Thor's kindness, his thought for her—everything but his love!

"It's ten minutes to nine," Kirsten warned. "Time to get ready. Thor will be on his way to the church by now. She paused at the door. "Can you manage alone for a minute, Meg, while I go along to my room and change?" she asked.

"Yes," Margaret said, "I can manage," but she was still sitting on the edge of the bed with Thor's flowers in her hands when Kirsten came back.

"Don't be late, whatever you do!" Kirsten admonished. "*We* think that's unlucky. In the country, up here in the mountains," she chattered on as she slipped the new dress over Margaret's head, "a bride's wedding outfit is generally passed down from mother to daughter over several generations, or else it is specially embroidered by the mother so that the daughter will be fittingly attired."

Thor had certainly seen to it that his bride should be "fittingly attired".

"How lovely you look, Meg!" Kirsten said huskily, kissing her impulsively when she stood ready to leave Solstua, at last, and only when she had to hand Margaret the stick without which she would not walk, did her bright eyes dim.

Outside there was a brave jangling of bells as the horses tossed their heads in the frosty air. Paul was already in the sleigh, but he jumped down to settle them comfortably in the back, with the white bearskin rugs over their knees. Margaret had noticed them hanging over a beam in the *stabbur* and had wondered then if she would ever see them in use, and now they were securely round her on her wedding day.

Don't look back, she told herself. Nothing is ever gained by looking back. Surely that was as true as Kirsten's firmly-held belief that it was useless to peer ahead into the future? Live this day, her heart pleaded. Your day. Your wedding day!

The swift drive down the valley was more wonderful than anything she could have imagined, and when they came to the village and the little *kirke* on the knoll above it, the whole world seemed to be stilled, waiting. All the hills were wrapped in a soft blanket of white, with the mountain peaks above them rearing their hoary heads against a sky of pure turquoise, and the only person to be seen was Thor, standing tall and erect in the dim wooden porch.

He looked at her for a long moment as the sleigh pulled up, and then he stepped quickly across the snow to help her up the half-dozen wooden steps.

Inside the *kirke* was cool and rather bare, the altar devoid of all ornamentation save for the lovely picture hanging above it, a masterpiece of the painter's skill.

Most of the villagers had gathered in the narrow, heavily-carved pews, the men on the right-hand side, the women sedately seated across the central aisle, but Margaret was hardly aware of custom. She felt Thor's hand on her arm, warm and reassuring even through the thick fur of her coat, guiding her firmly forward to where Olav Jorgensen was waiting.

The rather stern Calvinistic service was soon over. Thor's ring was on the third finger of her right hand, and she was his wife.

There was no formal reception. Kirsten and Paul and Olav Jorgensen joined them for an early lunch at the one small hotel the village boasted, and they caught the fjord steamer at one o'clock. Paul, it had been arranged, would follow them to Oslo in the morning.

Ellen had not been at the wedding ceremony. She had refused stubbornly to leave Laerdal and Margaret had tried not to think about her.

"She'll come round in time," Kirsten had said.

The fjord steamer was almost empty when they went on board, but on this clear, cold day it was wonderful to stay on deck. Thor came to stand beside Margaret when his car had been stowed away to his satisfaction.

"Not too cold?" he asked. "It will not take us long to cross the fjord, but we can go down to the cabin if you wish."

"I don't want to miss one minute of this!" Margaret told him. "The mountains have come so near!"

The great peaks of the Jotunheimen had never looked so majestic, riding the skyline in their fresh mantles of snow. Where the sun touched them they were flushed a delicate pink, and in shadow they were blue.

They stood leaning on the rail, until the steamer slipped into a narrower arm of the fjord and a wide, fertile valley lay before them.

They had reached Laerdal, and for a moment Margaret wondered if Ellen would come to meet them, but she could not mention Ellen to Thor. It was too much like mentioning Gerda.

"We'll have something to eat when we reach Gol," Thor decided. "That will be the worst part of our journey over. We will be in the Hallingdal then, and it is not far to Oslo."

Margaret did not want their magic journey to pass too quickly. Sitting beside Thor as he took the wheel of the big, powerful American car which had replaced the one Erik had wrecked, she felt that this would be something to remember always, this day when they had travelled together in a new companionship.

They drove for miles without a village or even a hamlet in sight, the road winding deep in a cleft between the mountains. It was their world, wrapped in a silence Margaret was reluctant to break. For the first time she felt that she was really getting to know Thor, that understanding between them might not be so impossible, after all.

They were in the Hallingdal before darkness

began to fall, which was what Thor had wanted. The main Oslo highway lay before them, winding deep among the trees he loved, and there could be no fear now of a road blocked by snow or too treacherous icing conditions.

"We'll push on, shall we?" he asked when they came to Honefoss. "We'll keep to the main road, I think."

From time to time he had given her a quick, searching scrutiny, checking up on her reactions to the lengthy journey, but Margaret did not feel in the least tired. The car was warm and comfortable, and the soft fur touching her cheek was like a caress. She drew it closer as the first lights of Oslo came into view, pricking out among the low foothills like fallen stars.

The city itself lay close to the water's edge, a fairy city backed by its snow-capped hills, with a glitter of light and a warmth about it which Margaret had not expecte l. It was not at all like Bergen, the only other city she had seen. They had an entirely different character. Oslo, she thought, was softer, kinder, perhaps.

Thor drove straight to the Grand Hotel in Karl Johans Gate. It was nine o'clock and most of the other guests were in the *spisesal*, laughing and talking over their evening meal.

"If you would prefer it, Margaret," he said, "we can have something sent up to our rooms."

The suggestion of intimacy, of a place of their own, made her pulses throb a little faster, but she wanted Thor to please himself.

"Whatever you would like to do," she answered. "I'm not in the least tired."

He turned from signing the register.

"It's immaterial to me," he said. "If you wish it, we will go into the dining-room. They have a good orchestra."

The clerk behind the reception desk held out a pen.

"If madame would sign?" he suggested.

Margaret's fingers shook as she bent over the

book and wrote Margaret Revold for the first time.

Margaret Revold! It seemed to have changed everything, and yet nothing had really changed. She was still without Thor's love.

Determined not to think about it, she followed her husband to the lift and they were whirled up in silence to their first-floor suite. There was a small sitting-room, a communal bathroom and two bed-rooms. Thor's luggage was taken into the smaller of the two.

Automatically Margaret washed, and tidied her hair. Her wedding dress was still fresh and un-crushed even after their long journey, and she did not attempt to change it. It was perfect for their simple meal together, and Thor looked his approval when they met in the sitting-room again.

"I haven't thanked you for—for all this," she said shyly. "Not properly."

She limped across the room and stood under the small crystal chandelier, its light picking out the tawny glints in her hair. and in that moment she looked curiously defenceless. Thor turned abruptly to the outer door.

"There's no need to thank me from now on, Margaret," he said. "You are entitled to these things as my wife."

Entitled! The strangely cold, almost formal word struck at her heart. Entitled, when she had thought that she had come by Thor's gifts through affection, at least!

The dining-room was crowded, but the head waiter had reserved a table for them at the far end of the room, a round table with a pink-shaded light which glistened on the embroidery of Margaret's wedding gown and made the pearls look like dew-drops—or tears.

On a cleared space in the centre of the floor several couples were dancing. Margaret watched them between the lofty pillars which supported the roof, wondering if she would ever dance again. Would it have been easy to dance with Thor, feeling his arms strongly about her, feeling his nearness and strength?

She thrust the thought from her. She did not even know if Thor danced at all.

Like all Norwegian meals, this was a leisurely one. Thor seemed in no hurry to end it, and they lingered over their coffee in the lounge. The other diners were thinning out, going towards the lift or speeding departing guests with a final drink and a final *"Skal!"* Margaret glanced at Thor. He was frowning.

Turning in her chair, she saw that someone was coming towards them, and her heart seemed to miss a beat and plunge on twice as quickly as she recognized her tardy visitor.

"Erik!"

The word had escaped her in a sort of sigh. It seemed years since she had set out with Erik in the big tourer for Laerdal that fateful afternoon when the tree had fallen. He looked confused and shamefaced as he halted before her.

"I saw Thor and you coming out of the dining-room," he said. "I've been celebrating with some very old friends. A birthday."

Behind him Margaret could see a small group of people about her own age, only they seemed so very, very young. There was a tall girl in a white frock, with a beautiful face and hard blue eyes which roamed restlessly about the foyer in search of nothing in particular, and another girl in green, accompanied by two young men and an older woman.

"I'm sorry," Erik was saying. "I'm terribly sorry about—all this. Ellen wrote and told me you were coming. Fred Sonsburg told her. She said you might be here quite soon." He was not quite looking at her, avoiding the thought of her crippled state, and suddenly Margaret realized why he had only written once since the accident. Erik could not bear to see anything defaced or broken. "I should have written again," he acknowledged. "I meant to come, later on."

"It's all right, Erik," Margaret said steadily. "You could not be held responsible for an accident."

Thor had not spoken. She could feel him standing, tensed and rigid, just behind her chair, waiting for Erik to go.

"You're—married, aren't you?" Erik asked. "Ellen wrote that it had been arranged."

"Yes," Thor said, "we're married. And now, if you will excuse us, Erik, Margaret is tired."

He put his hand under Margaret's arm to lead her towards the lift, but she could not tell from his expression what he thought.

She said, looking back at Erik and trying to be kind: "We'll see you again."

"I hope so," Erik murmured conventionally, but she knew that he could not bear to look at her hobbling away on her stick with Thor's strong arm to support her on the other side.

Yes, Erik was very young, and her own extreme youth had fallen away behind her.

Thor stood aside to let her into the lift.

"I've had a wonderful day," she told him unsteadily. "It has been—everything I could have wished."

"I'm glad," he answered, not looking at her.

When they reached their sitting-room he rang for a maid, speaking swiftly to the girl in Norwegian for several minutes before he lit a cigarette and went to stand by the window.

The maid was waiting and Margaret followed her into her bedroom. The girl was helpful, but Margaret did not feel that there had been any real need for her services. She could have managed alone, more slowly, perhaps. Yes, she could have managed, she thought, until she remembered that her wedding dress hooked intricately right down the back. Without help, she could not have struggled out of it, and Thor had been unwilling to give that help.

Lying between the thin sheets under the great white *dyne* which was twice as thick as the ones they used in the mountains, she wondered if she should have gone back to Thor to say goodnight, but the maid had expected her husband to come to her and had helped her into bed.

Thor was a long time in coming.

"I thought you were asleep," he said.

She lay looking at him, willing him to kiss her goodnight.

"No, I was not asleep."

He came and stood beside the bed.

"Is there anything I can get you? An aspirin or anything to let you sleep?"

"No," she said, turning her head on the pillow, "there is nothing, Thor."

He bent and kissed her cheek, so lightly that she scarcely felt his lips against her skin. Lightly—and coldly?

"Goodnight," he said. "Sleep well, *vesla*."

The final small endearment, so unexpected, so near to tenderness, rushed the tears to her eyes as he closed the door between them, and after an hour, when sleep would not come, she heard him cross the sitting-room floor and go out through the double doors. Out along the corridor, no doubt, and down in the lift to the emptying lounge, perhaps even out into the deserted streets, to walk alone.

CHAPTER EIGHT

"SKAL!" said Paul Loren, raising his glass to the level of his fine blue eyes. "We meet again!"

He had come in with the evening train and come straight to the hotel where Margaret and Thor were waiting. He had given Thor one long, searching look as they had gripped hands, but it was impossible for Margaret to guess what he had discovered from his scrutiny.

"What sort of day have you had?" he asked as he sat down facing her.

"Quiet, but lovely," she told him. "Thor drove me out to Bygdoy and we sat overlooking a little bay and watched the boats coming up the fjord. It seemed that we were almost on an island, with the sea everywhere."

"Then?" he prompted.

Margaret laughed.

"We drove right up to the top of the world!"

Paul's eyes sparkled.

"Do I know this place?"

"I expect you do!" she told him. "I expect you think it very ordinary, but it was lovely today because I was seeing it for the first time."

"And with Thor!" Paul seemed in no doubt about their affection—their mutual love. "My guess is that it was Holmenkollen or Frognerseteren. Did you have a clear view?"

"We saw everything, and came back by a thousand lakes! What a lot of water there is around Oslo, and everywhere is lovely!"

"Keep on your rose-coloured spectacles, Margaret!" Paul said more seriously, clasping her hand. "You look wonderfully well in them!"

"I do feel most gloriously well," she answered.

"Well enough to see a colleague of mine tonight?" he enquired almost casually.

"Tonight?" Margaret had not expected this. "If—you think I should," she faltered.

Thor moved almost defensively, standing between them.

"Is this absolutely necessary, Loren?" he asked.

"I think so." Paul looked straight up at him. "I have made the appointment for eight o'clock."

"I can go," Margaret said. "Don't worry about me, Thor. I am ready."

Paul drained his glass.

"Shall we go, then?" he asked.

"I'll get Margaret's coat."

Thor went towards the lift, leaving a small silence behind him.

"This will not take long," Paul consoled, sitting down by Margaret's side. "It is most essential that we have a fresh view—another opinion. Do not let it disturb you too much."

Margaret turned, looking at him squarely.

"Paul," she said, "will you tell me the truth? Am I always going to be—like this?"

"No," he answered vigorously. "No, you must not think it."

"But there will be—always a limp?"

She saw his kind mouth grow tight.

"I will not let you imagine that," he said. "So much can happen with the passage of time."

"But not the complete miracle? Is that it?"

"Time can complete anything," he told her, "and heal much."

"There's just one other question, Paul," she said. "Did Thor know—before we were married, I mean?"

"He knew that I did not think an operation advisable in the circumstances."

The answer had come with very little hesitation. Paul could not pretend to her at this stage.

"I see," she said as Thor came towards them with her coat.

Thor had married her out of pity or from some mistaken sense of obligation. The thing she had known in her heart for so long was true, the thing she had feared and fought against and crushed into the background because she had recognized its power to destroy her was confessed openly now and she had no defence against it.

Numbed by her discovery, she let Thor help her into the taxi he had summoned, sitting cold and silent by his side as it bore them the short distance to the hospital where Paul Loren's colleague was waiting.

He was a kind, middle-aged man, as tall as Thor but very thin, with a stoop which made him look old, the bright blue Nordic eyes, however, were clear and keen as he made his examination, the strong, lean hands firm and sure. Thor had waited downstairs, but Paul had come up with Margaret to the consulting room. The two doctors talked to her in a desultory way as they worked, but now and then there was a thoughtful pause in which Margaret felt that they must surely be able to hear the heavy pounding of her heart.

When the examination was complete Paul took her back to Thor.

"The Professor wants a couple of X-rays tomorrow morning," was all he said. "Will you come at nine o'clock?"

Emotionally exhausted by the events of the past two days, Margaret let Thor answer for her.

"We'll come back," he said.

Paul left them to return to the hotel on their own. He would go upstairs again, Margaret thought, and talk to the Professor, and by the morning he might know what hope, if any, the older man could hold out to her.

"I'm going to send you straight to bed," Thor told her. "Tomorrow will be your biggest day."

Obediently she crossed to the lift.

"Don't come up, Thor," she said. "It's early and you must want something to eat. I'll ring for the maid if I want anything."

He hesitated, and then he put his hand out and pressed the lift button.

"I'll send you something up," he said briefly. "Make sure that you ring the maid."

Going up in the silent elevator, Margaret wondered if it would always be like this. Ringing for maids because she needed help, never really able to lead a free and useful life, always being an embarrassment to Thor.

She had perhaps twenty-four hours to go on wondering before she knew whether she was to remain as a burden to the man she loved or whether fate had decreed that she might walk unhampered again. And, since Thor had married her out of pity and a sense of obligation, what would happen if she was suddenly set free from her lameness and could live her life to the full again?

She lay battling with the question till a pale dawn broke over the sleeping city, but even then she had not found her answer.

The maid brought her early-morning tea in the English manner, and Thor came in while she was drinking it.

"We must break you of this terrible habit!" he smiled, although his scrutiny was concerned and deeply penetrating. "A good Norse breakfast is what you want."

"Ugh! Raw fish and boiled eggs and onions!" She made a face at him. "I shall always want tea and toast and marmalade!"

"It has a nice warm sound," he admitted, crossing to her window to pull aside the heavy curtains. "It is snowing," he told her.

He was still in pyjamas and dressing-gown, and the suggestion of leashed energy about him as he stood there made her ask:

"Thor, are you worrying about Helmsdal? About this fresh fall of snow?"

"No," he replied immediately. "It is not likely to block the roads for a week or two yet."

"I could quite easily stay alone," she offered.

He swung round to face her.

"That is out of the question," he said. "My place is by your side."

She could not answer that.

They drove to the hospital and he sat with Paul while the X-rays were taken. When Margaret rejoined them they looked tensed, keyed up for some sort of decision which neither of them had really expected.

"We'll have lunch," Paul suggested, "and then we can come back and hear what the Professor has to say."

They could not eat. Even Paul could do no more than toy with the meal he ordered. They were all on edge, anxious to climb the hill again and confront the truth.

"It's ten minutes to three," he announced at last, consulting the elaborately-engraved watch he carried in his breast pocket, anchored by a gold chain into the buttonhole of his lapel. "Everything should be fixed. Shall we go?"

Margaret prayed for enough courage to walk to the door without trembling. In another half-hour—in less than that, perhaps—the way of the future would lie before her. Her own future and Thor's.

Paul left them in an ante-room at the end of a corridor. He seemed to stay away an interminable length of time, and then, suddenly, he was coming too soon. Margaret heard his footsteps approaching the closed door and wanted to bury her face in her hands and say: "Don't tell me! Don't make it harder for Thor! Don't tear my life apart!"

She said none of these things. She sat deathly still, staring at the door, staring and staring until Thor came behind her and put a firm hand on her shoulder.

Paul came in, followed by the Professor. They were both smiling firm, professional smiles.

"Margaret," Paul said, "we want you to go to Zurich. There's someone there who may be able to help you. The Professor can get into touch with him right away." He looked at Thor. "I know it will be all right with Thor if you agree to go," he added encouragingly.

"Of course she must go," Thor said. "If there is the slightest chance of complete recovery she must go at once."

"It is only a chance," the Professor warned, "but

one I would like your wife to take. She is young—much too young and too beautiful to remain like this. The operation I hope for has been done once or twice before, in England and in Zurich, but my colleague in Switzerland has the wider experience, I think."

When they were left alone, Paul was almost jubilant.

"This is better than I had dared to hope for," he confessed. "You see, in the mountains I was working a little in the dark, without X-rays and the proper hospital equipment. Apart from that, however, I don't think anyone could have given a complete verdict until now. Nature has a strange way of helping us, you know," he added with a smile. "And Margaret is young and fit."

Thor had crossed to the window and was looking down into the deserted quadrangle.

"How long is it going to take to fix up this appointment?" he asked.

"Not very long." Paul made a rapid calculation. "A week. Perhaps even less, if the Professor can get in touch with his colleague at once."

"I see." Thor was still standing with his back to the room. "And you will have no idea how long Margaret may have to remain in Zurich?" he asked.

"About three weeks, I should think, if all goes well."

Margaret's heart was pounding, slow, deliberate strokes which seemed to fill up all the silence.

"Thor," she said at last, "you must go back to Solstua. I can wait here till—till Paul has made the appointment."

Thor turned, dismissing her plea with a brief gesture.

"There's no need for either of us to return to Solstua before we go to Switzerland," he said.

Paul Loren looked relieved.

"Now you see, Margaret, how generous I am!" he laughed. "I have made it possible for you to have an extended honeymoon in Switzerland!"

Thor turned away, and Margaret could only

smile wanly.

"Yes," she said, "you are very kind."

Paul looked thoughtful.

"I know how you hate hotel life, Thor," he said as they went down to find a taxi. "Why not take Margaret to Hanko for a week? I know it is late in the season, but it is mild down there just now and the sea air will do her good."

Margaret, who knew nothing of Hanko, could only wait for Thor's reply with a fast beating heart.

"We can't put you to that trouble," he told Paul. "You must have closed the chalet for the winter."

"It is always open till Christmas," Paul assured him. "I am a solitary being at times, and I like my own company for a week-end now and then. So Hanko is the answer."

Thor looked at Margaret.

"Would you like to go?" he asked.

"If you refuse," Paul assured her, "you will regret it for the rest of your life! Hanko is my cure for everything!"

Paul has a summer chalet there," Thor explained, "and a sailing boat, but it will be very isolated at this time of year."

"No more so than Solstua," Paul pointed out. "I'm trying to sell you the idea of Hanko," he smiled, looking deeply into Margaret's eyes.

Did he know about their marriage? Did Paul believe that his summer chalet on a lovely island somewhere on the wide blue fjord would help to make it real?

"You've already done that, I think," she said as lightly as she could. "Now you must sell the idea to Thor!"

Thor smiled.

"It is quite settled, then," he said. "We will go."

They spent the afternoon shopping in Stortingsgate, Thor insisting that she should replenish her wardrobe with clothes suitable for Switzerland at the beginning of the winter. They would not come amiss, Margaret supposed, when they returned to Solstua.

She did not want to think so far ahead, however, and when Thor drove her southwards along the fjord the following morning with the sun shining on blue water and all the hills like frosted sugar cakes, she made up her mind to leave her doubts behind her and accept one perfect week.

Paul's chalet was built high above the fjord, several miles from the lovely little holiday resort itself, which was now almost deserted. It was surrounded by trees on the landward side, but it looked out across the island and the fjord to a wide vista of open sea and distant, snow-capped hills beyond.

There was a magic, crystalline quality in the air, and it was not wholly cold. Margaret felt that a new world had opened up before her eyes as Thor drew the car to a standstill on a narrow gravelled terrace high above a little, hidden bay and felt for the key to Paul's chalet.

"Welcome to Hanko," he said. "If it is warm enough, we might even use the boat.

He slipped the key into the lock and opened the door.

"It's lovely!" Margaret cried, her eyes shining. "It's the sort of place one dreams about."

"It is better than Oslo," he agreed.

That would be all it would mean to Thor, Margaret thought. An escape from the city, somewhere nearer to his beloved mountains. While to her it was the chalet of her dreams. Paul's kindness swept over her, bringing swift tears of gratitude to her eyes, so that she walked ahead of Thor into the little house in silence.

It was small and compact, a bachelor's retreat which yet contained everything that went with gracious living. There was no need for Thor to find wood to stoke up a stove to provide them with warmth. Everything was electric.

"All done by the turn of a switch!" he remarked. "This will spoil you when you return to Solstua, Margaret."

"It would not seem right there," she told him. "I love Solstua as it is, Thor."

He halted in the doorway of the sitting-room, looking back at her as if her impulsive confession had surprised him, and for the first time Margaret saw Thor unsure. He brought in their luggage, laying it down in the tiny hallway, contemplating the closed doors which led from it with an air almost of concern.

"I'm not sure about Paul's accommodation here," he said. "I should have asked, of course." He strode to the nearest door, opening it on a large, sunny bedroom overlooking the fjord. "Here you are," he announced with something like relief. "Obviously the guest room! I'll see what else I can find while you settle in."

He put her case and dressing-case just inside the door, leaving his own grip in the hall. Margaret went slowly into the room, crossing to the far wall, which was all window, holding the fjord and the distant hills imprisoned in its broad frame. The clear-cut beauty of it all seemed poignantly lovely, and her heart contracted at the thought that they were only here for a short time. Perhaps not even for a week.

Well, then, she must make that week perfect, with no regrets afterwards.

Thor had settled himself in Paul's room when she went back to the hall half an hour later. Her bedroom boasted a hand-basin with hot and cold running water, and she saw that there was also a wonderfully-appointed bathroom on the far side of Thor's door.

It could all have been really perfect, she thought, but she turned regret aside there, regret that could so easily poison the happiness she already possessed.

For the next two days Hanko did its best to enchant them. Margaret lived in a paradise of Thor's unconscious making. They cooked meals together on the electric stove in the miniature kitchen and he taught her to make *smorbrod* to his liking; they opened up the boathouse and spent a morning overhauling Paul's sailing dinghy, then drifted aimlessly across the sound in it till the sun plunged down behind the western hills, leaving them afloat on a molten fjord of greens and blues and deep sienna, which was a reflection of the brilliant, vermilion sky.

Margaret had never seen such sunsets, and when the colour died, almost too suddenly, leaving the water grey and chill and the distant mountains ice-blue, she looked away.

In many ways Thor was the ideal companion. His confidence when he handled the sails excluded fear and he was obviously at one with his surroundings. They even walked a little, although he would turn back imperiously when he considered they had gone far enough.

These golden days were something Margaret would never forget. They were days of near-friendship when she seemed to be getting to know Thor, when he spoke of the past almost without reservation, and if he did not discuss the future at any great length, she felt that it was only because he had sensed her own nervousness in that direction.

He wanted to give her confidence to face the coming operation, but he would not hold out the promise of ultimate fulfilment. That was the one reserve she sensed in him.

When the telephone in the chalet rang for the first time she felt suddenly chilled. They had been at Hanko for four days, and she knew that this must be their summons to return.

Slowly she walked out on to the terrace, feeling the weight of her dragging limbs as never before, and when Thor came to her she could not face him immediately. Her sense of loss was too great, and for a moment, he, too, seemed to be contemplating the scene of their strange honeymoon with regret.

"I have to go to Oslo," he said. "Will you wait here for me, Margaret? There doesn't seem to be much point in your making the journey just to sit in a hotel lounge till I see about our passage to Zurich. There are one or two other things, too, that I would like to fix up—about Solstua and the timber we brought down before it began to snow."

he had said "I am coming to see you". He would
have to walk from the main road high above the bay
and she had no idea when there would be a bus, but
suddenly she was walking to meet him. She did not
want Erik to come to the chalet where she had known
a fleeting happiness with Thor.

The path up to the main road was quite steep,
and once or twice she was forced to sit down on an
outcrop of rock or on one of the simple rustic benches
which Paul had placed here and there to command
a view. Erik found her seated on one of them,
flushed and a little breathless at sight of him.

"Meg," he said, "I had to come! I had to speak
to you alone."

She moved, thrusting her stick between them,
her hands clasped tightly over its carved handle.
The ugly little troll's face seemed to look up between
her fingers and laugh at her.

"I don't see why," she said steadily. "You could
have written anything you wanted to say, Erik."

"I meant to write," he confessed, "but I never did
after that first time. Perhaps I didn't have the
courage, Meg." He tried to come nearer. "I couldn't
bear the thought of you crippled for life—because of
me."

"It was an accident," she said coldly. "There
can be no blame attached to anyone, Erik."

"You know I did it in defiance of Thor," he said.
"I thought he was wrong about closing the road and
we were wasting time, but it proved otherwise. I
shall never forgive myself, Meg, even though I am
asking you to forgive me."

Margaret's face softened.

"You mustn't worry about it," she said. "It's
all over. I may not even walk like this much longer.
Thor and I are going to Zurich in the hope that something can be done for me there."

She saw him avert his eyes from her awkward
body, though he evidently already knew about their
hope of a cure.

"   seemed confident," he said. "It must come
        t must!" he declared in sudden passion.

"I'll stay," she agreed. "I feel that I want every minute here before we have to go."

He turned her to face him more fully, his hands strongly compelling on her arms.

"I don't think you need any of my courage to add to your own," he said, "but it's there, if you want it, Margaret."

Her eyes clung to his, asking more than courage, and suddenly he bent his head and kissed her full on the lips.

"I will not be long," he promised.

She watched him go, with the memory of his kiss burning her mouth and with a strange, wild ecstasy flowing through her that made waiting easy.

When the telephone rang for a second time she felt quite sure that it would be Thor. Perhaps there was something he had forgotten.

"Hullo!" said a voice. "So you *are* there!"

"Erik?" She could not mistake him, although his memory had almost faded. "Yes, we are at Paul's chalet, but Thor has gone."

"Gone!" he repeated. "Do you mean back to Solstua?"

"Oh, no!" She laughed. "He's in Oslo. We are getting ready to go to Zurich."

"I heard about that," he said. "I met Paul Loren two days ago and he told me." There was a brief pause. "Meg," Erik said, after a moment or two, "I'm at Ingierstrand. You won't know where that is, but it isn't so very far away. I am coming to see you."

"No, Erik!" There was sharp refusal in her voice and something like panic in her heart. "You mustn't. There's nothing we can have to say to each other—"

She heard his brief laugh at the far end of the line and the small click as he put down his receiver. Her refusal had been rejected. He had rung off.

Turning from the instrument, she limped back into the sitting-room, wondering how long it would take Erik to get there, and hoping that he would have come and gone before Thor ret—
course, he might even be coming to see

"I've lain awake at night praying for some sort of solution." He slipped down beside her, his fair head buried suddenly on her knee. "Meg, forgive me!" he cried. "For God's sake, forgive me! I didn't mean this to happen to you, to see you —crushed and broken like this. I wanted you as you were, lovely, perfect in every way. That was the selfishness in me, I suppose, but now I know I still want you—whatever you are like."

Margaret drew back, aghast, but there could be no doubt about Erik's sincerity—the sincerity of the moment. His handsome face was quite colourless, his eyes blue seas of regret, and rejected passion burned in him like a swiftly-ignited torch. He saw himself as the grand lover whom fate and his own folly had cheated, and he was miserable because of it.

"We can't discuss this, Erik," Margaret told him quite gently. "I am married to Thor. You've got to remember that."

He flung back his head, confronting her with hostile eyes, his arms still tight about her.

"Thor cheated you," he declared. "He cheated you if he told you he loved you! He married you because he felt obliged to—because I had let you down."

Margaret's whole being recoiled before the impassioned outburst and her body seemed to shrink in Erik's wild embrace.

"No," she said. "No, that isn't true!"

Somewhere far beneath them she heard the sound of a car, a powerful car reversing swiftly in a confined space. There was nowhere for a car to be but down on the narrow terrace in front of the chalet at the end of the winding drive into Paul's tiny, secret bay. Someone was down there. Someone was going away.

"Erik," she said, freeing herself, "we must forget about this. There is nothing we owe each other. I am in love with Thor."

He stood back, aghast in his turn.

"I don't believe it," he said. "You can't be in love with him."

"You will believe it," she said. "One day."

He let her go, standing aside as she limped back down the path towards the fjord, and somehow she knew that he would not follow her. When she came to the chalet the door stood open and a little wind was straying in from the sea. The sun had been pulled down a long way towards the west and the wind was already edged with ice.

She walked through the open doorway and saw that Thor had been there. The short sheepskin jacket which he wore for driving had been thrown down carelessly in a chair, and when she went to the kitchen there were flowers—a great sheaf of them— still lying in their stiff paper wrapping on the table.

"Thor!" she whispered. "Thor!" but he was far from hearing.

Why had he driven away again? Why had he gone without seeking her out?

He came back when it was dark and the lights were burning in the chalet. Margaret had prepared a meal and put the flowers in water, but when she heard the car there was no sudden ecstasy in her heart. She knew without looking at Thor that something had gone wrong.

"Is it—about Zurich?" she asked, aware that all the warmth between them had faded.

"No," he answered stonily, "Zurich is all arranged." He held her gaze for a moment with a burning intensity in his grey eyes which scorched her. "You have nothing to fear in that respect. I have made reservations for us both on the morning plane."

She drew back, chilled. This was the old Thor, the Thor who had thrust an unscalable barrier between himself and the world. And she was still on the wrong side of that barrier. For three days she had imagined that understanding and affection had broken it down, but now Thor seemed determined to prove how wrong she had been.

"Thank you for the flowers," she faltered. "It was kind of you to remember."

"Paul sent them," he returned briefly. "I met

him in Oslo. He is coming down later on, to say
au revoir."

"Shall we wait a meal for him?"

"Just as you like." He was going out again, and
he had not suggested she should go with him. "I'll
put the boat up. We can hardly go and leave it
anchored in the fjord," he said.

He stayed away till Paul came, thrusting the
doctor between them, even in conversation. The meal
was a fiasco, and Margaret was almost relieved when
he suggested that Paul should stay the night and travel
up to Oslo with them in the morning.

"You'll be coming to the airport, anyway," he
pointed out.

"It won't make much difference, and I can easily
vacate your room."

Paul avoided looking in Margaret's direction and
remarked that there was no need for anyone to
change rooms. There was, he reminded them, a
second guest room.

The evening seemed longer than any Margaret
had ever had to sit through. Thor appeared to be
avoiding anything in the nature of a personal contact. He remained withdrawn, as if he were fighting
some sort of battle within himself, and she knew that
the tension had even communicated itself to Paul.
He rose to say goodnight as the clock in the hall
chimed twelve, saying that he had a busy day before
him.

Thor had also got to his feet, and Margaret felt
for her stick. He came across the room to help her.

"Thor," she said, "I forgot to tell you about Erik.
He came this afternoon."

There was no change in his expression as he
answered her. It remained tight and cold.

"I met him," he said briefly, "on the high road—
after I had left your flowers."

She wanted to say so much more, to explain, if
she could, about Erik, but Thor stood waiting for her
to go as if she had been a stranger. She wondered if
something had happened in Oslo to send his thoughts
crashing back into the past, but he was too far away

from her now for her to question him. Once more he was the remote figure she had first met, polite to the point of aloofness, the stranger whom she had married believing that they might have something to give each other.

Paul saw them off at the airport the following morning. It was still bright and sunny and, as usual, he had brought a parting gift of flowers. He fastened two white gardenias into her coat with a reassuring smile.

"All will be well," he told her. "I have arranged everything in Zurich and—you have Thor!"

Yes, Margaret thought, she had Thor, but only the outward assurance of his support in this her time of need. The Thor she wanted, the inward reality, was as far removed from her as he had ever been. These past few days, which had been so wonderful for her, had meant nothing to him, a duty performed, perhaps, but nothing more.

The plane rose and circled above the fjord. She had never travelled by air before and the first magic held her as they sped southwards above the clouds. Everything was new, and for a moment she was able to forget the reason for their journey.

Once or twice she was aware of Thor watching her, studying the eager response in her flushed face to a new and exhilarating experience, but when she turned towards him he invariably looked away.

By the time they reached Zurich her excitement had tired her. She was paler than usual and her mouth drooped a little.

"Will you lie down?" Thor asked when they had reached their hotel on the edge of the lovely, placid Zurichsee. "There is still time before dinner."

Margaret shook her head.

"I'd like to go out," she said. "I'd like to see something of the lake and the mountains."

He did not argue against the suggestion, taking her arm as they walked along the lake shore. The night was dark and starless, but there was a luminosity behind the mountains which reminded Margaret of Norway. She turned her back on the artificial glow of the city nestling close to the water and looked towards the dark rampart of the Glarus Alps silhouetted blackly against the sky.

"All mountains are different, Thor," she said. "They have a personality of their own which one can't change, even in one's imagination. All this is lovely, but it is not quite the same as Helmsdal. The Jotunheimen are your mountains."

He looked at her sharply, but his reply was light.

"It may be a case of 'where the heart is,' Margaret. Do you wish so much to return to the Jotunheimen?"

"More than I can say." Her voice had trembled in spite of her effort to steady it. "That doesn't mean, of course, that I am ungrateful for—all this," she added.

In the uncertain light his eyes seemed to glitter.

"What does it mean?" he asked, his fingers hardening on her arm as if he were determined that she should not escape the question.

"It means that I am in love," the confession surprised her even as she made it. "I want to go back—all in one piece. I want to feel free."

The agonized appeal had come straight from her heart, but she could not have been prepared for Thor's reaction to it. He stiffened and his fingers relaxed their hold on her arm, although his eyes still gleamed coldly above her.

"Perhaps I should have foreseen this," he said, "when we made our hasty bargain."

His voice had held all the chilliness of ice, but Margaret could only remember that he had called their marriage a hasty bargain.

CHAPTER NINE

THEY had their first appointment with Professor Weber-Holtz the following morning, and two days later Margaret was transferred to his private clinic high on the Dolderstrasse.

Her bedroom gave her a wonderful view of the blue lake, but she could not see the mountains she had looked at that first evening with Thor.

Professor Weber-Holtz was a dapper little man with a deep, guttural voice which proclaimed his German origin, although he was now a naturalized Swiss citizen. He wore thick spectacles, peering from behind them in a way which was almost disconcerting to probe deep into the individual human soul.

Margaret felt that he knew all about her in five minutes.

"This operation we shall do means much to you, huh?" he asked. "All the future is—how do you say —coloured by it?"

Thor, who had been standing beside Margaret, turned away.

"That is so," he acknowledged. "It is something that must not fail."

The Professor looked at him and nodded.

"Time is precious, perhaps?" he suggested. "We must hurry you back to your own country."

Thor did not answer that.

"We will operate in the morning," the Professor decided. "All is in order here."

Margaret held her breath, wondering if Thor would go now, if she would not see him again until after the operation. She knew that they would not let her see him in the morning, because that was the rule of the clinic and even husbands were barred, but there was still the evening before her, an evening that might well prove long and nerve-racking without someone she knew to talk to.

She could not pretend now, at this eleventh hour, that she was not afraid, but it was mostly fear of the final verdict that mocked her and sent her heart beating wildly against her breast. She thought of Kirsten Moe, wishing that Kirsten could have been with her or, at least, not so utterly out of reach. Norway seemed suddenly very far away.

Thor went with the Professor to the door, and she heard them talking out in the corridor for several minutes before they walked on, each presumably in an opposite direction.

Her heart sank, but she would not give way to the tears of disappointment that rose too readily to her eyes.

When she had almost despaired of his coming and was preparing to go to bed, Thor knocked on her door.

"I'm not going to disturb you, Margaret," he said, "but I thought I would like you to know that I'll be—near at hand in the morning."

Her eyes flew to his, but there was nothing in them but the concern he felt for her, or the pity, perhaps.

"It was nice of you to come," she said, the convential words falling between them like drops of ice. "You have done—everything you could for me."

He crossed the room to stand looking down at her for a moment under the bright central light, and it seemed that he was about to add something purposeful to what he had already said. Then, abruptly, his mouth hardened and he bent and kissed her instead.

It was a kiss that anyone might have given her.

Surprisingly, she slept. A bright sun that came glancing over snow poured through her windows to waken her and a nurse came in, half hidden in a great sheaf of flowers.

"From your husband!" she announced in careful English.

Margaret held them in her arms, struggling with sudden tears. The card said "From Thor", but nothing more, yet she knew that the message would have been just as brief if he had been in love with her. The flowery phrase and ready compliment were far removed from the make-up of this giant of the mountains.

She kept her eyes fastened on the flowers as they brought the trolley and wheeled her away, and the last thing she remembered was the bronze glory of chrysanthemums fading slowly to an unrecognizable glow.

When she came out of the anaesthetic Thor was there. She turned her head, and a deep, reassuring voice said:

"It's all over now, Margaret. Everything is all right."

She stretched out her hand and Thor took it, his strong fingers fastening tightly over hers.

After that she must have slept, because when she woke again Thor had gone and it was quite dark.

Two days later he told her that he had to fly back to Oslo.

"I won't be away for long," he promised. "A week, perhaps."

Her heart sank.

"Will you go to Solstua?"

"No. This is a business deal which has cropped up unexpectedly," he explained. "A buyer who has come from Australia. It means a bulk sale of our timber, which we can't afford to lose."

Those seven days seemed endless to Margaret, lying there waiting for Thor's return and the verdict of her own future. The Professor had promised it by the end of the week and she knew that Thor was as tensed as she was when he walked into the room.

I don't want him to be here, she thought in sudden panic. I couldn't bear it if I am never to walk again.

That was the issue, really. She might walk upright, or she might even be more crippled than before. They had faced the possibility and decided to take the chance, and now, for the first time, she was conscious of a paralysing fear.

"Thor," she whispered, "will you wait outside?"

He looked as if he would refuse, his mouth tight and his chin thrust out as she had seen him look so many times in the past when he had made up his mind about something, and then he nodded briefly and went away.

The Professor came in with the doctor in the white coat who had been there when she had come from the operating theatre. He was young and pleasant-looking, with no English, but he smiled at her. It was a warm, reassuring smile which gave her new courage.

"Now," the Professor said, "I am going to stand here, beside the window, and you will come to me—alone and without your stick."

Margaret's heart quailed. She couldn't do it. The distance between her bed and the window might have been a dozen miles instead of a couple of yards. A nurse stood on either side of her as she sat on the edge of the bed, but they did not attempt to help her. This was something she must do alone. They were only there to help if she failed.

Trembling, she struggled to her feet, straightening slowly and painfully till she stood upright. The silence in the room could almost be felt.

"Now, come to me!" the Professor said.

She stood swaying for a moment and then she began to walk. He held out his hands to her and almost before she realized it, she was gripping them tightly, holding on, clinging to them as a drowning man might cling to a rock.

"Now, back again." The brisk, persuasive voice was inexorable. "Walk back to the bed and that will be enough."

She did it, aware that she was walking free and upright for the first time in weeks. The knowledge crumbled something within her and she collapsed on to the bed, weeping.

Shame scorched her as the nurses drew the clothes over her and Professor Weber-Holtz came to stand by her side.

"I'm sorry," she apologized. "I did not mean to go to pieces like that."

"It is only natural," he smiled. "But we have a great success performed! We must go now and tell your husband the good news, and then, tomorrow, you will walk for him, huh?"

Margaret was trembling.

"Yes," she said, but she looked away from the Professor's enquiring brown eyes.

Thor came almost immediately. There had only been time for him to hear that she would walk as freely as she had ever done, and Margaret's eyes sought his as soon as he appeared in the doorway. He came towards the bed, his face a mask, the eyes beneath the thick dark brows coldly grey.

"This is good news, Margaret," he said briefly. "It is more even than we expected. The Professor tells me that the accident might never have been for all the effect it will have now."

His frigid acceptance of the situation stunned her into silence. She lay gazing at him, unable to believe that he was not wholly glad—for both of them.

"When can we go home?" she asked unsteadily.

The word appeared to disconcert him for a moment.

"Back to Solstua? I haven't asked about that. Quite soon, I should think."

He seemed almost reluctant to take her back. Was he regretting his bargain? Was he sorry now that he had made such a hasty marriage in the belief that she would never walk freely again and that his was the real responsibility?

She could not ask him; she could not even look at him in that moment in case she might see such a truth written in his eyes. If she was a moral coward in that respect, she could not help it. She clung to her love a little longer and the comfort of Thor's protection.

There could be no doubt about that aspect of their strange relationship. Thor surrounded her with every comfort and his undivided attention for the next few days.

Gradually, as she grew stronger and her confidence increased, she was able to walk into the garden, leaning on Thor's arm.

"How soon do you think we can travel?" she asked one morning as they sat in the pale November sunshine facing the lake and the southern mountains. "I feel quite fit now, but I know it will depend on the Professor."

Thor looked at her with a strange smile in his eyes.

"When the Professor knows how anxious you are to return to Oslo," he said, "I am sure he will not stand in your way."

The dryness of his tone was unmistakable, although she could not understand the implication of his words.

"Will you ask him?" she said, quite sure that he, too, must be anxious to return. "We've been here for over three weeks now."

He spoke to Professor Weber-Holtz straight away, and by the beginning of the following week they were preparing to leave.

"I've written to Solstua," Thor said briefly. "Everything will be ready for our return. Unless," he added, "you wish to stay in Oslo for a few days. That, also, could be arranged."

"I would rather go straight to Helmsdal, Thor," she said. "You have been away so long, and all because of me."

He did not answer, but she supposed he was relieved as they said goodbye to the friends they had made at the clinic and boarded the north-bound plane.

Thor shook the Professor's hand, thanking him for all he had done.

"It is a pleasure," the little man beamed, "to do such a small service for one so young and—may I say—beautiful?" His brown eyes twinkled beneath their beetling grey brows. "All is as it was before. Your marriage is now secure."

Margaret looked quickly away. How could this beaming little man who had just worked a near-miracle know that their marriage was anything but secure, that it was and always had been a marriage in name only?

The journey seemed interminable. The plane was crowded and it bumped uncomfortably over the high Alpine regions, running into the edge of an electric storm before they reached Oslo. Thor had been reassuring, but she was glad when they finally touched down. In another minute or two, she felt, she would have been ignominiously sick.

It was snowing and the airport looked deserted at first, and then they were filing across the slushy tarmac to the administrative block and Paul was there to meet them. Paul and someone else.

It was a split second before she recognized Erik, and by that time he was holding out his hands to her.

"This is wonderful, Meg!" His eyes were aglow with relief and something more, and before she could stop him he had kissed her on the cheek. "You're completely cured, completely yourself again! The same Perfect Specimen!"

"So many pretty compliments, Erik!" she tried to say lightly. "You are quite expert at them!"

"You know how concerned I was," he protested, still holding her hands. "You are being unkind."

"Not intentionally," she told him rather coldly. "And here's Paul! How nice of you to come to meet us, Paul!" She freed her hands from Erik's lingering grasp, turning with relief to the doctor. "Thor said he had wired you, but we fully expected you to be too busy to come."

"Never too busy," Paul said, coming between her and Erik with a determination which Thor must have noticed, "to welcome Thor and you home."

Thor went to see about their luggage, supervising its transfer to the back of his car, which Paul had brought to the airport for him. He came back to them slowly, acknowledging Erik with the briefest of nods. It was impossible for him not to have seen Erik's welcome, yet he ignored it completely.

"You're staying overnight?" Paul asked.

"No." Thor was quite firm in his decision. "We'll push on as far as Gol, I think."

Erik looked taken aback.

"You're in a great hurry," he remarked.

"We've been away for a long time," Thor reminded him briefly.

Margaret got into the car, conscious of Erik watching her every movement with the greatest relief as he came to close the door behind her. Thor was already behind the wheel, waiting to start, and he must have seen Erik put a hand over Margaret's as he said:

"It won't be long before I'm back in Solstua, Meg. Soon the Christmas vacation will be here and we will all be in the mountains." He turned directly to Thor for the first time. "I have every reason to hope that I should have passed my finals by then," he added confidently.

Thor gave him a long, straight look.

"We will congratulate you when you come," he said. "In the meantime, it would be just as well if you worked as hard as you can."

Erik stepped back, laughing.

"Thor has no faith in me!" he observed. "He has no faith in anyone but himself."

Thor let in his clutch and with a silent movement the big car slid away.

The road to Gol was crisp and dry, but beyond the little town, Thor was warned, the snow-ploughs had been at work.

The following morning they drove into the mountain fastness at the edge of the Valdres, along a track already walled on either side by snow. It was a bitterly cold journey in spite of the car's heating system and Margaret was glad when it ended in the gradual descent to the fjord.

The steamer was waiting and they went aboard immediately. They were almost the only passengers. At mid-week, at this time of the year, traffic was mainly in goods and livestock, with the odd returning native making the journey home to see some distant and isolated dale.

Suddenly Margaret felt a new and strange warmth stealing over her, an inexplicable sense of welcome as she thought of Solstua. It was Thor's home. Perhaps one day it could be hers, also, in more than name. If Thor wanted nothing else from her, at least she could make him a home.

Kirsten was at the pier to meet them, but not Ellen.

"This is wonderful!" Kirsten declared, kissing Margaret on both cheeks while her shining eyes sought Thor's above her friend's head. "Better—far, far better—than we expected."

They had tea together. Kirsten had set it out in the English manner in her sitting-room in the school-house before an open log fire, and it was only then that Margaret became aware of a certain restraint in her manner. Kirsten seemed to have something to say to Thor which might prove difficult.

"Has Ellen come home?" Thor asked at last. "I expected to hear from her, but she has not written."

Kirsten took a deep breath.

"I think we're going to have difficulty with Ellen," she confessed, choosing her words carefully. "She's far too introspective for a young girl. There seems to be something weighing heavily on her mind and she won't make a confidant of anyone, I'm afraid. Not even Fred Sonsburg."

Thor looked up sharply.

"Has she been seeing a lot of Fred?" he asked.

"Quite a lot," Kirsten nodded. "Fred has been going to Laerdal, and he brought her back last week-end. That's one thing," she added. "Ellen wouldn't let you down, Thor. She came back to prepare Solstua for your return."

"Signe could have done that," Thor said, frowning. "Though I'm grateful for Ellen's—fidelity."

To Margaret his tone had seemed harsh, the words he had used uncharitable, but she knew so little of Ellen that she could not really judge.

They drove away from the school-house in a heavy silence.

"Ellen must go," Thor said when they were half-way to Solstua.

"No! Oh, Thor, please don't send her away because—because of me," Margaret begged.

"Solstua is your home," he said briefly.

"It is also Ellen's," Margaret protested earnestly. "It has been Ellen's home for as long as she can remember. I understand how she must feel, Thor, thinking of me as the intruder, but I can try to make things as easy as possible between us by not noticing."

"Ellen has a complex about the past." Thor's eyes were fixed on the road ahead, their expression remote. "And I suppose one can hardly blame her for her loyalty."

He meant Ellen's loyalty to Gerda, which was the same as his own loyalty. It was something she would never be able to break, Margaret thought, something she had no real wish to obscure. Ellen had loved Gerda, too. Her older sister—so sweet and lovely—had been the pivot of all her dreams, the ideal to which the young Ellen had turned eagerly and completely. If her love had bordered on worship, no one could have blamed her. Certainly not Thor.

"Please don't do anything just yet," she begged. "Let me give it a trial first."

He looked as if he might refuse, and then he shrugged.

"I doubt very much if you will succeed," he said.

Signe was out on the doorstep when they reached the house, her wrinkled old face wreathed in smiles. Margaret had spent a good deal of her convalescence with a dictionary and a Norwegian grammar, so that she was able to greet the old servant in her own tongue. Thor looked surprised.

"You've gone up in Signe's estimation by leaps and bounds," he smiled. "Your effort has bridged a tremendous gulf. Signe would never be able to express herself in a language which was not her own. When you get to know her better you will find her loyal and helpful."

Margaret wondered if Signe would be any help in her effort to understand Ellen, for Ellen, it seemed, was not to be easily won.

She presented herself at the sitting-room doorway with a frankly resentful expression in her blue eyes, not really looking at either of them, and her very words were guarded.

"Everything has been done as you wished it, Thor," she announced. "Fred Sonsburg saw to the alterations. The house is completely changed."

Thor picked up Margaret's luggage.

"I'll take these up for you," he said. "You must want to have a wash before you sit down to a meal."

Margaret followed him up the wide, uncarpeted staircase, their footsteps echoing on the polished wood. Ellen hung back in the hall, and when they reached the gallery overlooking the sitting-room, Margaret had the uneasy sense of being watched from below.

She did not look down, and in a moment she had forgotten Ellen because so much that had been Solstua had been changed.

The whole upstairs corridor had been taken away and the doors opened now from a spacious landing. It had displaced the rooms which had once been Gerda's.

Margaret's heart began to pound uncomfortably. It seemed that Thor had torn all the memory of his past love away. Was it because he had determined to start afresh, or because he could not bear the thought of someone else—Margaret herself—walking there? In loyalty to their marriage, perhaps, he had uprooted his former love. It was the sort of thing that Thor would do, but Margaret knew how tenacious love could be. The deliberate act of uprooting could never be enough.

"I thought we would get more light up here if we had a suite of rooms instead of half a dozen small, individual bedrooms, which we may never use," he explained. "When I planned it, I thought you might like to have a sitting-room with a view."

He had planned it all, in some kind of love, when he had looked ahead and faced the fact that she might be permanently crippled, and now it had not worked out that way. She had been given her release.

Margaret went through the door he had opened, trying to thank him.

"It was wonderful of you, Thor, to think of this," she said. "In a good many ways, it reminds me of Hanko."

"The idea was the same," he acknowledged. "Plenty of glass to let the sun in, but mountains instead of a fjord."

She crossed to the wide, semi-circular window, looking up at the snow-clad giants across the valley.

"I think I like them best," she said.

He turned away.

"You may come to think of them as a prison wall," he said, "shutting you in. When that happens, Margaret, I shall expect you to tell me."

He went out, leaving her to the deep silence of her room, the room he had chosen for her, which was not Gerda's room and not his own.

It was furnished simply, with comfortable chairs and a low table drawn close to the windows, and there was a communicating bedroom, the one she had used before they had gone to Oslo. A convenient door had been broken through to the bathroom beyond, and Thor's own room was on the far side of it. It had all been planned with meticulous care, an expensive concession to what might have been her need. And now, to Margaret, at least, it could only seem a monument to the incompleteness of her marriage.

Turning from the bitterness of such thoughts, she washed and changed into a woollen two-piece she had bought that day in Oslo on the first stage of her strange honeymoon. It was a deep, soft blue, the colour of the fjord on a summer's day, and it gave added depths and lustre to her eyes.

For the first time she walked without the aid of her stick, clinging to the banister rail as she went back down the stairs. Almost at the foot, she was aware of the tall, slim figure of a young girl, wraith like in the waning afternoon light, standing in the shadows, and her heart turned over convulsively. The figure moved and it was Ellen, but in that moment Margaret knew that Ellen and Gerda had been much alike.

What torment for Thor, then, to live with Ellen constantly in the house!

Ellen stood aside as she passed. At first it did not seem that she would speak, and then she followed Margaret into the sitting-room, saying fiercely:

"You see what he has done? He has tried to change Solstua because of you, but he will never be able to put my sister's memory away. She will always be there, deep in Thor's heart. Whatever you do, whatever you think may happen, you cannot alter that!"

Margaret was trembling. The encounter on the stairs and the realization that Ellen and Gerda might have been one and the same person, had confused and bewildered her, but she knew now that she had a right to fight for her love, at least against Ellen's attempt to preserve the past.

"Thor knows what he is doing, Ellen," she said quietly. "Neither you nor I can change what he feels. It would be like hurting ourselves against a rock to try. I have accepted the fact that I must live here without love—the sort of love you mean—but there are other things. Kindness and companionship and respect. These are part of love—the sort of love that endures."

She felt that she was repeating something Thor had already said. Kindness and companionship and respect. He had offered her these things and she must make them do.

Ellen laughed. It was a hollow sound and her face was completely colourless, so that she looked more than ever like the ghost Margaret had taken her for.

"Try to break Gerda's power!" she cried. "Try to break it, and you shall see!"

The echo of her impassioned challenge rang in the silent room as she fled from it and a movement above her drew Margaret's eyes to the gallery to see Thor standing there. How long he had been there, looking down at them, she did not know. He moved, disappearing in the direction of the staircase, and a second later he was in the room.

"This is intolerable," he said. "No one could expect you to live with it and be happy. Ellen must go."

"Give her time." Margaret hardly recognized her own voice. "She is young, Thor, and passionately attached to—the past."

"I have given her time," he answered grimly, his mouth set and hard. "I thought that she had got over the idea of our marriage, but apparently it is not so."

He had paced to the window and back again, and now he stood hesitating, one foot on the raised stone hearth, his arm resting along the sloping chimney hood, his eyes fixed intently on the glowing logs beneath it. It seemed that he was on the point of making some sort of confession, of tearing away at least one obscuring veil from the past.

Margaret waited, watching the firelight flickering on his dark hair and along the stern line of his jaw. The moment of indecision seemed to last for ever, but even before he turned sharply away she knew that he had changed his mind. Whatever intimacy they might have had, whatever he had been about to say, was lost to her, because of a scruple, maybe, but lost, just the same. Thor was determined to guard the past even more grimly than before.

CHAPTER TEN

"ONLY three more weeks till Christmas," Kirsten
Moe said, unfastening her skis. "And so much still
to be done!"

"You will be on holiday soon," Margaret reminded her. "But I'd love to help, Kirsten, if there's
anything I can do at the school."

"I wasn't only thinking about the school,"
Kirsten said. "Although I will admit that I have my
work cut out for me there." She paused. "I was
thinking of all you will have to do here if Ellen
really means to marry Fred Sonsburg."

Margaret knocked the loose snow from her skis
and stood them up against the *stabbur* wall.

"I don't think there's any doubt about it," she
said. "Fred came to see Thor last night and the
engagement was arranged."

Kirsten heaved a sigh which might have been
relief.

"What does Thor really feel about it?" she asked.

Margaret bit her lip. How could she tell even
Kirsten that she did not know what her husband
thought, that since the day of their return from
Switzerland they had remained strangers, almost,
although they lived together under the same roof and
she wore Thor's ring?

"I'm sure he thinks Fred is the sort of person
Ellen should marry," she answered lamely.

"You will, of course, give her an engagement
party."

Margaret nodded.

"I was going to ask you to help me," she confessed, leading the way into the house. "I don't want
Ellen to feel that she will miss anything because of
me. Solstua has always been her home, and if her
mother had been alive I understand that she would
have made great preparations for Ellen's betrothal.
Thor will not grudge the money for anything she
needs, but—but I thought that—just buying every-

thing might not be the same. Signe embroiders wonderfully well," she added, a little flush of excitement stealing into her pale cheeks, "and I could learn. We could make some of the things and buy the rest."

"Yes, indeed," Kirsten agreed, although her mind seemed to be on something else. "You could do all that, Meg, but whether Ellen would accept it in the spirit in which it was offered would be another matter."

They had come into the sitting-room, to a blazing log fire, and Margaret stood before it, looking down at her hands.

"I see," she said. "It makes one feel—rather useless, doesn't it?"

"I'm sorry," Kirsten apologized, moving restlessly about the room. "It was only that I thought we should face facts right from the beginning. I'm saying now, go ahead. Get Thor to give a party announcing the engagement, a pre-Christmas party with songs and dancing will be just the thing. It is a custom which goes back a thousand years, and I have heard Thor say it ought to be revived. He can revive it now for Ellen's engagement. People will come from all over the dale. You needn't be afraid of that," she smiled. "They will come because of Ellen and because of you."

"Because of me?"

"They will come to see Thor's bride."

Margaret's heart contracted. The sensation was almost one of physical pain as she thought how unlike a bride she really felt. The long dark evenings had thrown her and Thor into each other's company as never before, but there had always been Ellen to make an uneasy third at the fireside, and Thor's carving and metal work to take him off alone. There had been frequent forays, too, into the mountains or up to Drakensval to fit bear-proof locks on the new farm doors. The winter fodder for the cattle was left in the high farms, and no one was more aware of the fact than the prowling bear. His cunning, Thor said, was amazing.

He told her these things, but he did not offer to take her with him on his journeys. He had taught her to ski on the more gentle slopes near the house, but he did not encourage her to venture beyond them.

"Have a word with Signe about Ellen's trousseau," Kirsten advised when they had finished their coffee and she was ready to set off down the valley before nightfall beset her. "I'll see what I can do about getting help from the village women with the embroidery."

"Will you, Kirsten?" Margaret asked eagerly. "I'd like to do this. You see, I feel that I owe it to Thor."

"Yes," Kirsten said quietly, "Ellen would have had all these things if her mother had lived."

During the next few days Margaret hugged her secret to her and it warmed her. Signe and she were like two conspirators, smuggling all sorts of things into the house when Ellen was not about, and hiding them away in the *stabbur* when she was. When the goods waggon came up the valley it brought more than its ordinary consignment of goods for Solstua, ordered by Margaret with Thor's consent.

He had looked at her doubtfully when she had unfolded part of her plan to him, and then he had turned away with an odd expression in his eyes.

"Ellen should be grateful," he said, "for all you are doing for her. Has she invited Erik?"

"Erik?" Margaret had all but forgotten Erik. "Yes, I suppose he will come. It will be during his Christmas vacation."

He gave her an odd, searching look, going off almost immediately to see to some repair or other that was necessary on the sleigh.

Mention of Erik made Margaret think of him. As Ellen's brother he should be most actively connected with her engagement party, yet they had not heard from him since their return from Oslo. There was Paul Loren, too. She wondered if Thor would ask Paul to the mountains for Christmas to spend the festive season in their company. Paul had no real family ties in Oslo, and somehow Margaret felt that Kirsten would be pleased if he came.

Two days before the party Erik phoned to say that he was in the village.

"I've got quite a bit of luggage," he told Margaret, who had taken the call. "Can you send the car down to collect me?"

Thor and Fred Sonsburg were outside, carving a piece of furniture in the *stabbur*. Between them they were making much of the furniture for Ellen's new home.

"I'll see what Thor says." Margaret felt that it was going to be quite an effort to meet Erik again. "Someone will come. Where will you wait?"

"I'll look up Kirsten Moe," Erik decided lightly. "We were never exactly buddies, as the Americans say, but we can bear each other for an hour. Especially when I have so much to tell her!"

He was about to hang up when Margaret asked:

"Erik, is it about your exams? Have you passed?"

He chuckled.

"How like Thor you are becoming! No, I have given up the unequal struggle," he told her almost flippantly, "and taken a job instead."

Margaret's heart sank. This would be a terrible disappointment to Thor after all the effort he had made to give Erik a chance in life, all the benefits of an advanced education, which he himself had missed. And now it seemed that Erik had not cared about them. Her feet dragged as she crossed the hard-trodden snow between the side door and the *stabbur*.

"Erik is in the village," she told Thor. "He'd like the car sent down to pick him up."

"I'll get the jeep," Fred offered, laying down his chisel. "No need for you to turn out, Thor, and I can collect Ellen on my way back."

Thor nodded.

"If you will," he said briskly. He turned to Margaret. "You will want to go," he suggested.

"No. I have quite a lot to do, Thor, before Ellen comes.

He looked surprised by her refusal, not pressing the suggestion when she had made her decision, and Margaret went back to the house to put in an hour's work on Ellen's wedding dress, which Signe and a woman from the village had already made. The embroidery on bodice and skirt was almost completed now. It was lovely, intricate work, but Margaret had soon mastered the art, spending many hours with her needle when Ellen and Signe were busy about the farm.

Sometimes she wondered if Ellen was half aware of what was going on, or at least aware that some of the preparations for her marriage were already afoot. For days she had been moody and restless, rising early and long before it was light, and going to bed late, as if she were struggling with some deep, inward indecision which could not be resolved without help.

Margaret knew, however, that it would be useless to approach her. Ellen would not turn to a stranger for the consolation she needed.

Perhaps Erik would prove to be the confidant she could most easily approach. After all, they were brother and sister and had always been close in their friendship.

It was quite dark before the jeep returned. Thor switched on the light above the *stabbur* as soon as he heard the engine, and stood there waiting. The powerful electric glare illuminated the entire quadrangle between the snow-dusted buildings and the house, and when Erik jumped down from the jeep the two men met in its revealing brightness. Erik appeared to be defiant, and Thor, with his back to Margaret where she stood at the window of the firelit kitchen, looked enormous, dominating the situation as he always did. They spoke heatedly for several minutes before she saw Erik shrug his shoulders and turn away.

He came towards the side door, and she drew back from the window, her heart beating rapidly. He came directly into the kitchen, crossing the polished floor in two swift strides, as if he would kiss her again in greeting, as he had done in Oslo when they had come off the Zurich plane, but Margaret forestalled him by holding out both her hands.

"Welcome home, Erik," she said in a low, controlled voice. "The whole family is here now for Ellen's party."

He looked about to protest, and then he laughed.

"We are a strange family," he observed, "but if that is to be the way of it——!" He made her a mocking bow. "You must tell me, Meg, when you change your mind."

She chose to ignore the remark. Even if Erik believed that she had been in love with him in the past, if it was perhaps a little true that their youth had held out eager arms to one another when they had first met, there was nothing of that left now. Erik was a disappointment to her, just as he had proved a disappointment to Thor, but she would not upbraid him for it.

"Thor's furious about the job," he said casually as he drew off his gloves to warm his hands at the stove. "I don't see why he should be when it eases him of so much responsibility where I am concerned,"

"What sort of job is it?" Margaret asked, aware that none of the others seemed inclined to join them.

"Journalistic. I've been lucky, really. It means that I can travel, but I won't be stuck in one place for too long."

Margaret was remembering that he had once offered to be "stuck in one place," as he put it, by returning to Helmsdal to teach in order to be near her, but she did not seek to remind him of the fact. This new, unexpected job was perhaps the best sort of work for Erik, after all.

Thor did not speak about it. Whatever he had said to Erik out there in the fierce glare of the *stabbur* light had evidently been his last word on the subject. Erik was old enough and apparently wilful enough to choose for himself.

Margaret did not see very much of him, or Thor either, for that matter, till the day of the party. Inevitably she was caught up in Signe's enormous

preparations for the event. All morning piles of little
cakes and platters of *smorbrod* accumulated on the
white pine tables in the kitchen, and Thor's guests
began to appear as early as four o'clock.

With Fred Sonsburg's help, he had cleared the
stabbur for dancing and brought extra chairs and
benches to the sitting-room, where a bright log fire
had been burning all day.

Sleigh after sleigh drew up in the quadrangle and
soon the house was full to overflowing. So many
people had divested themselves of coats and scarves
and snow shoes in the hall that it looked like the
scene of a gigantic auction sale, and even Ellen was
smiling. She wore Fred Sonsburg's ring for the first
time, the plain gold band on the third finger of her
right hand which would also be her wedding ring,
and Thor had produced a similar ring for her to give
to Fred.

It was the custom, Kirsten told Margaret, coming
in with Paul Loren, who had just arrived from Oslo.
The diamonds came afterwards, she added, when the
babies came along.

Margaret had never given Thor a ring. The
customary exchange had either been overlooked or
had not been considered necessary in their case.
Thor's hands were bare of all trappings and, curiously
enough, she could not imagine him wearing a ring.
He was unconventional in so many ways.

It was impossible not to feel the excitement of the
party spirit, she discovered, as the evening wore on.
These grave-looking mountain people knew how to
play as well as work when occasion demanded, and
every one of them was prepared to do his or her part.
There was music for the dancing, fiddles and man-
dolins, and harmonicas wonderfully well played and
drums. Prost Jorgensen sat at the piano, as ef' cient
with his dance rhythms as when he played his
beloved Grieg or Chopin, although perhaps not quite
so happy.

Ellen had received a number of presents from
distances which seemed incredible in this snow-bound

land, and before the dancing began in earnest Margaret and Signe presented their masterpiece.

Ellen had come into the kitchen to replenish her tray of coffee cakes and Signe brought the dress from the cupboard.

"It is for you," she said, holding it out over her arm, "from the master and mistress."

Ellen stood gazing at the beautiful native costume with its matching white blouse like a drift of newly-fallen snow and the deep bands of embroidery on skirt and bodice which lifted it high out of the ordinary. It was hers to wear now that she was a woman. Hers to wear on her wedding day! The handiwork of a mother could not have fashioned it with greater care, and Ellen stared and stared till the tears came.

"You did it, Signe?" she asked.

Signe looked proudly in Margaret's direction.

"We did it together," she said.

Ellen did not thank Margaret. It seemed that she could not even look at her. With an inarticulate little gasp she turned and fled.

"Put the dress in her room, Signe," Margaret said. "I am sure she will wear it when the time comes."

She went slowly across the hall to where her guests were waiting, thinking that, if she had gained some sort of victory with Ellen, it was a purely personal one. It had nothing to do with Thor. Ellen's resentment might fade, but she knew now that it had not helped to fashion the barrier between herself and Thor. Ellen alone could not have produced anything so formidable.

"Come and dance," Erik invited, finding her standing in the doorway. "Almost everybody—even the old people—are in the *stabbur*."

They crossed the hard-trodden snow under a sky that was alive with starlight. There was no need for Thor's artificial light tonight. The scene in the vast, raftered barn was amazing. The men from the timber camp had decorated it until every inch of the pine-panelled walls was covered with evergreens and flags, and paper streamers hung from the dark rafters, looped and festooned in gay bunches of brilliant colour against the more sombre shade of the leaves. Much laughter and eager conversation drifted out to them, and Erik swung her on to the floor for her first dance. She had seen little of him during their preparations and he held her close.

"Meg, you look wonderful!" he said, smiling down at her. "Thank heaven, you are completely recovered!"

The words had been more an admission of personal relief than anything else, but she did not hold it against him.

"It's amazing that I can dance again," she said lightly. "But not too long, Erik, if you don't mind. I don't want to overdo things just at first when I feel so well."

He led her to a corner when the dance was over, leaving her to go in search of something to drink, and it was then that Margaret became aware of Thor standing just inside the big double door. There was a strange expression on his dark face, half pride and half regret, and she stood watching him until the lights were dimmed and someone started to sing. It was a man's voice, full and deep, and it filled the whole *stabbur* with its vigour. An old Viking song rose to the rafters, stirring the assembled company to respond and when it was finished there was an instant demand for more.

Surprisingly, the voice took up a more gentle refrain this time, the deep, pulsating notes of a love song. It throbbed out in the stillness like a personal challenge, and Margaret drew in her breath almost as if she would ward off some physical blow.

In that moment she knew that she was no longer alone. Someone was standing in the shadows behind her and she knew, without turning, that it was Thor. The music floated above them, round them, closing them in, but the words escaped her. Her knowledge of Thor's native tongue was not yet complete.

"What do the words mean?" she whispered,

wondering if the strangely-haunting love song might hold some message for them both.

"They say," he translated slowly, "that 'when the heart is once given, it is given for all time'. I am beginning to think, Margaret," he added, "that it is indeed true."

Before she could stop him he had left her, making his way through the applauding company as the love song ceased.

Watching them, Kirsten Moe turned her head away. This can't happen, she thought. It all just can't go up in smoke like this!

"Why have you so much to think about Kirsten?" Paul Loren asked, coming to stand beside her. "So much that is sad. I should have thought you would have been glad to see Ellen Borge safely engaged to be married."

"I am," Kirsten agreed forthrightly. "But it doesn't solve any of the other problems I'm interested in."

"The problem of Thor and Margaret, for instance?" he queried, brows raised. "That, my dear Kirsten, will right itself."

"I wish I could think so," Kirsten returned vigorously, "but I can't. Margaret looks near the end of her tether, and Thor, for that matter, looks much the same. Margaret will not stay here if she imagines that Thor is unhappy."

"A man is as miserable as a woman makes him," Paul remarked. "Take me, for instance. You will not marry me, although I have asked you a dozen times!"

"I want to be quite sure," Kirsten said only half-heartedly. "We've waited so long," she pointed out. "Perhaps too long."

He put his hands on her arms, turning her to face him in the now-deserted sitting-room.

"You know that isn't true," he said. "I need you, Kirsten."

"You have managed very well without me for the past fifteen years," she reminded him, but without bitterness.

"I have 'managed', as you say," he admitted, strengthening his hold on her arms, "but I have not been entirely happy. Not apart from my work. Neither have you," he added stubbornly. "You've gone on with it because it was all you had, but we need each other, Kirsten, and one of us must give up a career to be with the other. In the nature of things, it is generally the woman who does that."

He was not demanding, only stating a fact which Kirsten herself had recognized long ago.

"Yes," she acknowledged, "you are right."

"And you are not deceived any more?" He tilted back her head, forcing her to look at him. "You will marry me?"

"In a little while," Kirsten agreed. "I will come to Oslo in the spring."

He kissed her, long and tenderly, full on the lips.

"It is a promise," he said.

Two days later, Kirsten had a visitor. It was Christmas Eve and she was not entirely surprised to recognize Ellen Borge standing on the snow-covered step of the schoolhouse.

"I have to see you," Ellen said. "I want to ask your advice."

"Of course, Ellen." Kirsten flung the door wide, letting in a flurry of snow. "Come in quickly and don't let the heat escape. It has turned bitterly cold."

Ellen did not seem to notice the cold. Her mind was obviously taken up with something else. Kirsten pushed the ever-ready coffee pot further on to the stove and motioned to her guest to sit down.

"Take off your coat," she advised. "You'll need its extra warmth when you go out again. Have you much snow up at Solstua?"

"A great deal," Ellen answered automatically. "Thor thinks that the Drakensval road may be blocked quite soon."

It was early in the season for the valley to be completely cut off, but the harsh weather conditions in the mountains were nothing new to either of them.

It was not the possibility of Drakensval's early isolation which was troubling Ellen.

Kirsten poured the steaming coffee into two mugs, returning with them to the stove.

"What is it, Ellen?" she asked. "Can I help you?"

Ellen sat stiffly erect in her chair, her fingers closing over the mug she had accepted with a completely automatic gesture. She did not seem to feel the warmth of the dark liquid it contained even when it seeped through the numbness of her hands and brain.

"It's about Gerda," she said. "About Gerda and Thor."

Kirsten stiffened.

"I've got to tell you," Ellen persisted, seeing the look of distaste in the blue eyes opposite her. "I can't live with it any longer. She left him. She betrayed him that night. She was going away with someone else. That was what she was really like. All the times she was supposed to be visiting the Jules at Laerdal, she was really going on to Oslo to spend a gay time there with the sort of people she preferred. I didn't know. Nobody knew it here; nobody would have believed it if they had been told. Everybody worshipped her, including Thor. Words, a veritable spate of words came rushing out, bringing with them their own peculiar relief. "I loved her. She had always been all that was wonderful to me, and I was bitterly ashamed. I was ashamed and jealous. I wanted to keep—the other Gerda free from taint. I wanted her to stay the sort of person I had believed in all my life."

The young, high-pitched voice broke on the unexpected confession and Ellen buried her face in her hands.

"Poor Ellen!" Kirsten consoled. "You could not help it. You are not to blame for loving her."

Ellen looked up, her eyes bleak and so pale that they were almost colourless.

"But I am to blame for what I did," she protested.

Kirsten looked her curiosity.

"I kept back a letter," Ellen rushed on to confess. "Gerda wrote it to Thor that day—before she went away, before she took the boat to cross the fjord. It told him that she was going, that she had never loved him in the way he had wanted. It told him she was going to someone else, someone in Oslo who would free her from Thor's mountains. But it was someone she could not marry."

Ellen's voice faltered and failed once more. Her confession had exhausted her emotionally and she had no more feeling left.

"And you kept the letter when she was drowned?" Kirsten guessed. "You kept her memory as you would have wished it to be?"

Ellen nodded.

"I was so ashamed," she repeated.

"And now," Kirsten said, "what are you going to do?"

"I do not know. I have come to ask you what I should do."

It was a difficult moment for Kirsten Moe, that strongminded, practical creature who had proffered advice when it was asked so often in the past. She did not know what to say. She felt so utterly at a loss, because she could not see that giving that old letter to Thor could alter anything at this late date. She wondered, too, if she had really the right to make a decision in the matter. Ellen had hugged her secret to her for the best part of three long years and it might be better to let it remain in the past. The revelation of Gerda's unfaithfulness could only be another shattering blow to Thor, and it might not help Margaret at all to reveal it now.

Oh, what should she do? Kirsten had never felt so undecided in all her life. At her age—thirty-five next month!—she should have been able to cope with such a situation, to work it out to its logical conclusion, but she could not.

Believing that there was only one way, and wondering in the same breath if she were being a complete moral coward to suggest it, she advised Ellen to go to Margaret.

"Margaret is married to Thor," she said. "It must be her decision whether he has the letter now or not."

Ellen did not look at all happy as she went away, and for a split second Kirsten knew an almost overwhelming desire to call her back, to reverse her decision, to take responsibility somehow on her own broad shoulders, but something that went deeper than impulse, something that was surely intuition, held her back.

Ellen made the return journey to Solstua determined to carry out Kirsten's advice, yet it was almost more than she could bring herself to do. Margaret had been kind to her, seeming to forgive her quite freely for her violent outbursts of the past, but Ellen still laboured under the deeply-ingrained belief that Margaret was a stranger to the dale. The feeling persisted that, if she had never come to Solstua, Gerda's memory might have remained the spotless thing Thor believed it to be.

On the other hand, it was Margaret who had thought of making her a wedding dress, Margaret who had given her happiness beyond believing on her engagement. She had even given her Fred Sonsburg, in a way. If she had never fled to Laerdal because of Margaret, Ellen knew that she would never have come to understand Fred as intimately as she did.

Warring within herself, pulled this way and that by so many conflicting loyalties, Ellen reached home at last, and the first person she met was Margaret.

"Ellen, you look like a ghost!" Margaret exclaimed, seeing her pinched white face. "You have been out in the cold too long."

"I am warm," Ellen said. "I am burning inside."

Margaret gave her a quick, searching look.

"Take off your things," she said. "I'll make you something hot to drink."

Ellen followed her into the kitchen, watching while she filled a kettle and set it on the stove.

"Not tea," she said. "I do not like tea, and I do

not think that I want anything to drink. I—want to speak to you."

Margaret turned to face her.

"If it's something that's going to hurt," she said, "don't tell me, Ellen."

"Someone has to be hurt," Ellen answered stonily. "Even if it is only Gerda."

"Please," Margaret implored, "need we speak about this again, Ellen? It all happened so long ago——"

"And it was all so wrong." Ellen's voice was suddenly level and controlled. "What I did was wrong. Gerda left Thor. They were to be married within a week, and she went off to someone else. Someone who was very rich but who would never marry her. She did not want Thor's mountains. She did not want Thor in the end. Only, for a long time, she was afraid to tell him. In the end, she wrote him a letter. She entrusted it to me, and—and when she was drowned crossing the fjord, I kept it from Thor. I knew what was in it, you see. I knew that he would despise her if he found out about her going away for good."

Margaret got up from the wooden bench beside the stove where she had been waiting for the kettle to boil. She was as white now as Ellen, all the colour gone out of her face and an agony of pain darkening her eyes.

"Why have you told me this?" she asked. "It can't do either of us any good."

"Kirsten Moe said that you should hear the truth. She said that it must be your decision whether I am to give the letter to Thor after all this time."

"Can you trust me with it?" Margaret asked. "The letter, I mean."

"Yes."

Ellen fumbled in her muff and produced a crumpled envelope which she passed over without looking at it. When it was in her hands Margaret stood quite still. She did not hear Ellen go out or Signe come in through the woodshed door with fuel to replenish the fire; she did not see the old woman fill the wrought iron basket at her feet with yellow logs, the logs which Thor had felled and chopped for burning. She stood reviewing the past and trying to cope with the future all in one desperate half-hour of agonizing indecision which seemed like a lifetime before, slowly and deliberately, she opened the stove doors and dropped Gerda's letter into the fire.

She watched the tongues of orange flame lick it and burn it and turn it black before it fell into grey ash and disappeared.

CHAPTER ELEVEN

A WEEK later, on New Year's Day, Ellen Borge was married to Fred Sonsburg in the village *kirke*.

Margaret had thrown herself into the bustle of preparation which precedes every wedding, glad of the activity which kept her almost too busy to think, although a wedding like Ellen's could only strengthen the comparison with her own of two months ago.

There could be no question about Ellen and Fred being in love. It had given Fred a new confidence and transfigured the girl he was about to make his wife. Ellen was an eager, happy person at last, and Margaret could not denounce her because part of that happiness sprang from the fact that she was no longer the possessor of a guilty secret. When she had passed on her sister's letter, Ellen had shed her own responsibility in the matter.

By two o'clock she stood waiting for the sleigh in the lovely native costume which had been Margaret's gift, with the high bridal headdress covering her hair and a look in her eyes which every bride should wear. She was lovely, Margaret thought, young and sweet and tender now that all her unhappiness had been shed.

She would not think of her own unhappiness nor of the constant aching of her heart when Thor was near. Ellen's departure to her new home at the lumber camp would leave her virtually alone at Solstua with Thor, alone with the memory of that night at the party when he had told her so plainly that he could not forget, that love, once given, was for always.

When she had burned Gerda's letter, she had not thought about the future, but she knew that, after today, she must face it squarely and decide what should be done.

A jangle of bells took her to the window of Ellen's room to look down into the courtyard where Thor was preparing the sleigh. New snow had fallen thickly during the night and all the outbuildings were covered in a spotless canopy of white. Even the road, stretching away down the valley to the waiting village and the silent church, lay innocent of footmarks under the uncertain sun. It wound like a white ribbon—a satin wedding ribbon—between the trees, as fresh and new as the satin bows which Signe was tying on the gleaming harness while Thor stood aside to watch.

He gathered up the reins, throwing them across the horses' backs, and it seemed that his shoulders were stooped a little, as if the happy wedding trappings which had been prepared for his ward had given him room for thought. Unhappy speculation, perhaps, about his own marriage.

Margaret thrust the suggestion away with a grim determination. At least for today she would savour some of the joy of being Thor's wife.

"Now," said Signe, smoothing the bridal gown for the last time when she came to tell them that Thor was ready, "we will go! You will not catch cold in this," she added, holding out the magnificent fur cape which was Thor's gift to the bride. "A hundred squirrel skins must have gone to its making!"

Ellen smiled across the room at Margaret, a radiant, bridal smile.

"You, also, are wearing Thor's gift," she said. "It is your wedding dress."

Margaret had worn the dress again because it was still the loveliest thing she possessed, but now she could not be sure that Thor would approve. He might think that she was trying to remind him of the vows he had made, to love and to cherish her till death parted them.

"Hullo, there! Are you ready?" Erik called from the foot of the stairs. "Thor is impatient to be off."

Margaret crossed to Ellen and kissed her on the cheek.

"Be happy, Ellen," she said.

"Thor is worried about drifts," Erik explained when she joined him in the hall. "The way the wind has been blowing for the past three days, there are bound to be some between here and the fjord."

"I hope we're not going to be held up," Margaret said as they went out into the ice-keen air. "We've timed it rather finely."

"Prost Jorgensen will wait," Erik assured her casually. "Weddings are often postponed for days at this time of year."

Thor came round from the horses' heads. He looked pale and thinly-drawn about the mouth, his eyes deep-set and unfathomable as he looked at them. Erik had taken Margaret's arm to help her into the sleigh, and Thor asked abruptly:

"Has there been any sign of the Thunes? They have had time to get here from Drakensval by now."

"They must have gone direct," Erik suggested. "One of the lumbermen was supposed to collect them in the jeep."

Ellen appeared at the top of the steps.

"Happy bridal day, Ellen," Thor saluted her conventionally. "And happy future."

Ellen looked almost as if she might burst into tears, but she got into the wedding sleigh dry-eyed and Thor took his place beside her. Erik had escorted Signe and Margaret to the second sleigh, which was to go on ahead.

"Would you like the hood up?" he asked, tucking the great bearskin rug over Margaret's knees. "Or will you risk a blue nose in church?"

Margaret felt that she would smother in a closed sleigh.

"If Signe doesn't mind," she said, "I'd rather travel with it down."

"Signe is a countrywoman," Erik laughed, cracking his whip. "O.K.! We're off!"

Winding along the valley floor in a deep, soft silence, with the sleigh runners leaving two parallel shiny white tracks behind Margaret could have wished that she had been travelling with Thor, but convention demanded that she should be there to await the bride at the church.

The entire village had turned out in honour of Ellen, but Margaret was soon aware that she was sharing at least some of the limelight. It was the first time Thor Revold's wife had been seen at a function beyond the confines of Solstua, and the dale folk were naturally curious. Margaret felt shy and alone as she waited beside the snow-capped lych gate for the bridal sleigh to round the edge of the hill and come sweeping up the final stretch to the *kirke*. Erik had stayed out on the road to escort his sister, and she supposed that Kirsten and Paul Loren were already inside.

The sleigh came over the brow of the hill with a gay jangling of bells and a murmur from the crowd which was a signal for most of them to precede the bride into the church. Ellen, who had no small relatives of her own and no younger sister, had borrowed two of Kirsten's schoolchildren to act as bridesmaids, and they were waiting demurely under the canopied porch. They were so fair that the wreaths of white flowers on their heads scarcely showed up against their flaxen curls, and their dresses were miniature replicas of the bride's.

Margaret felt a firm hand on her arm.

"Shall we go in?" Thor said.

She had not been sure that he would take her into the church. He was Ellen's guardian, and it might have been his task to lead the bride up the aisle, but she supposed that Erik was really nearer to Ellen than Thor. As her brother, he had the prior right.

Thor did not speak after they had reached the porch. His face looked taut and colourless, and his mouth was grim. There was a sort of vital pride about him, however, as he walked beside her into the bare little church and put her into the pew beside Kirsten, taking his own place, with Paul, on the other side of the central aisle. All the men sat on one side, with their womenfolk on the other, yet during the simple ceremony, as Prost Jorgensen read the words which made Ellen and Fred Sonsburg man and wife, it seemed to Margaret that she and Thor stood side by side, as they had done two months ago, repeating these simple, well-remembered words, renewing their vows.

Shaken by the thought that had grown almost to a conviction, she stood at the end of the service till bride and groom came down the aisle, and then, slowly, to the strains of the wedding march, she was walking with Thor, his hand on her arm, the last rays of the dying sun striking in upon them through the open door.

A dinner had been prepared in the schoolroom, and toasts were proposed and drunk; toasts to the bride and bridegroom and to the bridesmaids, and a toast to the future.

Margaret found herself drinking the final toast with tears in her eyes.

When they rose from the table to circulate about the room she found herself separated from Thor. She saw him talking long and earnestly to Kirsten, who seemed to have lost much of her usual high colour since she had come from the church and looked almost as pale and tense as Thor himself, but she had no idea what they could be discussing. Thor was still worried about the Thunes from Drakensval. The old Lapp couple had not put in an appearance at the wedding, although they had been given a special invitation and had been looking forward to the trip for days, and the jeep had not turned up from the lumber camp. Three people had missed Ellen's wedding who should have been there, and Thor was concerned for their safety.

As soon as the bridal pair had left on the first stage of their honeymoon, he crossed the hall to where Margaret was standing with Erik.

"People are beginning to leave," he said. "I must get back to Solstua as quickly as I can. Do you think you and Erik could hold the fort alone?"

"I wouldn't worry about the Thunes," Erik said. "You know what Lapps are. They may have changed their minds about coming."

Thor gave him a withering look.

"I've known the Thunes for twenty years," he

told him. "When they make a bargain they stick to it, even though it might cost them their lives."

Erik looked slightly conscience-stricken.

"Yes, I suppose that's so," he agreed. "Look here, you can't go alone," he added as Thor turned away. "Not if you mean to go to Drakensval."

"I can manage," Thor said. "I need you to stay here to bring Margaret back to Solstua."

"Paul Loren can do that," Erik argued swiftly. "He and Kirsten were coming back with us, anyway."

Thor hesitated. It was obvious that he thought he might need Erik.

"I'll have a word with Paul," he said. "Will you harness the small sleigh? It will be faster."

"Can I do anything to help?" Margaret asked.

Thor looked at her directly for the first time.

"Just get our guests away without fuss," he said almost frigidly. "There may be nothing wrong at Drakensval, but I have to go and see."

An eternity seemed to pass before the final guest had gone and Paul Loren gathered up the reins on the bridal sleigh. He helped Margaret into the back, and then Kirsten; he himself sat outside with Signe, wrapped in furs to the ears and almost unrecognizable, sitting beside him.

The night was clear and starlit and they could see across the snow for a considerable distance, though the undulating nature of the road kept them from seeing Solstua until they were almost upon it.

"Margaret," Kirsten said uneasily, "there's something I have to confess. I have told Thor about Gerda's letter."

Margaret drew in a long, quivering breath.

"I wish you hadn't," she said in a choked whisper which just reached her companion in the darkened sleigh. "It can't help, Kirsten. It could only have wounded Thor needlessly."

"He knew about it," Kirsten said abruptly, as if there was no other way to tell her. "He knew all about Gerda."

Margaret twisted round in her seat, trying to see her friend's face in the uncertain light.

"He knew?"

"Apparently. He wanted to know what you had done with the letter."

"I burned it," Margaret confessed automatically.

"I told him you had probably destroyed it," Kirsten returned quietly.

Margaret was trembling.

"What am I to do, Kirsten?" she cried desperately. "How can I possibly go on living with Thor with this between us? I destroyed Gerda's letter because I love him, but I can't tell him that."

They had reached Solstua and through her tears she saw that it was unlit. Thor had gone on to Drakensval.

"You could try to tell him," Kirsten said as the sleigh stopped. "It might make a difference."

Signe went ahead into the empty house and lights sprang up, one by one.

"There's no message," Margaret said, looking round at the bare tables in the living-room. "Perhaps they didn't come here at all."

"I'll phone the camp," Paul dicided.

When he came back his mouth was set and grim.

"There has been some trouble," he said, knowing that it was quite useless trying to keep the truth from Kirsten. "One of the men set out in the jeep to bring the Thunes down and he didn't get back. When they tried to contact Drakensval by phone from the camp there was no reply."

"Don't they know by this time?" Kirsten demanded exasperated. "Surely someone went out to see what had happened?"

"They went out at three o'clock," Paul told her briefly.

"They've been digging ever since."

Kirsten could not control the small gasp of horror which escaped her lips.

"What was it?" she asked. "An avalanche?"

Paul nodded.

"They could see the jeep's tracks going in, but nothing on the other side."

"Coming or going?" Kirsten asked.

"Coming back from Drakensval. That was why there hadn't been a reply when they phoned."

"Have you been in touch with Thor?" was Kirsten's next question.

Paul shook his head.

"No. Everyone who can stand on two legs is up on the pass, except Alf Erikson, the telephonist. Thor's there, of course, and Erik. I've got to get there, too, as quickly as I can," he added, "in case I am needed."

"They may also need a nurse," Kirsten reminded him firmly. "I'm not one, but I can do as you tell me."

"Please let me come," Margaret begged. "I couldn't stay her, Paul—just waiting."

Paul looked across the room at Kirsten. She shrugged and he turned towards the door.

"You'll have to change, both of you," he said. "Get on something warm, something you can ski in, if need be."

It was a nightmare journey for Margaret. She knew, without Paul's having to admit to it, that there was danger. Anyone hacking away at one of those treacherous snowfalls that came careering down the mountainsides to bury everything in their track would be taking his life in his hands, but Thor was the last person to hold back out of any sense of personal danger. The Thunes were his trusted servants and they were buried alive up there on the pass. He would dig to release them till the last vestige of hope had ebbed.

Even with the sleigh, the road was difficult once they had left the valley and were climbing towards the pass. The great mountain barrier seemed to close in on them, white, treacherous and silently menacing. Paul's face began to grow sterner, his pleasant mouth more grim. Time and time again the sleigh would slip sideways like some drunken thing as the horses missed a foothold for a split second on the icy track.

and it seemed only by a miracle that it righted itself and they were not hurled several hundred feet through space to the valley floor.

Even before they came to the scene of the accident the horses seemed to sense catastrophe, pulling against the bits with their breath steaming from their nostrils and their ears laid back against their heads.

"Hadn't we better get down here?" Kirsten asked. "It would be easier to walk the rest of the way."

There were flares ahead of them, throwing up the elongated silhouettes of men toiling at a silent task. The most obvious thing was the lack of sound. A cry, Kirsten explained, or the rattle of a falling shovel, could bring down another fury of ice and rock and snow from the heights above.

Straining her eyes against the sudden brightness of the flares, Margaret searched for Thor but could not find him. Erik, too, was nowhere to be seen.

Paul went forward, speaking earnestly in Norwegian to the foremost workman. When he returned to where they waited, he looked shocked by a further calamity.

"What is it?" Margaret whispered. "What has happened?"

Paul hesitated.

"Please, Paul—if it is Thor don't keep it from me," she entreated. "I have a right to know."

Paul Loren drew in a deep breath.

"Thor and Erik went in over the top," he said, looking up to the narrow, ice-encrusted ridge which ran along the bare rock face where the avalanche had come down. "It was a magnificent thing to do."

And a wild, mad thing! A thousandth chance. Margaret followed Paul's gaze to the sheer face of black rock on the snowbound mountainside and shuddered.

"They could never get over there," she said.

"Thor might," Paul said. "And Erik would have a shot at it. There's not much wrong with Erik, really," he added. "He was bred in these mountains. Thor would think it was the quickest way of getting to the Thunes if they were still alive. He would start digging in from the Drakensval side."

After that, Margaret's brain became numb. She shovelled away snow with the others, carefully piling it into a little wall between what was left of the road and the drop to the valley below, but it seemed an aimless task. Nobody really thought that Thor and Erik had negotiated that bleak rock face leering down at them in the starlight, nobody believed that they were alive.

She could see it in the men's faces as they toiled, hour after hour; she could read it, at last, in Kirsten Moe's eyes.

Vaguely she realized that a tunnel was being cut in the snow, through which they might pass after another day had dawned, hours and hours ahead yet, when the stars had finally paled.

Then, almost too suddenly, the front of end the jeep was there. How slowly they dug after that, how desperately slowly, without a word!

She stood at the entrance to the tunnel, her hands clasped tightly, praying soundlessly. If only Thor were there. . . .

Paul went into the tunnel and Kirsten stood beside Margaret, waiting. It seemed ages before anyone came back to them, and then it was a lumberman in a soiled *anorak*, asking Kirsten if she could make some more coffee.

A truck had been sent up from camp with blocks and tackle and shores to make the snow tunnel, and the inevitable stove had been produced to make coffee on the spot. Kirsten and Margaret had made it twice that night, black and steaming hot, passing it to the men as they worked.

Margaret watched Kirsten talking to the lumberman in rapid Norwegian, which she could not follow.

Is there—any news?" she asked when Kirsten came back to the stove.

"They found the jeep—empty!" Kirsten said with a strange light in her eyes. "Someone had dug though to the Thunes from the Drakensval side."

Thor or Erik? Margaret asked the wordless question, her eyes fastened on Kirsten's.

"They don't know," Kirsten admitted. "Whoever it was Thor or Erik—wouldn't dare to shout in case the whole snow tunnel fell on the men working from this side. But the fact remains that they must have got whoever was in the jeep out of the snow and somewhere to safety. Probably back to Drakensval."

"How long will it be before we are through from this side?" Margaret asked.

"Not very long."

Kirsten had kept her hands busy while she talked and the coffee was ready. Margaret carried it to the tunnel entrance, and almost instantly there was a sort of funnel of wind against her face, blowing strongly from the far end.

She put down the coffee pot and ran. She did not need to be told that the men were through. Stumbling on the rutted roadway, she passed the silent lumberjacks, reached Paul and passed him, too. Dawn was breaking, flickering uncertainly above the dark scar where the avalanche had come down, but she could only see the narrow, deserted road to Drakensval. Somehow, the occupants of the jeep had been taken back to the chalet.

There was a single light twinkling in a downstairs window, like a final guiding star left behind by the night. She was almost sobbing as she crossed the orchard, and she could hear Paul and the lumbermen following close behind her, but she did not wait for them.

In the strengthening light, while she was still a dozen yards from the house, the door opened and Erik came out. He looked fantastically tall as he strode towards her, and for a moment she could not see beyond him. She did not want to see.

Then, in the next instant, she knew that Thor was there, too. Thor, needing her.

She passed Erik without even seeing him again, straight past him and into Thor's arms.

"Thor, Thor! Are you all right? I thought that

only one of you had come over the ridge. I thought I had lost you. . . ."

Long afterwards she wondered if she had really uttered these impassioned words which took her completely into Thor's arms. It was certain that he did not answer them. He stood in the ice-cold morning air, holding her to his heart, holding her as if he would never let her go.

Even when the others came, when the lumbermen and Kirsten and Paul reached the chalet steps and Erik had turned back with them, Thor held her.

The Thunes were safe, and so was the driver of the jeep. They had been buried for over six hours and the driver was slightly concussed, but Paul said, after a detailed examination of all three, that their injuries were slight and all external.

He looked at Kirsten when the last of the lumberjacks had left to carry their comrade back through the shored-up snow tunnel to the waiting lorry.

"You and I had better report back to the schoolhouse," he said. "Otherwise, there's going to be another search-party on its way up the valley." He looked at Erik with frank command in his blue eyes. "I think you should come, too," he suggested. "We'll need your sleigh, and you can drive it back to Solstua in the afternoon."

Erik shrugged. He was tired and wet and hungry, and he thought there were better places than a half-empty mountain chalet to look for a meal. Signe, he supposed, would have one ready for them at Solstua when they got there.

Thor watched them go. There had been no question of Margaret's going with them. When the last echo of voices had died against the mountain wall, the last foot imprinted itself on the snowbound track, he turned her to face him.

"Margaret," he said, "surely we must have known it was going to be like this from the beginning! In spite of Erik, in spite of everything, you were mine from the moment you stepped ashore at Bergen."

Her eyes were too full of love to question him. What did it matter if there had been misunderstanding and error and the pain of another love between them? She knew that Thor wanted her now, wholly and completely, his wife in every sense of the word. She lifted her lips to his and the warmth and tenderness of his kiss sank into her heart like balm.

They stood on the edge of the orchard, looking down across the little clearing where the grass had been burned in a wide circle, but the snow covered it now, and as if he had followed her in thought, Thor said:

"When you first came to Drakensval I was still wrestling with a memory. I had built this house for Gerda and furnished it to please her, but she had betrayed me, thrown my love back in my face. I came here afterwards and burned everything she had ever touched. I made a colossal pyre of it and I told myself I had destroyed all the love that would ever be in me for a woman. I wanted only to hate, to shut myself away with my hurt pride and my disillusionment." He stood for a moment looking down at the snow-covered grass. "And then you came." His arms tightened about her and his lips caressed her hair. "I didn't want to love you, Meg," he said. "I didn't want to love again, but you became part of Solstua—so easily. Then, that first day when you came here, I felt that we belonged, but the memory of Gerda thrust itself between us. Then, it seemed, there was Erik."

"Erik?" She moved in his arms, facing him. "Erik never mattered to me, Thor. From the very beginning—perhaps even from that day in Bergen when you were kind and I hadn't expected it—I loved you."

"Maybe I made it easy for Erik," he said with the slow smile that lit his dark eyes and curved his lips up at one corner. "Erik's youth and your youth! I took it for granted that you could not be other than attracted. Then"—his face darkened—"when he let you down, when he didn't want to marry you after the accident, I thought I might have something to offer you, after all."

"Not pity, Thor," she said unsteadily. "I thought you could only love me out of pity at the time and I accepted it, but now I know I could never have lived with your pity."

"Did pity ever love like this?" He bent her head back against his supporting arm, pressing a deep, impassioned kiss on her eager mouth. "I may have been arrogant enough to imagine that my love was big enough for both of us," he said, "but now I know that a one-sided love is only half a love. When we were at Hanko, I thought our love might one day be complete, and then it seemed that Erik had come back into your life and that you were in love with him, after all. I suffered the agonies of the damned then, Meg," he confessed. "Jealousy and anger burned in me like a consuming flame when I thought about your hopeless love. I told myself that one woman had deceived me, so why not another, but I knew that you were not made that way. I knew you would stick to your bargain, to your marriage vows, but that was not what I wanted. I wanted you, completely mine, and fate seemed to be laughing at me for a second time!"

"Was that why you—offered me my freedom, that day we came back from Oslo?" Margaret asked softly, seeing so much with the clear eyes of love. "Was that why you said I was never to let your mountains feel like a prison wall?"

"I suppose so. I blamed myself, you see, because Gerda had been afraid to tell me of her change of heart and it had all ended in a hopeless tragedy. But nothing matters that is in the past," he added firmly, leading her back towards the chalet where the carved dragons crouched protectingly on the ridges above the eaves. "Nothing matters so long as we can go on living here—together."

Margaret pulled his hand against her cheek, turning her lips to kiss it. Her eyes were on the wide valley beneath them, Thor's secret valley shut in by the white giants he loved.

"Drakensval!" she sighed. "It has an angry sound, but it is the loveliest place I know."

He held her close.

"We'll keep it that way, Meg," he promised.

THE EMERALD CUCKOO

THE
EMERALD
CUCKOO
Gwen Westwood

"Little child, don't marry. Young girl, don't fall in love" — strange words of warning from the green-winged bird, the emerald cuckoo. For Tracy they had come too late, at least as far as falling in love was concerned.

Tracy could not forget her adventure on the African wilderness trail, shared by Lester Cordell, the ruggedly handsome Game Reserve Ranger. And, loving Lester, how could she possibly marry someone else?

CHAPTER ONE

THE notice on the gate read 'Rhinos are dangerous. On no account must any visitor to this reserve proceed on foot unless accompanied by a game guard.' The gate itself was firmly padlocked. Tracy brought the small dusty car to a halt and waited for someone to discover she was there, but on this hot afternoon the whole wild world of Africa seemed to be sleeping and in the stillness, emphasized by the cessation of the car's engine, the only sound was the persistent chirrup of a grasshopper.

Her small passenger stirred and opened his eyes. They were heavy yet too bright and his cheeks had an unnatural brilliant flush that even Tracy, inexperienced as she was with children, could tell was not solely due to the heat of the journey.

'How do you feel, poppet?' she asked, trying to sound bright.

'My throat's sore. When are we going to get to my mummy? Are we there?'

'Not quite, but nearly. We'll soon have you tucked up in bed and you can have some nice stuff to make you feel better. Would you like to sound the horn?'

As he leaned his small bullet head across her, she touched his skin. It felt as if it were on fire. This alarmed her much more than any notices about wild animals could have done. She must have been crazy to take charge of a small boy on the long journey to this wild place, but she had had no alternative. However, she would soon be able to hand him over to his mother, she hoped.

She herself felt cramped and stiff after the long drive from the airport on roads which although well made seemed strange and lonely to someone who was used to city life. She longed for a hot bath or a cool shower, or both, and a change of clothing. The elegant navy silk town suit, which had seemed appropriate for jet travel when she set out from London, now clung to her body in dusty folds and the frilly blouse which she had chosen to make herself look feminine and pretty when for the first time in ten years she met her father had lost its freshness.

The sounding of the car's hooter seemed to have had the desired effect, for an African man, yawning and fastening the leather belt on his smart khaki uniform, had emerged from a small hut by the side of the gate and was making his way towards them.

'*Sakubona, Kosazana,*' he greeted her.

The formal words of greeting echoed in her memory like the sound of a deeptoned bell.

'Good afternoon, am I far from Mr. Bryant's house?' she asked.

'No, madam, not far. You will get there now-now if you follow this road,' the rich African voice replied. 'Madam must be a little bit careful and drive slowly. We have had rain today and in places the ground is soft. There has been no time yet to fill in.'

'I know you. You're Moses,' announced Julian, suddenly taking an interest in his surroundings.

'Hey, hey, you are right,' laughed the large Zulu, holding up his hands and putting them in front of his mouth to express astonishment and admiration. 'And who are you, little master?'

'I'm Julian Lockwood,' the eight-year-old replied

with pride. 'I've been with my grandparents, but now my mother wants me to visit her.'

'Oh, now I understand. I knew your father. He was a very good man.'

Tracy glanced at Julian, but obviously the reference to his late father did not upset him. After all, he had been with his grandparents for a year. Tracy put the car into gear, after thanking the guard, and drove slowly into the reserve. She had thought she would remember the way to the house, but the route of the road had been changed since she had lived here as a child.

On this side of the fence the bush was thicker with every so often a large flat-topped thorn tree higher than the other small acacias. There were open views as well so that sometimes it looked like a huge park, but Tracy was too busy handling the car on the sandy road to take much notice of her surroundings.

Julian had dozed off again, so promptly that it seemed to augur no good. She would be glad when she could hand him over to someone more responsible than herself. She noticed some movement in a tree with no leaves but vivid scarlet blossoms and saw that there were several monkeys feeding there. They seemed to be eating the blossom, reaching out little black hands and grasping the clusters greedily. The vivid crimson of the flowers and the grey forms of the monkeys were etched vividly against the deep blue of the sky like a Japanese painting.

She had forgotten how exotic this country would appear after an absence of so many years. She had been fourteen when she and her mother left, an impressionable age, yet her happy memories of a childhood spent in the wilds had somehow become overlaid by her mother's complaining reminiscences, for she had never liked the life they had led with her absentminded naturalist father, and had finally taken Tracy back to England with the firm intention never to return.

She had obtained a divorce and married a successful business man who had been as kind as he knew how in a limited way to young Tracy. But the conventional life they led, the comfortable home, the good school she had attended, had somehow never quite made up to Tracy for the loss of her vague, interesting, unmaterialistic father, and when, quite unexpectedly, she had received a letter asking her to visit him in order to help him with the preparation of a book, she had jumped at the chance to see him again.

'My dear girl,' Konrad had protested when she told him of her intention, 'it's a nonsensical idea. You say yourself you haven't seen or even heard from your father for ten years, so how can he demand now that you rejoin him?'

'He hasn't demanded it,' Tracy explained gently. 'He's just written a letter to suggest we should get to know each other again. It won't be for ever, Konrad dear.'

'I should hope not.'

'He suggests that it will take about three months to prepare the manuscript and help him with the photography. He has already done the bulk of the work himself, but he needs a good typist.'

'And so he has the effrontery to ask his daughter to be a secretary to him when he hasn't taken any interest in her for years.'

'He hasn't really had much chance to take an interest in me,' protested Tracy, thinking of the organized life she had led with her mother, the boarding school and the expensive secretarial college that had turned the tousleheaded youngster from Africa into an elegant young lady. Yes, her life in the wilds had been buried deep beneath years of more sophisticated living.

And yet when she had had this unexpected communication from her father it had made her realize that she had always wanted to return, even if it was just to lay a ghost, the ghost of the child who had thought Africa and its people were so wonderful. Perhaps now she was grown up she would see it with her mother's eyes and come back satisfied that the kind of life her father led was not for her.

She knew now that it was because of this dream of Africa that she had hesitated when Konrad pressed her to marry him, although he seemed to be everything that a girl could desire. Tracy had been his secretary for three years already. Young, handsome, sophisticated, he was a successful business man, the owner of numerous hotels in different parts of the world, the organizer of a travel bureau which planned tours in exotic places for wealthy people.

When she expressed some of these thoughts to him, he promised he would take her to Africa for a holiday when they were married. But it was not as Konrad's wife that she wished to go back, but as herself, Tracy, the successor of the young girl who had cried into her pillow for months after she had left, thinking of the freedom of the life she had led and dreaming of . . . who? At this stage in her thoughts she usually drew a veil over the past, but today, half-way along the road to her father's home, she allowed herself to think of the possibility of meeting Lester Cordell again.

She had been fourteen when she left. Could one be in love at fourteen? Could a hobbledehoy tomboy who apparently cared only for covering wilderness trails and nursing lame animals have emotions fine enough to last ten years? Even now at this distance of time she blushed a little when she thought how she had worshipped the young game ranger. She had followed him around with the unswerving devotion that only a child can give.

And yet although he had given her no encouragement, her feelings had been partly those of a woman. A Juliet in jeans, she thought wryly. He had been in his early twenties, she supposed, a tall lithe young man with whipcord body and dark hair and eyes of a curious golden brown. Her interest in caring for injured animals and birds had brought them together, for he was always willing to offer advice and practical help.

The only flaw in their relationship, she found, was that he displayed what to her seemed a most unnecessary interest in a girl of his own age, Evangeline Stott, a soppy kind of person in young Tracy's opinion, far more interested in dress and make-up than in wild life. However, when she tried to tell Lester what she thought of Evangeline, his reply was crushing. 'You wouldn't expect a girl as beautiful as Eve to be interested in roughing it.'

Tracy tried to recall the child she had been at fourteen, thin and angular with straight silky honey-blonde hair to her shoulders, usually untidy, and grey-blue eyes startlingly too large for the small face with its high cheekbones. Now, driving along the sandy road, her nostrils constantly assailed by the rich smell of damp earth, of blossoming trees, of sunbaked vegetation, she allowed her mind to dwell on their parting.

He had come to their home in the afternoon and

very correctly, almost formally in the presence of her mother, had said his farewells to them both. But that night after she had gone to bed in the small room with its open beams and thatched roof, she had sat in the deep window seat watching a golden moon rising above the thorn bush, hearing the sharp whistle of a reed-buck and a zebra's bark, shrill and querulous. The sound of a tree frog pulsated in her ears like her own heartbeat. How could she leave Lester without seeing him again? She would take the little buck she had found today in the bush and ask Lester if he would care for it. Her father had said he was willing, but he was rather absentminded. It would be best to ask Lester anyway. Thus she reasoned to herself so that now it seemed perfectly logical to visit Lester at midnight.

She was wearing thin cotton shortie pyjamas, but she did not think of changing. It was only when she was outside and releasing the little buck from its pen that she realized she should have put on shoes, for in the darkness she might tramp on a night adder. But she was afraid to go back in case someone might veto her visit.

The night was full of mystery and vague rustlings. Below near the river in the dark bush there was the crashing sound of a heavy body. Probably a hippo, thought Tracy, but she was not alarmed. She would have been more nervous in a city street. Lester's bachelor quarters were not far away, yet now that she was near her courage failed at the thought of waking him. But there was no need. He was sitting on the stoep in the faint glimmer of the rising moon's light. She could see the glow of his cigarette in the darkness, as she stood beside the jasmine bush at the gate hesitating. But the buck, impatient at the sudden halt, pawed at her awkwardly, giving a complaining bleat. Lester looked up sharply.

'Tracy, what on earth are you doing out at this time?'

'I brought Sandy to you. I. . . .' All her excuses died away at the sight of him and her mouth quivered. 'Oh, Lester, I'm so unhappy. I don't want to go away.'

He put his arm around her shoulders in a brotherly way, but she flung herself into his arms, sobbing and clinging closely to him. She had always hidden from him her feelings of adoration and had taken a pride in showing how boyish and independent she could be when they rode the wilderness trails together, but on this, their last night together, she was desperate.

'Little Tracy,' he said, 'I know it's tough your parents are separating. I'm terribly sorry about it, but it's decided now, and I can hardly see them changing their minds at this late hour.'

'I don't want to go,' wailed Tracy.

'You can hardly stay with your father. You know that. It would be an impossible task for him to be responsible for a little girl like you.'

'I'm not a little girl. Anyhow, you could look after me. I could stay with you. You know I can cook well. I've cooked for you when we've been camping with Papa.'

He gave her a little shake.

'Tracy girl, you know that's impossible.'

'But I love you, Lester. It's because of you that I'm so unhappy. I know I'm not old enough to marry yet, but I will be in a couple of years' time.'

He had turned the stoep light on and great soft moths were hurling their silver bodies against the wire screen. She surprised a rueful look of amusement on his face. It infuriated her.

'You think I'm a child, but I'm not, Lester. I love you much better than Evangeline does. She cares only for her silly looks.'

His face hardened. 'Be careful what you say, Tracy. Lord knows I don't want to quarrel with you when I won't see you again after tomorrow, but I think I should tell you I've become very fond of Evangeline. In fact I intend to ask her to be my wife.'

Even now ten years later Tracy remembered the agony of that last sleepless night in Africa. People forget, she thought, as they get older, how raw and defenceless are the emotions of the young. The years between had taught her discretion. Her association with Konrad was calm, level-headed on her side at least.

Now she felt suddenly overwhelmed with panic. What was she doing here at all? Why had she so eagerly seized the opportunity of visiting her father? Was it because of the last paragraph in her father's letter that her doubts about the wisdom of such a trip had become resolved? He had mentioned that if she came he hoped she would not mind accompanying a boy of eight who had been visiting his grandparents ever since his father had been killed in a shooting accident last year.

'He's the son of Evangeline Lockwood, whom you may remember as Evangeline Stott. She finds it hard to recover from the death of her husband and Lester Cordell thinks it might help her if the boy returned. He is very concerned for her because her husband, who owned a large sugar farm near here, was Lester's best friend.'

So Lester had not married Evangeline after all. Tracy remembered John Lockwood's farm, for it had seemed extremely luxurious in contrast to the restricted facilities of the game reserve. He sometimes gave large parties there to which even the youngsters were invited for day-long swimming, riding and tennis. She remembered him as a gay, lively person – and now he was dead.

Her thoughts were interrupted when a nyala bull with curving horns and long greyish white mane above its stripy hide leapt down from a thicket on the side of the road. Tracy had to brake sharply although she had been going very slowly. The car skidded a little in the soft sand and she felt the wheels subside somewhat. When she attempted to proceed, they spun ominously and the car settled deeper into the wet patch. At the same time Julian awoke and gave a little moan.

'Are we there, Tracy?' he croaked. 'My head aches and I feel so shivery and cold.'

Tracy looked desperately up and down the road. Not another vehicle in sight. The only sign of life she could see were a few small white cattle egrets intently looking for insects in the long grass. But she was sure they could not be far from the settlement now. She could not just sit there. She would have to go for help.

'I'm just going to walk up the road a few hundred yards,' she informed Julian. 'I'll tuck you under this blanket in the back of the car and you must stay there all nice and cosy until I come back. I promise I won't be away for more than a few minutes.'

Julian was drowsy again and raised no objections. He was a well-behaved child and would follow her instructions. In any case she would not leave him for long. If she could not see any signs of the camp beyond the bend of the road she would come back. How surprisingly the sights and sounds and smells of the wilderness obliterated the years between. All around her grasshoppers crackled with noisy persistence and somewhere near there must be a bush of wild jasmine, for its fragrance came on the breeze like that of a gardenia.

But she was confused by the similarity of the landscape or by the lack of landmarks that previously would have been familiar to her. Her patent leather pumps were certainly not meant for walking on this kind of track and her elegant suit was soon covered with red dust. When she turned the bend of the road however she breathed a sigh of relief. In front of her spread a valley made beautiful by clumps of green-topped thorns and tambootie trees, but beyond on the next ridge she could see the white wall of the square thatched cottages that made up the staff's living quarters.

She recollected where she was now and decided it would be a good idea to take a short cut across the valley along one of the game tracks. It would be quicker than making her way to the camp by the winding road. As she walked across, grasshoppers rose in clouds about her. Her city habits fell away and she glanced cautiously around as she proceeded. But there were no animals visible. It was too early yet, she supposed, for them to be stirring from their afternoon's drowsiness. When the heat of the sun subsided, they would rouse themselves to search for water down by the river, using their well-worn tracks, or they would go to the waterholes and timidly wait their turn, glancing around with extreme caution while they quenched their thirst.

Suddenly with no warning the whole landscape seemed to spring into violent life around her. About a hundred yards ahead a group of zebras raced from behind some bushes, tossing their heads and viciously kicking out at their companions in their efforts to speed ahead. A group of warthogs sped swiftly in the same direction, ugly and ash-grey, their tails ludicrously held aloft as they ran.

Now there was the sound of a heavy body crashing through breaking branches. From out of the thicket heading straight towards Tracy burst a white rhino, an enormous beast like a prehistoric monster. Its short legs thudded over the ground with surprising speed and its long front horn seemed like a scimitar above the square prehensile mouth. Running frantically, Tracy tried to escape from the juggernaut's path.

There was a group of bushes to the left and she headed in this direction, thinking fleetingly of discarding her shoes but not daring to do this because the ground was thick with thorns. She could hear the pounding reverberation of the animal's huge hooves. The noise seemed to surround her and she dared not look back to see how near it was.

Then suddenly there was a thundering crash. The ground underneath her feet seemed to quiver and then there was silence, broken only by the complaining shouts of a hornbill. She stopped her headlong attempt at escape and ventured to look around. The rhino lay on the ground in a cloud of dust and disturbed vegetation. It raised its head and struggled to rise, then flopped back as if exhausted.

What could be the cause of her sudden reprieve? She had heard no shot, and in any case it would be very unusual for anyone to use a gun in the reserve. Again she was startled by the sound of hooves and crashing branches, but this time the noise seemed more familiar and before she had time to panic afresh from out of the thicket burst a small sturdy horse ridden by a most odd apparition.

The rider was covered from head to foot in padding and his face was protected by a visor almost like that of a medieval knight. On seeing the prostrate rhino, he slid from his horse and cautiously approached it on foot. The great beast raised its head as the rider approached and Tracy held her breath. It struggled to rise, but the effort seemed beyond its strength and it flopped back again, relapsing into its former state of coma. The rider seemed satisfied and spoke into a radio apparatus that he carried with him, in the meantime soothing his horse which was protected by a thick canvas apron, felt leg guards and a mask with plastic eye shields.

'Good afternoon,' Tracy said to the medieval apparition.

The man swung around with a start. Tracy reflected that she seemed to scare him much more than the recumbent rhino.

'Good lord, how you startled me! What the devil are you doing here?'

'My car is stuck. I'm looking for some help.'

'Didn't you read the notice on the gate, madam? It's extremely dangerous to wander around a reserve with no guide. Surely you could have waited until someone came along?'

Tracy felt hot, not only with the heat of the blazing sun but also with irritation. Her feet ached in the elegant black pumps. Her face and hair were full of red dust and her mouth dry with thirst.

'I'm quite aware of the fact that it isn't safe,' she replied, 'but I have a sick child in the car. I couldn't just sit there.'

'I should have thought that was all the more reason not to take any chances. However, it's fortunate for you that you came across me.'

'Fortunate?' asked Tracy, 'with this in the vanguard?' as she indicated the rhino. She was still trembling a little from the shock of her first sight of the huge animal and this man's calm assumption that she should be grateful for his presence rasped on her nerves.

'Oh, don't worry about him. He's out for quite a while until the vet gives him an injection that will revive him sufficiently to be able to walk into a truck. However, it's a bit alarming to see him come to life again and I advise you to go back to your car. I'll send some help for you and your child as soon as possible, Mrs. . . . er. . . .'

While he was speaking he had taken off the helmet and revealed a shock of dark coppery hair. His face was turned away from her because he was looking at the recumbent rhino. But at the sight of that square-shaped dark head a thrill of shock and excitement ran through her. He turned towards her somewhat impatiently.

'The others will be here soon. For heaven's sake, madam, do as you're told and get back to the car. These animals are normally mild, but there's no accounting for what they'll do after they've been shot with a drugged dart and chased through the bush.'

The eyes that were gazing at her with barely concealed anger and no sign of recognition were a strange golden brown. The face now revealed by the removal of the mask was older, more mature, but had the rugged features of the young man she had once known.

She stepped forward, her hands outstretched. 'Lester. . . .' But at that moment his attention was distracted by a group of people emerging from the trees, two white men and a group of African guards. Beyond them on flatter ground she could see a four-wheel-drive vehicle enclosed with heavy mesh.

The man with a walkie-talkie apparatus was apparently the veterinary officer, for he advanced to the prostrate rhino and proceeded to examine it. The other man was a stocky person with greying hair and a fresh complexion. It was to him that Lester turned.

'Doctor, sorry to spoil your fun, but this young woman is stranded by the roadside with a sick child in the car. Do you think you could help her if I send a couple of guards to help push?'

The doctor gave a rather wistful look at the scene he had to leave on Tracy's account. The vet had swiftly given the rhino an injection and it was showing alarming signs of life already. But then the doctor turned politely to Tracy and introduced himself.

'I'm James Miller. Let's go, shall we? What seems to be wrong with your child?'

'He's very feverish. He has been like this the whole day. He complains that his throat is sore.'

'Well, we'll soon see,' said the doctor resignedly.

'I'm sorry I'm being a nuisance,' Tracy said. 'Am I taking you away from your duties?'

The doctor laughed goodnaturedly. He seemed a very pleasant character, thought Tracy, still smarting from her encounter with Lester. His blue eyes were very kindly.

'No, no, my dear, don't give it a thought. It's my afternoon off. My partner's in charge. Instead of my usual round of golf, I persuaded Lester to let me observe a rhino catch. It's most intriguing from a medical point of view, as you can imagine. The success of the thing depends entirely upon a correct dosage of drugs.'

'It looks pretty dangerous to me,' said Tracy.

'It is. But not half so dangerous as it was when they first began to experiment. They're getting it down to a fine art. However, that time between when the rhino is darted and when it collapses is still a pretty tricky time. Rangers like Lester Cordell need nerves of steel. But then they're tough chaps anyhow to carry out their normal jobs.'

'But why do they need to catch the rhinos?' asked Tracy.

'It's an odd situation. Years ago the white rhino nearly died out as a species, just as the quagga and the dodo did. So they gave them protection in this reserve and now they breed so fast that there are too many for the small area of the place, so they have to send some away to zoos and other reserves all over the world.'

By this time they had reached the car and to Tracy's relief Julian was still sleeping. He wakened when she opened the car door and gazed around, very flushed in the face and inclined to be a little tearful. Doctor Miller's kind manner soon reassured him, however.

'I'll examine him properly when we get to the rest camp,' he told Tracy. 'As far as I can tell you without a thorough examination, it looks as if he has tonsillitis.'

By this time the African guards had arrived and they had soon set the car back on to the firm ground again. The doctor offered to drive while Tracy held Julian. He glanced at Tracy's dishevelled appearance with kindly blue eyes.

'You look all in yourself, Mrs. . . .?'

'I'm Tracy Bryant,' replied Tracy hastily. 'And this is Julian Lockwood. I've brought him from England. I'm coming to visit my father here.'

'Good lord, old Tom Bryant's daughter! I'm glad you've come. Maybe you'll be able to knock a bit of sense into Tom.'

'Why do you say that?' asked Tracy, startled.

'Frankly, Miss Bryant, I'm not too pleased with your father's state of health. He has always led a very Spartan kind of existence and admittedly he's tough. But he's not getting any younger and this life in the bush is a bit hard on an older man. He tries to do too much. I hope now you've come you'll be able to persuade him to take things a bit easier. Another thing, he doesn't have much comfort the way he lives. He hardly notices what his servants do and they have a pretty easy time of it. However, I guess you'll see for yourself soon enough.'

'I suppose I will,' said Tracy with a sinking heart.

Her childish dream of the lovely exotic place she had known and her eager memories of her adored father faded before the reality of Doctor Miller's frank words of warning. And Lester? The man whose memory had come between herself and every other man she had ever met had not even recognized her.

CHAPTER TWO

THE settlement for those employed in the game reserve had changed somewhat from the place Tracy remembered. The adobe cottages painted white had been rebuilt and were more solidly constructed than the rather rough-and-ready round huts she recalled, and the roofs, although still made of thatch, were beautifully and expertly done. Except her father's one. When they stopped at the small gate of the overgrown garden, Tracy evidently was not able to conceal her expression of dismay, for James Miller patted her hand and said:

'You can see your father is inclined to neglect the things he doesn't consider are important, but cheer up. I'm sure you will soon get things sorted out. He was offered a new cottage when the others were rebuilt, but he said he was perfectly happy in this one and did not want the task of moving all his books and equipment.

'I suppose you will keep Julian until his mother can call for him,' he added. 'I will carry him inside where we can examine him properly. It's strange that I didn't hear that Evangeline was back.'

'Has she been away?' asked Tracy.

'Yes, she's a restless creature. The last I heard of her was that she was spending some time in Lourenço Marques. She seems to prefer city life in spite of having been a farmer's wife.'

'Well, I suppose she must be back, for she knew Julian was coming.'

Doctor Miller took the sleeping child in his arms and ushered Tracy in front of him along the weedy path of the tangled garden that led to a stable door which had once been painted green but was now peeling and blistered by the heat of the sun. He knocked at the door and, when there was no response, he hoisted Julian to his left arm and lifting the latch strode inside.

Tracy recalled the layout of the small house. She remembered the front door had led straight into a large airy living-room that her mother had furnished with handwoven rugs and one or two comfortable chintzy armchairs with a pattern of roses that matched the curtains in the small deeply recessed windows.

Now the thought crossed her mind that she had never seen such an untidy room in her whole life. Books lined the walls, but in haphazard piles not on shelves. The rose-patterned curtains hung in ribbons and the chairs had very odd-looking lumps on them that must be due to sagging springs.

But all thought of her surroundings vanished as she heard footsteps approaching and someone opened one of the inner doors that led from the bedrooms. How much older he looks, she thought, and her heart was wrung with the rush of affection and pity she felt for this elderly man, who, though wiry and deeply tanned, yet looked somehow helpless with his guileless blue eyes and the tuft of silver hair that resembled the topknot of some crested bird. It was she who put her arms around him and stood there smiling while tears rolled down her cheeks.

'It's so silly, I know, but I can't help it. It's so good to see you.'

'Tracy, my dear! I'd forgotten you would be grown up now. I was still thinking of you as you looked when you were fourteen. I didn't realize I'd have such a beautiful daughter.' He suddenly became aware of the doctor. 'Jim, what are you doing here?'

'Hello, Tom. I'm afraid we have a sick child on our hands here. Has Evangeline phoned, or would you like me to phone and tell her Julian has arrived?'

'Child? Oh, yes, Julian. I've forgotten what this is all about. Did Evangeline ask you to bring him?'

'No, Papa,' Tracy said patiently. How well she remembered his vague absentminded manner which had always annoyed her mother so much. 'You asked me to bring him. You said in the letter that Lester Cordell was anxious he should come back because he thought it would help to cheer his mother.'

'Did I? Ah, yes, no doubt Lester told me what to write. I'd be obliged, old chap, if you would phone his mother. Poor little scrap, he does look red, doesn't he?'

But when Dr. Miller phoned the farm he was informed that Evangeline was not due home until next week.

'He'd better stay here until we can get this sorted out,' said Tracy decisively.

Julian had awakened now and was inclined to be tearful.

'Where's my mummy? Why aren't you taking me to her?' he demanded.

'We'll find out soon, old boy,' the doctor reassured him.

'Meanwhile I'm going to get you into bed right here,' declared Tracy.

She noticed that the doctor looked a bit doubtful and, when she had carried Julian towards the second bedroom which she had concluded would have been prepared for her use, she realized the reason. This room too was piled with books and scientific apparatus. There was hardly room for the small unmade single bed in the middle and this in turn was covered by all kinds of things. There was even a large butterfly net upon it. Dust lay thick on the battered chest of drawers and on the chair that was leaning drunkenly supported by two bricks.

'But surely he was expecting me to stay here?' asked Tracy.

The doctor shrugged his houlders.

'Of course he was. He's talked of nothing else for weeks, but his mind is on this book all the time and I'm afraid he doesn't think of material comforts for himself or for anyone else. I'll go and speak to his servant.'

He disappeared into the kitchen which was a long room running the length of the cottage at the back, and she heard him talking in a quiet yet firm way in Zulu. Next she heard him having a conversation on the phone. When shortly he returned, his rather rubicund face was wreathed in smiles.

'We've solved your problems for the time being. I'm to take you and the child to Lester Cordell's house for the night. He's come back from his rhino chase and he offered to take Julian since he feels responsible for him to his mother. But I told him it would be a good idea if you were to attend to the child during the night. He objected to that. Didn't want to bother you any further, I suppose, but I overruled him. Told him that Julian needed someone with whom he was familiar. I hope you don't mind.'

What could she say? thought Tracy. Doctor Miller had been so kind and he was so pleased with himself that he had attended to her comfort and solved her problems. Besides, certainly she could not keep Julian here. The dust lying thickly around would be the worst possible thing for his sore throat.

It did not seem to strike the doctor as unconventional that she should spend the night at Lester Cordell's house. Perhaps the conventions were not so strictly observed in the wilds of Africa. Well, she would go. She was curious to observe Lester's reaction now that he had been informed of her true identity. Did he have any recollection of the child who had practically thrown herself at his head or had that scene which had meant so much to an adolescent girl held so little significance that he had forgotten it almost as soon as it had happened? She was inclined to hope so.

She bade farewell to her father, promising to come back tomorrow. He seemed quite content with this. 'We're going to have plenty of time to get to know each other again,' he said.

Arriving at the house, she realized that it was new and so did not hold any embarrassing recollections for her. Lester was not there when they arrived. The Zulu male servant informed them that he had gone to the boma to see the rhino settled in its temporary home, but he had said they must ask for anything they required. He showed them into a room that was sparkling clean, comfortable without being luxurious with two beds showing white sheets underneath the brown blankets, and a shining parquet floor in small blocks of dark and light coloured wood. The small table, wardrobe and chest of drawers were enamelled white, and dark blue curtains and rugs completed the somewhat austere effect.

She quickly settled Julian into bed and Dr. Miller examined him thoroughly. He was able to supply tablets from the bag he carried in the boot of his car, and promised to look in again in the morning. Julian's throat was inflamed but would probably clear quite quickly, the doctor promised optimistically.

'He will probably sleep well tonight, but may wake wanting a drink or some attention. It's best that you should stay here. More convenient for you too. I told your father's servant he must get your room cleared tomorrow. He isn't a bad chap, but he's young and needs someone to give him instructions. You'll find he'll be glad to have you around to tell him what to do. It's just that your father never worries about domestic comfort. He never even notices if anything's wrong. He lives in a world of his own.'

'Thank you for everything, Dr. Miller. I hate to think what I would have done without you,' acknowledged Tracy.

'Not at all. Glad to be of use,' said the doctor as he went towards the door. 'Well, now I'll be off. Can't wait for Lester. Tell him I'm sorry I missed him, but I must be back for my evening surgery. Good-bye, my dear, I'll see you tomorrow. Don't worry about the boy.'

She was supplied with water by a smiling Zulu servant and proceeded to wash Julian, then gave him a warm drink with the prescribed tablets. Only when this was finished did she have time to realize how very weary and tired she herself was. She had brought with her her small overnight case and now she was able to have the hot bath she had been longing for since early afternoon.

The delicate apricot-coloured peignoir trimmed with coffee-coloured lace looked far too luxurious for her surroundings. It had been a present from her mother who always loved feminine expensive clothes. She had packed it without considering her destination. She must try to buy a cotton housecoat when she got the opportunity.

She decided to ask the Zulu servant to bring her a tray to the room. Toast and tea would suffice and in this way she need not see anything of her reluctant host. But as she entered the living-room intending to go into the kitchen, she heard firm steps upon the stoep and within seconds Lester was in the room.

He had discarded the padded guards that he had worn during the rhino chase and was wearing khaki jodhpurs and an open-necked shirt. His arms below the rolled-up sleeves, the broad column of his neck and the face with its strong features and square jaw were all of a uniform colour of brown. The heavy brows and thick-fringed lashes were so dark that they made the golden eyes look even more startling, those eyes that seemed to Tracy to be gazing at her with a half amused, half scornful expression.

Her hand felt small and delicate in his large brown one. He did not let it go but kept it in his own, examining it with an enigmatic smile.

'Tracy Bryant, who would have ever believed you could have hands that resembled an advertisement for some kind of lotion? When we used to ride through the bush, they were tanned, strong hands that could handle a horse or a sick kudu with equal ease.'

'Ten years ago, Lester. It seems a lifetime. We're both different people now.'

'So it seems,' said Lester dryly. His glance took in the fragile apricot gown, the shining, sleek, honey-blonde hair. He put his hands on her shoulders and drew her towards the window where the last rays of the setting sun were filling the room with golden light.

'Let me look at you. The same enormous grey eyes. They were your one beauty when you were a scrawny little girl, following me around like a lost steenbuck. And now you're entirely beautiful, but the Tracy I knew has gone.'

Tracy closed her eyes. She felt herself drowning in waves of violent emotion. Good heavens! He still had the same effect upon her as when she was a vulnerable child of fourteen. The mere touch of his hands grasping her shoulders had been enough to make her feel again the desperate passion she had schooled herself during ten years to forget entirely.

'Yes, she's gone,' she replied firmly. 'And what a foolish little girl she was, wasn't she, Lester?'

His hands dropped from her shoulders.

'I beg your pardon. I must get used to this new Tracy. You were a funny, lovable child, as I remember you. Who would have thought you could become so. . . .' He shrugged, looking faintly puzzled.

'You can't leave it at that, Lester. Please go on.'

'No, I'm being stupid. Naturally you had to grow up and, knowing the kind of life your mother liked to lead, of course I should have realized you would be . . . well, worldly.'

Tracy turned aside and blinked her eyes rapidly. She dared not show her hurt.

'Let's agree that it's nonsense to expect people to be the same after ten years, Lester. We're both different people and I for one have forgotten my childhood here. I hope you have too, for as I remember it I was a stupid, emotional child.'

'Perhaps . . .' said Lester, 'but very sweet.'

The Zulu servant came in to the room with a tray of

drinks, and Tracy suddenly recalled her original plan.

'I don't want to be a nuisance, Lester. I can have supper in my room. That's why I haven't dressed.'

'Nonsense,' said Lester in a tone that brooked no argument. 'You'll dine with me. You say we're strangers, so we must remedy that. Don't bother to dress. I'm sure you're quite aware that this garment looks charming on you.'

His cynical smile infuriated Tracy. What an arrogant man Lester had become! Did he think she had worn this frivolous negligée on purpose to charm him? Well, she would show him quite clearly that he was mistaken.

Without a word she went back into the room and changed into a plain pair of navy slacks and a blue and white striped cotton sweater. Then she tied her hair back with a large navy bow. When she came back he was sitting in one of the comfortable basket armchairs with the tray of drinks beside him. He eyed the slacks with amused eyes, but made no comment.

She accepted a lime juice and soda from him while he drank whisky.

'How's the boy?' he asked.

'Julian? He seems a little cooler. Doctor Miller said he should be over the worst by morning. Naturally he's disappointed that his mother isn't here. When will she be coming?'

Lester frowned. 'I have no idea. Evangeline is a law unto herself. She seemed delighted when I suggested sending for Julian, but something must have delayed her. I'll put a call through to her this evening. Naturally she knows the boy can be left with me.'

Why naturally? thought Tracy. They must still be

very friendly. Why didn't they marry ten years ago, and is he hoping now . . . a year must have passed since John Lockwood died. . . .

'You remember Eve, of course, she used to be Evangeline Stott when you lived here.'

'I remember her. I didn't realize it then, but as I recall her she must have been very beautiful.'

'She still is,' said Lester, and the admiring tone in his voice gave her an unaccountable stab of pain, for after all what had it to do with her? 'She's a courageous person. She was remarkably brave at the time of her husband's death, perhaps too brave, for now she seems to be suffering some kind of reaction and is very restless, continually travelling, not wanting or seeming able to settle down.

'That's why I thought it best to send for the child,' he continued. 'I thought he would help. Perhaps it was a mistake to send him away in the first place, but she was determined to get him away from the atmosphere of mourning. She thought only of his good, not of her own wishes.'

Tracy had some reservation about this statement. It seemed odd to her that a mother who had not seen her only child for a year should not be on the spot to meet him, but as Lester said, there must be some simple explanation. But it was rather hard on Julian.

'I asked your father to join us, but he says he's working on his book tonight and is looking forward to seeing you tomorrow,' Lester informed her, as they ate the simple meal the servant had prepared.

'That was kind of you. How is my father, Lester? Doctor Miller alarmed me by saying he needs to take things easier.'

Lester's eyes gazed very directly into her own. His

expression was hard.

'Yes, Tracy, I'm afraid I agree with James. It's high time someone took an interest in his welfare. He's had ten years of living on his own, and he's so absentminded and completely unworldly that he isn't the kind of fellow who should be left to look after himself. It didn't help either that his family completely lost touch with him. For heaven's sake, Tracy, an occasional letter wouldn't have cost you anything!'

'But I did write,' Tracy protested. 'I wrote every week at first, but he never replied. A child is easily discouraged, Lester. When I had no response from him, my mother said he obviously wasn't interested in us any more.'

'That wasn't his story, Tracy. He said you stopped writing to him. He would never come to supper on Sunday when I asked him because he said that was his night for writing to you.'

'But I only ever received one or two letters from him. Sometimes there would be a Christmas card. . . .' Tracy broke off, alarmed by the expression on Lester's face. 'Don't you believe me?'

'I think you probably believe now that you wrote more often than you did. A letter is an effort to a child. But I do know that he wrote regularly to you and I suspect that he aged quicker than he should have done because he thought he'd lost you.'

Tracy could not think how to reply to Lester's accusations. Obviously he thought she had neglected her father, and this was borne out by his next words.

'Oh, I realize well enough that you were leading a busy, highly sophisticated life in London. How could you be expected to realize how much it would have meant to your father to have news of you?'

'But I'm here now,' said Tracy, trying to justify herself against his obdurate convictions. 'I came as soon as he asked me.'

'Yes, I must confess I was very surprised when I heard you'd consented to come. But if your idea is to have a holiday at your father's expense, I hope you realize how much he's looking forward to your helping him with this book, and that it will entail quite a lot of work.'

Tracy gasped. She felt as if he had struck her.

'Ten years seem to have done very little to improve your manners, Lester. I don't remember that they were always so insufferable.'

To her surprise, he grinned.

'Perhaps your own were not so smooth in those days. That was before you'd been finished at a young lady's school, remember? You were not so critical then. In fact you thought rather highly of me. But I could hardly hope to please you now you've grown up into a sophisticated young lady, could I?'

'No, you could not,' said Tracy, rising from the table. 'And now if you'll excuse me I'd better go to see how Julian is.'

But she was not to get rid of his presence so easily.

'I'll come too,' he offered.

Tracy had left a small nightlight burning, and they could see that Julian was sleeping peacefully. His breathing seemed more regular and his skin was slightly damp instead of hot, dry and burning with fever as it had been earlier. Lester touched the short cropped hair.

'He's very like John,' he murmured to himself. 'There seems nothing of Evangeline in him.'

Did he regret this? thought Tracy.

'He seems well enough,' Lester commented. 'Come, Tracy, I'm sorry if I offended you. Sometimes I say more than I should, and you, of course, are used to more suave manners than mine. Show me you forgive me by giving me a little more of your company. Let's sit on the stoep and you can listen to the sounds of the wilds. It must be a long time since you heard anything more exciting than hooting taxis.'

Too long, thought Tracy. As a child she had known no fear of her surroundings. She had realized the beauty but not the terror of the night hours in Africa. But now, used as she was to the homely sounds of the city, the darkness seemed full of mystery and ominous noises.

Then gradually, as she sat quietly with Lester by her side, the threat of the unknown lifted and again she began to recognize the things that had been familiar to her so long ago. That hollow call and its ghostly answer was only the sound of two small owls, the ones the Zulus called *mabengwane*, calling and answering for companionship as they floated above, soft as moths in their flight. That querulous bark like the yelp of a sea-lion was the shrill cry of a zebra and the same sound farther away was mellowed by distance into clear musical notes. That gruff menacing cough was a wildebeest that had been separated from its herd, and much nearer in the trees below the house, that sound like the lamentations of a witch's baby, was the cry of a galago, the enchanting bush baby with its silky fur and huge yellow eyes.

'So,' said Lester, when she identified these sounds, 'ten years in the city have not made you forget this life entirely. But I must insist, Tracy, that when you and your father go out on these photography expeditions,

you must take a guide. There are many more rhinos
now than there were ten years ago. In fact, much more
game of every kind. Conservation has seen to that.'

'I'll follow my father's wishes,' said Tracy, resenting
Lester's tone.

'I'm responsible for people's welfare here,' said Lester adamantly. 'You'll follow mine.'

The phone rang before she could respond to his
statement.

'That will be the call I booked to Evangeline,' said
Lester.

He came back looking pleased.

'She says she's dreadfully sorry you're having all this
trouble with Julian. She didn't realize he was coming so
soon. Evidently his grandparents put the wrong date in
their letter to her.'

'But. . . .' said Tracy, and stopped. Julian's grandmother had insisted upon writing the letter while she
was there when she had gone to see her about the arrangements. In fact they had composed that part of the
letter together. There had been no mistake.

'She's coming as soon as she can get a booking.
When I told her you were young and attractive she was
most eager to meet you. She doesn't have many friends
of her own kind around here, I'm afraid.'

'I was so sorry to hear of John's death,' said Tracy,
finding herself unable to respond to Evangeline's wish
to meet her.

'Yes, it was a bad show. He was a very good friend of
mine. I don't suppose you remember because you were
just a child, not interested in love affairs at that stage,
as I remember, but John and I were both keen on
Evangeline. I thought at one stage that I was to be the
lucky one, but it was John she preferred. I could hardly

blame her. He was older, more sophisticated with lots of charm. I was just a brash youngster.'

And he had a beautiful sugar farm and was very wealthy, thought Tracy, then felt horrified at herself for her spiteful thoughts. After all, she had scarcely known Evangeline in those days and she had looked at her with the eyes of a jealous child. If everything Lester said was true, she was a most admirable woman, so why wasn't she, Tracy, looking forward to meeting her?

As she said good night to Lester he told her he probably would not see her in the morning, for he got up and was about his work very early. In spite of her weariness, she lay sleepless for a long time, thinking over rather sadly the change she found in Lester. Or is it the change in myself? she thought. Obviously he thinks so.

She was awakened from a deep sleep some few hours later by a sound she could not define. Was it Julian? She got up and went to his bed. The nightlight was still burning and she could see he had hardly moved during the night but was sleeping peacefully. Then what had wakened her? It must have been the cry of some animal in the bush, but now all she could hear was the persistent grating noise of a cricket.

She was just about to return to her bed when she heard and recognized the sound again. It was a low tormented moan and it seemed to come from the direction of Lester's room. Terrified, not knowing what she could expect to see, she took the few steps to his open door. To her relief she saw that he was sleeping, lying on top of the bed wearing only brief shorts. But as she looked at him, his chest heaved and the low moan came again. He sat up and she saw that his eyes were open but unfocused.

'John, look out!' he shouted in agonized tones. 'For God's sake, listen to me. Don't tempt fate, John. Don't be a fool. Oh, God, he's dead . . . dead, and it's all my fault!'

The pain in his voice was more than Tracy could bear and without thought she put her arms around him, soothing him as she would have done with Julian. Gradually his breathing quietened and his body that had been taut against her relaxed. She eased him back upon the pillow and covered him with a sheet. His eyes which had closed flickered and opened and he stared at her in apparent surprise. Quickly she slipped away from him, but as she went quietly through the door, she heard him speak again.

'Evangeline,' he said, 'must I take all the blame?'

CHAPTER THREE

A FEW days later, Tracy stood at a window of her father's house. The sun had scarcely risen, but although it was still dark in the valleys with drifts of blue mist near the gleaming silver of the river, the distant rolling hills were tipped with pink and over all the land the torn trees looked black, mysterious and exciting.

In the kitchen, George, the young Zulu boy, was preparing coffee to be served with rusks, for Tracy and her father planned to do some photography work before breakfast, since the animals would be astir at this hour before the heat forced them into the cover of the bush.

As Doctor Miller had predicted, Tracy had found the young Zulu servant quite amenable to carrying out her instructions. Before her coming, he had lacked guidance, but now, within days, the house was cleaned and made more tidy, though Tracy had still not ventured to interfere with Mr. Bryant's working area. Tracy had kept Julian with her as there was still no word of his mother's arrival, and he was recovering rapidly from the attack of tonsilitis. James Miller had proved most attentive and kind both with Julian and her father.

It was good to have someone she could turn to, thought Tracy, for she felt too awkward and embarrassed with Lester to dream of asking him for help. Although of course he was not aware of what had happened the night she had stayed with him, she had been puzzled and scared by this unwitting glimpse into his innermost feelings. Did he feel himself responsible for John Lockwood's death, and if so, why? Dr. Miller could perhaps enlighten her, but in spite of his friendliness she hesitated to ask him, feeling she had discovered something that was secret, and that it would be disloyal to discuss it with someone else. And yet curiosity to know the circumstances of Eve's husband's tragic death nagged at her mind. She knew she would not be satisfied until she was enlightened.

Time and again she regretted the impulse that had brought her back to her childhood home as she tried in vain to quell the feelings that had been aroused in her during the first evening. She admitted to herself that she had hoped she would find that Lester's attraction for her had vanished and that she could return to make her calm life with Konrad, satisfied that the violent emotions she remembered had all been part of a youthful dream.

She had planned that in her life this three months of helping her father was to be an interlude and nothing more, and had hoped it would resolve all doubt and she could go back to a pleasant civilized life, including marriage to an eligible young man with whom she had much in common. She had visualized herself and Konrad living in some elegantly furnished apartment in Chelsea or Regent's Park, entertaining their friends, enjoying dining out at small luxurious restaurants, going to plays and concerts.

And now what had happened? One evening with Lester Cordell seemed to have turned her neat plans upside down. But what was she thinking of? That life in London was the reality, not this, and it was a foolish dream to think she could ever mean anything in Lester's life, though she admitted to herself that in one evening he had aroused feelings in her of which she had thought herself incapable. And yet she had to confess, humiliating as it seemed, that she had received no encouragement from him. So here she was back in the same position in which she had been at the age of fourteen. But now she was more mature and could deal with the situation. It was ridiculous. She must shorten her stay and go back to Konrad as soon as possible.

Her thoughts were interrupted by her father who came in at that moment looking, since he had forgotten to comb his hair, a little like one of those mahem cranes with their fluffy blond topknots. His blue eyes gleamed with pleasurable anticipation.

'Well, Tracy, this is good. I can't tell you how much I've been looking forward to making these expeditions with my daughter. Lester has become a little fierce with me of late about going off on my own. But now I have you with me, I expect he'll relax his restrictions. As I remember it you were pretty much of an expert at these wilderness trails when you were still a child. I don't expect Lester has forgotten that. No, indeed.'

Tracy put her arm around him. He was tall and thin with a bony frame. His tan gave a false impression of health. Since she had returned she was constantly alarmed by his fragility.

'We'll make a grand success of this book, Papa, just wait and see. You must tell me exactly what you have in mind and I'll try to follow your instructions.'

'Yes, well, my idea is to show the general public just how important conservation of wild animals is. We'll try to get rather sentimental portraits of some of the animals. You know how important it is to find funds for our work here. Touch their hearts and you touch their pockets.'

'Why, Papa, I would never have thought you could be so materialistic!' laughed Tracy.

'I must confess, Lester put the idea into my head. But as usual, he's quite right. Don't you agree?'

'I suppose so,' said Tracy. 'But it's not just to be full of sentimental photographs, is it?'

'By no means,' said Mr. Bryant. An air of authority shone through his vagueness when he was speaking upon his own subject. 'We'll give the public lots of information, facts about animals that are little known, but we'll do it in a readable way. That's where you can help me. You can prevent me from being boring, tell me when I'm being too obscure or prosy. I've roughed out the main plan, but I hope you will help me with refining it. Now, if you're ready, I think we can start.'

Tracy hesitated. She remembered that Lester had spoken very severely about their taking a guard for protection.

'What about a guard, Papa? Lester mentioned that we should take one with us.'

'Did he? Of course, so he did. I should have arranged something with him yesterday. Oh, well, we should be all right just for once. I'll arrange about a guard when I see him.'

Tracy did not want to disappoint her father. He was obviously looking forward very much to their first outing. She thought fleetingly of taking George, their servant, but he was not qualified to give protection in the bush, and besides, someone had to stay at home to look after Julian. She thought to herself that she would take care to keep to the main roads and discourage her father from getting out of the car.

Taking up the photography equipment, which included a large telephoto lens, she made her way out to the high truck with which her father had been provided for viewing and photographing game. The sun was just rising and the distant hills were tipped with colour like the heart of a rose, but the bush still lay in dusky shadow. Spiders' webs beaded with drops of moisture hung from the spikes of the aloe plants and somewhere hidden in a tree a bush robin whistled its loud clear call.

It was good to be here, thought Tracy, all her doubts dissolving in the joyous atmosphere of early morning in this place that was like a scene from the first week of creation. They stopped to photograph a group of impala with their glossy red coats and lighter stripes. Though so common, they were one of the prettiest of African antelopes. They stood dead still when they saw the car, obligingly freezing into immobility so that Tracy got what she hoped would be a perfect photograph of the gracefully horned ram together with its group of does and fawns, then in sudden alarm they all bounded away with marvellous leaps until they were hidden in the leafy foliage.

Two bushbuck, usually the shyest of animals, were fighting by the side of the road. When at last they sensed the presence of the car, they bounded away tossing their heads and barking loudly like asthmatic old men, the distinctive white circles on their rumps showing through the dark bush like the fading smile of the Cheshire cat in *Alice in Wonderland*.

While Tracy had been photographing the fight of the waterbuck, her father, used to these scenes of wild life, had been scanning the parklike countryside with his binoculars looking out for signs of more game. Suddenly he gave a low whistle.

'Cheetah! My goodness, Tracy, we're in luck this morning. There are not many cheetah in the reserve and they usually keep away from the public roads. We simply must try to get a picture of them.'

Two grown animals with a cub were strolling across the veld, seemingly unaware of their presence. As they watched, the cub bounded forward and the mother gave it a sharp cuff, then apparently repenting of her severity, she lay down and caressed the small spotted creature with her paws. They were such beautiful animals that Tracy was completely enchanted. Their bodies were long and lithe and they were very tall and long-legged with the most wonderful tawny pelts shining black and gold in the early rays of sunlight.

'You stay in the car,' she said to her father. 'I'm going to get out. I must get a little closer.'

'Be careful,' he said, but he too was completely enthralled by the sight of the handsome beasts and oblivious to any danger.

Tracy edged forward. The animals were unaware of her presence, absorbed as they were in their teasing play with the young offspring. She got behind a bush and pointing the tele-lens was able to take some wonderful shots of the golden-furred creatures with their dappled coats. But suddenly the click of the camera aroused the male to a sense of danger. He turned towards Tracy's hiding place and, before she had a chance to conceal herself properly, he was approaching curiously. Nearer and nearer he came. Should she start to retreat to the car? She had not realized how far she had ventured away from it.

The mother cheetah mewed warningly to its cub and retreated towards some bushes, but the male stood stock still, angrily lashing its tail and glaring with yellow-green eyes in Tracy's direction. Tracy remembered reading that the cheetah is the swiftest animal there is. It would be useless for her to attempt to run back to the car. Suddenly to her horror she realized that her father had emerged from the truck and was making his way towards her, obviously hoping to divert the attention of the animal.

What chance would this frail old man have against the rippling muscles of this creature of the wilds? She shouted a warning, but he still advanced, armed only with a stout stick. The cheetah, its attention diverted, snarled at him, its mouth open in a menacing grin. So absorbed was Tracy in the immediate danger that she had not noticed the arrival of another truck. But suddenly a whipcord figure walked with determined pace between her, her father and the male cheetah.

Lester, his body taut, waved his arms threateningly at the snarling beast and after a moment's hesitation it retreated, growling in a low voice and casting many a backward glance at the humans who were apparently threatening its mate and cub. No word was spoken until they regained the road, and then it was Tracy, not Mr. Bryant, whom Lester addressed.

'I thought I warned you that you must take a guard. Why did you not tell me you intended to come out this morning?'

'I . . . we . . . I'm sorry, Lester. I thought we'd be all right. I didn't intend that we should leave the car. But it was so tempting to try to get photographs of the cheetah.'

'Tempting – when you or your father might have been mauled? Really, Tracy, you had more sense when you were fourteen. It was madness to approach cheetah when you could see they had a young cub.'

Mr. Bryant intervened, 'I'm sorry, Lester, our enthusiasm ran away with us, I admit. In future I promise Tracy shall have a guard.'

'Meanwhile I insist I must accompany you for the rest of this morning's expedition. I can't risk a recurrence of this episode,' said Lester sternly.

'But, Lester, surely you have other work to do,' protested Tracy. 'We can't take up your time like this.'

'That's for me to decide.'

Lester's face was stern, his jaw rigidly set. He gave instructions to the African who was driving his truck, then came to take his place in their vehicle. Obviously he's furious with me, thought Tracy, first for risking my father's safety and now for wasting his time. Her hands trembled as she set the camera. How could she take photographs successfully with this grim-faced man sitting beside her and watching her every move?

In spite of her feeling of humiliation, she was glad of his company she had to admit when they came upon the rhinos. There were eight of them together, so large that they looked from the distance like a herd of elephants. They were disporting themselves in a shallow pool, letting themselves down into the mud back feet first with ludicrous caution, like old ladies not sure of the temperature of the water. They were so enormous that the effect of seeing eight of these large animals together was, Tracey found, quite stupefying.

Lester had taken over the driving, saying briefly to her that she would have more opportunity for photography if he did this, but really she was sure he did not trust her ability to drive on these roads. Now he quietly stopped and turned to her.

'Well, I suppose you want to get out to be a little nearer for your photographs,' he said challengingly.

It was the last thing Tracy wanted to do. The cheetahs had seemed quite a different proposition. Even though at the back of her mind she had known they were dangerous, they were so beautiful and gentle in their play with their young cub that she had felt no fear until the male had threatened them. But these huge beasts seemed like something from a different world, a prehistoric place populated with mammoths and dinosaurs. There was something completely unreal about them with their fantastic bulk and small eyes set in a head that bore one immense curved horn and one smaller straight one above the truculent square jaw.

But she was determined she would not show fear in front of Lester. He seemed to have recovered from his anger, but it was almost worse now that he was regarding her with bright amused eyes. Of course he expected she would refuse, but he would soon find out he was wrong.

'I'm ready to go if you are,' she said, trying to make her voice strong and determined when she felt it quavering. Leaving Mr. Bryant in the car, they cautiously approached to within a few feet of the playful animals. Lester put his hand firmly on her arm. She supposed he was trying to reassure her. How could he know that his touch confused her to such an extent that the thought of danger from the rhinos receded and she could only marvel that this angry man, who seemed to condemn her every move, could by the simple action of holding her arm make her feel cherished and send her soaring into some high heaven of tender emotion?

With his help she obtained some very good action shots of the bathing rhino. With him near at hand she felt there was very little cause for fear. He knew the rhinos and had studied their every move, and if he felt there was no danger, then she was content to trust his judgement.

'They're fairly timid beasts,' he explained as they made their way back to the car. 'Only if they feel them-selves attacked, they can be aggressive. These are young ones. One has to be more careful, obviously, with the family groups.'

However, they even managed to photograph one of these later. A huge bull rhino stood with mother and calf and obligingly let himself be photographed, but maddeningly the calf kept going behind the mother, who snorted and turned to face Tracy every time she thought she was getting a good sideways shot.

'Their necks aren't pliable, so they can't swivel them,' said Lester. 'That's why they turn to face what they consider might be danger.'

He seemed to have recovered from his ill temper completely and discussed the forthcoming book with Mr. Bryant with great interest, suggesting photographs they might try to get of the more unusual aspects of wild life, the way giraffes fight with their necks and the manner in which the hornbill imprisons its mate in their nest.

'How horrible, like being in purdah,' Tracy shud-dered.

'Very good for independent females,' said Lester with a teasing smile. 'The hornbill has found a good way to discipline them.'

The part of the reserve to which Lester had driven them seemed bushier and more remote. The open parklands had given way to low forest; small tambootie trees, their wood wrinkled like an elephant's hide, grew amongst thorn trees, and occasionally the sickly green bark of the fever tree could be seen.

For some time Tracy had been trying to get a photograph of a steenbok; one of the most lovable animals, with its dainty stance, large eyes and elliptical winglike ears, it looks as if it has stepped out of a fairytale illustration. Each time they stopped, the little animal eluded them. It would stand, ears pricked, eyes wide and curious, then, just as she thought she was going to get a perfect shot, it would turn tail and all she could see would be a fluffy white scut as it ran nimbly behind a bush.

They had just stopped again and this time Tracy really thought her efforts were going to meet with success, when Lester gave a loud exclamation that amounted to a curse. She turned around to him feeling justifiably annoyed while the dainty animal disappeared into the middle distance, but he was staring into the trees, his face set and grim.

'Stay in the car, both of you, and don't move,' he commanded.

'Why, Lester, what is it?' asked Mr. Bryant.

'Something odd going on over there. I won't be long.'

With that Lester bounded out of the truck, not worrying about the noise he made when he slammed the door. Now as Tracy strained to look through the screen of trees, she could see a truck like the one Lester had left with his African assistant. It was parked off the road and it must have been this that had attracted Lester's attention.

She watched Lester's lithe figure striding towards the truck and when he drew nearer she could hear him calling the guard by name and saying something in Zulu. Then suddenly when he was only a few yards from the vehicle, a group of figures broke away from its shelter and dashed for cover. She heard his shout, but the figures did not look back.

She saw him stoop to look at something on the ground. Was it an animal? She was too far away to be able to see. Mr. Bryant stirred on the back seat.

'I'd better go to see if I can help Lester. It looks to me as if there's trouble of some kind.'

'No, you stay here. I'll go,' said Tracy.

She did not know what to expect, but was filled with nameless dread. As she came nearer Lester saw her and shouted: 'Tracy, I'd be glad of your help if you can stand the sight of blood.'

He was bending over the African guard, the one she had seen with him in the truck. The guard was bleeding freely from an ugly head wound and seemed unconscious.

'These cursed poachers!' muttered Lester.

Glancing around, Tracy became aware of a dead buck caught in a snare. The African must have come upon the poachers while they were getting it ready for transport.

'He seems in a bad way,' said Lester, getting a first-aid box from the truck and trying to staunch the bleeding with a pad. 'Let's try to get him back into this truck and you can drive while I hold him still.'

When they explained the position to Mr. Bryant, he offered to drive their own truck and together they slowly made their way back to the camp. It was a nightmare journey for Tracy. She was not used to driving so large a vehicle and added to this was the necessity to go smoothly so that the injured man should not be jolted. Every time she made a mistake with the gears, Lester seemed to take out his bad temper on her.

'For heaven's sake, Tracy, we have a very sick man

with us, try to go carefully.'

After all the nerve-racking experience of the morning, she was ready to cry with worry and exasperation, but she drove on steadily, refusing to respond to his chiding remarks, for she knew that they were only a cloak for his desperate anxiety. When at last they arrived back at the camp, William had lost a fair quantity of blood, but fortunately James Miller had arrived to have a look at Julian and he was able to render first aid, before packing him off to the village hospital.

'If I remember correctly you have the same blood group,' he said to Lester. 'We'll take you along just in case he needs a transfusion.'

Watching them go off in the doctor's large station wagon, the back seat of which had been transformed into a bed for the injured man, Tracy felt sad and useless. The last thing she had heard Lester say to the doctor were words of self-reproach.

'If only I hadn't left him! Two of us could have dealt with the poachers. He was too rash to tackle them on his own. He was probably foolhardy because he wanted to impress me. I should have stuck to my normal duties instead of. . . .'

The rest was lost to Tracy because he was getting into the car, but she knew well enough what he meant. If she had taken his advice and insisted upon the company of a guard, there would have been no need for him to come with them and the accident need never have happened. She felt sure that Lester blamed her for the whole disastrous episode.

CHAPTER FOUR

SHORTLY afterwards Tracy received her first mail from overseas. When she saw the correspondence, she felt as if she had been away from home for a year instead of the comparatively few days she had really been absent. How far away Konrad seemed and the sedate life she led in London! She opened his letter reluctantly, not wanting to read the words of love she felt sure would be there.

But she was surprised by the contents of his letter. Certainly he wrote in a very loving manner, telling her how much he was missing her and how when she came back they must make arrangements to be married as soon as possible, but he also gave details of a scheme he had thought out in which she could help him. Trust Konrad to have an eye for business, thought Tracy.

'I have had an idea,' wrote Konrad, 'I can't think why I did not think of it sooner. Would you have time to make inquiries about buying land to build a luxury hotel near your game reserve? Africa is the "in" thing with the jet set, and the remoter places are the most popular. If I could offer luxury accommodation, very close to the reserve, and could take tourists in by mini-bus, while they lived in more five-star circumstances than they do in the game reserve camps, it would attract a wealthy type of tourist. My agents tell me that there is an estate dealer in the nearest town whom you might contact, a Mr. Vincent Pringle, who would be able to help you by telling you where land is available. Please consider doing this for me, my darling love.'

Tracy felt infinitely cut off from the world of business, but she supposed she would have to try to help Konrad. After all, he had been very patient about her wanting to come to spend three months with her father, admittedly with some initial argument. She owed it to him to do her best to find him a site for his new scheme. It would please him and make up a little for her absence. She had a feeling of guilt that she had banished the thought of Konrad to the back of her mind and felt she must do her best for him now.

Julian had received postcards from his grandparents which had been redelivered to their address. She called him from the sandy stretch of garden where he was busily absorbed in some task of his own. It seemed to consist of sitting on the ground, his fair lock of hair falling forward over his eyes, and stirring a hole in the loose earth with his index finger while chanting some rhythmic words.

'What are you doing, Julian?' she called. He looked up, his blue eyes twinkling.

'I'm finding coolie cumbers,' he replied.

'What?'

'Come and see.'

She descended the steps of the small stoep and went to investigate.

'They're easy to find,' Julian informed her authoritatively. 'You look for a tiny hole, then stir the ground and say "Coolie, coolie cumber, come out before the doctor comes!" and they do.'

Much to Tracy's astonishment in response to Julian's mystic chant, a large lion ant came out of the ground.

'Good heavens, what next?' she said.

'What next? What next?' shouted Julian, dancing

along in front of her.

He was not a troublesome child, for he seemed to be able to occupy himself for long periods with various games. This was fortunate, for she really did not have much time to devote to him. She was kept busy sorting out her father's notes and papers, getting them into some kind of order before they could begin the real task of composing the book.

Julian leaned against her, pressing his round hard head into her shoulder while she read the cards. He looked sturdy and independent in his brief blue shorts and striped T-shirt. He had fully recovered from his illness and was becoming brown already from playing around in the sunny garden, following the Zulu servant about his tasks.

'How can I give my mummy a big hug and kiss from them if she isn't here?' he asked, when she had read the final greeting on the cards. 'When is she coming, Tracy? You said she'd be here when we came.'

'Something must have delayed her, but I'm sure she'll be home soon,' Tracy assured him. It seemed very strange that after not having him here for a whole year Evangeline should be willing to leave her only child to be cared for by strangers. Except of course that she thought Lester was looking after him.

Tracy had volunteered to keep him with her and Evangeline probably did not even know this. Still, it would have been a difficult task for Lester. He had to be away in the Reserve most of the day. Julian seemed used to being left with servants and seemed pleased with any small attentions he got from Tracy. She found him a very lovable child and would miss him when his mother returned to claim him.

He was eager and willing now to help her with the

task of sorting out her father's books, though not a very expert assistant. She had made makeshift bookshelves by ordering bricks and pieces of wood shelving from the nearby town and was busy sorting and cataloguing her father's massive collection in a rough attempt at librarianship. It had puzzled her that he seemed to have so many new books, but when she asked him he had explained that his previous collection had suffered a disaster having been attacked by termites.

'I intend to be more careful in future,' he had said, though Tracy thought this did not seem very likely when she regarded the haphazard way he stored the volumes. He really had an enormous number of new technical books, which must be extremely valuable. She said as much to her father and he agreed in his vague way. She had understood her mother to say he had to live frugally because he existed on a very small pension, but the books and the fact that he had paid for her air fare belied this. Still, it was none of her business how he came to afford such a collection. Nevertheless she thought she must guard them against further depredations by the ever-present termites, as well as cockroaches and other pests.

She occupied herself the whole day going through the books and listing them. Julian slept during the long hot afternoon, but she was eager to finish her task. The sooner she accomplished all she had to do here, the sooner she could return to England and a recovery of her peace of mind. This infatuation she felt for Lester whenever she was in his company was truly ridiculous when she thought about it sensibly. All she had to do was to get away in order to banish him out of her mind, and from now on while she was here she would spend as little time as possible with him.

But at tea-time when he strode in to the house looking like some illustration of a Rudyard Kipling hero, lean, bronzed and extremely tough in his khaki uniform with the green beret, all her good resolutions seemed to vanish, and she weakly agreed to accompany himself and Julian to the hide near the small lake where they could watch the animals although they themselves would be unseen. He had promised Julian this treat some time previously and this evening seemed to hold a promise of perfect weather for their game viewing.

'Tracy must come too,' the child had insisted, so Tracy accompanied them, although she was not at all sure that Lester desired this. But he seemed quite cheerful when he handed her into the car. Perhaps on account of Julian, his moody silence seemed to have vanished this evening and he answered the boy's questions and chatter with interesting information about the various animals they might see.

He's more like the man I knew, thought Tracy wistfully; if only we could leap the barrier of the intervening years and become the people we were then! Hesitantly she asked after the game guard and was rewarded with a smile.

'He's doing fine. They're pretty tough, these guards. They have to be. There's a tremendous amount of poaching in the reserve lately, much more than usual, though heaven knows there's always been a lot. But somehow this latest batch of poaching episodes seems more organized, more connected. I suspect that it's not just being run haphazardly by stray Africans who want the game for food. It seems to me there's a master mind behind it. I've heard lately that a quantity of biltong and game has appeared on markets as far away as the

Transvaal. If someone is selling it to the city markets, they're getting high prices and almost clear profit, of course. It's worth risking a couple of fines, undoubtedly. Impala can be sold for three rand a beast plus five rand for the skin, but there's also a more undercover kind of trade in rhinos. The Africans believe there's some magic property in the animal's horn.'

'What kind of magic?' asked Tracy.

Lester smiled a little ironically. 'Well, you would hardly believe this. Certainly the rhino doesn't look an object of romance, but the Africans attribute some aphrodisiac quality to the powdered horn. Slipped into the food of a loved one, it's supposed to have the effect of making him or her return one's love.'

Tracy laughed. 'I must remember that! It seems rather a high price to pay for love. First catch your rhino, as Mrs. Beeton would have advised.'

It was late afternoon, calm and sunny. The shadows of trees were long upon the grass and the heat, which at noon had made the blue hills shimmer in a distant haze, had given way to a balmy warmth with the scent of white jasmine upon a welcome breeze. Lester braked the car quietly as they arrived at a reed-covered passage leading to the 'hide' that had been built in order to allow visitors to the reserve to observe the animals drinking.

It was midweek and no other people were there. Admonishing Julian to keep as quiet as he could, they emerged out from the passageway on to a platform built high on one side of a small natural lake or 'pan' as they called it here. There were rough benches set in the reed-covered structure and a slit at eye level to make observation easy. Lester and Julian sat on one of the benches while Tracy busied herself arranging her photographic equipment, then sat by herself on the other bench.

'Sit by us, Tracy,' commanded Julian.

'Yes, why are you so unfriendly?' Lester teased.

'Lester must be in the middle,' Julian instructed her.

So Tracy obediently sat beside Lester. In the shadowy hide, with its dusky green gloom dappled here and there by flecks of late sunlight, she felt overwhelmingly conscious of this man at her side with the dark rugged face and eyes golden as those of some creature of the wilds. His lean brown arm, covered with silky golden hairs, brushed against hers as he pointed across the water to indicate to Julian where he must watch for the animals.

At first, the only occupants of the pool were two birds, a hammerkop and a woolly-necked stork. The hammerhead, a short bird with a peculiarly wedge-shaped head, stood on one leg and seemed to gaze at himself in the water with rapt concentration.

'Do you know what the Zulus think he is saying?' asked Lester.

'Yes, George told me,' answered Julian triumphantly. 'I should have been a handsome chap, but I'm spoiled by this and this and that.'

There was a flash of green as a bird swooped over the water, looking with its bright plumage like some enamelled toy. Tracy remembered that long ago Lester had told her how the Africans interpreted its call.

'*Umtwanyana, ungendi,*' she murmured to herself, but Lester heard her.

He turned laughing towards her as he had done all those years ago.

'So you still remember the advice of the emerald cuckoo, "Young girl, don't fall in love." Have you heeded her warning, Tracy?'

Tracy was grateful to Julian at that moment for diverting Lester's attention. Now with the shadows lengthening the animals began to arrive, first a group of graceful impala, one buck and eight does with their kids. They moved around quietly until they found a place where they wished to drink and then, splaying their legs to accommodate their short necks, they slowly reached for water. The buck in gentlemanly fashion waited until his family's needs were satisfied before drinking himself.

But the zebra when they arrived on the scene were not so polite and Julian had to be restrained from laughing out loud at their circus-like appearance and antics. The wildebeest too who arrived with the zebras pushed their way in rudely, looking grotesque with their Roman-nosed profiles which made them seem too solemn to be capable of their skittish, ludicrous prancings.

Nyala bulls walked slowly and sedately, coming to quench their thirst; beautiful animals with black coats, lighter legs of golden hair and black hooves, they held themselves with stiff dignity.

'Nothing could be more different than the nyala cow,' Lester explained. 'It's a soft golden colour with lots of white stripes and butterfly-shaped ears. It's unusual to find such a contrast in the animal world, though of course I suppose when you think of it amongst humans you find very ill-matched couples.'

'Do you think people should be alike to make a success of marriage, then?' Tracy could not resist asking.

'Possibly. I haven't really given the matter much thought,' Lester said, turning towards her and smiling in the hard, amused way with which he seemed to meet any attempt she made at communication with him. 'I suppose people should seek out wives or husbands with similar interests. Certainly a sophisticated person wouldn't be happy married to someone in a profession like mine. But of course you know that from experience.'

He was referring of course to her parents. She must have looked sad, for he added immediately, 'Forgive me. I'm afraid that was tactless.'

She brushed aside his apology and plunged into an explanation that seemed to get her still more deeply involved.

'My parents couldn't have made a success of their marriage in any environment,' she said. 'In their own way they were both completely unyielding one to the other in their determination to lead the kind of life they wanted. Even my father, mild as he seems, has a fixed idea about his interests which really precludes any kind of family life.'

'You're right, and that all goes to bear out what I said. People who are entirely absorbed in their professions find it hard to lead any kind of family life unless the wife is as interested in the profession as they are. This applies particularly when somebody's work involves living in lonely places. No, Tracy, it might have suited you ten years ago, but not the new Tracy.'

'I wasn't aware that we were discussing me,' said Tracy. She was alarmed, for she wondered whether he could have sensed some of her feeling for him and was taking this opportunity to warn her off. But no, that was impossible. For a moment the reflection of the large kudu bull she had been watching wavered indistinctly in the water, its magnificent horns merging into one as she blinked the sudden tears from her eyes.

'Naturally, I'm not referring to marriage in your case,' Lester continued in an adamant tone of voice. 'I meant that if you're considering staying with your father, it would hardly be fair to yourself. If you can get his life more organized and possibly visit him at shorter intervals, that should suffice. I can't imagine that it would suit you to make your life here.'

She was silent, not knowing how to reply without betraying too much feeling, and yet saddened by his opinion of herself. Did he want her to go? It seemed a different story from his accusation of neglect of her father that he had made on that first night she was here.

She was glad of the interruption when the deep peace of the evening scene was shattered by the arrival of a troop of chacma baboons. With raucous din they jumped from the trees, squabbling and pushing each other in an endeavour to find the most advantageous place for themselves at the waterhole. They crouched down, thrusting their mouths into the welcome cool of the water, lapping greedily like cats. The huge leader sat on a log, with his legs stretched in front of him and his hands on his knees, watching the behaviour of his charges.

When they had finished drinking they were in no hurry to leave but lingered on the bank chasing each other and playing amongst the branches of the trees. The younger baboons teased the adults until they ended by getting soundly slapped. Julian was so amused that he went off into peals of laughter, but the noise of squealing and shouting from the baboons was so loud that the humans' presence was not even noticed.

A few Hadada ibis arrived and contributed to the clamour with their ear-splitting calls. They drank and bathed in the water, then sat on a nearby stump preening their bronze-blue plumage. The scene at the waterhole was constantly changing with all kinds of animals coming and going. Families of warthogs ran into the water, their tails ludicrously upright, swallowed deeply, then wallowed in the mud before running back into the bush. The first stars had begun to appear before Lester suggested moving, and then only because Julian gave an enormous yawn.

Driving back in the dusk, Tracy felt in herself a rising panic that she was letting herself become too involved, not only with the people here but with the enchantment of the place itself. In the tambootie trees fireflies moved in iridescent patterns forming threads of light against the black velvet of the tropical night, and plovers, disturbed, rose from the grass, calling clearly and melodiously. The African nightjar intoned its litany, 'Good Lord Deliver Us.' Tracy smiled as she remembered the bird's supposed prayer. Another recollection from her childhood. This nostalgia was too dangerous!

Be sensible, she admonished herself. This is no place for you now, fascinating as you may find it for a while. Remember how unhappy your mother was here. Think how calm and ordered your life could be with Konrad, how pleasant and comfortable. She glanced at the man at her side, rugged, suntanned, completely at home with the wild and its creatures. I don't want to feel like this about him, her heart cried rebelliously.

She recalled the shout of the emerald cuckoo, 'Young girl, don't fall in love,' and thought that for herself this warning was true.

CHAPTER FIVE

TRACY had spent a peaceful morning going through her father's manuscript with him. She had started typing now and he was seated at the large table doing some re-writing, his silky grey hair erect, his rimmed glasses on the end of his aquiline nose. He was completely absorbed in his task, his pencil gripped between his teeth in a childlike manner. Tracy glanced at him fondly. It was all very well for Lester to say she must not consider changing her way of life because she thought her father needed her, but she was becoming increasingly attached to him day by day, and he seemed to depend on her for so many things, help with domestic matters as well as with the book.

Little things he said made her realize that he appreciated the extra comfort that her presence here had brought to his home life, yet it was not so much the material things that mattered but their increasing affection for each other which made Tracy realize how difficult it would be to part from him when the time came.

George interrupted her meditations by coming in with a cardboard box from which issued loud indignant squeaks.

'Whatever have you got there, George?' she asked.

'*In-dlazi*,' George answered.

'A mousebird – *colius striatus*,' Mr. Bryant translated. 'Let's have a look at it.'

A fledgling, presumably fallen from its nest, the little

creature was a bundle of mouselike feathers that looked like soft fur, with two bright eyes peering from amongst them and two enormous long legs ending in claws out of all proportion to the size of its minute body.

'What an odd fascinating creature,' said Tracy. 'What are we to do with it?'

'Feed it, I suppose,' said her father resignedly, for life in the wilds had made him accustomed to these happenings. 'Julian could probably be taught to be useful with it. I warn you, fledglings claim a lot of attention.'

When Julian came he was enchanted with the new arrival and christened it Coly because Mr. Bryant said its scientific name was *colius*. Typing was forgotten and they spent the rest of the morning feeding the mouse-bird with milk and an eye lotion dropper. It seemed so hungry that eventually they decided to try a kind of patent porridge that could be mixed with water. The little bird frantically absorbed as much as he could, but at the end of his feed Tracy and Julian could not decide which one of them was splattered with the most drying porridge, themselves or Coly.

They spent the next half hour carefully washing all traces of porridge from his feathers, though they realized that in a little while the whole process would have to be gone through again. Tracy was laughing almost as hilariously as Julian and even Mr. Bryant was joining in the merriment. They were making so much noise that they did not realize that Lester had knocked at the door and, getting no response, had walked in. He had come to ask them if they would like to see the rhinos departing from the boma and being loaded on trucks to go to their new home.

'May I bring Coly?' asked Julian.

'Yes, if you like,' said Tracy, 'but bring his box along too.'

'Well, at least,' thought Tracy, as she looked in the mirror, trying to remove traces of porridge from her hair, 'he can't complain that I look too sophisticated at the moment!'

She was dressed in slacks and striped cotton sweater, her hair loose around her shoulders. The huge grey eyes looked back at her reflection, startlingly joyful and sparkling. Was that because Lester had taken the trouble to come and fetch them?

The boma was an enclosure made of sapling trees woven into a fence, strong enough to keep in the captive rhinos. But actually they were amazingly docile once enclosed. Fed and made much of by the attendant guards, they soon became reconciled to their present life. If they did not, Lester explained, especially if they refused to eat, they were returned to their wild state.

But with Lester, the rhinos had become not only docile but even affectionate. It was very amusing to see half-grown calves gambolling towards him in eager recognition. He had to be skilful at sidestepping, for it was like being charged by a small tank. They butted at him playfully, making small plaintive noises that seemed ill suited to such large animals and were rather touching, Tracy thought.

They were all so busy watching the huge animals being loaded on to the crates that were waiting for them in the trucks, that they failed to notice the arrival of a small red sports car. The first thing Tracy knew about it was when Evangeline sauntered in a leisurely way towards the group of spectators.

It was true, thought Tracy, with a sudden jolt of the heart, she was more beautiful than ever. Maturity had given her added grace and rounded the curves of her lovely body. She was tall and vibrant with flaming Titian hair, the kind of thick white magnolia skin that the sun does not affect, and her slightly almond-shaped eyes were brilliant as emeralds. With a swift glance she took in the group of people standing near to the trucks, then, singling out Lester, she walked swiftly towards him with the long-legged grace of a cheetah and placed her hands on his shoulders. Her touch was light, but the sensation in Tracy's heart was almost as if she had seen them in a passionate embrace. She saw Lester's face light up with gay recognition.

'Why, Evangeline, this is a pleasant surprise! Why didn't you phone? I would have come to meet you.'

'Lester darling, I left my car at a garage near the airport. I know how busy you always are. I wouldn't dream of taking up your time. A widow soon learns to be independent.' She gave a slight shrug and made as if to turn aside, for her lovely eyes were brimming with tears.

Julian was clinging tightly to Tracy's hand. He hung back shyly watching his mother. He was an affectionate, impulsive child and Tracy was surprised now at his diffidence.

Lester took Evangeline's arm. 'And so you came rushing straight here to see Julian. Well, here he is, as you can see, very well, safe and sound, all thanks to Tracy.'

Evangeline whirled around. 'Julian, of course! Is he here?'

Julian came from Tracy's side and walked rather slowly towards his mother.

'You took a long time to come,' he said rather accusingly. 'But you're a very pretty mummy just like I thought.'

'Isn't he charming?' asked Evangeline, laughing. 'I'm so glad I have a son who appreciates me.'

She gave him a butterfly kiss, setting him down when his embrace threatened to ruffle her hair.

'Would you like to see my mousebird?' asked Julian, and started telling her a long story about it. Released from his first shyness, he was bent upon holding her whole attention. But Tracy noticed that she was not listening to his childish chatter, but was regarding herself, Tracy, with a curious stare that was almost rude in its aloof concentration.

'So this is Tracy. No one seems to be introducing us.'

Julian was left behind and his conversation died away as Evangeline advanced towards Tracy with hands outstretched.

'I don't suppose they consider it strictly necessary. We used to meet ten years ago, didn't we?' asked Tracy, trying to sound friendly.

'Oh, my dear, it sounds like a lifetime. You were just a little girl, and I myself was very little older,' she hastened to add. 'Your looks have certainly improved, Tracy, if you don't mind my saying so. No wonder Lester told me you were attractive. Don't I recollect that you had rather a pash on him, as we used to say in those days? But there, that's a long time ago, isn't it? We mustn't remind you about things best forgotten, must we, Lester?'

Lester's attention had been momentarily diverted by one of his guards looking after the rhinos on the trucks and fortunately he had not heard this conversation, but now he came forward smiling.

'What's best forgotten, Evangeline?' he inquired.

'Ah, that can be a secret between Tracy and myself, can't it, Tracy? How charming she has grown, hasn't she, Lester? She must have had many men in her life since she used to devote her time to you and sick animals, mustn't she?'

'I suppose so,' replied Lester, rather brusquely. 'What are your plans, Evangeline? Are you taking Julian now?'

'I will have to pack his clothes,' said Tracy.

'I have a wonderful idea,' said Eve, her brilliant eyes alight. 'You, Tracy, and Lester must come to dinner with me. Julian will settle down much better with you there and I'll ask Doctor Miller if he can come too. Please come. Otherwise I'm going to be bored stiff on my first evening at home.'

Lester glanced at Tracy. 'Very well, we'll come. Is that all right with you, Tracy?'

'But, darling, you will come now, won't you? I haven't seen you for so long. I'll get Dr. Miller to call for Tracy.'

'No, Eve, you take Julian with you now. I'll bring Tracy later. I must finish trucking the rhinos before the sun sets.'

Eve gave a small grimace of disgust.

'How would you like to have rhinos for rivals?' she asked Tracy. 'I'll see you later. Come, Julian baby.'

'May I bring Coly?' asked Julian, still tightly clutching his box.

'Who, darling?' asked Evangeline vaguely.

'My mousebird. I told you all about him,' Julian replied in a slightly injured tone, thrusting the occupant of the box towards his mother's face. She gave a small shriek and pushed it away none too gently, giving a grimace of distaste.

'Good heavens, child, wherever did you get such an ugly little thing? What are you going to do with it?'

'It's my pet. I'm going to feed it and look after it until it's big.'

Tracy intervened hastily.

'Perhaps you should leave it with me, Julian, until it's learned to take food properly. You can come to see it as often as you want to.'

She was afraid the child would not be able to cope with the feeding, and it did not seem as if Evangeline would take much interest in the little creature.

Evangeline gave a sigh of relief. 'Yes, do, darling. Leave it with Tracy. She'll be able to cope with it. It's far too dirty for you to handle. Think of the mess it will make around your room.'

'I'd clean up after it,' said Julian truculently.

He looked at his mother, then, apparently not seeing any sign of relenting, he sighed and handed over the box to Tracy.

'I'll feed him before we come to dinner with your mother and you can come to see him any time you want to,' Tracy promised.

Julian's eyes brightened and he looked even more cheerful when he sat next to Eve in the bright red sports car. He was so busy inspecting the dashboard that he forgot to say good-bye to Tracy. She felt curiously reluctant to part with the child, for she had grown fond of him and become used to his company. When, with a wave of her hand, Evangeline had gone, Lester seemed eager to get back to the rhinos. 'I'll call for you at six-thirty,' he promised Tracy hastily, and, feeling a little in the way, she slowly retraced her steps to her father's home, meditating a little ironically upon the fact that none could be more sophisticated than Evangeline and yet Lester did not seem to object to this.

That evening she dressed with care, selecting a black voile dress with medieval puffed sleeves and adornment of white broderie anglaise threaded through with black ribbon. Her honey-gold hair was tied back with a bow of black chiffon. She felt she looked a little more elegant than usual, yet the dress was suitable for a country dinner. Lester seemed to approve of her choice when he called for her.

'You're looking very sweet, Tracy,' he said.

'Thank you, I'm glad.' Then to hide the joy she felt she said, 'Did you get the rhinos off safely?'

'The rhinos ... oh, yes. One day you must come with me when I go to see them loaded on to their boat. You must find life dull here after London.'

It was no use arguing with him, thought Tracy. He was quite convinced that she was bored here and that her only natural habitat was London. So what was the use of disputing it? He would never believe her if she said that she found the life here fascinating. She made up her mind to enjoy this little time with him, and sat back in her seat, gazing at the countryside while all the time painfully conscious of his vivid physical presence.

Driving out of the reserve, they came to the farmlands, acre upon rolling acre of sugar-cane lands, shimmering in the evening light of the setting sun. The homestead was set high upon a hill, built to withstand the sub-tropical heat, its white wall and wide patios sheltered by huge mango trees. Evangeline rushed out to greet them as soon as she saw the car. She had changed into an exotic culotte suit of some thin silky material in bright kingfisher colours. The trouser skirt was voluminous and yet in a subtle way the garment emphasized her lovely body.

Her manner was vibrant, vivid, very alive and yet so highly strung that it made Tracy feel slightly exhausted. No wonder Lester had felt she needed some calming influence, and yet, wondered Tracy, what would be the effect of such a personality upon a child like Julian?

Dr. James Miller rose smiling from a seat on the patio. Having evidently managed to tear himself away from the demands of his patients, he was looking very relaxed, drink in hand. The paved terrace was furnished with white wrought-iron chairs, gaily cushioned in shades of orange and yellow. Beyond this were the vivid green lawns surrounding the homestead edged by clumps of bamboo, and immediately below them a large bed of canna lilies flaunted its flowers of bright scarlet.

Although it was not particularly late, there was no sign of Julian. Tracy wondered whether he was still awake and if she dared ask to say good night to him. When he was staying with her she had always given him a little mothering before putting him to bed, reading a story or telling something about the animals that lived in the reserve. But perhaps Evangeline had put him to bed before the arrival of her guests.

'Did Julian settle in well?' Tracy asked finally when nothing had been said about him.

'Julian? Yes, Tracy dear, he's somewhere around. I told one of the servants to run his bath when he wanted it. I suppose they'll have given him his supper by now.'

'May I go to say good night?' Tracy requested.

'Certainly, my sweet,' said Eve, looking slightly surprised. 'But don't be long, will you? We're going to celebrate my return with champagne cocktails before dinner. Why, James, where are you going?' This was to Doctor Miller who had risen and come to stand near Tracy.

'I'd like to say good night to your young man too. I'll go with Tracy.'

'You know the way, then – the old nursery suite. Or if he's still in the kitchen, go through the green baize door. There's no hurry,' said Evangeline, contradicting her instructions of a few seconds earlier. 'Take your time. I have lots to talk over with Lester.'

The nursery suite and kitchen were both placed towards the back of the house which was, Tracy supposed, sensible when the servants had to be able to hear the children, but it was rather lonely and isolated when there was only one child as in this case. They found Julian kneeling beside the window of the small white room, gazing up into a clump of palm trees nearby.

'Oh, hello,' he greeted them in a rather abstracted way, 'I was just looking at some mousebirds in those palm trees. Do you think Coly will grow as big as they are?'

'I'm sure he will,' Tracy assured him.

'I would have liked to have kept him for myself,' said Julian a trifle wistfully.

'Perhaps when he's bigger, you can keep him.'

Julian shook his head. 'No. Mummy says they're a pest. What's a pest, Tracy?'

'Oh, I suppose – a nuisance. They steal fruit from orchards.'

'But that's what she said I was, a nuisance. It can't mean the same thing, Tracy. I don't steal fruit.'

'Oh, well,' Tracy replied, feeling she was getting rather involved in her explanations, 'I don't suppose she really meant it either about you or Coly. You must try to be very well-behaved for Mummy, Julian. After all, she has to get used to having a little boy around again.'

'But you'd never looked after a little boy before. You said so. And you didn't call me a nuisance and shout, "Keep quiet for heaven's sake!" '

'Hm, hm,' Doctor James coughed. 'Well, that's something that happens when little boys do too much chattering. Say good night to Tracy, now, there's a good lad, and go to sleep.'

Tracy was glad of the doctor's sturdy common sense, for she herself felt worried by Julian's remarks, but of course Evangeline was not used to having a small child around and she well knew that Julian could be very wearying with his inquiring mind that led to endless questions.

Tucked into his narrow white bed, he looked small and defenceless. His large eyes followed their progress to the door and, if it had not been for Doctor James' presence, Tracy felt sure he would have used some form of delaying tactics like a request for a drink of water, but he meekly submitted to their departure.

Doctor James took Tracy's arm and led her through a door at the back of the house into the garden. It was almost dark and there was a smell of wet grass where the gardener had been watering the lawns. From the lily pond a large frog was giving out loud resonant booming notes and somewhere in the trees a fruit bat was calling with the insistent sound of a metronome.

'You mustn't worry about the boy. He's a fine independent wee chap and he got over that attack of tonsilitis very well.'

What a nice sort of person the doctor was, thought

Tracy, a comfortable man to have around with his kindly expression and courteous manner. He asked after her father and she was able to tell him that his health seemed to have improved since she arrived.

'And no wonder. I thought your visit would do him good even from a practical point of view like taking regular meals. Half the time he forgets about eating when he's on his own. You've been a tonic to him, my dear,' said the doctor as they walked up the terrace steps, smiling together.

'Now where have you two been? They look very pleased with themselves, don't they, Lester? I thought you went to see Julian and here I find you have been flirting in the garden!' declared Evangeline. Her tone sounded amused, but Lester raised his eyebrows and seemed to study them closely. How foolish of Evangeline to insinuate that she, Tracy, could be interested in Doctor James in that way! Why, she had always thought of him as of a similar generation to her father. But coming to think of it, he was probably only about twelve years older than herself. It was his rather heavy figure that gave him a more mature appearance.

A servant in white uniform and red fez hat came in response to Evangeline's ring and handed round thin tulip-shaped glasses of champagne cocktail. Evangeline persistently kept Lester in conversation with herself while Tracy made small talk with James – but I mustn't be uncharitable, thought Tracy. After all, she hasn't seen him for a while and they must have a lot to say to each other. But she found it difficult to keep her eyes from the vivacious beauty of the other woman's face, with its smiling mouth only a few inches from Lester's as he bent his head towards her, his dark copper head a contrast to her red-blonde upswept hair.

During a pause in the conversation, above the shrilling noise of the tree frogs, came the noise of a car approaching along the drive.

'Another guest?' Lester asked Evangeline.

'Vincent Pringle said he would drop in if he had time. Have you met him yet, Tracy?'

'No,' Tracy replied, 'but I've heard of him.'

In a small community such as this it was not a startling coincidence to meet socially the man Konrad had asked her to contact, but it was fortunate. Maybe she would have an opportunity to arrange to visit him at his place of work. In any case she would be able to approach him not as a complete stranger.

'What a pity we have to spoil a perfectly good evening by meeting that rogue!' said Lester, frowning.

'Oh, Lester darling, don't be like that. We can't all be open-air types. Someone has to do business and be commercial.'

'I don't argue about that. It's just that I don't like the way he conducts his business.'

'Just because he indulges in a little sharp practice, you don't have to condemn him out of hand. After all, what business man doesn't?' asked Evangeline, putting her white hand in Lester's brown one. 'But hush, here he comes. Do be polite to him, Lester, for my sake.'

The man who was ascending the steps of the patio had blond curly hair and looked very much the well-groomed business man, more familiar to a city than a small town, but he was well tanned as if he spent plenty of time in the open, and this was emphasized by the rather expressionless china blue eyes. He was very good-looking in a suave, sophisticated way, a very different type of appearance from Lester's rugged handsomeness or the doctor's pleasant average looks.

He was the kind of man, Tracy realized when she was introduced to him, who thought himself irresistible to women. He tried to hold her attention by a meaningful gaze and, keeping her hand in his, led her to one of the swinging double seats, imploring her to tell him all about herself and informing the rest of the company that he had been wanting to meet her ever since she arrived, but that no one had previously given him the opportunity.

'So now you've met her, I hope you're grateful to me,' Evangeline responded, somewhat dryly.

'Naturally, darling. How lovely you look, my dear. Isn't she looking gorgeous, Lester? East Africa must suit you, or was it all those romantic Portuguese men who've put that shine in your eyes?'

'A little of both,' said Evangeline, signalling to the servant to bring more champagne cocktails.

Before they were summoned to dinner, Tracy found an opportunity to speak to Vincent about Konrad's desire to find land, and they made an appointment to meet a few days later. Fortunately they were out of earshot of the rest of the company, though Tracy was conscious every now and again of being the subject of Lester's rather disapproving stare. Of course he could not realize that she and Vincent were talking business. She supposed it looked to an observer as if she had very rapidly become on intimate terms with the newcomer, especially when Vincent took her hand, squeezed it and assured her in louder tones that could be heard across the patio, 'Well, that's settled then, my dear. We'll meet as soon as possible.'

'Really, Vincent, you're a quick worker,' drawled Evangeline.

Vincent preened himself, quite willing for them to

believe that he had made a date with a pretty girl in double quick time. Lester frowned grimly and even James looked a little surprised. Tracy was placed next to Vincent at dinner and she noticed that he took every opportunity to caress her, lightly touching her shoulders when he had placed her chair in position and touching her arm whenever he wished to emphasize a point in the conversation.

Her heart sank when she realized this, for it was going to be difficult to discuss business with a man of his nature. But her guilty feelings about Konrad made her eager to come to some agreement. She glanced across the table at Lester. In the glow of the candlelight he looked even more bronzed than he did in full daylight. He was laughing at something Evangeline had whispered to him, but suddenly he turned aside and looked across the wide polished table at Tracy.

Her glance was caught and held by his, and she was startled and dismayed by the sudden transformation from laughter to a kind of brooding sadness. In a flash she recalled the scene during her first night here. Could he be concealing some deep unhappiness completely alien to his normal disposition? He was talking again, smiling with lively interest at something James had said. Had it been a trick of the candlelight aided by her imagination? Looking away, she caught Vincent's glance. Her heart gave a small jolt of dismay for she felt sure he had noticed her absorbed study of Lester and his sly smile showed he was putting his own interpretation on it.

Vincent was drinking glass after glass of the excellent claret that Evangeline had had served to accompany the roast sirloin. And after dinner he accepted whisky very little diluted with a dash of soda, although everyone else refused anything further to drink. When it was time to go, Evangeline urged Lester to stay longer.

'But I was going to take Tracy home,' he demurred.

'Oh, I'm sure Tracy wouldn't object to some other escort. She gets on easy terms with people so quickly,' she added, glancing significantly at Vincent. 'We have so much to talk about. You do understand?' she explained sweetly.

'I'll take Tracy home,' declared Vincent, springing up with such alacrity that he swayed a little, but James announced firmly that Tracy had promised the pleasure of her company to him. Although this was news to Tracy, she was surprised and touched by his thoughtfulness. Obviously he had observed her look of dismay at the prospect of Vincent as an escort.

'It's been such a joy meeting you,' declared Evangeline, taking her farewell of Tracy. 'I suppose we'll see you at the yacht club dance next week. Anyway, you won't mind if I send Julian to keep you company sometimes, will you? He seems to have taken a great fancy to you.'

Tracy was glad that Eve was willing to part with Julian occasionally and assured her that he could come to her at any time. She was a rather silent companion to the doctor on the way home, but he seemed quite content, only remarking to her that Vincent never knew when to stop either with liquor or with girls and that he did not blame Lester for criticizing him – a dictum which Tracy heard with dismay, as she had already arranged to meet him in a few days' time to visit likely places for the proposed hotel. Well, she would endeavour to keep the meeting firmly on a business basis.

Mr. Bryant was still working, deeply absorbed in writing, surrounded by pictures and photographs, but she persuaded him to come and have coffee with James, and the half hour spent with her father and the doctor seemed to Tracy to be the best part of the evening.

As he was leaving, James asked Tracy rather diffidently if she would care to accompany him to the yacht club dance.

'If, meanwhile, you're asked by anyone else, I mean someone younger and more gay than an old stick-in-the-mud like me, don't hesitate to tell me. I certainly won't be offended, but it would give me great pleasure if you came with me, needless to say.'

Tracy thought how self-effacing he was. No wonder he had never married if he was so diffident, yet he was very pleasant company and with him she was sure there would be no emotional complications. Lester, of course, would be sure to be going with Eve. As for Vincent, she dreaded having to meet him again considering the bad impression she had gained of him this evening.

When she came back to the living-room, after James had gone, she poured another cup of coffee for her father and told him something about the dinner party and the people she had met there. When she said she had not cared over-much for Vincent, her father hastened to assure her that he was 'really not such a bad sort'.

'He's helped me now and again in various ways. I wouldn't like you to show too plainly that you dislike him. After all, first impressions are often erroneous, don't you agree, Tracy?'

Tracy found this surprising. Why should her father

be so eager to impress upon her that she should not snub Vincent? What possible association could her quiet scholastic father have with the brash estate agent? His blue eyes were gazing at her with an expression of uneasiness. Or on second thoughts, could it be fear?

CHAPTER SIX

THE day she was to meet Vincent, Tracy asked her father if he would mind if she took the truck to town during the afternoon. It was the only form of transport they had now, as she had sent the small hired car back almost immediately after her arrival. Mr. Bryant seemed worried about Tracy taking the truck and driving alone through the reserve, although as she thought to herself she usually did the driving anyway. However, at lunchtime she saw him wandering across to the other houses and when he came back he was beaming as if well pleased.

'I've arranged that you should go in to town with Lester,' he announced, smiling triumphantly, like a child who has done a good deed. 'He mentioned that he was going in and I asked if he would take you as you had an appointment you must keep.'

'But how will I get back?' asked Tracy, dismayed by this turn of events. Konrad had pledged her to silence until her inquiries bore some fruit, and how could she account to Lester for the fact that she was going to meet Vincent?

'You can arrange to meet Lester when you've finished whatever you have to do. I'm sure he'll accommodate himself to your plans. He's a very good-natured fellow, I've always found.'

Good-natured, no doubt, with her father, whose kindly absentminded manner brought out the best in people, Tracy thought, but not with her, of whom he never seemed to approve. However, she could not disappoint her father who seemed so pleased about his arrangements, so she changed from her slacks into a cool lime green dress, loosened her honey-gold hair from its severe ponytail and knotted it into a cool style, applied a little more make-up than usual, rose-coloured lipstick and a faintly green eye-shadow, and began to look forward to her expedition into the little town. In spite of the fact that she had not liked Vincent, it would be a pleasant change to see something of the village life and be able to step out of the car without cautiously looking around for rhinos.

Lester had changed from his uniform into a cream-coloured safari suit that emphasized the deep tan of face and limbs. He seemed in a good humour and teased her about not being able to keep away from the shops even in Zululand. He advised her to bring a swimming costume because they might be able to have a swim at the hotel pool.

It was a day of high summer. In the Reserve, the air quivered with waves of heat above the roads and the sunlight in the open glades was dazzling. The trees were beginning to look parched and shrivelled, and the feathery leaves of the thorn bushes were folded against the heat. Even the river, set between its banks of dark flat-crowned thorn trees, looked hot and sluggish.

Beyond the hills the cumulus clouds were massing in great towering fortresses and there was the sound of thunder like the guns of a distant army, but near at hand the sun blazed down from a white hot sky. In the Reserve no animals were to be seen, for they had all sought the shade. The usual bird song was absent except for an occasional gasping whistle from a bulbul.

Lester said little during the journey, but Tracy was overwhelmingly conscious of the man at her side. Any attempt at small talk seemed futile when so much had to be left unsaid. Why, why had she come here at all? Now she had met her father and become fond of him again it was going to be doubly difficult to leave him, but in the heat and dust of this sultry afternoon she felt a longing to be done with Africa for ever. Looking back on it, her ordered life in London seemed so peaceful and free of violent emotion, her feelings for Konrad so calm and controlled.

What on earth had possessed her to wish to see Lester again? He regarded her as a transient visitor. If he had any feelings towards her at all they seemed to be hostile. It was obvious to the merest onlooker that he was involved with Evangeline. So why was she so foolish as to get this heady intoxicating mixture of emotions whenever she was at his side?

He has a kind of physical magnetism, she argued with herself. That's all. It affects me because I've been unused to this tough masculine kind of man for so long. He's so close to nature all the time that one senses a primitive ruthless streak and that kind of thing appeals to most women. But surely, she admonished herself, if you're able to recognize this, you should have the common sense to fight it. It's sheer stupidity on your part to feel thrilled when you're in his company. She resolved to be sensible in future and to refuse to recognize the overwhelming attraction he held for her.

Just as she had made this admirable resolution, a brown lean hand grasped hers across the seat.

'You look so far away and serious. Are you thinking of someone in London? Whoever it is, he's a very lucky man to occasion that dreamy look.'

The topaz eyes held teasing laughter as the brown hand gave hers an affectionate squeeze and returned to the wheel. Why did he have to be at his most attractive when she had just made her stern resolve?

Lester had some business to negotiate at the bank, so she asked to be dropped near the chemist's shop. She did not want him to realize she intended to see Vincent. They arranged to meet later for tea at the hotel before driving back. Emerging from the chemist's shop after making her purchases, she glanced up the street and saw no sign of Lester, so felt free to go in to Vincent's office. When she had been ushered in, he gave her an effusive welcome, grasping her hands for too long a time and putting his arm around her as he offered her a seat.

'I had a letter from Mr. Young,' he said, 'in which he explained his requirements, but I understand that this is all very hush-hush.'

'Naturally, my ... Mr. Young wouldn't want his business discussed before it's finalized.'

Tracy had intended to say 'my employer', but Vincent, who did not miss anything, took her slip of the tongue to have another meaning. His glance wandered to her ringless hands.

'I've heard of Mr. Young, naturally. Even in this back-of-the-woods joint we know about his string of luxury hotels around the world. It would be a fine thing if we could get one here. I take it you have some influence with him? Lucky man!'

Tracy liked neither the tone of his voice nor his leering smile, but she pretended to ignore it, and repressed any further probings by rising briskly to her feet and asking if he had any available sites to show her.

'I was just going to tell you, my dear, that I think I have an ideal spot for you. I think with a little negotiation we could do a deal. Can you come with me now? It's not far away and quite a pleasant drive on a hot afternoon.'

His car was parked in the shade at the back of the building, so fortunately they did not have to go out again into the main street. Although it made her feel very underhand, Tracy did not relish the fact that she might encounter Lester while she was with Vincent. He evidently disapproved of him and Tracy hardly blamed him. But in this small town she did not know of anyone else who conducted this kind of business, and in any case Konrad had specially mentioned him.

She thought regretfully how different this drive was from the previous one. How happy she had been to be with Lester, and how uneasy she felt in this man's company. After a few miles they came to a gate which opened on to a track into ground which had the park-like aspect she had noticed in some parts of the Game Reserve. Open tracts of grass were dotted with flat-topped thorn trees and thickets of bamboo. The track climbed steadily upwards until Vincent brought the car to a halt on a high plateau. Far below the river glinted silver, curving between dark bushy banks, and on a golden stretch of sand, crocodiles sunned themselves surrounded by white egrets.

'Too hot now for sightseeing, but you do see game from the Reserve on the opposite bank, and if the place was stocked with a certain amount of impala and other buck it would give a bit of local colour. It's fairly level ground on this plateau and if the road was improved the building trucks could get up quite easily. There would be no difficulty about building materials. You could use the same construction as the huts at the Game Reserve but in a more elaborate style.'

'It seems fairly suitable,' Tracy replied cautiously.

'Is it for sale? Does a farmer own it?'

'Not a farmer, no,' said Vincent a little cagily. 'It isn't actually for sale at the moment, but I don't think I would have much difficulty in persuading my client to part with it. Would you like me to make inquiries?'

'Yes, please, I should be glad if you could do that,' Tracy answered.

She was puzzled, because by his expression he seemed to be enjoying some kind of private joke, and yet he was not a man who seemed to find many things humorous. She turned away to take a last look at the view. On the high hilltop a breeze had sprung up, cool and refreshing. It caught Tracy's thin dress, pressing it against the curves of her slender body. She gave a start of surprise as Vincent came up behind her and placed his hands around her waist, then bent his head so that his face was against hers.

'Lovely view, eh?' he asked. She tried gently to disengage herself, not wanting to make an issue of an incident that probably meant nothing to someone who was obviously used to being too familiar with women. He laughed without mirth.

'Come on,' he said. 'Surely all my trouble in bringing you here on a hot day is worth a little kiss. Konrad Young is half a world away.'

Tracy managed to disengage herself and tried to speak in cool level tones, ignoring his words.

'I would be glad if you could take me back, Mr. Pringle. I have an appointment to meet Lester at four o'clock.'

'Oh, so he's the lucky man, is he? You'd better be careful, Miss Bryant. You'll have Eve scratching your eyes out.'

'I'm merely meeting Lester to get a lift home,' Tracy

replied. 'I think we've concluded our business here, Mr. Pringle and I would be glad to get back to town as soon as possible.'

Vincent's china blue eyes were bloodshot from the heat and his face flushed. With his curly topknot of fair hair he looked like an angry bull. But recognizing Tracy's strength of will, he acquiesced to her request and slowly they made their way back to the car. He looked very hot, sulky and bad-tempered, and yet, reflected Tracy, the business side of their meeting had gone well. He was a self-opinionated man and it was evident that she had angered him deeply by repulsing his advances. When finally they were sitting in the car he made no attempt to touch her again but sat apparently in deep thought.

'All very well for you to give me the brush-off, Tracy dear,' he said finally, 'but if you have any ideas about Lester Cordell, a little offside flirtation maybe while away from Konrad Young, I would advise you to forget it.'

'I have no interest in Lester,' denied Tracy, furious that this boorish man should be probing her most secret thoughts.

'No? I'm pretty observant, Tracy darling, and I noticed the way you gazed at him the other night when you thought no one else was looking. But take a word of friendly advice from one who knows. He's after Evangeline and all that goes with her. And who am I to blame him? If I had the chance of a beautiful woman and a rich sugar farm thrown in as a bonus, I'd not scruple at what I did to get it. And he hasn't either. Take it from me.'

'What do you mean?' Tracy asked faintly.

'It was mighty convenient the way John Lockwood

was killed by poachers, just when Evangeline was getting a bit bored with him, and had started casting her eyes elsewhere. Only witness the man's best friend and some unknown poachers who've never yet been found. How do we know there ever were any poachers? They made a grand excuse to explain the man's death.'

'What you're saying is slander. Let me have a turn at giving advice and warn you not to go spreading this scandal around.'

Vincent laughed sarcastically as he started the engine and drove towards town.

'Slander, is it? In that case you would have to charge the whole district. Even Lester's friends couldn't deny that there seemed something fishy about John Lockwood's death.'

The rest of the short journey was finished in silence, but just before they parted he reverted to the subject again.

'Take my advice, Tracy. I don't wish you any harm and you're a stranger around here. What better way could there be to divert gossip from Evangeline than to pretend to make a play for you?'

Slowly and thoughtfully Tracy made her way to the hotel, a simple building by no means luxurious in aspect but with a wide verandah and a green lawn in the midst of which was a small swimming pool. She explained to the hotel manager that she was waiting for Lester and he suggested she might like a swim. There was a small changing room and making use of this she put on the gaily flowered bikini that she had packed hardly thinking she would use it.

Then she did a neat swallow-dive into the pool, feeling as if she was being cleansed not only of the heat of the sultry day, but also of the cruel implications of her conversation with Vincent. Up and down, up and down the pool she swam as if she were taking part in an Olympic race, but the words pursued her, 'Only witness the man's best friend and some unknown poachers. You'd have to charge the whole district.' And deep in her heart she remembered Lester's nightmare and the tragic plea, 'Must I take all the blame?'

But Vincent's idea that Lester was pretending to make a play for her was absurd, a wild surmise from his observation of the glance that had passed between her and Lester at the dinner party. Little did he know that Lester's attitude towards herself had been the reverse of flirtatious. How could Vincent possibly imagine that Lester might feign a romantic interest to protect Evangeline from gossip? Certainly there had been nothing of the kind so far.

'Hold on there! You *are* energetic for such a hot day! You look as if you're being pursued by the Furies.'

And there was Lester, his strong arms cleaving the water at her side. He swam as smoothly as a seal, matching his pace to hers, but the sight of him and the break in the continuity of her milling thoughts made her realize that she was utterly exhausted. She faltered in her stroke and tried to disguise from him the fact that she was trembling, but he looked with concern at her white face.

'You've done too much today, Tracy, and now you've exhausted yourself. Away you go and sit under one of those beach umbrellas. You aren't used to the heat. You'll feel fine again when you've had some strong tea and one of the cream and jam crumpets that are this hotel's pride and joy.'

He insisted on getting out of the water with her and

seizing a towel he rubbed her vigorously in an attempt to allay the fit of involuntary shivering that had afflicted her. In her confused state of mind she was highly embarrassed by this enforced intimacy, but soon the warmth of the sun had its effect and as she sat drinking tea with her head in the shade of the umbrella and her legs stretched out to the sun, she began to revive and even to feel a little more cheerful.

There was nothing but kind concern in the golden eyes with their dark water-tipped lashes turned towards her. Surely it was ridiculous to take any notice of words spoken by someone Lester himself had called a rogue. But Lester's own words, the mystery of that nightmare, weighed on her too. It was like those dark shadows of clouds she had seen that day upon the horizon together with the distant thunder threatening a storm.

As if echoing her thoughts, Lester glanced at the sky and said, 'If you're feeling better, Tracy, I think we should go. I'm afraid we might run into a storm before we arrive home.'

The small wind she had felt upon the hillside had dropped and the air was sultry and still as it had been before. The cumulus clouds were piling up dark and brassy in the vivid sky. Tracy changed quickly and came out to the car, her hair still damp and escaping from its knot into curling tendrils. Already on the dusty side-paths large splashes of rain were being absorbed as if they were falling on blotting paper, and when they were well into the Reserve the storm broke in all its fury.

The roads were awash and Lester was forced to stop the car because the landscape had become practically invisible. The electric storm was directly overhead and blinding white flashes of lightning were followed instantaneously by clashing drum rolls of thunder. Tracy was not usually nervous of storms, but this direct contact with the elements was different from sitting in Konrad's penthouse in light and warmth while watching a summer storm like a pyrotechnic display of fireworks especially staged for their entertainment. She could not restrain herself from a nervous movement when a particularly bright flash was followed by a crack of thunder that seemed directly on top of the car roof.

Lester put his arms around her and held her firmly.

'Poor Tracy, you're not used to thunderstorms, are you? Try not to think about it. Let's talk about something pleasant. Do you like dancing?'

She nodded, trying to respond to his attempt at comfort.

'Yes, we ... I ... often go to a pleasant place by the river to dine and dance.'

'I can't promise that my standard will be up to that of your London friends, Tracy, but how about coming to the yacht club dance with me next week?'

If he had asked her before her encounter with Vincent, she would have accepted joyously, for James had not tied her down to going with him and she was sure it was only his kindness of heart that had led him to offer himself as a partner, for he admitted that with his busy practice he did not have much time for social frivolities.

But now, confronted by Lester's invitation, she thought that two hours ago it would have thrilled her indescribably, but since then all her emotions about Lester had been smeared by Vincent's suggestions.

How could she accompany Lester to the dance feeling that there was the possibility that he was using her to allay the small town gossip? And Evangeline would be furious. That was another consideration. She had grown fond of Julian and did not want to be denied access to the child. Nevertheless, encircled by his arm in the close intimacy of the small car, with his smiling mouth so close to hers, she hesitated.

'The whole district will be there,' he urged, sounding a little puzzled by her lack of response. 'It will be a good opportunity for you to meet people, Tracy.'

The black thoughts in her mind said that it would also be a good opportunity to stop scandal if Lester appeared with another partner in front of the whole community.

'I'm sorry, Lester,' she answered firmly, 'I've already promised to go with someone else.'

Lester withdrew his arm and shrugged his shoulders.

'Bad luck for me. I should have realized a newcomer would be in demand. My grapevine whispered that you'd been seen with Vincent this afternoon.'

'Does that matter to you?' asked Tracy. She was hurt by his assumption that she could have any interest in a man like Vincent but too proud to deny it. After all, what had it to do with him?

'I know I haven't any right to advise you, Tracy,' said Lester, echoing her thought. 'I realize that type of man can be attractive to women and I wouldn't like to see you get involved with him. Of course he's interested in you. Newcomers to a place like this are always a novelty, particularly young attractive girls like you, but he's a bad egg and for your father's sake I would not like Vincent to cause any scandal about you. In a small place like this people can be very unkind.'

Tracy started to laugh a little hysterically. Lester regarded her with amazement. 'I seem to have appealed to your sense of humour,' he said somewhat stiffly. 'Let me in on the joke. It appears to be a good one.'

Tracy felt it was best to appear flippant rather than to burst into tears. Everyone she met seemed bent on giving her advice and warning her about something or someone. Vincent had warned her about Lester and here was Lester warning her about Vincent. She felt she had endured too much confusion for one day.

'The storm seems to have quietened, Lester,' she said. 'Could we go on?'

'Certainly,' Lester said formally. 'I told your father we wouldn't be late returning.'

Of course, thought Tracy, the afternoon in Lester's company had not been of his choosing, but due to her father's request. Well, she would take care to avoid his company in future, for she was inclined to the opinion that Vincent, hateful as he seemed, was right in thinking that Lester was intent to scotch any scandal about himself and Evangeline. Why otherwise should he have asked herself to the dance when hitherto all his interest had seemed centred upon the beautiful widow of his best friend?

CHAPTER SEVEN

DOCTOR JAMES' friendly receptionist had informed Tracy over the phone that culottes and trouser suits were very popular for informal dances at the yacht club, so she was glad she had packed one, thrusting it in at the last minute mainly because it was very light in weight and she had not expected to need any formal clothes.

Now, peering at herself in the long mirror that since her former time here had become marked with spots of mildew, she felt well pleased with the effect. Her slight tall figure looked well in the long lines of the white culotte suit with its flowing white trousers and long silver and white tunic bodice. With it she wore low-heeled thonged silver sandals, and her hair was drawn away from her face and ornamented with an antique silver clasp.

She was looking forward to meeting some new people and having an evening's relaxation from the many duties that she had undertaken to help her father produce his book, so when the phone rang her heart sank, for she thought James had been called out to a case and their pleasant expedition would have to be delayed or cancelled. But it was Evangeline's honeyed tones she heard when she lifted the receiver. 'Tracy, thank goodness you're still there!'

'Why, Eve, is something wrong?'

'It's Julian. I'm afraid he's sickening for something. He's been so restless and naughty all day. I can't do anything with him and he keeps asking for you.'

'I'm sorry, Evangeline, is he feverish?'

'He won't let me take his temperature. Really, Tracy, he's so naughty and disobedient with me lately. I think he was thoroughly spoiled while he was away from me. Not that I mean you spoiled him, Tracy darling,' Eve hastened to add, 'but you know what grandparents are like with an only grandchild.'

'Is there anything I can do? I could come to see him tomorrow morning if you like,' said Tracy, glancing at the clock and thinking that James would be here to call for her at any moment now.

'Tracy darling,' Evangeline hesitated, then spoke in a coaxing tone, 'I'm so worried about him, but I had looked forward to meeting people again after my long vacation, and I've had so little pleasure up to now. You know it's only a year since dear John died and I've only just begun to venture out again. I know you can't be terribly keen about going to the dance. After all, you must go to much more amusing affairs in London. So would it worry you terribly if I asked you to come and keep Julian company this evening? I know you wouldn't mind making a small sacrifice for him. I hate the idea of leaving him alone with the servants.'

Tracy was reluctant to disappoint James who had looked quite pleased and gay when she had informed him she would like to have him as an escort, but on the other hand she could not bear the thought of a sick and unhappy Julian being left alone, for she knew for certain in her own mind that Evangeline would never sacrifice her own pleasure for her small son.

'Very well,' she said resignedly, 'I'll make arrangements to come, Evangeline. I'll phone my partner to say I won't be coming to the dance.'

'How very sweet of you, Tracy dear. I know how

fond you are of Julian. You're the only one I would trust him with. You do understand, don't you? It really is a social duty for me to put in an appearance after all these months.'

'Yes, Evangeline, I'll come as soon as possible,' Tracy replied, a little tired of her extensive explanations.

'What a darling you are! I'm sure Lester won't mind, when he knows you can't come because you're helping Julian. He's quite devoted to the child himself. I'll explain to him when we get there. I expect he'll come in any case. There's always a dearth of men at these affairs and I know he's keen to sail in the race.'

Tracy was puzzled. Evidently Eve thought that Lester was bringing her to the dance and did not know she was promised to James. But if that was so, who was escorting Evangeline? Perhaps they had decided to avoid further scandal by seeking other partners. Anyhow, it did not concern Tracy any longer, for she had promised to care for Julian and she would have to break the news to the kindly doctor.

Just as she was about to pick up the phone again, she heard his car stop in front of the house. She ran out to meet him, her silky culottes fluttering around her.

'Why, Tracy, you look like a pretty white moth,' exclaimed James, beaming at her with his hands outstretched.

'I'm so terribly sorry, James, I've just found out I won't be able to come.'

'What's all this? Oh, no, you must be joking. You're dressed already – and looking, if I may say so, remarkably lovely.' A look of concern crossed his round face. 'Is it your father? Perhaps I can do something.'

Tracy shook her head. 'No, Evangeline just phoned

and implored me to go there to be with Julian. She says she doesn't like to leave him by himself. He's not too well and she feels she should go to the dance since it's her first social outing since she returned.'

'Julian ill? What nonsense! I called by there only this afternoon and he was as bright as a cricket.'

'But, James, I needn't tell you, surely, that children get ill very quickly.'

'Well, if you feel uneasy we'll go past Eve's house and see Julian, but in any case why didn't she phone me if she was worried? I'm not going to be done out of a dance with a charming partner so easily,' declared James stubbornly. 'I tell you what we'll do. I'll phone my nurse-receptionist from here and ask her to sit with Julian this evening. She's a kind soul and will do anything to please me,' he said with naïve pride.

When they arrived at the house, Evangeline had already left and Julian was lying peacefully in his bedroom looking at picture books with not a sign of fever. James examined him and said, 'What's the meaning of this, young fellow? I hear you wanted to claim Tracy's company when I'd already got in first and booked her for this evening.'

'It was Mummy's idea,' explained Julian. 'She said would I like Tracy to come this evening and of course I said "yes", but I didn't know she was supposed to be going to the dance too. You look fabulous, Tracy, doesn't she, Dr. James? You must go to the dance. You will be like Cinderella when she thought she wasn't going and then the fairy godmother came.'

'Well, in this case, Julian, I'll be the fairy godmother,' said Eileen, the nursing sister, whom James had phoned. 'And I'll stay with you just to make sure everything is all right with you.'

'Can you read?' asked Julian.

'I'll try,' said Eileen.

'And I'll tell you about my mousebird. It's getting almost tame enough to come home to me, isn't it, Tracy?'

'Perhaps next week,' promised Tracy.

She felt no qualms about leaving Julian in Sister Eileen's care, since it seemed that Evangeline had tried to trick her into not going to the dance. But then she had thought Lester was to be her partner and she would find out her mistake soon enough. Surely she could not object to Tracy's going with the good-natured doctor? Even if Lester and Evangeline had decided to scotch gossip by going with different part-ners it seemed the beautiful widow was too possessive to take kindly to the idea of Lester accompanying Tracy. Well, thought Tracy, Eve had little to fear from her, for she and Lester invariably seemed to be at cross purposes when in each other's company.

The Yacht Club was a pleasant modern building set high above the waters of a large reservoir that stretched, a man-made lake, for several miles bordered by reeds in which Nile geese and other wild waterfowl had made their home. Coloured lanterns were strung around the large open deck where chairs and tables were placed, and several ships' binnacles, a large wooden steering wheel, together with an old figure head, gave some local colour to the place.

It was a lovely balmy evening with a soft breeze just strong enough to cool the air and make dancing pleasant. The whole district seemed to have turned out for the occasion and there was a mixture of all ages, older people sitting at the tables and younger ones disporting themselves in energetic fashion on the dance floor.

Many of the men wore white mess jackets though the younger ones were less formal, some in white polo-necked shirts. There was considerable variety amongst the women's dress, though Tracy was relieved to see her advice had been sound and the evening culotte suit predominated.

The doctor seemed popular and was hailed and greeted by several groups with pressing invitations to join them, but rather to Tracy's surprise, for he seemed a naturally gregarious man, he led her to a small table for two.

'We'll join the others later,' he explained. 'It's not often I have the chance to be alone with a charming young woman and I must make the most of it.'

'He really is very sweet,' thought Tracy, as they ordered drinks, a Pimm's cup for her and a whisky and soda for him. 'I wonder why he's never married?'

As if in answer to her thoughts, James told her briefly, 'I never had much time for gaiety. The girl I loved at college married someone else and since then I always seem to have been far too busy to give much thought to relaxation, but sometimes, it's true, we let life slip by and wake up too late to a realization of what we've missed.'

He looked at her very affectionately with his kind brown eyes and for the first time Tracy had a small qualm of wondering whether he felt for her more than the almost fatherly interest he had so far displayed. Surely not. She admonished herself that she must not start getting stupid ideas, for life here had become complicated enough already.

Her thoughts were interrupted by the arrival of

Evangeline and Vincent. The emerald green culottes with gold-embroidered bodice, deeply plunging, enhanced Eve's Titian beauty. She looked very vibrant and sparkling as she threaded her way through the throng, laughingly greeting people she knew. But when she caught sight of Tracy, her face clouded in a quick frown and she came across to their table with her rapid panther stride.

'Tracy, you've let me down, then! I thought you were with Julian.'

Tracy felt acutely embarrassed, though really it should have been herself who was doing the accusing, but before she could reply, James, who had sprung up and was standing at Eve's side, patted her shoulder and said diplomatically, 'Ah, you young mothers, you're all alike, panicking at the slightest little cough. And all credit to you for being a careful parent, Evangeline, but I couldn't let you take my partner away so easily. I hope you'll forgive me for taking it upon myself to examine Julian. I found there was little to worry about, but I took the precaution of leaving Sister Eileen there. We left him chatting very happily to her. You know her, and I was sure you'd thank me for not spoiling Tracy's evening.'

For two seconds Eve looked as fierce as a witch who has just been handed the wrong ingredient, but almost immediately she recovered her equanimity and said smoothly, 'How kind of you, James. You shouldn't have gone to such a lot of trouble. Certainly I would never have dreamed of asking Tracy to stay with Julian if I'd known she was so set on coming to the dance. Where is Lester, by the way?'

'I've no idea. We haven't seen him. Does he intend coming?'

'Yes, certainly. He isn't so keen on dancing, but he usually takes part in the midnight race. So he didn't tell you anything of his plans?' she asked, turning to Tracy.

'No,' Tracy answered. 'Why should he?'

'Why, indeed?' answered Eve, and smiled brilliantly. 'Come, Vincent. You at least can't be accused of not liking dancing,' and she caught his arm and led him very willingly into an energetic and fiery version of the samba.

James smiled ruefully. 'I'm afraid I'm not very good at these modern dances. Would you like to come and look at the boats? I see some of the competitors are preparing for the midnight sail already.'

There was a kind of concrete quay below the club and here it looked rather odd to see formally dressed men in white mess jackets rigging their boats.

'They'll change later,' James informed her. 'Naturally they don't sail like this, but some of them are so keen that they like to get everything shipshape before enjoying the dancing. Hello there, here's the man we were just talking about. Talk of the devil, hey, Lester?'

Tracy had never seen him formally dressed before, and in the light of the ship's lanterns on the quay, his face and hair looked very dark against the white of his mess jacket, as he hoisted the jib and set the head of the mainsail into the mast track.

'Oh, hello, you two,' he hailed them. 'Ever done any sailing, Tracy? I know James here hasn't.'

'You're right there,' agreed James. 'I won't sail with you until they make a yacht with at least two funnels.'

'And you, Tracy?' He turned to her and for the first

time seemed to register her changed appearance, the gauzy white trousers and the silver tunic. 'Though I must say, you hardly looked suitably dressed for what I had in mind.'

'What was that, Lester?' asked James.

'I'm looking for a crew, because my usual man had to back down this evening. His wife is ill and everyone else is booked. What about it, Tracy? Do you know how to sail?'

'Yes, I do,' said Tracy hesitantly, looking doubtfully at James. 'But....' she glanced down at her culottes.

'Don't worry about the clothes. I'm sure someone will be able to lend you some shorts and a shirt or swim suit. And old James can spare you for a little while, can't you, James?'

'I'm not so sure about that. You'll have to ask me nicely,' said the doctor. 'If Tracy will save me the next quickstep, which is the only kind of rhythm I seem to register, I'll consent to give her to you for the race.'

It seemed Tracy had no chance to refuse. They had settled everything between them before she could say a word. In spite of herself she was delighted at the prospect of taking part in the contest. Apparently quicksteps were out of fashion, but the doctor managed to achieve one by his urgent request to the band, and Tracy thoroughly enjoyed dancing with him. In spite of his tendency to weightiness he was very light and agile on his feet and he swung her around the floor until she begged for a little respite.

'Not enjoyed anything so much for years,' he assured her. 'Thank you very much, my dear, and now you deserve some supper and a glass of champagne.' They helped themselves to the delicious smorgasbord that had been arranged on trestle tables, in an alcove. There was smoked salmon, langoustines, crayfish, and many small seafood delicacies together with all kinds of cold meats and delicious salads. The champagne was ice cold in its frosty glasses, sparkling like captured sunbeams. Tracy felt happy and released from care, almost as if she were really Cinderella as Julian had said, and she laughed gaily with James, enjoying his company that was pleasant and undemanding. But all the time at the back of her mind she was thrilled and delighted that she was to have Lester's company for part of this evening in an unexpected adventure.

'Dr. Miller,' suddenly boomed the loudspeaker. 'Dr. Miller wanted on the phone!'

James' face fell and he excused himself from the table. On his return he looked somewhat glum. 'I thought my luck couldn't hold for the whole of this delightful evening. I have to go, Tracy dear, I'm awfully sorry. Let's find Lester, shall we? I'm sure he would be delighted to look after you.'

'Oh, please, don't bother, James. I'll gladly come home now. It's quite late already.'

'No, no, I can't let you miss the race for my sake. Besides, I hope I may be able to return to see the finish.'

At this point in their argument, Lester appeared on the upper deck of the club and, before Tracy could stop James, he had explained their dilemma.

'Oh, come, Tracy, I can't lose my crew again,' Lester protested, smiling and taking her hand.

'There's a perfectly good bottle of champagne in the ice bucket there,' James informed them. 'Why not drink to the success of the race while I'm gone?'

'No, we'll toast ourselves after we have won, won't

we, Tracy? Right now I'm going to claim a dance.'

Lester swung her on to the floor to the romantic strains of an old waltz tune. To Tracy, the other dancers seemed like shadows; this man in whose arms she was enfolded seemed the only reality. They were perfectly matched, his strong whipcord physique lending itself equally well to a graceful waltz as it did to swimming or any form of physical exercise. Tracy felt she would like this dance to last for ever. Little as she thought it meant to him, she was in his arms and close enough to observe the curious darker flecks in his golden eyes, and the thick black lashes and heavy quizzically tilted brows.

'I could have danced all night,' carolled the vocalist, and Tracy agreed, but it was plain that Lester had more practical ideas, for as soon as the lovely waltz stopped, he hurried her over to borrow some suitable shorts and a T-shirt from a woman member who was of about the same build as Tracy and then gave her strict instructions to go and change and not to keep him waiting. 'We must be on the water soon if we're to make a good start.'

'Still more like Cinderella,' smiled Tracy to herself as she changed from her glamorous culottes into brief navy shorts and a white and red striped cotton sweater. Then, re-knotting her hair more severely, she hastened to join Lester at his boat. He had already got it on the slipway and was waiting his turn to float it upon the water before returning the cradle to its mooring place.

'In you get,' he commanded, and Tracy, stepping into the water, found herself being hoisted not too ceremoniously over the side. He jumped in after her and they were away, with a great flapping of sail and putting down of centreboard. Almost immediately the light breeze took their sails and they were skimming over to the deeper part of the lak where the starters were waiting ready to give the signal.

Their conversation was confined to low words of command from Lester and brief queries from Tracy, but after a few minutes she felt perfectly at home on the boat and the night was so calm that there was little else to do but hold the ropes lightly as Lester steered over the moonlit water. She was able to look around now and caught her breath at the beauty of the scene. Far back, whence they had come, the coloured lights of the clubhouse cast wavering luminous ribbons over the dark waters. But near at hand the fleet of yachts glided over the lake like lovely swans.

Tracy had often sailed during the daytime, but this was different, infinitely glamorous and exciting. In the front of the boat, Lester was a dark shadow, his craggy features barely discernible, his face only to be distinguished by the flash of his smile as he encouraged her to follow his instructions. Then they were at the starting buoy and the fleet of boats strung themselves out into a long line, manoeuvring for position as they awaited the gun. Sleepy cluckings came from the reeds on the lakeside as the echoing calls from one boat to another awakened the sleeping geese. Lester lit a match to look at his watch and in the small golden glow Tracy saw his dark face, intent and serious.

'A few seconds to go,' he whispered to her, then leaning over took her hand in his and gave it a squeeze. 'All right, Tracy?' he asked. 'Everything shipshape?'

'Aye, aye, skipper,' she responded, laughing.

He grinned and turned away, and at that moment

the gun resounded over the silver-dark waters, echoing across to the distant shore and arousing flocks of Nile geese which flew with indignant honkings in high swirling circles across the moon's path.

By skilful manoeuvring, Lester caught the breeze that had become a little stronger as they moved to the centre of the lake. He crossed the line on starboard, which gave him right of way, so soon he was able to put two of his opponents about. Almost immediately after this he went on to the port tack and Tracy, very excited, realized that now the boat was steadily gaining, nosing its way ahead of the others.

Their nearest rival was hot on their transom, but they were able to keep a half boat-length ahead. Soon, however, the opposition started to contest their lead strongly, but Lester evidently knew all the old sailing tricks. He tacked at short intervals to maintain his lead, keeping his boat between his rivals and the finishing line. Another shot rang out over the water.

'We got the gun!' shouted Lester, grinning triumphantly. 'Well done, Tracy! If only our handicap is right we'll be celebrating with that champagne just as I said.'

He turned the boat and headed it out to the upper reaches of the lake as if reluctant to return to the noisy shouting of the crowd and the blare of dance music coming from the brightly lit club. Tracy sat quietly. For once when she was with Lester, the wildly conflicting emotions had disappeared leaving her heart beautifully at rest. They skimmed over the silver path of moonlight, the only noises, the hissing spurt of small waves as the keel cleaved through the water and the occasional splash of a fish jumping.

'Where did you learn to sail?' asked Lester. 'I don't

recollect that you did any here. Of course you couldn't have done, because ten years ago the dam wasn't in existence.'

'At school,' replied Tracy. 'My mother sent me to one of those finishing places where you're supposed to be made into an accomplished young lady, and in these active times sailing is considered a sport essential even to them.'

'You surprise me. I'd imagined that all those establishments would teach you was how to find a husband.'

Tracy smiled. She was determined that on this perfect evening she would not let herself be offended by anything Lester said.

'I imagine it's considered one way to catch one, Lester.'

'I suppose so. If you make an obedient crew, then it follows you'd make a good wife. Is that the idea?'

'Well,' said Tracy, slowly considering this, 'that isn't altogether true. In a boat you have to be obedient for self-protection, otherwise you're likely to find yourself in deep water.'

'But isn't that true of marriage too?' asked Lester. 'The wife needs someone to guide her and give her good advice. Otherwise. . . .'

'That seems to me a somewhat antiquated idea of marriage,' ventured Tracy.

'Why, what's your idea, then? Don't you believe in including the word "obey" in the marriage service?'

'I believe in mutual help, companionship,' said Tracy, evading the question. 'And I believe that in this day and age people can marry but still retain their own individuality. For instance I have many friends in London who pursue their own careers when they're married and make a wonderful success of both lives.'

Lester shook his head. 'I couldn't live like that. The girl that I marry must be so much in love with me that she thinks everything I do is wonderful. Her home must be the centre of her life, not just consist of household chores that are a nuisance to her and keep her from her own interests.'

'To me that sounds very arrogant,' said Tracy. Her good resolutions not to quarrel were fading fast in the light of the present conversation.

'But then,' said Lester, placatingly, seeming to become aware that he was spoiling their sail and its peaceful atmosphere, 'our way of life is totally separated, isn't it? You couldn't be expected to lead the life that's expected of a game ranger's wife here. Why, if you go to some of the more remote reserves, a wife often spends weeks, even months, without seeing anyone but her husband and her African servants. But of course you know that. I remember how unhappy your mother was in her life here. You were just a child, but she made me deeply impressed with the fact that it was unfair to demand that a woman who had been used to big cities and was beautiful and cultured should put up with living in the bush. As a young man I vowed I would never take a wife who was unsuited to the kind of life we lead here.'

A loudhailer interrupted their conversation, calling across the lake, 'Here, you two, what are you up to? Come and celebrate your win with us. Don't be so exclusive!'

They turned about the wind caught the sail and swiftly brought them back to the clubhouse. Tracy changed quickly into her previous costume, and as she combed her hair and applied a little make-up she noticed that her cheeks were rose pink and her eyes sparkling. And yet it was stupid to have enjoyed the race so much, for it was obvious that Lester still held the same opinion of her that he had always had. And when she thought of it sensibly, perhaps he was right, and they were completely unsuited, she to his way of life and he to hers.

But, she admitted to herself, it's difficult to think sensibly when, however much we may differ, he has the power to arouse emotions in me that I've never before felt for any man I've ever met. Oh, Konrad, how can I be so unfair to you? In a few brief weeks the idea of marriage with him had faded into the background and her life in London appeared to her infinitely remote.

She had no time for further introspection as she was caught up in the noisy exuberance of the returned yachtsmen and their crews. There were hearty congratulations all round and Lester and Tracy were called up to receive a silver cup.

Make it a loving cup!' shouted one of the men, and a steward was summoned to pour champagne and stout into the silver container. 'The captain has to kiss his crew!' shouted another person, and, in front of the large crowd of onlookers, Tracy felt herself swept up into Lester's arms and very emphatically kissed. Then she was sipping the loving cup and it was being passed around from one to another.

Only afterwards did she have a chance to look around at the spectators and then she noticed that Evangeline was standing a little apart, her bright hair glowing under one of the binnacle lights, an icy expression upon her straight thin lips. As Tracy looked, the other woman caught her gaze and for a moment bitter hatred showed in her expression, but then she turned and spoke to Vincent and they began to push their way through the crowd towards herself and Lester.

Now Evangeline's expression was all sweetness and Tracy could almost have thought she had imagined the savage glimpse of her true feelings.

'Congratulations, Lester darling, and you too, Tracy dear.' She kissed Tracy and it was like being kissed by the ice maiden in the fair story. But when she kissed Lester her lips lingered as if she wished to blot out all memory of any previous embrace.

'I've hardly seen you this evening, Lester. Vincent here is very anxious to dance with Tracy. Shall we change partners? It was bad luck that James had to go, wasn't it, Tracy? Poor James, I thought you were a kind girl and would keep him company, not desert him to stay here.'

There was little Tracy could answer to this veiled barb, for Evangeline had turned and was preceding Lester to the dance floor. She was left with Vincent, who put his arms around her very promptly and led her towards the dance floor, but after a few turns, still dancing, he guided her out on to that part of the deck that was uncovered and open to the stars. The crowd had thinned now that the excitement of the race was over and they had the place to themselves.

Tracy was reluctant to be alone with Vincent, but it seemed difficult to object and her father's words came back to her, 'I wouldn't like you to show too plainly that you dislike him,' puzzling, odd statement for her father to have made, he who had as far as she knew never thought of business concerns in his whole life nor had any dealings with a man like Vincent who was obviously keen to make money and to do a little sharp dealing as Lester had said that first night she and Vincent met.

'So, little lady, you see I was right and the plot thickens,' said Vincent. He had led her to the balcony rails overlooking the moonlit water and Tracy could not help feeling it was a pity this beautiful scene was being wasted in such hateful company.

'What do you mean?'

He had retained his grasp on her and she could not keep herself from shying away as his inquisitive hands wandered over her thinly clad body.

'I mean Lester made a great play for you tonight in the most public place he could find. Clever of him to keep you out on the lake after the race had finished. Needless to say, everyone was convinced you were . . . well, you get what I mean.'

His smile was odious, at once leering and understanding. It smeared Tracy's picture of the peaceful moonlit lake by placing in front of her the vision of the gossiping suggestions of the crowd.

'Even Evangeline herself was fooled, but not me. Take it from me, Tracy, Lester is a cunning man when it comes to protecting himself from ugly rumours. If I were you I wouldn't trust him as far as you could throw him.'

'But you don't happen to be me, Vincent, and thank goodness for that,' Tracy was stung to retort. 'I should have thought you had better things to do than talk scandal about Lester.'

'Oh, certainly, darling, if you put it like that,' drawled Vincent, and to her dismay he turned her to face him, taking her into his arms and covering her face and neck with rough kisses.

'Why so stingy?' he asked as she turned her mouth

aside from his seeking lips and tried in vain to escape from his burning grasp.

Suddenly she was free and almost fell as Vincent was wrested from her. Lester had appeared like a whirl-wind and had grasped the other man by the scruff of his neck. He shook him like a terrier shaking a rat and before anyone could stop him had heaved Vincent over the balcony and dropped him into the water that was lapping at the quay a few feet below.

'Good heavens, Lester,' drawled Evangeline's voice behind them, 'there was no need for that. How could you be so foolish? Tracy is well able to protect herself, I should imagine. If not, she should not have come out here alone with him. Poor Vincent! Aren't you afraid he might drown?'

Tracy felt too numb to speak. Lester still looked be-side himself with fury and obviously was in no mood to care whether he had endangered Vincent. There were sounds of splashings down below and she saw some of the yachtsmen helping a very wet Vincent up the steps. She heard laughter and someone shouted, 'Drunk again, Vincent?' Then she heard Evangeline still talk-ing furiously to Lester.

'How could you be so foolish? Surely there's been enough talk already about you?'

Tracy saw her stride to the rail and stand beating her fists against it as she watched the scene below. Vincent had only been a few feet from the edge and could hardly have drowned, she thought, with all these people around, and yet she felt very shaken. She could not forget Lester's anger. If he was capable of losing his temper to such an extent over a comparatively minor episode, was it not possible that the rumours about his best friend's death could be ... but no, she must not think of it.

Lester's peremptory voice cut across her thoughts.

'Are you ready to go, Tracy? I promised James I would take you home if he couldn't return.'

She would have liked to refuse, but there seemed no alternative. Evangeline had turned and was giving her a glance of pure hatred.

'You certainly managed to create a stir at your first appearance in public here, didn't you, Tracy? First, you keep Lester out on the lake for hours and keep everyone waiting for the prizegiving, and thinking the worst of you, then you get involved with my partner too. Is this an example of that permissive society that we hear so much about from London?'

Tracy had no means of knowing whether Lester agreed with Evangeline's opinion of her behaviour. He bade farewell to the widow rather abruptly and taking Tracy's arm practically forced her to go along with him. She felt he was treating her like a child in disgrace. Silently she got into the car and they drove away. As they rounded a bend in the road, Tracy turned and looked back at the clubhouse. Strains of music floated across the moonlit water. She sighed, remembering how happy the evening had been until Vincent had ruined it by his boorish behaviour. But it was not her fault that Lester had created a scene.

It was like being in an enchanted forest, driving through the Game Reserve at night. Once they saw a bushbuck, majestically crossing the road, its scimitar-shaped horns silver in the moonlight, its coat like the sheen of pewter. A pair of porcupines scuttled along followed by their small family and in the car's headlights owls lifted themselves silently in light-feathered flight. When they reached her father's house, Lester halted the car, but as she made a move to get out he put out a restraining hand.

'No, wait, Tracy. I must talk to you, though I suppose you'll say it's none of my business.'

'What is it, Lester?' asked Tracy. In the moonlight his face looked paler, and a little strained. She felt a sharp pang, a puzzling bittersweet emotion, compounded of love and regret, and she remembered how she had once comforted him in her arms, though he was unaware of it.

'I quite realize that a long time has passed since we knew each other before, and that you're grown-up now and presumably able to take care of yourself, but I can't help remembering that other Tracy, the little girl whose affection was so easily aroused, who flung herself into the arms of the first young man she knew.'

Tracy's heart began to beat wildly. Could he have noticed. . . .

'I've warned you once before, but I'm venturing to warn you for a second time, Tracy, because I know how easily you used to fall in love, steer clear of Vincent. He's not your type.'

'Who is my type, Lester?'

'How should I know? Some clever bloke in London, I dare say, but definitely not Vincent. He's all out for the main chance. The only person he's capable of loving is Mr. Vincent Pringle.'

'Lester,' said Tracy gently, and she even ventured to touch his hand as it lay on the steering wheel, 'I . . . I don't even like Vincent. You needn't warn me about him.'

'Then for heaven's sake steer clear of him. I simply can't understand, if you're telling the truth, why you seem to go out of your way to attract him. Promise me you'll try not to see him again.'

Tracy withdrew her hand. 'I can't promise you that, Lester.'

'And why not? For your father's sake if not for your own you should avoid the man.'

Tracy was very tempted to tell Lester that her association with Vincent was purely a matter of business. She felt if he knew that fact it would clear up all his suspicions and doubt. After all, Lester would be interested in a scheme to enable more people to see his beloved Reserve. He might even be able to give her help and advice on the matter. But Konrad in his letters had pledged her to silence. It was not her secret and therefore she must not reveal it until she had permission from him.

She looked regretfully at Lester's expression, dark and saturnine in the moonlight.

'I'm sorry, Lester, as you said before it's my own business whether I see Vincent again or not.'

Lester gave an angry exclamation.

'And it's my business to stop you making a fool of yourself with him. I realize he has a certain fascination for women, but have you thought how it would hurt your father to realize that you were becoming involved with a man like Pringle?'

'Strangely enough, he seems to have a liking for Vincent. Perhaps he's less hasty or more charitable than you.'

'You can't be serious. I know your father too well. Mr. Bryant could never like a rat like that.'

Had he but known it his disbelief echoed Tracy's own incredulity when her father had first asked her to treat Vincent well. Suddenly she felt utterly weary of the whole business. She could stand no more discussion and stepping out of the car started to walk hurriedly towards the door of the house. But he came up behind her and forced her to stop, saying, 'Why are you leaving me so abruptly?'

'Because it's useless to argue with you, Lester, if you're not prepared to believe anything I say. We'd better say good night. Thank you for bringing me home.'

The cool words died on her lips as he drew her into his arms. Then he was bruising her lips with angry, passionate kisses. A million stars seemed to spin dizzily around her head. Suddenly he released her so abruptly that she stumbled.

'You really are the most infuriating woman I've ever come across, Tracy, obstinate as the devil! I suppose it's your stupid ideas about independence and equal rights and all that trash that forbids you to promise such a simple thing as not seeing Vincent Pringle again.'

'Yes, it is!' exclaimed Tracy furiously. 'By what right do you think you can rule my life? What on earth has it got to do with you what company I keep? I'll choose my own friends without asking your advice. And as for you, Lester – why, you're just as much a philanderer as Vincent Pringle!'

And before he could reply, she had fled into the house.

CHAPTER EIGHT

TRACY had written to Konrad about the land that Vincent had offered, but so far she had had no reply from him, for there had hardly been time. She felt she should get more definite information from Vincent, because he had been rather vague about the ownership of the ground, but in spite of her verbal defiance of Lester's edicts, she felt unwilling to meet Vincent again.

So she put it off, saying to herself that she must wait to hear from Konrad about his plans, and in the meanwhile she busied herself preparing her father's manuscript, typing this as well as developing photographs with him and arranging his extensive library of books.

His photographic equipment was remarkably modern and of the most expensive type and again she wondered how he managed to buy such costly things, but on second thoughts of course he had not had a family to support for years and his living costs were low. Goodness knows he lives frugally enough otherwise, she thought.

She had one letter, however, which solved a problem which had puzzled her but gave her cause for sadness. Her mother was evidently a little alarmed at her enthusiasm for the reserve as evinced in her letters home and warned her against any thought of making her life there.

'Though I realize I'm being silly, Tracy dear, it's unbelievable that you could really take to life in the wilds after all these years of civilization. Perhaps I was wrong to keep you separated from anything to do with your father, for now I am afraid the novelty of the life has attracted you afresh. But I thought it best at the time to keep his correspondence with you to the minimum, so I'm afraid I didn't always show you his letters. Forgive me, Tracy, but I was only thinking of your own good, and it's all a long time ago.'

So that was what had happened! That was why Lester had accused her of not replying to her father's letters. But most of the time she had never received them, and as she had said to Lester, a child is easily discouraged from writing. Knowing the way her mother's mind worked, she realized that she would think her actions justifiable when it came to protecting her only child from too much involvement in the life that she herself had abandoned because she hated it. Tracy could not feel angry about it, only immensely sad for all the wasted years when she had believed her father was uninterested in her existence.

This morning Julian had arrived early. Evangeline often sent him over and they were giving the mousebird a meal of fruit before Tracy started her work on the book. Coly had long since abandoned his diet of porridge. The odd-looking little creature had developed from a scrawny fledgling all feet and beak to a bird with a body covered with mouse-coloured fluff almost like fur, a long tail, and two bright inquiring intelligent eyes set beneath a rather comical topknot.

Tracy would never have believed a bird could be so attractive and lovable. She left him completely free and now he even flew into the bushes in the garden sometimes, and yet always came back to the house eventually. It was only at night that she kept him in a cage in case he fell victim to marauding cats from the compound when sleeping.

The golden pawpaws hanging from their thin-stemmed supporting trees were at the mercy of Coly, but he defiantly kept away all other trespassers. Tracy was afraid he would get injured, for he did not seem to know what fear was and attacked bigger birds than himself with reckless courage, coming back to tell her all about it in a twittering language of his own. Julian had resigned himself to the fact that his mother would never allow him to keep the bird and was happy to play with Coly on his frequent visits to Tracy.

Just as she had finished preparing the bird's food, and leaving it to Julian to complete the task, was about to start work on the book, her father came in from his morning stroll. He looked much more healthy because since she came he was getting regular meals, but there was still a fragile look about the thin tall old man with the silky tuft of white hair.

'Ah, Tracy, my dear,' he said, 'I've been talking to Lester about this Wilderness Trail.'

'What Wilderness Trail is that, Papa?' asked Tracy. He often thought he had told her about things when really he had merely pondered over them in his own mind.

'Didn't I tell you? That was very remiss of me, but I'm sure you'll agree it's a good idea. I'm proposing that you and I should go on a Wilderness Trail – that is, we'll go walking into the heart of the reserve away from the roads and the tourist area. That way we will see much more of the animals in their natural habitat and we should be able to get superb photographs.'

'And was Lester agreeable to our going?' asked Tracy, thinking of the restrictions he usually seemed to put on their activities.

'Yes, yes, quite agreeable. Naturally we will take a couple of Africans with us, but we'll be very glad of Lester's company, won't we?'

'What?' asked Tracy. 'Do you mean he's coming with us?'

'Yes. Very good of him, I must say. He said he has wanted to do this particular trail for some time as he wondered whether he could pick up any clues about the poachers. He suspects they've been operating in that area.'

'But if that's so, isn't it unsafe for us to go there?'

The old man shook his head emphatically.

'No, no, even if they're around they'll be much more afraid of being seen by us than we will be by them, specially in Lester's company.'

'I suppose it will be all right if you're really keen to go,' Tracy said slowly.

Her father was looking so pleased at the prospect of the excursion, and she herself was very interested to take part in it too, but the expectation of the two to three days in Lester's company filled her with dread. And yet in spite of her hesitation, she would feel much safer if he were there. She tried to drag her thoughts down to practical matters and went to the pantry to inspect her supply of tinned food.

She left her father to make their arrangements with Lester, knowing that in spite of the old man's vagueness she could rely on Lester to give him the requisite instructions. She had not seen him again since the disastrous night of the dance, though in spite of herself she had thought about him often enough. But now, if she had to go on this wilderness trail, she made up her mind she would be polite but cool and have as little to do with him as possible. How she was going to do this when she was never to leave his company by day or night she did not know, but she made her firm resolutions nevertheless.

In spite of her doubts, however, when at last they started upon the expedition, Tracy could feel nothing but excitement at the prospect of the next three days. Dawn was just breaking when the truck left them after they had unloaded their equipment. Before them lay the wilderness, hundreds of bush-covered hills intersected by dark valleys where the curving river was covered by cottony sheets of mist.

Lester distributed their packs according to his estimate of his company's capabilities, giving comparatively light loads to Mr. Bryant and Tracy and heavier burdens to the two African guides and himself. They had food for three days and sleeping bags but no tents and they had cut their baggage down to basic necessities. As they waved farewell to the truck-driver, the dark distant hills took on a shade of deep rose and there was a damp early morning smell of growing things. A fragrance like lemon verbena arose from the ground as they crushed the leaves of the umsuzane bush underfoot. Clamorous bird song assailed their ears on every side. From deep in the bush the brown robin whistled clear and loud and the clanging cry of the drongo shrike was like the sound of a squeaky wheelbarrow.

Tracy had had no chance of carrying out her intention of being polite but cool to Lester. It is difficult to be cool to anyone who is helping you with your haversack and adjusting straps, especially if he is bending his face close to yours as he does so. Tracy tried to look stern as she thanked him, but his ready smile and the intoxicating atmosphere of her present surroundings made it

very difficult to be cold and forbidding. She found it
hard to meet his quizzical gaze and was glad when he
took the lead leaving herself and her father to follow
and the Africans to bring up the rear.

They walked in the direction of the valley, walking
silently along a track still damp with dew. On either
side of them there were furtive rustlings and once a
small grey duiker rushed across their path before fleeing
with plunging, leaping run into the nearby bush and
quickly vanishing from sight.

By eight o'clock the sun was hot and they were glad
when their path led into the thin shade of an acacia
forest. Between the trees a herd of zebra grazed like live
rocking horses and Tracy was able to get some good
shots of these fat little animals with their sleek striped
coats. As usual there were several wildebeeste keeping
them company and she got near enough to these to take
a picture of their noble Roman noses before they scam-
pered away, kicking up their heels and showing their
backs that were so small and at variance with their
large frontal appearance.

Lester was helpful. It was as if the furious man in the
moonlight had never existed. But of course he was being like this for her father's sake, thought Tracy. By
noon, after a successful morning's photography, they
were glad to stop for a cold snack and a rest under the
trees, though Lester was careful to post one of the
guides to keep watch.

'Best to do so, even during the day,' he told them.
'Though if they're wise most of the animals will be
resting too.'

Mr. Bryant chose some shade a little apart from
them. Tracy glanced over at him, feeling a little
worried.

'Do you think my father is standing up all right to the walking?' she asked Lester, who had come and cast himself down by her side, flinging his slouch hat to one side and running his fingers through his dark chestnut hair.

'He seems to be standing up to it remarkably well so far,' he replied. 'If you notice he's tiring, just tell me and we'll slacken the pace. No need to make it a marathon, is there?'

No, thought Tracy, there was no need to race. In this luminous landscape, quivering with beauty in the noonday heat, time seemed to stand still. There was a peace here that she had never found during her life in the city. Near at hand she could hear the constant chirping of insects in the grass, and deep in the bush a grey dove boasted to anyone who was awake in this heat, '*Sikidi, sikula, sikidi, sikula,*' 'I am a great one.' But a wood pigeon answered forlornly, singing her mournful lament on waves of shimmering air, 'My mother is dead, my father is dead, all my children are dead, and so my heart goes doo-doo-doo-doo.'

Above the trees the African sun blazed high in a dazzle of yellow-white. She closed her eyes and must have dozed for a while, and when she woke Lester was lying upon his elbows, his golden eyes studying her face. She felt herself flush, not only with the heat. His eyes were brooding and melancholy, but when he met her glance he smiled and turned aside the emotion-fraught moment by saying, 'I was wondering when you were going to wake. It's time we moved on now if we're to reach the plain before sunset.'

They had been walking on a flat plateau of land thickly wooded, but now began to descend to the plain below. Even from this distance they could see it was thickly populated with game.

'This must be like the whole of Africa used to be,' Tracy said to her father, 'a land of golden plains crowded with fabulous animals.'

Lester overheard her and gave her a rather surprised glance.

'How strange that you should say that, Tracy. I've often thought the same thing myself. What sins those first white hunters committed when they shot out the game just for the fun of the thing and not from necessity.'

'Of course,' said Tom Bryant, 'I suppose you both realize that a hundred years ago this was the royal hunting ground of Shaka, the Zulu king, than whom there's never been any tyrant more terrible. The young men of his court used to have to tackle ferocious animals barehanded just to prove themselves.'

'Yes, it's true,' said Lester. 'He was everything you say, but give him his due, he organized the Zulu nation into a first-class power that once defied, successfully, the might of Victoria's British army.'

Suddenly the African guides exclaimed together excitedly in their own language. Lester joined in, then went to examine some trees further ahead. There was every sign that this part of the bush had been visited by black rhinos. Branches were bare of leaves and small thorn bushes had been uprooted.

'They've visited here fairly recently,' Lester said. 'Perhaps if we got to the small waterhole near at hand we might see them.'

When they found it, it seemed a very small waterhole to Tracy and she did not feel by any means as safe as when she had watched the animals in the hide with Lester and Julian. She started to set up her camera and they crouched behind a rather inadequate bush while the African guides went stealthily to investigate.

Suddenly there were loud shouts from the Africans on the other side of the pool. '*Ubejane*!' – 'Black rhino!' and at the same time Tracy could see they were making frantic gesticulations at the bush immediately behind their hiding place. The rhinos had appeared in exactly the opposite place to that which they had expected.

'Run!' shouted Lester, and they seized the camera equipment and splashed through the muddy shallow pool, not even daring to take a backward glance. When they had reached the bushes on the other side, Lester gestured to them to stop, and said calmly to a very breathless Tracy, 'You can take photographs now. We're downwind and they don't know we're here.'

With a crackling of twigs, the rhinos broke cover out of the bushes and trotted towards the edge of the water. Tracy's hands trembled as she held the camera, but with a great effort of will she managed to hold it steadily enough to photograph the weird beasts. Not as big as the white rhino, nevertheless they appeared colossal to a person on foot not elevated by the superior height of a car. Their parrot-like upper lips were entirely different from the square mouth of the white rhino, but the horn looked just as threatening between those small malevolent eyes. Although she was getting some wonderful shots, Tracy was not sorry when the three animals took to the bush again on the other side of the water.

'Good work, Tracy,' said Lester approvingly as they ventured to raise themselves from their cramped positions.

Her father added his words of praise, 'I'm proud of

you, my dear.'

'Well, you needn't be,' said Tracy. 'My legs were trembling all the time I was doing it.'

She expected Lester to smile a little scornfully, but instead he said, 'And whose wouldn't? Take it from me, Tracy, a black rhino is a very excitable, bad-tempered beast, and if you've ever seen a rhino charge you'd never forget it. It's the very epitome of hatred.'

Gradually the land became more level and the thicker bush gave way to parklike surroundings with more open grassland. Here herds of animals were grazing like ordinary domestic cattle, but when they came closer, they could identify zebra, wildebeeste and in the far distance a huge group of buffalo. Tracy looked at them through the glasses and could see the shaggy coats and fierce domed heads with their large horns.

It was strange how when she was with Lester she felt completely free from fear, secure in the knowledge that if he felt there was any danger in approaching the animals he would be the first to think of their protection. Wild animals seemed completely unpredictable to most people, but it was as if knowledge of their habits was ingrained in his very being.

They took cover behind a ridiculously small bush to watch some white rhinos who were grazing peacefully. There were three mothers with their young, almost, thought Tracy, like some afternoon tea party, a social gathering. Some slight noise must have warned one of the cows, for she lifted her head and gazed in the direction of the bush. At that a dark bird perched upon her back uttered a shrill note of warning, and immediately the rhinos formed a circle, facing outwards in three directions. A small calf tried curiously to approach nearer to the bush but was quickly nudged back by his anxious mother. Then suddenly all taking fright they tossed their heads and dashed away.

'They're more scared than I am,' Tracy whispered, amazed. 'That makes me feel much better!'

Lester grinned. 'What did I tell you? They're timid beasts. It's only if they're attacked that they can turn nasty. They have a completely different temperament from the black rhino, which is a good thing when you consider their size.'

Well before sunset Lester chose a camping place where they could stay for the night. It was near to the river in a grove of wild fig trees that had their roots splayed over boulders, brought down by these waters in ages past. Tracy bathed in the shallow running water of a pool that was completely enclosed by rocks, because Lester had expressly forbidden a venture into the deeper river although after the long day's walk it looked very tempting.

'As you would to a crocodile,' smiled Lester, shaking his head when she remonstrated.

'I'd forgotten about them,' Tracy confessed.

'But I hadn't,' said Lester. 'There's always the risk of them in these rivers.'

As she splashed in the water that was now pink and gold with the colours of the sunset, she contemplated her own state of mind. 'I'm happy, happy, happy!' she told herself. And when she came to the fireside in the dusk of evening something of her feelings must have shown in her face, for her father said, 'You look very pleased with life, Tracy.'

'I am, Papa, I'm loving this. I never realized it would be so wonderful.'

Lester, supervising the Africans' preparation of the

stew, heard her. His dark gaze across the glow of the
fire was surprised and quizzical. 'I hope you'll still be
saying that, Tracy, by the time we've finished. I must
confess I was a little worried in case you should be unfit
for a trail as strenuous as this one.'

'She's fit enough,' smiled Tom Bryant. 'I'm proud of
my city-bred daughter.' Then he sighed. 'I'm afraid
the boot's on the other foot. It's I who am finding it a
bit hard to take.'

Tracy turned to him anxiously.

'Are you very tired, Papa? Don't you feel well?'

'Don't worry about me. It's stupid old Anno Domini
catching up with me. I'm not as young as I was and I'm
only just beginning to realize the fact. I'll be all right
after a night's rest.'

Soon after supper Tracy and her father retired to
their sleeping bags placed well inside the light of the
fire. Beyond the encircling glow, the darkness was alive
with noise, shrill singing of crickets, calling of birds,
punctuated by more sinister noises, the sound of genets
growling and spitting like cats, the cackling of a hyena,
the mournful distant howl of a jackal, the alarmed yelp
of a baboon.

Every time Tracy opened her eyes from her snatched
attempts at sleep, she saw Lester, sitting beside the fire,
his features dark and silhouetted against its rosy glow.
So that was why he had rested in the noonday heat. It
was because he did not intend to sleep through the
night. He was protecting their camp in the same way
that primitive man had looked after his family millions
of years ago, guarding them against the dangers that
lurked in darkness. What a long way she seemed to
have journeyed from that other Tracy, the one who had
dreamed of a safe, comfortable life with Konrad, the

little house in Chelsea, the small dinner parties!

She looked up at the sky where a million stars swept across the great deep blue bowl of night. There was the Southern Cross with its two pointer stars. Tomorrow she must remember to ask Lester about the other constellations, but now, with the knowledge that he was there watching over them, she slept.

Next morning, emerging a little stiffly from his sleeping bag, Tracy's father confessed that he still felt very exhausted.

'I've decided I can't be a drag on the expedition,' he informed Tracy, and when she said that they would all turn back he very vigorously denied the necessity of this.

'I'm very anxious you should do this trail,' he told her. 'I know you're enjoying it, but you mustn't think my motives are purely unselfish. It's essential for my book that you should get as many photographs as possible and I'm quite sure you'll get more opportunities to take good ones the deeper you penetrate into the wilds.'

'But we can't leave you alone,' Tracy protested. She was appalled at the idea of continuing the expedition on her own with Lester.

'I won't be alone. I'll take one of the guides and we'll make our way slowly back to the road. Lester has a radio set with him and can easily send a message and get a truck to pick me up at the nearest point.'

As Tracy had expected, Lester protested over her father's decision. She was quite sure he was as reluctant as she was that they should continue the journey in each other's company. But he was overruled by Mr. Bryant.

'I'm trusting you with my dearest possession,' he

joked with Lester. 'See that you look after her well.'

Tracy made one last attempt to get herself out of this predicament.

'Papa,' she said when they were alone, 'don't you think it's a little unconventional for me to go on alone with Lester?'

To her surprise, her father seemed a little nettled at her question, but quickly recovered his good humour and assured her, 'You don't realize what a good chap Lester is. I'd stake my life on his honour and integrity. Good heavens, you don't think I would leave you with him if I didn't trust him implicitly, do you?'

'No, Papa, I realize you do think a lot of him, but. . . .'

But how am I going to keep up a front of coolness and indifference when I'm all alone with him? she thought to herself with desperation.

Next morning from the river she walked with her father until she could see an open view of the plain. Then she stood watching his fragile figure and that of the stalwart guide gradually growing smaller and smaller until they faded away into the distance. She was so pensive that she did not even hear Lester's footsteps coming along the path and turned with a start when aware of the crackling of twigs near at hand.

'Come, Tracy,' said Lester, 'we must be on our way. It's unfortunate it's happened this way, but your father was most adamant about our continuing the trail.'

She turned without a word and followed him. When they got back to the camping place, she found that everything had been neatly packed and that they were in fact ready to go.

'Just a word of warning, before we start off again,'

said Lester. Here we go again, Tracy thought rebelliously. Now we're alone, he's sure to put lots of restrictions on me.

'Your father left you in my care, so please oblige me by not wandering away as you did just now. I realize you wanted to take leave of your father, but it was highly dangerous to go, knowing that you would have to come back through thick bush on your own.'

'Very well,' said Tracy. 'I promise I won't go so far away again.' She felt she must keep the peace for her father's sake since so much depended on her getting good photographs on this expedition. 'But Lester,' she added, 'I'll have to go off by myself occasionally, you must admit.'

'Then don't go far, and tell us which way you're going,' Lester insisted.

Her companion's sternness could not dampen Tracy's spirits on that radiant morning as they walked beside the rippling eddies of the sparkling river with its stretches of silver sand. A kingfisher with vivid feathers quartered the water, hovering for a few seconds, beating its wings swiftly until it saw a fish, then hurtling itself like a bullet into the water, and terrapins, small water tortoises, swam hurriedly downstream, their small heads raised above the waves.

Suddenly the guide who was walking ahead gave an exclamation of surprise and gestured to Lester to come quickly. Tracy, stumbling behind in the soft sand of the river bank, was surprised by their sudden excitement. But when she arrived at the spot where they stood and looked at the sand, even to a city dweller the story in the sand was plain to interpret. There were the deep pug-marks of a family of lions, three full-grown ones and the smaller more delicate flowerlike prints of a family of cubs.

'But when were they here?' asked Tracy, quite breathless with excitement.

'Probably early this morning.'

'If only we'd seen them!'

'We may do so yet,' promised Lester.

At midday when they sought the shade, William, the guide, brewed tea and Lester took his rest. But Tracy found she could not relax. She glanced across to where Lester lay, his thin shirt rising and falling with the steady rhythm of his breath. When William noiselessly came back from some private excursion of his own and stood at her side she saw that his eyes gleamed with unaccustomed excitement.

'I have found the trees near the river where the lions are,' he informed her.

'What are they doing?' asked Tracy.

'They are on the other side of the river. They sleep quietly like the master here.'

'Could you take me near enough to see them?' asked Tracy.

William looked doubtfully at the sleeping form of his master.

'The *bas inkulu* would not like it, *kosazana*. We must wake him before you go.'

'No, he needs the rest. Let's go to see them. I won't go near them, just look at them across the river. I can take photographs from far away. My camera makes big pictures.'

It was her way of explaining to him that she had a telephoto lens. William still looked doubtful, but finally yielded to her persuasion. The fact was that he was proud of the lions in the Reserve and wanted to show them off. As Lester had explained to Tracy, the return of the lions to Zululand was a fascinating story. Within living memory no lions had been heard of in this part of the world, until some years ago a lone male lion had made the long journey from Mozambique territory, eluding would-be captors and hiding up in the bush at night until at last it found refuge in the Reserve. Later it was joined by a lioness, who must have journeyed in the same way, and over several years the pride increased. But still the Zulu guides admired most the old lion, the one who came first, and they referred to him affectionately as '*Lendoda yakhile*' meaning 'that man of ours'. Now William's desire to show him to the *Kosanza* overrode his normal caution and he led her quietly along the path back to the river.

Through the telephoto lens, the animals looked startlingly near, but as he had said, they were on the other bank of the river, peacefully drowsing under a tree, the sandy gold of their pelts blending perfectly with the dry golden grass, the brownish stones and the sandy soil. The Old Man was sleeping, stretched out in a relaxed abandon, and one lioness drowsed like a sleepy cat, but the other played sleepily and gently with her cubs, patting them back to obedience when they became too boisterous.

Tracy was able to photograph them and get what her father called sentimental poses and they were about to turn back when suddenly the peace of the hot somnolent afternoon was broken by the sound of a rifle shot. As a host of blue starlings rose shouting shrill disapproval from the trees nearby, the lions vanished into the bush as if they had never existed, but Tracy was able to get a magnificent shot of the old man standing in silhouette against the sky before they disappeared.

William watched her impatiently. He was afraid the

noise would have aroused Lester and he would get into trouble.

'Quick, *kosazana*, we must go back,' he whispered, and they hurried along the path. So enthralled had Tracy been with the spectacle of the lions that she had not given a thought to what Lester's reaction would be if he woke and found she had gone off on her own. Now her steps lagged. With his alert faculties he could not fail to have wakened at the sound of gunfire and he would be furious with her when he knew she had gone to see the lions even though she had been accompanied by William. She tried to steel herself to face his anger, but an icy dread made her tremble even in the afternoon's heat.

Now she looked up and saw him standing framed by the trees at the end of the path. She saw him before he was aware of their presence and his expression was everything that she had expected, dark and frowning. Then he caught sight of them and in a few strides he had reached her. His tall spare form was shadowing her path, towering over her, blocking out the sunlight. And then she was in his arms, but it was difficult to tell whether he intended to embrace her or shake her. There seemed to be a little of both, but she was only overwhelmingly conscious of the frantic drumming of his heart beneath the thin stuff of his bushjacket.

'Tracy, thank God you're here! I heard a shot ... for a moment I thought. . . .'

She smiled up into his face, thankful and happy that he did not seem angry.

'I'm truly sorry, Lester. I persuaded William to take me to photograph the lions. We came back when we heard the shots.'

'What?' Lester released her and stood for a few mo-

ments gazing at her with those frowning golden eyes
and apparently struggling for composure. 'Good lord,
Tracy, do you like to provoke me on purpose? Your
father left you in my care and I'm going to see that I
keep my word to him even if I have to chain you to my
side. And as for William. . . .' he looked around for him,
but the African had very wisely disappeared.

'William!' he bellowed, and Tracy thought that if
there were any poachers in the vicinity they would not
stay long if they heard that voice. William appeared
sheepishly from where he had been making a pretence
of collecting wood for the fire. Lester spoke rapidly in
Zulu, but as far as Tracy could tell he did not seem to
be very angry with William. She apparently was the
one who was considered the culprit. They seemed to be
having a consultation about the gunfire, then Lester
turned to her.

'William is anxious to find the poachers, but I've
forbidden him to try. It would be madness to attempt
it, especially as we have you in our care.'

Again Tracy felt that she was a burden to him. Oh,
why had she let her father persuade her to stay with
Lester? She was beginning to wish she had gone back
with him and she felt sure Lester felt the same way.

'What do you intend to do about it?' she asked.

'I'll radio the camp and tell them poachers are in
this vicinity and that they should send people to investigate, but I'm afraid they'll be too late. By the time
they can get here, the poachers will be gone. However,
at least it gives us some idea where they're operating at
present.'

'Lester, I know you want to do this yourself. Please
don't consider me.'

But Lester shook his head. He had given his word to

her father and as far as he was concerned that was final. He would not take any unnecessary risks while she was here.

'But suppose we come upon them by chance?' she persisted. 'What then?'

Lester looked grim. 'I have my gun with me. If we come across them by chance, it's going to be unfortunate . . . for them.'

The sun was reaching towards the horizon when they set off again on their path through the wilderness. In the reeds weaverbirds were coming back to their nests that were like small baskets hanging over the water. A paradise flycatcher with long tail flashed in and out of a mimosa bush like a small red flame, shouting *'Swei! Swei-aaah!'* Lester pointed out its nest that was shaped like a wineglass in the fork of a twig. It looked like a small clump of fine driftwood that had been deposited there by the river. In a deep pool they saw a diving anhinga or snake bird, cruising slowly under the surface of the water, its wings held streamlined at its sides, its snake-like neck propelling its head forward in a hunt for its fishy prey.

It was almost dusk when they finally made camp, and Lester insisted that she should rest while he and William prepared the fire and the meal. When she had bathed, she sat quietly watching the pearl-breasted swallows wheel in flashing blue flight against the darkness of the bush. The air seemed spangled with glittering wings and she asked Lester what they were hunting.

'Have you forgotten? Of course it's a long time since you saw them. Don't you remember the termite ants?'

Of course, the beautiful silver wings belonged to the

termites which spent their lives in the dark earth, only emerging for this, their nuptial flight. For only a few minutes they were transformed into swift airborne creatures and in that short time they were the prey of birds, lizards and bats. Finally dropping their wings, they sank to the ground and frantically, blindly, searched for a mate before the dark earth claimed them again.

'Poor blind creatures,' said Lester. 'It happens in life too. Man soars after his dreams only to be dragged down by commonplace physical appetites.'

She wondered if he was thinking of Evangeline. Did he rebel against the physical attraction he felt for her and had he fallen in love when she still belonged to John?

When darkness came she was painfully aware of the fact that they were alone, deprived of the gentle restraint her father's presence imposed. William had long since retired to his place of rest, but she sat on, reluctant to leave the comforting glow of the fire and the reassurance his presence gave her against the eerie noises of the night. What was Lester thinking of? In the glow of the firelight his face looked dark, closed and mysterious.

To their left suddenly came a tremor of ghostly noise, followed by a weird screech. She started and he came out of his brown study and smiled at her.

'That's only an eagle owl. Poor Tracy, I expect you're wishing this was the Thames Embankment — confess it now?'

His blithe assumption that she would be more at home in the city angered her and she said, 'No, I'm not. Haven't I convinced you at all, Lester, that I like this life and that when the time comes I'll be very reluctant to leave it?'

'Do you really mean that? I believe you do. But I can't believe it myself. I still think you're perhaps intrigued by the novelty of all this, just as many city people are who come on wilderness trails, but when you get back to London you'll think, "However did I put up with it?" ' He took her hands in his and examined them in the light of the fire. 'That's better,' he said.

'What is?' asked Tracy breathlessly. She was overwhelmed by the sense of his nearness, the touch of the lean brown hands holding her own.

'These are the hands of the girl I knew, sunburned, a little scratched, capable hands that could tend a sick animal . . . oh, Tracy. . . .'

He put his face down on her hands and she felt a rush of tenderness with his dark springing hair so close, the strong brown neck within reach of her lips.

'If we could take away those years,' she heard his muffled voice, 'go back to those days when we were both still so very young. But we can't. It's foolish even to think of it. We're two people totally committed to different ways of existence, and I bear a burden of guilt and scandal.'

He rose abruptly and sat down near the fire some distance away from her. 'Forgive me, I didn't mean to involve you in an emotional scene. Heaven knows our lives here and their complications can mean very little to you. But even you must have heard the gossip that revolves around my name.'

She sat dumbly, neither confirming nor denying his words.

'It's a wonder no one thought fit to warn Tom Bryant about me. Your father, bless him, is one of the few who refuse to believe bad of anyone. But others aren't so tolerant. Aren't you afraid to be alone with a killer, a person who deals out death to his best friend?'

She looked at the light golden eyes, staring intensely at her, like the fierce eyes of the lion as he stood proudly upon the bank before vanishing into the wilderness.

'I don't believe the story for a moment,' she asserted.

'No?'

She hated his mocking tone and turned aside, shading her eyes from the leaping flames and from his inscrutable stare.

'But the majority of people do believe it. John Lockwood was killed with my gun. That was rather hard to explain. I told them I'd dropped it in the struggle and the murderer must have seized it. They had to accept that story for lack of further proof, but although some members of the poaching gang were subsequently arrested, my gun was never found, nor did the true culprit ever come forward.'

'But didn't you yourself see him?' asked Tracy.

'No, the shot came from a totally different direction from the one where the other members of the gang had been. I was busy attending to John, and by the time I could pursue him, the slayer had vanished.'

Lester shrugged his shoulders.

'Firelight makes one talk too much. It's high time you went to sleep, Tracy. Forget my troubles. Other people have lived through this kind of thing and survived.'

'But isn't there anything to be done?' asked Tracy.

'Not a thing. Forget it. I guess I confided in you because tonight you seemed more like the Tracy I knew long ago.'

'Why do you see such a difference in me?' asked Tracy desperately. 'There isn't really, Lester, you know.'

'No?' asked Lester, the old quizzical look back on his face. 'Well, I must admit you've stood up to the trail remarkably well. But you need your rest. We have a long way to go tomorrow.'

Watching his rugged profile in the light of the flames, Tracy thought over their conversation. She believed him when he said he had no part in his friend's killing, but he had missed out one thing. What part had Evangeline played in the events he had related, and what did she mean to him now?

The stars were fading when Tracy woke to the sound of the old lion, shattering the silence with his deep-chested grating roar.

'That man of ours!' said William proudly when he brought her some coffee. It was amazing how the sound of the king of beasts silenced all noise from lesser animals. There was absolute silence for a few seconds and again came the awesome roar followed by the deep grunts of a lioness.

'They roar after they've eaten,' Lester informed her while they were having their simple breakfast, 'so you needn't feel too scared if we happen to see them.'

'I won't be,' she vowed stoutly, and then, glancing at his charming grin, realized he had been testing her. He seemed determined she should forget the intensity of emotion he had shown to her the night before, and kept up a light banter for the duration of their morning walk.

They were making their way back to the camp by a

different route, one which would enable them to return home by this evening. They had seen the lions from a distance, gorged and sleepy after enjoying their night's kill, and Tracy had managed to take more photographs as they lazily licked both jaw and paw.

Now that they were on their homeward journey, Tracy felt wild regret that the wonderful experience was almost over. She looked around her, trying to engrave some memories in her heart for ever, sights and sounds, yellow-billed kites turning and calling in the clear blue air, small klipspringer buck standing like statues staring at them in wide-eyed amazement, a flappet lark rising from its nest, its vibrating wings making a sound like the opening of a door, and, most thrilling of all, the piercing, challenging call of a fish eagle, lord of the African sky.

Yes, she thought, she would remember these three days in the wilderness as long as she lived, but how could she if at the same time she must forget her companion? Yet, if she failed to do this, her peace of mind would be gone for ever.

On this their last day of the trail, the weather had become ominously sultry and in the afternoon great banks of cloud piled in mountainous cumulus formation upon the horizon. Lester instructed William to go on ahead in order to alert the truck driver when he came to the meeting place and possibly to ask him to bring it a little further along the road in case they were caught in the storm.

But when they were still a few miles from their destination a tempest seemed imminent. Great ragged grey clouds scudded across the sky and the wind howled like a hyena, flattening small bushes to the ground and thrashing the taller trees.

'We must find somewhere to shelter,' Lester said. 'I remember last time the storm frightened you more than the rhinos. Or has the trail toughened you up so much that you're prepared to disregard the weather?'

'Perhaps we could shelter under a tree,' suggested Tracy.

'Surely even you know that a tree is the worst place to find shelter when you can expect lightning. No, Tracy, I have a better idea. There's a ranger's hut, disused, but still a roof over our heads, somewhere in this vicinity. If I can just hit upon the track ... ah, yes, I remember that fever tree. It should be along there.'

They soon came upon the small two-roomed cottage. By this time the rain was pouring down and as they ran across the clearing in front of the hut they became soaked to the skin. Fortunately the place was not locked and Lester swung the stable door open with a terrific crash, which was echoed by the peals of thunder and the loud drumming of rain upon the tin roof.

'This is better,' said Lester. 'Can't take you home to your father with pneumonia, can we?'

Tracy reflected that this might still happen. Her thin shirt was plastered against her body, although her tough denim jeans seemed to have discarded the rain. There were some logs and branches in the hearth and Lester put a match to this, and, pulling up an old mattress to the fire, told her to sit down while he produced a towel from her haversack and started to dry her face and hair as if, thought Tracy, she was still fifteen.

What a disconcerting man he was, and how contradictory. It hardly seemed possible that this man who was gently rubbing her hair until the wet rat-tails became a shining aureole could be the same man who had shaken Vincent Pringle like a shark seizing its victim before he had thrown him into the lake.

The logs had caught alight now and a cheerful glow was cast across the gloomy room.

'What's this place used for?' asked Tracy.

'Nothing really now. Another hut was built in a more convenient place and this was abandoned.'

The worst of the storm seemed to be over now and the noise had abated. There was only the steady drip of water from the eaves. Tracy sat gazing into the orange heart of the fire; her face with its lovely shape and high cheekbones was shadowy, her enormous grey eyes dreamy. Lester slid down beside her upon the old mattress and put his arm around her.

'Are you weary, Tracy?' he asked gently. 'It's been a hard slog for a city girl, hasn't it? But I want to tell you before we get back to civilization that I've felt really proud of you. I never expected you to stand up to it so well.'

The smiling mobile lips were very close to hers, and afterwards she was unsure whether she herself had been the first to lean forward, but all at once she was in his arms and this time there was no drawing back and she was responding eagerly to his ardent embrace. It was he who drew away and springing up, began to stride the narrow length of the room like an angry panther.

'Forgive me, Tracy. I shouldn't have done that. Your father trusted me and I ... well, you can see now why I seem to attract scandal, and I wouldn't blame you for saying I deserve it.'

Tracy was bewildered. Slung down from ecstasy to this revelation of self-hate, she found it hard to understand him.

'Blame it on proximity,' he was saying. 'It's just as well we're going home, Tracy. You're altogether too attractive.'

So he found her attractive, but he blamed it on her nearness, or physical allure, and whatever attraction she had for him he felt he must resist it. There was no hint of the abiding love for which she yearned. At the cost of betraying herself she must discuss this with him.

'Lester,' she said, her eyes large and pleading, 'don't you feel any. . . .'

There was a loud crash from the direction of the other room, and they both sprang startled towards the closed door. Lester was there first.

'Keep back, Tracy!' he shouted, and flung it open. But there was no one there. The shutters of the window swung with the remaining momentum of some previous violent opening. Lester rushed across and looked out. Behind him Tracy could see the vague outline of a man's figure fleeing rapidly and disappearing into the bush. Lester shrugged his shoulders.

'Too late. We'll never catch up with him. Besides, I can't leave you here alone. He might double back if he sees I've gone in search of him.'

'But who could it be?'

'Some stray poacher, I suppose. How infuriating that he must have been hiding in this room all the time! I suppose the noise of the storm prevented us from hearing anything, but he must have heard us and then he decided to make a dash for it.'

'Did he leave anything behind?' asked Tracy.

'Doesn't look like it,' said Lester, who had been searching methodically. He went outside and examined the ground for footprints.

'Odd – it doesn't look as if it was an African. Here's the imprint of rubber boots. The African poacher is usually barefoot.'

He went towards the track by which the stranger had disappeared and Tracy heard him give a startled exclamation.

'What is it?' she asked fearfully, as she ran across the clearing to join him.

Lester was standing holding a gun that he had picked up on the pathway. His expression was grim.

'It's mine,' he explained. 'The gun that killed John Lockwood.'

CHAPTER NINE

AFTER all it would be good to be home again, thought Tracy, smiling when she realized that her definition of home had become her father's cottage in the reserve. The last day had contained too much confusing emotion, too many unsolved riddles. The magic of the wilderness trail had been broken by the odd matter of the gun. Lester was abstracted now, deep in thought, and he said good-bye to Tracy almost absent-mindedly when he dropped her at her father's home.

Would she ever again, she wondered, reach the stage that she had arrived at in the deserted hut, when she had almost screwed up her courage to discuss her true feelings? She doubted it, and now that the moment of passion had gone, she realized that she was glad there had been an interruption. Who knew what humiliation she would have courted if their discussion had continued? She had been carried away by the enchantment of their embrace, and now that she could think about it soberly she realized that he had been overcome merely by the romantic atmosphere of their surroundings and the physical attraction he said she possessed. Love did not come into it at all.

Her father was out when she returned, but she supposed he would return presently. Meanwhile she lay in a warm bath, wondering when she would be able to go back to England. She had only to develop the photographs now and arrange them in their order amongst the text of the book. Soon her task would be over, for during her absence her father had been very energetic in preparing the last of the manuscript.

After days of wearing bush shirts and jeans, it was good to change into a cool leaf-green cotton dress and to arrange her newly washed hair into a golden top-knot. She went to give orders to George and was surprised to see that he had anticipated her wish and was preparing a meal of roast chicken, roast potatoes, yellow raisin rice, and green beans.

'Why, George, how clever of you to prepare a nice meal for my homecoming,' she smiled at him. George grinned back.

'Master Bryant he say so. He says the *baas* from London will need good meal.'

Tracy was puzzled. She must have misunderstood him.

'The *baas* from London? Who is that, George?'

'This *baas* he came yesterday. He say he send telegram, but *kosazana* away when it came. Here on dresser.'

Puzzled, Tracy took up the cable that was lying on an old tray on which George was accustomed to place any letters that came.

'Thrilled at prospect of land sale. Expect me on first possible plane. Love. Konrad,' it read.

Konrad ... he was here! She had completely forgotten about the business of the luxury hotel during her days in the wilderness, and now she had difficulty in concentrating on the incredible fact that Konrad had already arrived and was presumbaly staying at the hotel in the village and coming to dinner this evening. She was seized with panic at this new complication. But why? Surely she should be pleased to see Konrad, whom she had considered as her future husband? She should be thrilled and excited, not filled with terrible apprehension.

But perhaps this new development would solve her problems. Perhaps when she met Konrad again she would realize that he was the one for her and that this feeling she had for Lester was just infatuation. So she argued with herself, knowing all the time deep in her heart that it could never happen that way.

A little while later Tom Bryant came into the cottage smiling happily.

'Tracy, my dear, how good it is to see you again! I feel as if we've been parted for a week instead of a couple of days. I'm getting too used to having a daughter around. I missed you very much.'

Tracy embraced and kissed him. His white silky hair was in wild disarray and he had a couple of buttons missing from his shirt. She sighed. How incapable he was of looking after himself properly, even if it was only for two days! Why did he have to catch at her heart so much when soon she would have to leave him for ever?

'I missed you too, Papa. We both did. What's this that George tells me about Konrad? I had no idea he intended to come. I'm sorry you were left to receive him. Has it been any trouble to you?'

Mr. Bryant waved this aside. His innocent blue eyes shone with pleasure.

'No trouble, Tracy darling, no trouble at all. Your Konrad is a charming young man, and very wide awake too. He seems devoted to you by his own account and apparently he has some wonderful scheme in hand which he intends to reveal to us soon.'

There was no denying Konrad's practised charm. It seemed to have won her father over completely.

'Yes, well, we'll see,' said Tracy. She wondered if

Konrad had seen Vincent, but of course he would have got in contact with him straight away. Konrad in a business deal wasted no time.

She made herself busy arranging the table and sorting out their small array of drinks, but all the time, in spite of her memories of Konrad's charm, an icy weight seemed to lie around her heart as she thought of meeting him again. What would he expect of her? Would he want their association to be on the same footing? But of course he would. How was he to know that half the world away she had been fighting an infatuation that had dimmed his memory to such an extent that now she was afraid to meet him?

When at last he walked down the pathway on to the small verandah and seized her hands in his, she was trembling. But he evidently took this as a compliment.

'Why, Tracy dear, your hands are ice cold. Have you missed me, darling?'

There was no chance to reply, for he had enfolded her in his arms and his mouth was upon hers. With a distinct effort of will she prevented herself from an instinctive withdrawal.

'It's good to see you, Konrad,' she managed to say.

But what had this suave, well-dressed man to do with the life she was leading here? With his understated good looks, his fashionable haircut, his dark city suit, he looked very much the successful London businessman. And she felt she had travelled light years away from the life that marriage with him would imply. But it was too early for him to sense any change in her.

During dinner he set himself to charm Mr. Bryant, and obviously succeeded. He listened respectfully to the old man's opinions about the changing world and talked earnestly about his book, the subject nearest to his heart. Nothing was said of the project which had brought him here until the old man had retired to bed and Konrad and Tracy were sitting on the stoep in the bland warm velvet of the summer's night.

Konrad put out his hand and stroked Tracy's arm.

'What have they been doing to you here, my love? Where did you get all these scratches and scars?'

Tracy withdrew her hands a little too quickly.

'They're battle-scars, Konrad. You can't do a wilderness trail and retain a lilywhite skin!'

Konrad looked slightly hurt at her swift withdrawal.

'Evidently not. But surely you must have had servants with you? I've always thought that your slender hands and perfect filbert nails are one of your greatest beauties. There was no need for such rough treatment of them, was there?'

She remembered Lester's taking her hand in his strong brown ones. 'These are the hands of the girl I knew,' he had said, but they were not those of the girl Konrad loved. He would think it eccentric that she had borne the scars of the wilderness trail like a badge of courage knowing that Lester was proud that she could endure the hardships entailed.

'Fascinating place,' Konrad was saying. 'Just as I thought, it has great possibilities. The wealthy tourist is bored with the usual European tour, and much of Africa is undeveloped, but this place, combining scenery and animals, yet not so far away from airfields and a large seaport, is fantastically right.'

Fresh from the enchantment of the wilderness trail,

Tracy for the first time experienced a qualm of doubt about Konrad's scheme. The people who worked here, Lester for instance, were more concerned with preserving the wild life than encouraging tourists. To them the tourists were a necessary nuisance but not a source of wealth. What would Lester think of Konrad's plans for a luxury hotel?

'They do cater for tourists already, Konrad,' she ventured. 'Do you really feel there's any need for a hotel?'

'Tracy darling, you ought to know that I don't cater for the ordinary type. No, these will be people who can pay, jaded, bored men of the world to whom the sight of rhinos will be an extraordinary thrill. We might even give them some excitement like staging a charge. I believe a black rhino's temper is very easily aroused. Perhaps we could persuade them to stock up with a few more lions. I'm told the lions here keep right off the beaten track and stay in the more isolated parts of the reserve. That's ridiculous. If you want to attract tourists they should be able to see them.'

'But there are reserves in Africa where you can see lions easily,' said Tracy. 'The charm of this place is its wildness, the sense that here is Africa as it used to be, untouched by civilization.'

'Yes,' Konrad agreed, 'there is that too. We'll keep it like that, Tracy, with a few modifications of course.'

Tracy sighed. She was so used to obeying Konrad's wishes as far as business was concerned that it had not occurred to her before that this scheme could alter the very nature of the reserve. It was only now, hearing him talk in a way that seemed in complete antipathy to the ideas she had gained from her days in the wilderness, that she realized she should have tried to discourage him.

When he left, she kissed him lightly, but before she could slip away as she had intended, he had taken her into his arms. He took her chin and looked into her eyes without attempting to kiss her.

'What is it, Tracy? What's happened to you?'

She shook her head, her grey eyes brimming with tears.

'It's time you came home. Come back with me. The book is almost finished. Your father has no excuse to keep you any longer.'

'I can't come, Konrad. Don't ask me.'

'But of course you can come. This is nonsense. This is no life for you in a shabby cottage with no comforts. I'm amazed that you've put up with it for so long. You've been an angel to your father, but he's done without you before. He'll have to learn to do without you again. I need you, Tracy.'

'He needs me too, but, Konrad, it isn't just that. Give me time.'

'Time for what? This isn't your life, Tracy. Your life is in London with me. We suit each other. You know we'll have a wonderful life together. We'll travel ... you can even come back here if you want to, when my hotel is built. But for heaven's sake, jaunts like this wilderness trail are not for you. How could your father have let you go on alone?'

'I wasn't alone,' said Tracy. She had stepped away from his encircling arms and was in the shadow of the kaffirboom near the gate. She hoped he could not see her expression.

'Your father told me he left you with two reliable guides, but all the same it was risky. He seems to have

put a lot of trust in this ... what was his name ...
Lester Cordell?'

'He is trustworthy. He knows a lot about the kind of
life here.'

'That may be so, but according to Vincent Pringle
...'

'I wouldn't believe too much that he says.'

'No? He seems quite a go-ahead fellow for such a
sleepy hollow as this. I must say his business acumen
impressed me. But I only met him for the first time
today. I would like to meet Lester Cordell too. He
seems to have made a good impression on you and I
must establish cordial relations with the Game Reserve
staff. Perhaps he could join us for dinner at the hotel
tomorrow night.'

There was nothing Tracy wanted less than that she
should have to dine with Konrad and Lester together,
but there was little she could do. She was even relieved
when she arrived and realized that Konrad had invited
Vincent and Evangeline too. Knowing Konrad, Tracy
was not surprised that he had persuaded the chef of the
small hotel to perform extraordinary culinary achieve-
ments and raided the cellar to find some interesting
French wines.

The table was set on a small sheltered patio, its roof
festooned with bright scarlet bougainvillea. Tubs of
exotically fragrant lilies perfumed the warm air and a
bank of blue hydrangeas formed a natural screen. Soles
poached in white wine were served with a cream sauce
and a garnish of shrimps and caviar, and this was followed by a saddle of lamb roasted and served with
small young vegetables. Knowing how difficult it was
to get good fresh ingredients for a meal, Tracy mused
that Konrad had a knack of getting his own way and

performing miracles in the way of organization. It was no wonder that he was such a success in his particular field.

It seemed odd to see Lester formally dressed. He had arrived wearing a dark suit, but Konrad, apparently determined to put everyone at their ease on this warm evening, had suggested to the men that they discard their jackets, and the brilliant white of his shirt emphasized the game ranger's deep brown tan. Nothing, thought Tracy, could present a stronger contrast than the sight of the two men talking together, Konrad with his pale distinction, Lester with his rugged features and outdoor appearance.

'I understand you asked me here tonight because you said you had something to discuss with me that would be of interest to the Reserve.'

'Pleasure before business, Mr. Cordell, or would you object if I called you Lester, since I understand from Mr. Bryant that you are an old friend of Tracy's. Let's enjoy our meal first. Time enough to state my business when we're at the coffee stage.'

'As you wish,' said Lester rather abruptly.

He glanced, frowning, at Tracy. A simply cut but elegant white dress showed off the golden shade of her arms and neck, and the honey-coloured hair twisted into a sophisticated knot enhanced the lovely heart shape of her face and the slender neck.

'What a dark horse you are, Tracy,' said Evangeline, radiant in a shining cocktail dress of copper bronze that emphasized the luminous quality of her Titian hair and the alabaster whiteness of her skin. 'You didn't tell us you were a friend of the famous Konrad Young, and a very close one, it would appear.'

Konrad raised his glass to Tracy and silently toasted her as if by this gesture he was closing them off into an intimate little world of their own. When Tracy ventured a look at Lester his expression was difficult to define. For a moment he looked coldly at her and then, apparently recovering himself, he began an animated conversation with Eve. Tracy felt embarrassed by Vincent's knowing scrutiny and wished Konrad had not shown so plainly that he considered there was an intimate bond between them.

It was her own fault, she thought. She had drifted into the belief that she might consider marriage with Konrad one day, but that seemed to have been in another life. Perhaps it was true as he said that she should go back. What was the good of staying here in an alien place eating her heart out for a man who considered her unsuitable as a game ranger's wife?

The table had been cleared and coffee and liqueurs served before Konrad outlined his plan. As always his explanation was concise and well thought out, and although, as Tracy well knew, his ambition was to develop his own empire of exotic holiday hotels, he spoke feelingly of the benefit this new hotel would bring to the small community. Lester's voice cut harshly across Konrad's persuasive exposition.

'You'll forgive my criticism, but I can't see what possible benefit the Game Reserve can gain by turning it into a circus for the momentary pleasure of a handful of bored businessmen.'

'My dear fellow,' Konrad turned to him, mustering all his charm of manner, 'don't for one moment think I mean to ruin the Reserve. By no means . . . just a few gradual improvements, that's all that I have in mind. Don't imagine I'm going to set up souvenir shops and refreshment stands. I fully realize that the Reserve's natural wildness is its chief attraction.'

'And it can only keep that by remaining untouched, unspoiled. No, Mr. Young, I'm afraid I don't agree with your scheme at all.'

Evangeline leaned towards him, her beautiful mouth pouting mischievously.

'Lester darling, don't be so difficult. Think what fun it would be to have distinguished rich people here. It would give the old place such a lift. Don't be so conservative!'

Lester turned on her savagely.

'For God's sake, Eve, you know how we've had to work to repair the damage done in the name of civilization. In 1920 there were only twenty white rhinos left in Zululand. Now there are hundreds. This reserve exists for the conservation of animals, not for a rich man's pleasure or for the financial benefit of hotel owners.'

'I take it that that remark includes me,' said Konrad smoothly. 'I fully appreciate your feelings, Lester, but I'm sure, when you've given this matter a little more thought, you'll realize that my work not only benefits myself but other people. Why, when more people have heard of your reserve you yourself will become known all over the world. You'll be asked to do T.V. programmes. In fact you may find my new hotel is your road to fame and fortune.'

No, Konrad, don't try that kind of persuasion with Lester, thought Tracy, noting the proud scorn in the golden eyes. That's the last thing that would tempt him.

'Where do you propose to build this hotel?' he said, obviously trying to restrain his hostility.

'There's an ideal place high above the river. We're negotiating for that.'

Reluctantly Lester turned to Vincent for more details.

'You know the place,' said Vincent, 'the level ground where the bend of the river occurs. There are large thickets of bamboo and plenty of trees there.'

'But that is ... if I'm not mistaken ... doesn't it belong to your father, Tracy?'

Tracy could only stare dumbfounded at Lester's furious face. An icy chill seemed to seize her as she realized the implications of this astonishing news.

'Yes, I believe it does belong to old Tom Bryant,' Vincent interjected smoothly.

'So now I understand,' said Lester, rising to his feet. 'I must confess, Tracy, it puzzled me all along why you should come half-way across the world to see your father after all these years of neglect. I see now it was not for love of him but merely for material gain. As for your scheme, Konrad, and you too, Tracy, I can assure you that I will fight against it even if I have to get it thrown out by the Government itself.'

And with this he strode out of the hotel.

'I had no idea you were such an astute little business woman, Tracy,' said Evangeline, breaking the silence. 'What a clever idea to get Konrad interested in your father's land! I must say I think it's brilliant. I'm looking forward to all these changes. Life may prove to be still worth living here, when you build your luxury hotel.'

CHAPTER TEN

TRACY was tired out, exhausted by the reaction from the physical hardships of the wilderness trail, but still more so from the shattering revelation that it was her father's land and because of the violent contempt she had seen in Lester's eyes before he had flung out of the room as if he wished he could get out of her life for ever.

Her father, the innocent cause of her worry, was sleeping soundly. She had had some wild thought when she returned of rousing him and asking him about the matter, but he looked so peaceful when she glanced into his room that she had not the heart to wake him. Besides, in his frail state of health she did not want to startle him.

But in spite of her exhaustion she found it difficult to sleep. She was torn between humiliation and fury that Lester should so easily believe her motives in coming here were purely for gain. She sat in the deep window seat of her room watching a golden moon riding high above the dark bush, hearing the sharp whistle of a reedbuck and the sound of a tree frog penetrating the silence like the sound of her own heartbeat. How could she endure it that Lester thought the worst of her? She remembered the enchantment of their sweet embrace on that last day of the trail and she determined that whatever the consequences she would try to convince him of the innocence of her intentions as regarded Konrad's scheme.

The lonely sounds from the bush reminded her of

that night long ago, when as a fourteen-year-old girl, she had dared to confront Lester at midnight, rather than leave without explaining to him that she loved him. Now she was grown-up and mature, but the same ardent nature that had scarcely been able to tolerate their parting then now urged her to resolve this misunderstanding. She could not sit quietly here listening to the shuddering sadness of a jackal, the lament of a curlew. She would go at once and confront him, not wait until morning.

She slipped on the apricot-coloured housecoat with its fragile coffee-coloured lace, hardly conscious of its impractical nature for a midnight walk across the sleeping moonlit compound. She did not even pause to tie back the sweep of honey-gold hair that fell in a silky screen around her pointed face. She disregarded her appearance entirely, for she was totally absorbed in the desire to clear herself in Lester's eyes.

The heavy fragrance of flowering shrubs scented the air as she halted beside the gate that led to Lester's cottage. So far she had walked swiftly before her resolution should fail, but now she hesitated and looked about her. She knew he slept with his doors unlocked, but it would be embarrassing to have to wake him, and yet she was determined to have this business out with him and felt prepared to do even that.

But there was no need. She saw the glow of his pipe where he sat upon the stoep. He too must have had difficulty in sleeping. He looked startled by the sudden apparition. To him, scarcely roused from his brooding mood, Tracy looked not quite real, with her floating robe and shimmering long hair. Then he realized her identity.

'Tracy, what on earth. . . .

'Lester, I had to come. I wanted to discuss . . .'

'Surely Konrad hasn't sent you at this hour? It seems an odd time to do business.'

'This has nothing to do with Konrad. I want to tell you, Lester, that when I negotiated this business with Vincent Pringle I had no idea that the land belonged to my father.'

There was no belief in her statement, only utter contempt in the cold eyes and bitter mouth.

'Forget it, Tracy. There's no need to come here trying to justify yourself to me. I realize clearly now, far too clearly, that you've been playing a double game the whole time. You came simply because your lover needed a new site, a bigger and better and more exotic place for his latest line in luxury hotels.'

'That isn't true! I came because I wanted to help my father, because I wanted to see him again after all these years of separation.'

'And you expect me to believe that? That a sophisticated girl would give up her way of life and come to a shabby cottage in the wilds of Africa to see a father she had neglected for years? No, Tracy, it's all too pat. Perhaps you didn't realize at first that your father owned the ground, but when you did find out it all worked out very nicely and conveniently, didn't it?'

'I keep trying to tell you. I didn't know, I didn't realize that you would feel so strongly about the hotel. It was only when we went on the wilderness trail that. . . .'

How could she say it, without betraying that she had fallen hopelessly in love not only with him but with the kind of life he led, that she realized now how he felt about the kind of people who would come to a luxury hotel expecting a thrill for their jaded palates.

'The wilderness trail. . . . Good God, I believed you when you seemed enchanted with it. I thought you really meant it when you said it was wonderful!'

'But I did, Lester, I did think it was the most thrilling thing I've ever experienced.'

Lester smiled bitterly.

'In the same way that Konrad's city people will get a thrill. It was a change from your usual mode of life, wasn't it? Your life with Konrad, the suave, rich business man. It was an interlude, something you can talk about when you go back to London. And will I make an entertaining subject for dinner party conversation too?'

'Please, Lester, stop tearing me to pieces. I can't stand it!'

'I don't think you have any right to say what you can stand. Lord knows I've stood enough from you. I gave you my confidence, and all the time you must have been laughing at this dumb back-of-the-woods person being so dramatic. I really believed you when you said you didn't credit the scandal about my name, but I realize now that you didn't give a damn about it because you simply didn't care sufficiently one way or the other. All you cared about was getting a site for your damned hotel and making money out of it!'

'That isn't true! Oh, how can I convince you that I never for a moment had any thought of material gain in this business? How can I make you believe that I love the reserve as it is, not as a resort for tired businessmen? When Konrad asked me to inquire about land, I didn't think . . . I never dreamed. . . .'

'But you were damned cagey about it, nevertheless. It would have been the logical thing to do to ask me for advice, but no, you went to that crook, Vincent

Pringle, and as soon as you found out your father owned ground around here in a suitable place naturally you recommended that with great enthusiasm. I suppose you felt if your father was well provided for you could disclaim further responsibility.'

'How can you be so cruel? I adore my father. I have no wish to disclaim responsibility. It breaks my heart to think of having to leave him.'

'Don't give me that story. You left him for ten years and hardly even wrote to him. How can you say now that you adore him? It's just part of the exaggerated way of speech you have. No, Tracy, when you stood up to the trail so well, I was beginning to believe that you really meant what you said, and that you were enthusiastic about the life here, but now I realize that it was all so much pretence. Your interests are not here.'

'They are. They are! I don't care if I never see a big city again.'

'And Konrad? It's obvious, Tracy, to the most casual observer that you're deeply involved with each other. Can you deny that?'

How could Tracy explain to Lester that she had drifted into this affair because it seemed calm and comfortable and completely dissociated from those passionate emotions she had felt for him when she was only fourteen? She was silent, unable to meet Lester's scornful, golden gaze.

'I must congratulate you, Tracy. In spite of our differences, he seems a charming fellow, as well as an astute business man. Just the kind of man you need, I would say.'

'You don't know anything about me. How do you know what kind of man I need?' Tracy demanded.

'Why, one only has to look at you to see you need

someone who can supply you with a luxurious life. That is what your life with your mother accustomed you to. This pretty garment you're wearing, for instance – I dare say it cost the equivalent of a week's salary for a game ranger.'

'None of that matters to me any more!' Tracy almost shouted.

She felt at breaking point. How could she convince him that she cared nothing any longer for Konrad or for the life she had previously led?

'Tell me then, what does matter to you?' asked Lester.

Impossible to answer. Almost she was tempted to fling herself into his arms as she had done on that night long ago. But she was no longer fourteen and the thought of his possible scorn and anger was too hard to face.

'It matters to me that you have a good opinion of me,' she murmured.

He looked surprised.

'It doesn't seem a very logical way to go about achieving that when you deceive me about the purchase of land for a hotel and then come to see me after midnight dressed as you are. Or was that meant to distract me? Were you relying on the fact that in a weak moment I told you I find you physically attractive?'

'I wanted to see you. I wanted to explain. Believe me, Lester, I never gave a thought to how I would appear to you.'

'No?' asked Lester. His smile was disillusioned, cynical. 'Well, Tracy, if it gives you any satisfaction let me tell you that you look very beautiful, very seductive. Isn't that what you wanted?'

As he swept her into his arms, his hard hand bruised her back in its burning grasp. He covered her mouth with angry kisses, then just as swiftly let her go.

'Satisfied now?' he asked. 'You'd better go back to Konrad if you want more civilized behaviour.'

'It's no use trying to convince you,' Tracy shouted angrily, rubbing her bruised mouth as if to wipe away all trace of contact with him. 'I came here hoping to make you see reason, but you're impossible – I see that now. It would give me great pleasure if I were never to see you again.'

'That goes for me too,' said Lester.

They stood staring at each other like two angry cheetahs. This was the end, thought Tracy. She was finished with him. She had suffered enough humiliation in her foolish infatuation for him. All she wanted now was to go away and put him out of her life for ever.

The phone rang shrilly, breaking in upon them like a messenger from some foreign country. He strode swiftly to answer it.

'Oh, Gavin, hello. Poachers ... yes ... you say there's a big gang? Yes, get as many African guides as you can. I'll come straight away. See you bring your revolver as well as your rifle. We may need them.'

He looked at Tracy as vaguely as if she were a stranger visiting him and he could not think what she was there for.

'I'll have to go. Can you get home by yourself? They think they're on to a large gang. We can't waste a minute.'

She nodded dumbly as he put on his boots and equipped himself with a rifle and a revolver. She wanted to say, 'Take care of yourself,' but no words came. When he was half-way to the truck, she started to go after him with some wild idea of reconciliation, of imploring him for one word of tenderness, but she could not match his long stride. Before she could reach him he had started the engine and driven away without a backward glance.

CHAPTER ELEVEN

FAR below the silver outline of the river showed between its dark bushes as Tracy made her way back to
her father's cottage. A grey dawn was being heralded
by the nervous shouts of baboons and the raucous cries
of the hornbills screaming like cracked trumpets. There
was no hope of sleep now. Tracy felt raw with anxiety.
Yet dealing with poachers was all in the day's work to
Lester. He would be the first to scoff at her fears.

Oh, it was true that she was completely unsuited by
temperament to endure the life of a game ranger's wife
with its constant anxiety as well as loneliness. She must
put him out of her mind for ever. She gave up any idea
of rest, and dressed hurriedly in slacks and shirt, then
sat at her desk busily typing the last of the manuscript.
It was nearly finished. She could leave her father to
check it, finish off the development of the photographs
and mail it. If she wished she could return to London
with Konrad.

Why not? She would phone him this morning and
tell him she had changed her mind. That would be the
sensible thing to do. As if in answer to this idea, the
phone rang. Tracy realized that while she had been
working the red glow had disappeared from the east
and the sky was pale turquoise overhead. She wondered who could be phoning so early in the morning
and was even more surprised when she found it was
Evangeline.

'Tracy darling, could you be an angel and take
Julian for a couple of days? I find I have to go to

Lourenço Marques again.'

Tracy hesitated. If she carried out her plan it would be highly inconvenient to have to look after Julian while she prepared hurriedly for her return to London. But on the other hand she would like to spend some time with him before she left.

'I've decided to return to England with Konrad,' she informed Evangeline. Saying it out loud seemed to make it very final. 'But certainly I'll have Julian as long as I can. Perhaps you could make some alternative arrangement in case I go before you return.'

'Tracy darling, what a surprise! But I suppose it's only to be expected. I do congratulate you. He's so charming, not to mention the worldly goods. Some people have all the luck, don't they? I hope you aren't leaving any broken hearts around the neighbourhood. Our dear Doctor James is going to miss you, I would say.'

Tracy chose to ignore this. Her anxiety about Lester was so great that she felt she must mention it to someone even if it was only Evangeline. In some vague way she hoped for reassurance.

'Lester went out last night after a poaching gang. Did you hear anything about it, Eve? They seem to have been gone for hours.'

'Really? Not to worry, Tracy. It's all in the day's work and he's sure to have plenty of people with him. They've been extra careful since John died.'

Tracy realized it had been rather tactless to mention poaching at all to the widow. She had forgotten this in her anxiety. But Eve's casual manner had done the trick. She felt she was being foolish to experience such nervousness on Lester's behalf. If you lived here long enough, she supposed, you got used to happenings that seemed too dramatic to a stranger.

Just as she returned to her desk, she heard the rangers' trucks going past the cottage and was in time to catch a glimpse of them as they slowed down near the main office some distance away. She heard the penetrating noise of African voices raised in excited chatter. Good, they were back. As she had thought at the back of her mind, she was being foolish to worry about Lester. The expedition had ended and she would hear later, she supposed, whether it had been successful, but at least she knew now that they had returned.

By the time her father had risen, she saw Doctor James' car arriving with Julian in it. The little boy rushed into the room where the mousebird was and James accepted a cup of coffee.

'What's this I hear?' he demanded, but she waved to him to be quiet until her father had gone into the study, saying, 'I haven't told him yet. I only decided this morning, but I had to tell Eve because of this arrangement about Julian.'

'Your father is going to be very sad, and let me tell you, Tracy, he won't be the only one.'

Tracy felt a pang of guilt when she saw his expression. He was usually so placid and good-natured, and he now had the look of a spaniel that knows it is going to be left at home when the family go on holiday.

'I had hoped . . .' he said, rather heavily. Then he laughed without humour as if making fun of himself. 'No, that's a lie. Of course I knew you weren't for me, Tracy. No such luck. But once in a while even a practical country doctor can dream, can't he?'

'Dear James,' said Tracy, and took his hand gently. 'Thank you for everything, for the dance, for your help with Julian, and please look after my father for me. You're such a darling ... I wish it had been different.'

'Why, you sound as if you're going right this minute.'

'I feel as if I am,' said Tracy sadly.

She watched him go, smiling to reassure him when he looked back in her direction before starting the car. Why couldn't she fall in love with a man like James? He would be a wonderful husband and never give her a moment's anxiety. Why was her heart so foolish as to give itself to that most impossible man?

She went back inside the house and joined Julian as he fed the mousebird. It was becoming more and more difficult to keep Coly in the house because he slept in a cage at night to keep him safe from marauding cats in the compound, but his tail was by now so long that it was liable to break in the small confined space. Twice already he had lost one of his quills and had to re-grow it. It was getting to be quite a problem. When she had explained this to Julian, sne suggested that one day they would have to give him his freedom.

'The trouble is,' she said, 'that he's a grown-up bird now and should be with his own kind. But he's become attached to us and won't leave us; although he does fly around with other mousebirds near here, he always comes back to us.'

'Perhaps he needs to go somewhere else, Tracy,' suggested Julian. 'Perhaps we should take him somewhere that's further away. He's quite happy with other mousebirds. If he hasn't got us near, he'll forget us more easily.'

Tracy thought sadly that this philosophy fitted her own case too. She needed to go back to find her own kind of people. Being near the person she loved, she would always have difficulty in forgetting her attachment, but if she went far away and resumed her own way of life surely one day she would learn to be happy again?

'Let's take him this morning,' suggested Julian, always ready for a jaunt in the reserve. 'We needn't go far. Let's leave him where there are other mousebirds and see what happens.'

Tracy had grown attached to the little creature, but now she thought Julian's idea might be the right one. She could hardly give her father the trouble of caring for the bird after she had left. She asked Mr. Bryant if he would like to come with them, but he was eager to develop her photographs and said he would stay at home.

'I won't be getting out of the car,' Tracy explained, 'not with Julian here, so I don't need a guide. In any case they're all busy at the moment.'

It was true. The guides could be seen in the distance talking excitedly and crowding around the returned trucks. She caught a glimpse of the rangers' uniforms, but could not distinguish Lester at this distance. She allowed Julian to hold the little bird gently while she drove the truck. She would miss Coly with his cheeky ways and his bright intelligent eyes, but certainly there was no place for him in her life overseas.

It was mid-morning now and there were few animals to be seen. Only several zebras glanced disinterestedly at the truck, then resumed their grazing, and a few white cattle egrets stalked with dignity after the insects in the grass. Deep in the reeds near the distant river could be heard the coucal, the shy bird whose call was like a bubbling stream of low liquid notes. Impossible to believe that in a few days she would be back in London and this enchanting part of Africa would know her no more.

They found a little glade, its wild bushes laden with berries, where flocks of mousebirds were feeding. There were palm trees too, with ripening dates, plenty of food even for the most fastidious of home-bred birds. Coly lingered with them for a few minutes, but then, excited by the unusually large crowd of his fellows, he flew towards them. Tracy and Julian stayed there for half an hour and in all this time he never once attempted to rejoin them. They could not even distinguish their own pet amongst the score or more of identical birds.

Tracy sighed a little. So that was the end of that. One more link broken in the chain that bound her to this wild paradise. She started the engine and drove a little way, remembering that this was the same road she and Lester had taken on their way back from the wilderness trail. Julian had turned to catch a last glimpse of the flock of mousebirds and it was he who spied the small vehicle down the road driven by an African.

'Look, Tracy, isn't that William, the guard who usually goes with Lester?' he said. 'He's waving as if he wants us to stop.'

Tracy drew to the side of the road.

'Yes, it is William,' she replied. 'I wonder what he's doing here. I thought all the guards who were after the poachers had returned.'

William had stopped his car near theirs and was walking swiftly towards them.

'I am looking for my *baas*. I got separated from him before day came, and I have not been able to find him.'

'But I thought he'd returned with the others.'

'No, *kosazana*, we were on our own. We saw one of the poachers going through the trees. He had a gun. I wanted to go too, but my *baas* told me to stay near the truck. He said if he did not return, I was to go to fetch help. But later I heard shots, so I did not do what my *baas* say. Instead I look and look long time, but I found no one. So now I do not know whether it is best to return to camp. But I not like to leave my *baas*. Suppose he is lying hurt, shot maybe?'

'Where did this happen?' asked Tracy. An icy hand seemed to be clutching her heart and involuntarily her whole body trembled.

'It was near the path where the big fever tree is, a little way further on from here.'

The path of the fever tree – that was where the disused hut was. If he had been shot, maybe he would try to find his way there, always assuming he was still able to. . . . She made a quick decision.

'William, take Julian back to the camp as quickly as you can. Tell George to look after him, then get help and come back with more guards. I'll go to look for him in the meantime.'

William looked worried. '*Kosazana*, I don't know whether the *baas* would say. . . .'

'Quickly, William, do as I say! You won't take long and you will be able to see where I have left the truck. I promise I won't do anything rash. It's just that I think I may know where he may be. Come back as soon as you can.'

Julian submitted without protest to her change of plan, but Tracy scarcely waited for them to be out of sight before she turned the truck and headed in the direction of the path that led to the hut. She felt sure that the deserted place might hold some clue to the mystery of the poachers and of Lester's disappearance.

But when she reached the cottage it appeared to be deserted. She crept noiselessly up to the windows and peered inside. No one there. She let herself in and proceeded to inspect the place. It did not seem as if anyone could be living here permanently, yet in the cupboard of the inner room there were blankets, and stranger still, in the kitchen dresser was a bottle of whisky and two bottles of wine. If it was a poacher who hid there, he certainly did himself well!

She was just about to let herself out again and go back to the road to await the arrival of William and his helpers when she happened to glance out of a window. Someone was coming swiftly along the pathway and into the clearing, displaying little of the caution she herself had shown. Evidently this person was familiar with the place and did not expect to meet strangers. As the figure came out of the shadow of the trees, Tracy saw with a gasp of surprise that it was a woman, and as she drew nearer she recognized the curving, willowy grace of Evangeline. What was she doing here? Tracy had understood her to say she was leaving for Lourenço Marques almost immediately.

There was no time to get away, yet Tracy felt reluctant to confront Eve in these circumstances. She withdrew into the inner room and slid the bolt across the door hoping that Eve would soon go, otherwise she would have to climb through the window as the intruder had done. She was wild with anxiety to go on with her search for Lester, yet something held her back from revealing her presence to Eve. She heard the widow moving about restlessly in the other room, then soon afterwards she heard her call, 'I'm here, Vincent!'

'Not so loud, for God's sake!' she heard Vincent's cautious reply.

'There's no one else for miles around.'

Through the window Tracy could see the small clearing in front of the hut where Evangeline was hurrying towards Vincent. He made as if to draw her into his arms, but she drew away impatiently, exclaiming, 'Why did you send for me? You knew I was going to Lourenço Marques. I was just ready to start off . . . I almost didn't come.'

'It's a good thing you did, my girl, because after last night I must get out fast. This place is too hot for me at the moment.'

'What have you done? What's happened?' Tracy heard Eve demand.

'Nothing much, but Cordell's been on my trail for hours. I've only just shaken him off. Took a couple of pots shots at him, but that didn't help. I'm afraid he recognized me this time, so I'd better come with you until things have quietened down.'

'You can't do that,' Eve replied harshly.

'What do you mean? You know we've always been in this together.'

'Not any more.' Eve's voice was high and a little frightened, for Vincent's expression was ugly. She seemed to force herself to go on. 'When I said I was going to Lourenço Marques, I meant I was pulling out of here.'

'What? You don't mean for good?'

'I think so. The whole set-up here bores me stiff.'

'By that crack I take it you mean me?'

Vincent's voice was ugly. Tracy could imagine the

truculent, good-looking face flushed red.

'Take it how you like. I'm telling you I've had enough. There's no future in the life here.'

'Honey, I thought I was your future.'

Vincent sounded ardent and more persuasive now.

'I can't believe you thought that. You knew, you must have always known that our affair was bound to be brief. No, Vincent, it was fun while it lasted, but I can't put up with this small town existence any longer. I'll write to you from Lourenço Marques if I decide to sell the farm. I met someone there. . . .'

'So that's it! You've met someone else. One of these smooth dago types, I suppose. You seem to have forgotten one or two facts, Eve darling.'

'Don't adopt that threatening tone to me, Vincent. What facts are you talking about?'

'You seem to be overlooking the fact that we've been in business together for a long time.'

'The poaching? Oh, Vincent, what's the odds? You know I only had a share in the disposal of the skins just for the fun of it. You know it gave me a thrill to be doing something against the law.'

'You think that's nothing? Let me tell you, Eve, I have enough evidence to convict you even if I have to involve myself.'

'So you're trying a little blackmail now, Vincent? That's no way to keep me. I'm free as air and I intend to remain so. Your threats don't impress me one iota.'

At this Vincent seemed to explode with rage.

'Oh, don't they? Well, let me tell you something. I'm not going to stand for this. You have no right to come here and casually tell me you intend to leave me after all I've done for your sake.'

'What do you mean?' Evangeline sounded frightened now. Her voice was no longer harsh and scornful.

'Who rid you of an unwanted husband, just tell me that?'

'I don't understand you. John was shot by a stray bullet from a poacher's gun, you know that.'

'The stray poacher was me.'

'You!'

'Nobody ever suspected it, but it's true. Very conveniently it was Lester's gun that he had dropped that I used, so I've been able to foster the rumour of his involvement with you ever since. It doesn't take much for gossip to grow. Just a bit of self-protection on my part. Not that I need have bothered, really. No one ever suspected. Now what do you say? Don't you consider you owe me something?'

Eve's voice sounded faint. 'I owe you nothing. If I'd known . . . no, don't touch me . . . to think that I've allowed you to make love to me . . . my husband's murderer!'

'Oh, come off it, Eve.' Vincent's voice was brutal and unfeeling. 'We know each other too well for you to come the high and mighty with me, but don't talk of leaving me for someone else again, I warn you. It was bad enough having to pretend I liked your interest in Lester.'

'Oh, God, I wish that had been true. I wish Lester had been interested in me. Then I would never have become involved with you. He's worth much more than you and always has been. When I meet him I intend to tell him everything.'

There was the sound of sobbing and footsteps running towards the door.

'I don't believe you. You wouldn't dare,' said Vincent's voice. 'You'll soon come running back to me. I know you too well. There are some things you just can't do without. As for Lester whom you think is so wonderful, let him come near me. I've done it once, and perhaps we could arrange another little accident.'

There was quiet now in the cottage save for the sound of Vincent's heavy breathing. Tracy, cautiously looked out of the window, saw the running figure of Evangeline disappearing down the path. She heard the sound of a car's engine and then silence. How could she get out of this room without betraying her presence? She was trembling and emotionally shattered by the revelations she had been forced to hear. Somehow she must get to Lester before he came here and met Vincent. In Vincent's present frame of mind it seemed anything could happen. He was like a dangerous buffalo intent on goring anyone who got in his way.

She waited for a while hoping Vincent would depart, but she could hear him still striding angrily about the small outer room. If he tried this door and found it bolted, he would be suspicious. She decided that there was nothing for it but to try to get out of the window with as little noise as possible. She hoisted herself above the sill and looked carefully around. Dared she make a run for it, knowing that Vincent was in the other room with a gun and might see her before she reached the shelter of the trees? There seemed nothing else to do. She lowered herself down on to the grass and started to run across the clearing.

Her heart was pounding so loudly that at first she did not hear the thud of footsteps behind her, but all at once she was aware of a cruel grasp around her waist and Vincent whirled her around to face him, bruising her body with his rough hands.

'So . . . what are you doing here, Tracy? You'd better come back inside and give me an explanation, and I'm telling you it had better be a good one!'

He dragged her inside and slammed the door.

'Now let's see, how much of my conversation with Eve did you overhear? I take it you were hiding in that room?'

She could only stare dumbly at him and nod her head.

'Cat got your tongue, eh? But I suppose you'll have plenty to tell the wonderful Mr. Cordell when he arrives. But let me warn you, if he does come anywhere near here he might be sorry – and you too.' He produced his gun and motioned her to stand near the open window. 'Just in case we have visitors interrupting us. Now what am I to do with you . . . you know far too much for your own good.'

He sat on an old packing case nonchalantly swinging his revolver.

'I have to shut your mouth somehow.' He snapped his fingers. 'I have it! So long as you keep quiet about what you've heard here, your boy-friend will be safe, but if you say one word to him against me then his life is in danger. Like I said to Eve, accidents are easy to stage, specially when poachers make a good excuse. How about it now, do you promise?'

Tracy nodded, rubbing her bruised arms. Anything would be better than that this man should threaten Lester's life.

'Then I'll make a dash for it. Remember now, don't tell anyone you've seen me.'

'It's too late,' said Tracy. 'They're here.'

Vincent sprang up from his seat.

'You're bluffing me!' he snarled, and came to stand at the window behind Tracy. From the trees into the clearing Lester was walking followed by William and a handful of other guards.

'Stay where you are, Cordell, or I shoot!' Vincent shouted. He grasped hold of Tracy, his arm like a steel vice, and he held her against him sheltering his own body.

'Do as he says, Lester,' shouted Tracy. 'He's dangerous!'

'So I gather,' shouted Lester grimly. 'Eve has just told me, but I've suspected it for some time.' He lifted his gun. 'Let her go, Pringle!'

'You've got a hope! If you shoot, someone's going to get hurt, and it isn't going to be me.'

She saw Lester consulting with the other guards. They were shaking their heads and appeared to be trying to restrain him.

Finally she heard him shout, 'Tell us what you want, Pringle, but if you harm Tracy, I warn you, hell is going to be too good for you.'

'It's quite simple. All I want is to get out,' Vincent said truculently. 'If you let me go I'll make a run for the Mozambique border. I'm not the only one who can hotfoot it to L.M. Otherwise we'll shoot it out, and both you and Tracy here are liable to get hurt.'

Tracy's body was bruised in his grasp. The arm that was holding her seemed like an iron band. But it was with no thought of her own safety that she shouted, 'Please, Lester, let him go free!' She was petrified by the threat of the wicked-looking revolver pointed directly at Lester's skull.

Lester again had a consultation with his companions, but Tracy saw them shake their heads, then he shouted again, his voice coming harshly across the intervening space.

'Very well, we'll give you a chance to run for it. What do you want us to do?'

'Put your guns down in the clearing and walk back five hundred yards until you're out of sight. No funny business now or else I vow Tracy will be the first one to get hurt.'

The little group of guards disappeared from sight after leaving the heap of guns in front of the hut.

'Go and get them,' Vincent instructed Tracy. 'Lock them in the cupboard and give me the key.'

She did as she was told, desperately afraid all the time that the guns might go off, for she found it difficult to hold them steady because she was trembling so much.

'I'm off now. Just see that no one follows,' Vincent told her, and in a few moments she saw him running through the trees. He must have left his car some distance away, for she did not hear the engine starting. Soon she saw Lester returning, walking cautiously, and she called to him through the window when she saw him searching the ground for the guns.

'They're here! He made me lock them in the cupboard.'

Hearing her voice, Lester bounded into the room.

'Are you all right? That damned Pringle! I always knew he was up to no good. And now we've had to let him get away. But there was no alternative.'

Again Tracy was overwhelmed by the feeling that she always seemed to be a hindrance to him. If she had not been there, she knew he would have attempted to arrest Vincent. But then the chance was that he might have got hurt. She could not help feeling that Vincent's escape was the lesser of two evils.

'Well, if he makes for the border, we shouldn't have much trouble from him again. It was he who controlled the poachers and organized it into a big business. And Eve was involved in it too.' His smile was wry. 'Just like her to go in for a thing like this to cure her boredom, but who would have thought it?'

Tracy felt a sharp pang of jealousy that, even though he knew Eve was guilty of helping Vincent with the poaching, it seemed she still exercised some fascination over Lester. Was he still attracted to her in spite of the fact that she had been involved with Vincent?

He had succeeded in breaking the lock by now and was taking the guns out.

'What do you intend to do?' she asked.

He looked surprised.

'Why, follow him, of course.'

Tracy's heart sank. 'But I thought you said. . . .

'I must at least try to get him. He hasn't reached the border yet, has he?'

Tracy wanted to fling herself at him and implore him 'Don't go!' but instead she asked, 'Can I come with you?'

He grinned.

'Haven't you had enough adventure? What's Konrad going to say about all this?'

But before she could reply, two of the Zulu guards came running across the grass. They spoke rapidly to Lester and his face became grave. He questioned them sharply and they replied by waving their hands in the direction of the trees. Tracy could not understand the rapid Zulu language, but obviously something dreadful had happened.

After giving some instructions to the guards, Lester turned to Tracy.

'I'm afraid it's bad news. Vincent was a crook and a murderer, but I wouldn't wish such a thing to happen even to my worst enemy. I suppose in his haste he wasn't keeping a proper lookout on the way to his car. He disturbed a black rhino in the bush. They're the most evil-tempered creatures in existence when they think they're being attacked, utterly vicious. Once they start to charge, they go for their prey over and over again. The guards say Vincent is dead.'

CHAPTER TWELVE

TRACY had finished her father's manuscript now. The book was ready for the publishers and she intended to take it with her when she left tomorrow with Konrad.

How little she had to pack! A small suitcase held everything she had brought from London, for there was little she had acquired here, a small rhinoceros carved in wood, a bracelet of red lucky beans, a few mats in Zulu beadwork . . . that was all she had to show for her trip to the wilds of Africa. She folded the white culotte suit she had worn at the yacht club dance. How objectionable Vincent had been that night – and yet she wished he had not met such a horrible death. She remembered the race, recalling the time when she had sailed over the moonlit water with Lester and had wished it could last for ever.

Well, it was all over now and she was going back to London. Perhaps when she left these surroundings and took up her own kind of life again she would eventually learn to forget Lester. Why, oh, why had she taken the risk of meeting him again when it had only led to heartbreak? It would have been better if she had stayed in her own environment and eventually married Konrad, for then she would never have known this pain, or known what it was like to be enthralled by a way of life that was not meant for her. Nor would she have known the bitter ecstasy of loving a man who did not consider her in the least suitable to be his wife.

Would she ever be able to forget this life in the wilds

of Africa that she had grown to love? What was that poem that described the yearning for another place and well-loved sounds? 'While I stand in the roadway or on the pavement grey, I hear it in the deep heart's core.' So she would feel when she remembered the sights and sounds of this part of Africa. Beyond the sounds of traffic, the squealing of brakes she would hear the piercing triumphant call of the fish eagle, throwing back his head as he uttered his challenging shout, and she would remember the low bubbling call of the coucal like shallow water running over sunlit pebbles.

She thought of the day when Lester took them to see the animals drinking at the pan and smiled wryly as she thought of that green-winged flashing bird, the emerald cuckoo, with his warning words, '*Umtwanyana ungendi*', 'Little child, don't marry. Young girl, don't fall in love.'

Now, when it was too late, she would heed the bird's warning. It would be a long time, if ever, before she fell in love again or considered marriage, even though Konrad was urging her to set a date for their wedding on their return to England.

That reminded her that she must speak to her father about this question of the land. Although she realized he probably needed the money, she would try to dissuade him from selling it, even though it meant being disloyal to Konrad. She went in search of him, finding him looking a little forlorn and lost now that his book was completed.

'Tracy my dear, I know you have a busy life and must go, but I do wish you could have stayed a little longer. However, I mustn't be selfish. I'm lucky to have had you to help me. It's only that I thought you might grow to like life in Africa as much as I do. But I suppose that was rather a foolish idea.'

'No, Papa, it wasn't foolish. I love it here. It's just that. . . .'

'I know. I realize that you must lead a very exciting life in London, associated by your work with a man like Konrad.'

'It's something to do with Konrad's business that I want to talk to you about, Papa,' Tracy said. 'Are you quite sure it's the best thing to do to sell that land to him? Of course I realize you probably need the money but. . . .'

Mr. Bryant looked puzzled. He ran his thin hands through his white silky tuft of hair and shook his head.

'I know I'm getting very absentminded, but I can't recollect . . . what piece of land are you talking about, Tracy?'

'The piece that belongs to you that Konrad is interested in buying in order to build the luxury hotel. Really, Daddy, I don't know whether it's a good idea.'

'But I know nothing of this plan, do I?'

Tracy tried not to sigh. Really, Papa was getting very absentminded these days, as he had said. His memory was shocking. She felt very worried about leaving him. Patiently she explained where the plot of land was situated.

'But it doesn't belong to me,' said Mr. Bryant.

'Are you sure?' asked Tracy. She was certain he had become confused over her explanation.

Mr. Bryant looked shamefaced.

'I hadn't intended to tell you, but during the last few years I've not been earning very much and I was very short of funds to continue with the plan for my book.

As well as this I was very anxious to see you again and wanted to be able to offer you the air fare to come out here. I happened to mention to Vincent once that I needed funds and he offered to lend me money. I'm afraid I became a bit carried away by having available ready cash and I was rather extravagant about replacing my library when it was damaged.

'Vincent said he was in no hurry for repayment and implied I could wait until I made some money from the book before refunding him, but later he changed his mind and demanded some security. Eventually I surrendered that piece of land to him. Before his death it belonged to Vincent, not to me, Tracy. I don't understand why you look so worried. Is it so important?'

'No, Papa. Don't worry, I'll talk to Konrad about it.'

Is it so important? he had asked. Not really, Tracy thought. The muddle over the ownership gave Lester a bad opinion of me, but then he never had a very good one, did he? She felt sad that Vincent had cheated her poor muddleheaded father, for surely the land must have been worth far more than the small loan? It was just the kind of sharp practice one would have expected of him. She wondered what the position was about the proposed hotel since Vincent's death.

Her brooding thoughts were interrupted by Konrad who came eagerly up the path, bounded on to the stoep and embraced her affectionately.

'Tracy darling, have you packed? I'm afraid there's a small change of plan, but I don't think it will inconvenience you.'

'What is that, Konrad?'

'Vincent's affairs are in such a muddle that there's liable to be a lot of dispute over the sale of this piece of land that we'd chosen for the hotel.'

'I understand that it doesn't belong to my father, but to Vincent.'

'There seems to be some doubt on the subject, but, Tracy, you know me. I can't wait a year until his estate is cleared up. I must get going now. What you said about being able to see lions easily influenced me too, I must admit. I've been thinking that perhaps this reserve is a bit too tame for the wealthy jet set. I understand you see game much more easily in the Kruger National Park, so I thought I would go to investigate the land question around its borders. Don't you think that's a good idea?'

'Very good,' Tracy agreed.

So the problem was solved and Lester would not have a luxury hotel on his doorstep.

'I'm hoping you'll come with me. We should be able to find something suitable within a few days. It won't hold us up much. I know you must be dying to get back to London. It's been pretty rough for you here, hasn't it?'

'Very well, Konrad, perhaps that would be a good idea,' Tracy said.

After all, what was there to stay for? The sooner she got away from here the better.

'I'll book a flight on the evening plane to Johannesburg,' Konrad said. 'Who knows? Perhaps we would have time to stop off and buy a diamond there.'

She went back to finish her packing. This time she would not be travelling with Julian. A rather subdued Evangeline had taken him with her to Lourenço Marques. Somehow Tracy thought Julian would get more attention in future. Evangeline seemed to have tired of her desire for excitement. Thinking of Julian made her recall the little mousebird. She supposed she would never know what had happened to him, but she hoped he was safe and happy with his fellows.

The gate squeaked and she heard someone walking swiftly up the path. It could only be Lester. She would know that light yet vigorous footstep anywhere. She heard him greet her father and left them talking for a few moments while she tried to collect herself. In the spotted mirror, her eyes gazed back at her, very large and grey. She must try to speak to him coolly, try to control this agitation.

She went into the living-room and for a moment before he was aware of her presence she was able to look at him with her full attention. All morning she had been assuring herself that she must try to forget him, yet now he was here she felt she must engrave his image in her memory for ever, the strong whipcord strength of his body, the rugged tanned features, the dark copper hair, and those golden eyes which seemed to possess the wild passion, the proud dignity of the lion.

Now that she had come her father left them alone and Lester came towards her and took both her hands in his.

'You've come to say good-bye, I suppose, Lester. I'm to go this afternoon.'

'So soon? I hadn't realized.'

'There's been a change of plan. Konrad has decided to inquire about land near the Kruger Park. After all, the land here didn't belong to my father.'

'So I'm told. Tracy, I want to say I'm sorry about that.'

Tracy shrugged.

'What does it matter? You never had much opinion of me anyway, did you, Lester?'

'There you're wrong.' He put his arms about her and gave her a little shake. 'I was astounded how brave you were the other day. No game ranger could have shown more courage.'

'But I was in the way. I was a hindrance to you.'

'You were wonderful. You made me feel I'd been wrong all the time when I said you weren't suited to the life here.'

'I'm glad about that,' said Tracy, gently removing herself from his arms. She could not endure being so near to him and yet knowing she was so far from his heart. 'But it can't matter one way or the other any more, can it? In a few days I'll be back in the city.'

He turned away frowning.

'Konrad – I'd forgotten about him. I suppose you'll be married quite soon?'

'I suppose so,' Tracy said.

Not for a long time, not until I've forgotten you with your reckless courage that's so much a part of Africa, your gentleness that you can show for any animal in distress, but never for me.

'Well, I'd better go,' said Lester.

He kissed her, a light brotherly kiss, and walked to the door. She watched his tall figure disappearing down the path, but he did not turn his head. The tears that she had restrained for so long blurred her last sight of him then spilled over, wetting her cheeks. Suddenly she noticed that he had stopped and was examining something at the fence. Then he turned to call her.

'Tracy, come and see what we have here!'

His voice was excited, his face alight with tender amusement.

'I can't go,' she thought, but the next moment, brushing her face with her hands, she was running down the path. There upon the palings of the fence was the little mousebird, Coly, come back home. It flew on to Tracy's shoulder, twittering indignantly as if to scold her for her desertion.

'Well, I'm damned, whoever heard of a homing mousebird?' asked Lester, smiling.

'I thought he'd be happier living with his own kind,' Tracy explained, still trying to wipe away the traces of her tears. 'But evidently I was wrong.'

'Wise bird,' said Lester, watching Coly putting his quaint topknotted head against Tracy's face. 'He knows what he wants and nothing will stop him from getting it.'

Something in his tone made her look up into his face. He took the mousebird from her hands and it flew with indignant twitterings towards the open window of her room. But Tracy did not even notice, because now she was in his arms and the golden eyes were watching her with the tenderness she had desired for so long.

'Are those tears for me, Tracy?'

She nodded soundlessly.

'The mousebird won't let you go,' said Lester, 'and neither will I. I can't take it any longer, this loving you in silence, keeping quiet about it because Konrad seems so much more your type. It's no use your saying you're going back to your own kind, Tracy, because I'm determined that you shall stay with me.'

'You're my kind, Lester,' Tracy said, holding up her mouth to be kissed. 'I've known that since I was fourteen.'

A NIGHT FOR POSSUMS

Dorothy Cork

A NIGHT
FOR
POSSUMS

"I want to warn you—in a friendly way," Pam said. "Everything will be all right as long as you don't fall in love with my brother, Mitch."

Rae knew the possibility of that was unlikely. After all, she'd started working for the wealthy Gilcrist family to forget a broken love affair.

Besides, conceited, domineering Mitchell Gilcrist was the last person she would ever be likely to fall in love with!

CHAPTER I

It was a night for possums, Rae Lambert thought. Still, bright moonlight, the big gum trees making pools of shadow across the track. She let Monkey break into a canter, then at the gates swung down and led the horse on to the road.

Tarmaroo. As she turned to close the gates, the letters on the mailbox confronted her—black letters in the dazzling white moonlight of the early spring night. Rae looked back across the paddocks towards the homestead almost hidden in its grove of orange trees, and without knowing it she sighed. Was Tarmaroo to be her home for the rest of her life? And would she one day come to love it? If she and Ralph had children—of course she would. It would be really home, then . . .

Back in the saddle, she wondered why she had this vague feeling of melancholy—almost of foreboding—when she should be full of joy and excitement with her marriage to Ralph only three weeks away. Then she would belong to someone again as she had not belonged since her mother died on the day they arrived in Australia over two years ago.

Rae glanced west to the paddocks of Greentrees, where Ralph was station manager. Like those of Tarmaroo they seemed to go on into endless distance, their monotony broken here and there by a group of wilga trees, or by the moonlit glitter from the water of a dam. She had never learned to love these red, scrub-covered outback plains, and deep in her heart she sympathized with her mother, who had run away from home and married an Englishman. Rae wondered again why her widowed mother had ever come back; whether there was some thing in the land that refused to be forgotten; whether it was a longing to see her own people again—her mother, her brother Jack. Or whether she had known there was not much time left to her, and wanted security for Rae.

Estelle Lambert had never reached her old home. She had been rushed from the ship to Sydney Hospital, and less than six hours later she was dead. Rae, nineteen years old, bewildered and grief-stricken, had been thankful to have Uncle Jack fly in from the west and take charge of everything—and finally take her back with him to Tarmaroo and her grandmother, Gertrude Steele, a woman as hard and uncompromising as her name. Rae found it hard to believe that her mother, so gay and fun-loving, could have been the daughter of this stern old lady.

But Uncle Jack was kind and good-humoured, and Rae had liked him from the start. Perhaps he had been too good-humoured, for he allowed the old lady to dominate him almost completely. Rae would never forget how Granny Steele had looked at her on that bitter, windy afternoon when she arrived at Tarmaroo exhausted from all she had been through, and said harshly, ' So you've come home—home to Tarmaroo.' Rae was a little frightened by the fierce old lady leaning on a stick and staring at her in an unfriendly way. She had tried to smile, not knowing what to say.

' You're very like your mother when she was a girl,' her grandmother had said after a moment, seeming to recollect herself. ' Let me look at you.'

That was the beginning. And for two years, until she and Uncle Jack were both killed outright in a car crash, Granny Steele had treated Rae as if she were her erring daughter come home to be punished for her naughtiness of long ago. It was she who called her Irene—with three syllables—though Rae had been named Irène after her father's French mother, and at home the name had been converted to an anglicized 'Rae'. Rae, helping the old lady who was crippled with arthritis, reading to her, fetching and carrying, listening to her long tales of early days, found pity mixed with her natural feelings of rebellion. Granny had loved her mother, but it had been the wrong kind of loving—possessive, demanding, selfish. And it was almost impossible to offer love in return.

Rae had not been really happy, though there had been happy times. She had not adjusted well to the red country, to the searing winds of winter, the burning heat of summer, the dust, the monotony, the loneliness. Uncle Jack had taught her to ride, and to drive a car, both of which she loved. Mrs Stacy, the housekeeper, had taught her to cook and to manage a household. She had met Ralph Stevens perhaps half a dozen times. He was the manager of Greentrees, a neighbouring sheep station. 'Overworked,' Granny had said—meaning the property, not Ralph. Too much of the scrub had been cleared from it, and now half of it was little more than desert. 'Greentrees! The name's laughable. Tarmaroo —do you know what that means? It's an aboriginal word for possum.'

Ralph was lean and brown—brown-haired, brown-skinned, with narrow light greenish eyes that fascinated Rae, they looked so knowing. Uncle Jack said that one day Ralph would inherit enough money from an uncle to buy a decent sized place of his own. Meanwhile he was gaining good experience. Uncle Jack's wife had died childless fifteen years ago. 'And that makes you,' he had told Rae seriously, 'the heir to all these lands.'

It didn't mean much to Rae. She could not imagine herself as the owner of a huge sheep station. At all events, Uncle Jack was barely fifty, and Rae certainly did not intend to live here always. She dreamed of being where there were hills and rivers instead of the flat horizon of the never-ending plains.

How differently fate had planned things, she reflected now as she cantered along the road towards Greentrees. The death of her uncle and her grandmother had been so sudden. Mrs Stacy, a motherly woman, had looked after her, and Harry Sanders, her son-in-law, and the overseer, took on the job of manager. Before long, Ralph Stevens and his sister Peggy befriended Rae. She suspected they had kept away before because old Mrs Steele had the reputation for being something of a dragon —as indeed she had been, though Rae tried to remember only the good things about her: her generosity with money, the great strength of character that prevented her from being querulous or peevish or from giving in to the failings of her old body, her ability to recall the past and recount it so vividly . . .

Now, as well as being the owner of Tarmaroo, Rae had a considerable amount of money, even after most of Uncle Jack's mining shares had been sold to pay probate on the estate. There was a bungalow too, that Uncle Jack had recently acquired, in one of Sydney's northern seaside suburbs and where he had planned to take Rae for a holiday in the coming summer.

The only thing Rae had lacked was personal friends. Granny had not given her sufficient freedom to get to know anyone more than casually, and in the outback, one's circle was necessarily limited. It was while she was out riding that Rae encountered Ralph and Peggy Stevens again, and from that chance meeting her friendship with Ralph had developed until now they were to be married and her future was settled.

Rae was now riding across Greentrees paddocks, and ahead of her, beyond the clumps of pepper trees, she could see lights shining from the house. She tethered Monkey to a tree outside the home garden, and in a moment was walking along the path towards the front verandah. She heard a rustling in the branches of the big gum tree that Peggy insisted on leaving standing in the garden, and that Ralph cursed because of the mess its leaves made in summer on the lawn, and paused. Glancing up, she saw a brush-tailed possum that had swung down from a higher branch and was now staring down at her with bright friendly eyes. Rae wished she had a piece of fruit to give it. There was a brush-tailed possum at Tarmaroo that came often to the side verandah near the kitchen to be fed.

Because she paused then, she realized later, the whole of her future life was changed.

In that moment of stillness, as Rae stood beneath the big tree, Ralph's voice floated to her from the verandah where he and Peggy sat smoking. His words came clearly and distinctly, carrying as sounds do on a still night.

' Three weeks more, Peg, and we'll be shot of this rundown dump and sitting pretty over at Tarmaroo.'

Rae stiffened, shocked by his tone as well as his words.

' I feel a bit sorry for that little pommie kid,' came Peggy's slightly husky voice. ' All on her own and grabbing at straws.'

' Oh, Irene will be all right,' Ralph said with a laugh, and Rae put out a hand to steady herself against the gum-tree. Her heart was pounding hard and painfully in her chest. ' She's not a bad sort of a girl, and if we want Tarmaroo then we must take her with it. We've no option.'

' If only Uncle Charlie hadn't married that nurse and altered his will you'd never have had to bother about her,' Peggy said. ' I wish—'

'Well, just stop wishing. Irene's perfectly happy, we'll get what we want and everything will be just hunky dory.'

Almost, Rae could hear Peggy sigh. 'I suppose you're right. But I still don't like it.'

With an effort, Rae made herself move. She had heard enough—too much—and she felt almost paralysed. Somehow she forced herself to go, silently, almost blindly, back across the garden and through the gate, and presently to her relief she found herself sitting limp and shaken in the saddle while Monkey carried her home.

Her mind went over and over what she had heard. There was no mistaking its meaning. Ralph didn't love her. He wanted Tarmaroo—because his other hopes had gone. Because Uncle Charlie had married his nurse before he died. She felt sick, nauseated. In three weeks' time she'd have been married to him.

Despite the mildness of the spring night she shivered.

She wondered, as she let herself into the big, low moon-washed stone homestead, if anyone knew that Ralph's expected inheritance had come to nothing. She thought not. She thought that he had kept it very quiet. Mrs Stacy would have mentioned it if she had known. A new wave of nausea overtook Rae. The verandah outside her bedroom was flooded with moonlight and she sank down in a cane chair and put her hands over her aching eyes. She felt unutterably alone. The house was so empty. Mrs Stacy, knowing she had ridden over Greentrees, was probably at the Sanders' cottage, listening to the radio or playing cards with Harry and Enid. Or helping put the children to bed.

Suddenly Rae's eyes flooded with tears and she wept forlornly and copiously. With the tears came a wild rush of thoughts. 'I'll go away—I'll never come back. I can't bear it here a minute longer.' In her mind she saw the flat endless plains, stretching away for ever, hostile, weird, withdrawn—as perhaps her mother had seen them.

Presently, a little ashamed of her abandon, she went to the bathroom to bathe her eyes.

'You should be glad you found out in time,' she told her reflection, as she combed out the long silky light brown hair that had slipped out of its clip. Her lashes were stuck together in points, and her dark grey eyes looked full of grief. She would have to let Ralph know that she wasn't going to marry him.

She went to the small writing desk in the sitting room and slowly, carefully, wrote him a letter. Ridiculously, she felt mean as she wrote it. Poor Ralph! It would be a terrible blow to him not to have Tarmaroo after all! What would he do?

'Ralph,' she wrote, 'When I rode over to see you to-night I heard you talking to Peggy. I couldn't marry you now. I'm sorry, but you will understand. I don't want ever to see you again.' She signed herself Irène Lambert, then slipped the opal ring from her finger. 'Opals are unlucky,' Mrs Stacy had said when Rae showed her the ring, and Rae had laughed as though superstitions didn't bother her. She wrapped the ring carefully in a piece of tissue and put it with the letter in an envelope on which she had written Ralph's name.

'Mrs Stacy can see he gets it,' she thought.

It was only then that she realized she had made up her mind to go away. How else could she expect never to see Ralph again?

She went to her room and took the big suitcase down from the cupboard above the wardrobe. Then she began to pack. She would leave as soon as it was daylight. She would go to the holiday cottage on the coast. And from there she would plan her next move.

Her packing was almost done when she heard Mrs Stacy come through from the back of the house and call in her friendly way, ' Is that you, Irene? Would you like a cup of tea?'

' Yes, please,' Rae called back. There was a lump in her throat. Although she had never confided much in the housekeeper, she was very fond of her and very much aware of her integrity, her loyalty. She went out at once to the big kitchen with its shining tiled floor and old-fashioned scrubbed deal table.

' Mrs Stacy,' she said, quickly, definitely, ' I'm not going to marry Ralph.' She saw the concern in the housekeeper's brown eyes and added at once, ' It's all right—please don't worry. I haven't told Ralph yet. But I think I'll go away for a little while.'

' Best thing,' Mrs Stacy said, pouring the tea and pushing a cup over to Rae. ' I'm sorry, Irene.' She didn't ask any questions, and Rae knew that although she had never really taken to Ralph, she was sorry.

' I've packed,' said Rae, her voice tight. ' When I've drunk my tea I'll go to bed. I want to leave as soon as it's light. If Ralph comes, there's a letter for him on the writing bureau.'

' I'll see he gets it, my dear. Where will you go? Sydney?'

' Yes. To Uncle Jack's house at the beach.' She drank some of the hot tea and felt steadier, even managed a smile. ' You won't have to keep it a secret. I don't think Ralph will follow me.'

' Still, I shan't tell him,' decided Mrs Stacy. ' And that means no one must know. Unless there's someone you'd like me to contact?'

Rae shook her head. There was no one.

' How long will you stay away?'

' I don't know.' Rae lifted her head. Her eyes were

very dark. 'I haven't made any plans yet. I'll let you know.'

Mrs Stacy nodded as if she understood. 'I'll take good care of things here. I'll move in with Harry and Enid perhaps, but I'll keep the house aired and clean so it's ready any time you want to come back . . . Better let Mr Belrose know where you are.'

'I'll do that,' said Rae. Mr Belrose was the solicitor. 'And thank you, Mrs Stacy.' She finished her tea, and when she had showered went to bed on the sleepout where she always slept in warm weather. She had a drive of over four hundred miles ahead of her and she didn't know the road. She had been over part of it with Uncle Jack over a year ago, but only as far as Trangie. She would need her sleep, and resolutely tried to stop herself from thinking.

But her mind would not be still. She remembered Ralph's kisses, and the night over at Greentrees when he had asked her to marry him. It had been unexpected, yet she had said 'Yes' at once. And afterwards he had called Peggy and they had drunk a toast in, of all things, champagne.

What had made her fall in love with Ralph? Had it been nothing more than proximity and her own need for love? She remembered Mrs Stacy saying once, 'Ralph's not my idea of a good manager. He knows it's killing the land to clear the scrub, yet he takes no heed.' Had it been a veiled warning? Rae wondered now.

The words of an old ballad ran mockingly through her mind:

> ' " He does not love me for my birth
> Nor for my lands so broad and fair.
> He loves me for my own true worth,
> And that is well," said Lady Claire.'

There were tears on her cheeks when at last she slept.

Rae lay flat on her stomach on the white sand. The morning sun caressed her back, and the sea breeze stirred tendrils of her long hair. The sound of the surf was in her ears, her eyes were closed, one cheek rested on her forearm. She felt lazy, drugged, and very much of an escapist, and she knew dimly that it could not—must not—go on. She had been nearly a week at the bungalow now, and she had done nothing but sleep, eat, swim, and lie in the sun of an exceptionally warm September. It had been as though some healing balm were poured on her spirit, so that her unhappiness, her bitterness, had almost dissolved away. But it was an unreal existence. She would have to start living again, and this morning she had awakened full of determination to look for some way of justifying her existence.

So far she had done nothing.

The thought made her feel uncomfortable, and she opened her eyes, blinked in the bright sunshine, and sat up. Nearby two girls were sunbathing. Both had smooth brown limbs, but while one had short curly brown locks, the other had long smooth dark hair. Rae wished suddenly that they would talk to her. She was hungry for companionship, and when the curly-haired girl began to speak she listened unthinkingly to what she was saying.

' I wonder how things are going for dear old Gran. I hope to heaven *someone* suitable answered the ad. Those two who were waiting when we left didn't look a day under fifty.'

' Fifty's not old, Pam,' the dark girl demurred. ' And I think Mitch was right to stipulate middle-aged or elderly. That way there's much more chance of finding someone who'll be devoted and kindly and unselfish.'

' Devoted! Paid companions aren't likely to be devoted these days, Helen—it's no use pretending. Look at Alison!'

' Oh, Alison! But the older ones may be,' the girl called Helen argued.

' Anyhow, Gran doesn't like doormats any more than she likes nannies—or dragons.'

' Mitch will see she gets someone suitable,' Helen insisted.

' Trust you to champion Mitch! Seeing that it was his fault Alison left, it's certainly up to him to do something. But Gran's on her dignity, and she won't sit back and meekly do whatever he tells her. She enjoyed Alison's company—even if she did complain that she wasn't always there when she was wanted. She likes someone young and lively around her.'

Helen said slowly, ' I sometimes feel guilty that we don't do more to help. The office could do without you, I suppose, and my pupils don't take up that much of my time.'

Rae, listening, was quite caught up. Surely the fragile-looking Helen wasn't some kind of a teacher! She was really quite lovely, with classical features and high, delicate cheekbones.

Pam said decidedly, ' Family arrangements are never satisfactory—they make so easily for disagreements. And after all, money's no object.'

' It's a comfort to remember that,' Helen agreed a little dryly. She sat up and pulled a beach coat around her shoulders. ' I've had enough sun. Let's go back to Illalangi and see what's happened.'

The other girl agreed and Rae watched them gather up their towels and beach gear and felt regret to see them go. The curly-haired one—Pam—caught her eye, and Rae thought she smiled faintly. Her eyes followed them as they crossed the sand to the esplanade, and then with a sigh she began to think of going home herself. Home to what? To the silence of the bungalow and a lunch she would prepare herself and eat alone. As she stood up, her eye caught a glitter in the sand where the girls had been lying. She went to investigate, and found a small diamond-studded gold watch.

The girls had disappeared, and for a moment Rae was at a loss. Then she remembered they had mentioned the name of their home—a name with a liquid sound about it. Rae searched her mind and came up with Illalinga.

Which turned out, she discovered later when she called in at the local news agency to try her luck, to be not far wrong.

'You mean Illalangi. That's Gilcrists' place,' the newsagent told her when she had explained her dilemma. ' Go right up to the northern end of the beach, miss, then take the first road on your left and follow that up the hill. Vista Street—it's a cul-de-sac—is on the right, at the top. Gilcrists' place is on the high side—a big two-storied white house with a terraced garden and a double garage on the road. You can't miss it.'

Rae thanked him and went back to her bungalow. It was at this end of the beach—the southern end—in a quiet road that led directly down to the sand. In fact, Rae's garden—if you could call it that—was half inundated by sand, that, in spite of the paling fence, had blown or drifted into it. There was a back gate, but it no longer opened because of the white sand banked up on either side of it. It was a real holiday place.

Rae found it easier to jump over the fence than to climb on to the road and use the other entrance, and she did so now. Suddenly, life seemed to be more interesting. She was eager to shower and change, have her salad lunch, and be off to the house on the hill.

She ate at a small table on the wide verandah that faced the sea. It was a delightful verandah and the view was magnificent. Rae, after so long on the western plains with its red sandy soil, never tired of that view. And as her eyes took it in now, she thought of those girls on the beach, Pam and Helen Gilcrist, almost as though they were friends. She thought of 'dear old Gran,' and of Mitch—whoever he might be—who had stipulated middle-aged or elderly for Gran's new companion, and whose fault it was that Alison had left.

Rae's mind played round agreeably with thoughts of the Gilcrist family, and later, when her dishes were washed, she prepared to drive up to Illalangi. She put the little watch, safely wrapped in a clean tissue, in her handbag, locked the house, got her car from the garage and drove off. As she drove, she reflected how pleasant it would be to see the two girls again. She wondered if she would be asked into the house, and if Gran would have found a suitable companion. It would be wonderful to sit and talk to people again. She was very tired of her own company and of the monotonous regularity with which her thoughts returned to Ralph and that moonlit night when she had discovered the truth about his feelings for her. She no longer recalled his kisses with nostalgia. Rather, she was inclined to think she had been all sorts of an idiot to be so easily fooled by them. It would never happen again . . .

Rae found Vista Street and the big white house called Illalangi. She parked her car in the street, opened the wrought iron gate and climbed the path through the terraced garden where brilliant torrents of bougainvillea cascaded over bush rock. On this side of the house there were no tall trees, so as not to obstruct the ocean view, no doubt, but behind and at the sides, thickly leafed

trees and tall palms gave shelter and shade. At the top
of the garden was a wide stone-paved terrace shaded by
a vine-covered pergola. Rae noted that it was a grapevine. There was a long low wrought iron table at one
end with chairs to match, and at the other end a small
bubbling fountain whose waters spilled into a fern-
fringed pool. From here, the view over the shimmering
blue ocean was magnificent, and made Rae catch her
breath with delight. Before she had reached the front
door, the girl called Pam came on to the terrace through
one of the french doors. She looked at Rae smilingly.

' Hello, I should know you, shouldn't I? But I'm
awfully sorry, I've forgotten your name—and where we
met. Was it at the Valley?' She stopped face to face
with Rae, who thought she was prettier than ever in her
simply cut yellow and white linen dress. Her eyes were
cornflower blue, and beneath a short upper lip very white
teeth showed as she smiled.

Rae, who had removed her sunglasses, smiled back
but shook her head. ' No—we didn't meet anywhere,
really. But I was sunbaking on the beach near you this
morning and I found this after you'd gone.' She opened
her handbag and handed over the tiny parcel. ' A watch.
It still seems to be going.'

' Oh, you child wonder!' exclaimed the other girl in
amazed delight. ' I thought it had gone for good this
time. I'm always mislaying my most treasured posses-
sions—a fact that probably has some fearful psycho-
pathological significance! Please do come into the house
and have a drink while I thank you properly.'

She showed Rae into a big airy room with a floor of
dark polished jarrah and a scattering of off-white rugs.
' Sit down while I dash out to the fridge. I shan't be a
moment. Oh—you haven't told me your name.'

' Rae—Rae Lambert.'

'Rae?' the girl repeated enquiringly.

'Irène really. After my father's mother who was French.'

'How beaut! I love the French. I'm Pam Gilcrist.' Another bright look and she flashed off. Rae sat down by long glass doors that opened on to the terrace with its cool green shade from the trailing vine leaves, and looked over to the sea. The house was very quiet and she wondered where everyone was. Where were Gran— and Helen—and the mysterious Mitch on this Saturday afternoon?

Pam came back with a tray holding a jug of frosty-looking lemon drink and two tall glasses.

'Will this do or would you rather have something with a kick?' she asked. 'The house is loaded with it, of course, so say if you would. Personally I'm not much of a drinker. I prefer the innocuous lemon or orange.'

A little amused, Rae said a lemon drink was just what she needed, and accepted one of the tall glasses. Pam sat down at one end of a couch upholstered in a soft apricot colour and gave her a slightly quizzical look.

'Rae, I don't quite know how to say this, but—what can I do to thank you for bringing back my watch? If I'd advertised I'd have offered a reward—'

Rae smiled. 'I don't want a reward. Forget it, please.'

'I shan't *forget* it,' said Pam with a faint frown. 'Tell me anyhow how you knew where to find me. That's been intriguing me a little.'

'I'm afraid I listened to you talking to—your sister, wasn't it?' Rae confessed.

'Yes—Helen.'

'You mentioned going back to Illalangi, and though I didn't remember the name exactly I got through to the man at the news agency, and he did the rest.'

'That was very clever of you,' Pam said. 'I'm sure I should never have remembered such a name at all. It means—would you believe it—house on a hill!' She laughed gaily. 'Of course I should fall over backwards if you told me you knew that. You're English, aren't you?'

'Yes. And it's very nice of you not to show that you think me bad-mannered for listening to other people's conversations.'

'Oh, I do it myself when I'm alone,' Pam said with a shrug. 'It's one way of finding out how the other half lives.'

Rae let that pass, but asked, 'Did your grandmother find a companion? I couldn't help being interested.'

'Poor old Gran!' Pam looked ruefully amused. 'I'm afraid she had no luck. Or at least, she got very stubborn and dug her toes in and refused to consider any of the applicants. You see, Mitch had dealt with the written replies and weeded them out and those who came this morning were on his short list. All more or less elderly. And Gran has quite made up her mind she's going to have somebody young.'

'I rather gathered that this morning.'

Pam gave her a sudden stare and exclaimed, 'Of course! You're looking for a job. Why didn't I think of that before?'

CHAPTER II

Rae, startled, was about to protest that Pam was wrong when she stopped herself. Maybe she was looking for a job! She decided to play it by ear. She said calmly, ' I didn't come because of that. I came to return your watch. I only asked about your grandmother out of interest.'

Pam was hardly listening, but the cornflower blue eyes watched her with a lively and amused interest. ' You English girls are certainly enterprising,' she commented. ' One's always reading books by girls who've come out here and worked as cooks or governesses or jilleroos and heaven knows what else in the outback. Is that the sort of thing *you*'re doing, Rae?'

' I've been in the outback,' said Rae cautiously. ' Out on the western plains. But I haven't done anything adventurous.'

' I take it you've had enough of the bush for a while.'

' Something like that,' Rae agreed. It was true enough as far as it went. ' But as I'm only twenty-one, I don't imagine I'd stand a chance to get this particular job. *Mitch* wouldn't consider me.'

Pam laughed. ' Don't worry about Mitch. He's my half-brother—and in a way our guardian. There are three of us: Helen, then me, then Joan who's nineteen . . . But tell me—is this the sort of thing you're looking for?'

Rae said carefully, ' I don't know what's required.'

' Then I'll tell you.' Pam leaned back on the couch and, having disposed of her glass, ticked off a few points on the fingers of her well-manicured hands.

' Gran wants someone to drive her about—to the

hairdresser, the library, on shopping sprees and so on;
to escort her to tea-parties with her friends (she's eighty-
three, by the way, but pretty active); to read to her when
her eyes are tired; to *co-operate* in her knitting and
embroidery; to fetch her snacks when Mrs McPhail, the
housekeeper, is up to her ears in something and hasn't
the time, and we girls, who should be such a comfort to
her in her old age, are careering about with no thought
for anyone but ourselves (ask Mitch).' Her blue eyes
were rueful now, her hands fell into her lap and she told
Rae honestly, 'It's not what you would call a really
cushy job. Frankly, it would drive me round the bend,
always having to be on call. And there are times when
Gran needs help even with dressing—doing her hair—'

'I know,' said Rae understandingly. She was thinking of her own grandmother. 'Old people often need
more help than they like to admit.'

Pam sat up with a pleased look. 'You mean you've
done this kind of thing before? You can knit—drive a
car—?'

'Well, yes,' said Rae with a laugh. She felt excited.
It really was the sort of job she could do.

'Terrific!' Pam exclaimed. 'You'd have to live here,
you know, but you'd have time off. And the pay, I
promise you, is good. There's only one thing—' She
paused, and Rae sighed.

'Your brother. Mitch. He wants someone middle-
aged. And I can't pretend to be that.'

'Not that,' Pam said. 'I was just going to warn you
—in a friendly way. Everything will be all right as
long as you don't go and fall in love with Mitch. You
see, the last one—Alison Campbell—*did*, and that,
eventually, was the end of her. Even Gran knew it was
hopeless. Poor Alison was so demented she'd reached
the stage where she'd forgotten why she was here. And

in actual fact, she wasn't here that much. She'd pack Gran up at the drop of a hat and take her up to the Valley. And Mitch thinks Gran should be here, to keep an eye on *us*—though I've moved into a flat nearer town now. He was right to send Alison packing, I suppose —it was embarrassing for him having her chase after him the way she did. Still, it left us in a bit of a spot.'

Rae, who had begun to wonder if Mitch was conceited as well as dictatorial, said coolly, 'Well, I'm sure I shouldn't fall in love with him.'

'Why not? You haven't met Mitch yet! Or are you engaged?'

'No. I was engaged, but it's been broken off.'

'Oh—I'm sorry. But you mean you're not likely to lose your heart again in a hurry?'

'That's what I mean,' said Rae firmly. She thought how Ralph had deceived her and knew that it was true. She would be very cautious, very level-headed, before committing herself again.

Pam slipped off the couch and smiled down at her. 'Well, what are we waiting for? Let's go and beard Gran in her den. But first—you *have* done this kind of thing before, haven't you? I don't want to say you have if you haven't.'

'I looked after an old lady out west,' Rae assured her. 'I'll tell your grandmother about it if she wants to know.'

'That's fine then. Come along. Gran's in her own little sitting room upstairs, and Mitch has gone out, so we have a clear field.'

Rae, though relieved to hear this, felt guilty about it too—as if she were going behind his back. But after all, a companion was needed, Pam had said they were in a spot—and even if she didn't stay long, at least she could help out. All the same, she was surprised at the strength of her own determination to get this job and to hold it, as she followed Pam up the stairway with its fine gold coloured carpeting.

'Here's hoping,' whispered Pam as they approached an open door from which came the sound of pop music.

Gran—Mrs Gilcrist, Rae reminded herself—was a slender bright-eyed old lady. She sat with her feet up on an old-fashioned sofa—all the furniture in her room was old-fashioned, not antique, but very well cared for, and, Rae had the impression, very much loved. In spite of the music which came from a small transistor radio, she was intent on her knitting with which she seemed to be having some trouble, and didn't look up when Pam said, 'Hi, Gran!' But when she added, 'This is Rae Lambert and she's come about the job,' her head jerked up sharply. Rae was sure she had a rejection ready on her tongue, but when she saw Rae, young with long shining brown hair and a slender figure, she let her knitting fall on to her lap and gave a sudden wicked little laugh.

'Has she indeed? Doesn't she know that one of the conditions is that she should be middle-aged and ugly, with a mouth that turns down at the corners?' She snapped off the transistor and patted the sofa enticingly. 'Come here, Miss—Miss Rae Lambert, sit down and let's have your credentials.'

Rae's eyes were on the knitting, on the stitches that before her eyes were sliding slowly off the needle. As she sat down she reached for it and started rectifying matters while Pam said, sitting on the arm of the sofa and putting her arm around her grandmother's shoulders, 'Her credentials, Gran darling, are that she found my little watch on the beach—the one you gave me for my last birthday—and brought it back to me. She wants a job and she's used to looking after people—she minded a sweet old lady in the outback. Who was it again, Rae?'

'Mrs Steele,' Rae said. 'Of Tarmaroo Station out west.' She was sure it would mean nothing to them. 'I'm afraid I haven't any references with me, Mrs Gilcrist, but I could get one for you.'

'References?' The old lady was smiling to herself. 'Why would I want references when you've brought back my silly granddaughter's watch? You're young and pretty and I like the sound of your voice, and you've righted my knitting without even being asked. The last girl I had—Alison—wasn't nearly so adept, dear girl though she was. Can you manage patterns?'

'Yes, I'm quite good at patterns,' Rae smiled. She liked the old lady immediately, and decided that she didn't look as if she would be any sort of a tyrant.

'Can you drive a car, Rae?'

'Yes,' said Rae, and was surprised when Mrs Gilcrist said briskly, 'That's settled, then,' and shot an impish look across the room. Following her gaze, Rae found herself staring at the photograph of a very good-looking dark-browed man who was just not smiling. There seemed little doubt that this was Mitch, and Rae quailed, for there was a strong and purposeful air about him. He was certainly not going to be pleased if Mrs Gilcrist engaged her. She looked back at the old lady who said, 'Suppose you move in tomorrow some time, then you can be ready to start work on Monday. Or is that too soon for you? What are you doing now?'

Rae swallowed. 'That will suit me perfectly, Mrs Gilcrist. I'm not actually doing anything just now except—well, I'm looking after a house down by the beach. But are you sure '—she glanced uneasily at the photograph—'that you don't want to investigate me further?'

'Quite sure. I'm perfectly satisfied that we shall get along splendidly together. That is, if you really want the job.'

'I do,' said Rae, and meant it. She added prudently, 'I'll leave my address and telephone number in case you should want to contact me.' Then, she thought, if Mitch put his foot down—and he looked as if he might easily do that—they would be able to notify her without trouble and it would save embarrassment all round. Pam offered her a small writing tablet, and a few moments later she had said goodbye and was about to leave the room when a gentle question called her back.

'Mrs Steele of Tamaroo Station, I think you said?'

Rae turned back, colouring. 'Yes.'

'She and her son were killed in an accident not so very long ago. I remember Alison reading it to me from the *Herald*. I never met the Steeles, but I heard of them from time to time from various people. What became of the property? Put up for sale, I suppose?'

Rae hesitated. She could feel her cheeks paling now. She said evenly, 'No. It was left to a grandchild.'

'A grandchild? That would be—I remember, there was a girl who eloped.' Mrs Gilcrist crinkled up her eyes in an effort to remember, but to Rae's relief nothing more seemed to come to her. 'We must talk about it some day. . . . Well now, I'll expect you some time tomorrow and I'm certain we'll get along together splendidly. Middle-aged indeed!'

In the hallway, Pam laughed aloud.

'There, what did I tell you? I'm so glad you got the job, Rae. Gran is delighted, and let's face it, so am I. No more guilt feelings. I can go back to my flat with a clear conscience.' They were descending the stairs now, and Rae felt anxious to get away before Mitch came back and caught her red-handed, as it were.

'You've been rewarded nicely for bringing back my watch,' Pam said, at the front door. 'I really do treasure it, even if I am careless.'

'I hope your brother won't be angry,' Rae said ruefully. 'Was that his photograph in Mrs Gilcrist's sitting room?'

'It was. And wasn't Gran as pleased as a dog with two tails to be scoring over him? But don't worry, Rae. After all, it's Gran who must be considered in this matter, not Mitch. Anyhow, he spends most of his time at the Valley.'

'And I shall stay here,' said Rae, wondering where the Valley was. 'I shan't do an Alison!'

They both laughed, and on that happy friendly note they parted.

That night after she had eaten, Rae sat down to write to Mrs Stacy. It occurred to her that the housekeeper, let into her confidence, would be able to send her a personal reference, and vouch for the fact that she had looked after Mrs Steele satisfactorily for two years. 'Please refer to me as *Rae* Lambert,' she added in a postscript, and had just sealed the envelope when there was a ring at the front door.

Her immediate fear was that it was Ralph, but when she opened the door, she found herself looking into the dark unsmiling face of the man in the photograph. Mitch! Her heart gave a lurch.

'Miss Rae Lambert?' he queried, his voice hard.

'Yes,' said Rae, as coolly as she could. But she thought ruefully that this looked like the end of her job.

'I'm Mitchell Gilcrist. I believe my grandmother engaged you as her companion, this afternoon.'

'That's so,' Rae agreed pleasantly, as though everything were quite in order. It flashed through her mind that it was perhaps no wonder Alison Campbell had fallen in love with him. He was devastatingly handsome—more so in the flesh than in the photograph—and there was a very vital quality about him. His face was deeply bronzed, his eyes a brilliant blue—darker than his sister Pam's. His teeth were very white, though so far she had caught only a glimpse of them, for he had given her not the vestige of a smile. 'Would you like to come in, Mr Gilcrist?'

He hesitated for a second, then declined. 'No, thank you, I shan't take up much of your time, Miss Lambert. I just want to offer you my apologies and explain that my grandmother engaged you in a fit of pique. You're not at all the sort of person we're looking for—not in the least suitable. And far too young.'

'Agreed I am young,' Rae said with a smile. She looked him very straight in the face. 'But I must disagree as to my suitability. Mrs Gilcrist considered I would answer her needs very well.'

He drew his thick brows down. 'The advertisement stated, quite definitely, middle-aged or elderly.'

'So I believe. But I didn't come in answer to the advertisement,' said Rae mildly.

He stared at her for a moment, then to her surprise said, 'Perhaps I shall come in after all. If we're to discuss this we may as well do so privately.

Rae felt she had gained a little ground, and feeling more determined than ever to hang on to her job, showed him into the sitting room. It was a simple room, but it was well and tastefully furnished, with just the right air of casualness that a holiday cottage at the beach should have. As Mitchell Gilcrist sat down, he sent her a very penetrating look that took her in from her shining brown hair to her pretty Italian sandals.

'I understand you came to Illalangi to return my

sister's watch to her. And I think, Miss Lambert, that you are what I would call an opportunist.'

Rae flushed angrily. 'And I think you are being insulting, Mr Gilcrist. Just what do you mean?'

'Surely you know.' The blue eyes watched her with a cool amusement. 'But if you want it, I shall put it in plain words.'

'Do,' said Rae tightly.

'Briefly then, you saw a cosy little niche for yourself in the Gilcrist family.' He glanced round the charming sitting room. 'If I may say so, it would appear you have quite a talent for finding cosy little niches for yourself.'

'Whether you may or may not, you've said so. And if I may say so, I take exception to the things you're implying. The Gilcrist family means nothing to me. It's your grandmother I'm interested in.'

'Really?' He didn't look as though he cared a cent about her feelings or believed a word she said. 'My grandmother tells me you are minding this bungalow. But you are only too ready to walk out on whoever it is you're minding it for when you see a better opportunity for yourself.'

Rae bit her lip. She shouldn't have told that lie. She put her chin up. 'I'm sorry I told Mrs Gilcrist that, it wasn't true. Actually, the bungalow belongs to me.'

'It's yours?' He sounded so incredulous that Rae said haughtily, 'It was left me by the son of the old lady I looked after until recently.' Immediately she realized she had only made things worse for herself, for he said hatefully, 'You did well for yourself. And you haven't had another position since then?'

'No. But I thought I'd found a job for myself today.'

'Found is a well chosen word,' he said thoughtfully. 'As far as I can see, you have no right to this job, Miss

Lambert. No references, no qualifications. You must think we're a lot of fools, or that it's a very easy job.'

'I have had experience,' Rae said, bristling with antagonism and beginning to feel she hated Mitchell Gilcrist thoroughly. He was handsome, yes—but horrid! 'And I can drive a car.'

'We'll come to that later,' he said. 'Or we may possibly do so. Meanwhile—references, Miss Lambert.'

'You shall have my reference as soon as I receive it,' Rae said with as much assurance as she could manage. Oddly enough, he now seemed to be considering her— which seemed quite amazing, in the circumstances. Rae could only think that the necessity to find a companion must be urgent.

'Mrs Steele, for whom you say you worked, is dead.'

'Her housekeeper, Mrs Stacy, will vouch for me,' said Rae quickly. 'She's been at Tarmaroo for about fifteen years.'

'We'll see, then,' he conceded. 'How long is it since you left the country?'

Rae's eyes fell. 'Not—not long.'

'You stayed on after your employer died?'

'Yes.' Rae faced him again. 'I was engaged to be married to the manager of a neighbouring property.'

'What went wrong, then? Or did you think you could do better for yourself in the city?'

How she hated him! His opinion of her seemed to be as low as it possibly could be, and for no reason at all expect that he was insufferably conceited and had some inflated opinion of the status of his family. Rae said, 'I hardly think the matter's relevant. We're discussing my suitability—or otherwise—as companion to Mrs Gilcrist. Who, by the way, I thought was a very sweet old lady. It amazes me that you are actually her grandson.'

For some reason that made him smile and his blue eyes

were full of good-humour and friendliness. Then the smile vanished, and he said, ' Let us return to our moutons by all means, and presently we'll see if you're what I would call a responsible driver. Meanwhile, I'd like to explain that working for my grandmother is not the easy job you probably expect. She may be a sweet old lady, but she'll ask a great deal of you, and you won't always find her thoughtful or considerate. Those are qualities that will be expected of *you*. In my opinion, it's not at all a suitable job for a girl of your age. I have sisters, and I know a lot more about the girls of your generation than you may imagine.'

Rae narrowed her eyes and caught herself calculating how old he must be. Perhaps thirty-five—thirty-seven at the most. It had not occurred to her for a moment that he wouldn't know a great deal about girls and women of all ages. She said, ' Still, Mrs Gilcrist's last companion was young.'

' Exactly,' he said dryly. ' Miss Campbell also was an opportunist. Nevertheless, let me repeat that girls of your age don't as a rule devote themselves whole-heartedly to the interests of the aged unless they have a vocation—which is rare—or an ulterior motive, which is more common. My grandmother will try your patience. She will expect you to spend endless and boring hours with her when you long to be down at the beach with a crowd of young friends. You'll wait for her at the hairdressers, you'll fall asleep at dress-fittings ; you'll be driven to despair over finding suitable books at the library. You'll sit in on tea-parties with garrulous old ladies, and even your evenings will be spent dancing attendance on her. My sisters, whom I asked to do their bit to tide us over, would tell you if they were honest how demanding our grandmother is. You won't see much of them, you know. Pam is sometimes here at weekends, but has a flat at Wollstonecraft. And I spend most of my time in the Valley.' He broke off and eyed her sardonically. 'Are you still interested, Miss Lambert?'

Rae shrugged lightly. He seemed to be doing his best to frighten her off, and she was irritated that he had thought that little bit of information about his own whereabouts was relevant. She said, 'I've already agreed to take the job, Mr Gilcrist. I see no reason to change my mind.'

'Even though I advise quite strongly against it?'

So he was only advising now! Rae was suddenly amused. He had come to give her her marching orders, and now he was only offering advice.

'Even though you advise against it,' she agreed gravely.

He stood up. 'There still remains your driving test.'

'I have a licence, I assure you,' said Rae, rising too.

'I daresay. But to hold a licence is not enough. I'm certainly not allowing my grandmother to go out in the care of an incompetent or unreliable driver. The car I have outside is the one she uses. Are you ready?'

Rae said that she must first fetch her handbag which held her licence. In her bedroom, she glanced quickly in the mirror, ran a comb through her hair and clipped it back so that it would not blow in her eyes. She was not worried over her driving. Uncle Jack had said she had good natural road sense, and she had gained plenty of practice taking her grandmother into the town on just such errands as Mitch Gilcrist was so sure would bore her to tears. She was quite certain that compared with the life she had led at Tarmaroo she would find her new existence even colourful! She was sure to see something of the three Gilcrist girls. All in all, she felt the job was hers, and concluded that Mitch—she thought of him as that—had capitulated because he could see that *she* was not inclined to fall for his looks or his fortune or anything else. She had surely made that plain enough!

Mrs Gilcrist's car was an automatic. Uncle Jack's had been an automatic and Rae had driven it often enough to be familiar with it. This car was a different make, and more up to date, and Rae listened carefully while Mitchell briefed her on it. Sitting beside him in the car with the cool night wind blowing in through the open window, and the sound of the sea, as it rushed over the sand, in her ears, Rae felt more alive than she had for a long time, full of a sense of excitement and happiness. Mitchell, explaining something impersonal to her, seemed friendly and pleasant, and she reflected that he probably had his good qualities like anybody else. When he had done, she started up the car and drove along the road as he directed her. She concentrated all her attention on her driving, but soon began to enjoy herself. It was an easy car to drive and it was a beautiful night, with the sea so close and the night sky stretching vast and starry above.

Mitch was certainly testing her thoroughly. Following his abrupt commands, she negotiated sharp turns into narrow roads, accepted sudden changes of order without faltering—it was the sort of thing she could expect of Mrs Gilcrist, she supposed—and demonstrated to him that she could park neatly and make a faultless start even on a steep hill. As at last she drove down the hill towards the sea again, she was moved to say with a sigh, 'This is all so lovely after the plains out west! Hills and heights, and that marvellous ocean! I could go on driving for ever.'

'There'll be no need for that, Miss Lambert.' His voice was shatteringly cold. 'The object of our drive was not exactly to discuss or enjoy the beauties of the night.'

'No, of course not. I was more or less thinking aloud.'

'I'm not particularly interested in your thoughts. You can save those to entertain my grandmother. You can turn right at the foot of the hill and we'll go back.'

'Just as you say, sir,' said Rae jauntily, and put her foot on the accelerator rather harder than she had intended, so that they took the last of the downward grade in double quick time. She managed to slow to a stop at the corner of the main road and they completed the drive back to the bungalow in silence.

Mitchell politely accompanied her to the bungalow.

'Well,' Rae said then, feeling anxious now, 'am I to come to Illalangi tomorrow?'

'Yes, if that's what's been arranged. But don't imagine you've charmed me into accepting you.'

'No, I hardly think I've done that,' Rae agreed dryly, and was rewarded by a sharp look.

'It's possible you'll decide not to stay, but meanwhile my sisters will be relieved of duties they found irksome, and Grandmother will feel she has had her little victory.'

'Perhaps I shall stay longer than you think,' said Rae as she went up the steps.

'That we shall see,' he said, following her. 'But remember this, Miss Lambert—no matter how friendly you become with my grandmother, you are not one of the family. You will be at Illalangi to give service. I shall want to see your references when you have them —I'll make a point of coming down at the end of the week for that express purpose. As well, I shall want to check up on your performance. And I shall have no hesitation in sacking you if I'm dissatisfied in any way. So let's say that we're giving you a week's trial.'

'You're too kind,' said Rae coolly.

He ignored that. 'In the event that you do stay on,

I shall continue to keep a personal check on you. Not for your delight, but because I am responsible for my grandmother and sisters, and it's my practice to keep closely in touch with them. Is that understood?'

'Perfectly. Though it's rather a mystery to me why you should point out that you won't be visiting Illalangi for my delight.'

In the starlight they looked at one another, and Rae thought he smiled slightly.

'Perhaps it was unnecessary,' he agreed good-humouredly. 'Will you be able to manage the move tomorrow on your own, or would you like someone to come down and fetch you? Though on second thoughts, it might be better if you were to take a cab. I'll see that your fare is refunded.'

'I'm not all that hard up,' said Rae, smiling a little. 'As a matter of fact, I have a car of my own.' She saw his eyebrows go up and some imp made her explain airily, 'Another gift from my last employers.'

'You did well indeed,' he said, sounding disagreeable again. 'However, you won't be able to garage it at Illalangi.'

'I'll bring it back here when I'm able,' said Rae agreeably. 'Goodnight, Mr Gilcrist—and I'm truly glad I've passed muster. I'm looking forward to this job!'

CHAPTER III

Rae moved into Illalangi the next evening at about six o'clock. She had planned to go later, but Pam called in at the bungalow with a specific invitation from Gran —backed up by herself—for Rae to come to dinner.

'That way you'll meet everyone at once. Besides, I'm going back to the flat tonight, and Mitch will be leaving for the Valley first thing in the morning, and if you come late we shall scarcely see you.'

'It might be better that way,' said Rae honestly. 'At least as far as Mitch is concerned.'

'Oh, Mitch has capitulated. I'm afraid I couldn't help seeing the funny side when he said he'd agreed for you to come on trial. If you'd seen the grim look on his face when he came down here to tackle you! How did you win him over, Rae?'

'Sheer will-power,' said Rae cheerfully. 'Though I can't pretend I *won* him over. I think it was nine parts necessity and one part downright rudeness on my part. I don't think he's under the illusion that I'll follow in Alison's footsteps.'

Pam was amused, but came loyally to her brother's defence. 'You've started off with a bad impression of Mitch. I'm sorry about that because he's really a terrific person. It's just that he takes his responsibilities as far as his womenfolk are concerned rather seriously. I'll have to tell you about it some time. Meanwhile, I have a bit of running around to do for Gran. Joanie was supposed to be on call this afternoon, but she's disappeared. See you later anyhow. 'Bye for now!'

That evening as Rae made her way up through the terraced garden, a suitcase in each hand, Mitch came to meet her and relieve her of her burden.

'I'll take those, Miss Lambert. Is this the lot, or is there more to come?'

'Only my coat and a small travel bag, Mr Gilcrist,' said Rae. 'Thank you very much. I'll go down and fetch them.'

'You do that.'

He was waiting for her at the door when she got back.

'Mrs McPhail's busy in the kitchen and my sisters have rather prematurely returned to their own pursuits, so I'll show you to your room.' He preceded her up the stairs, saying over his shoulder, 'I'm afraid we can't offer you a sitting room of your own or your own personal TV, but I imagine you'll be fairly comfortable.' In the hall at the top of the stairs he flung open a door. 'This is where you sleep.'

Rae went in. It was a big room with low-silled windows shaded by outside blue and white awnings. There was a thick blue carpet on the polished floor and the furniture was light-coloured and modern. As well as the usual bedroom furniture there was a writing desk and a small settee covered in rose-coloured velvet. Mitchell deposited her luggage inside the door.

'My grandmother's rooms are directly opposite. She's resting at the moment, but that needn't concern you— you don't start work till tomorrow. The bathroom you'll use is next door. You might like to come down in an hour and have a drink before dinner. By that time, we should all be here.'

He looked grim, but this time Rae had a feeling that the grimness was not entirely on her account, and he even managed a brief smile for her before he left her. She occupied herself with her unpacking, then changed into a sleeveless turquoise dress of synthetic silk that had a sash with a long white silk fringe. Her grandmother had always been generous and Rae had plenty of good pretty up-to-date clothes that had scarcely been worn. Some of the things she had with her had been bought with Ralph in mind, but she refused to think of that now. She brushed her hair and arranged it in a style that she liked—a loose knot high on her head with a few curly tendrils falling against her cheeks and neck. She was wondering if she should go and see if Mrs Gilcrist needed her when she heard Pam's voice and knew that she was assisting her grandmother.

By the time she went downstairs to the sitting room, they were all gathered there and Mitch was pouring drinks at a side table.

'Ah, there you are, Miss Lambert. Will you have sherry or French vermouth?'

'Have a sherry, Rae,' said Pam, coming to link her arm through Rae's. 'The vermouth's not ours.'

Rae looked a question as she said, 'I'll have a dry sherry, thank you,' but her question was not answered, for no one seemed aware of it. Rae had meant, 'What do you mean by "not ours"?'

While Mitch poured her drink she spoke to Mrs Gilcrist, and Pam introduced her to Helen, whom she knew by sight. She smiled at Rae, but with a certain reservation, and Rae had the impression that she was more inclined to side with Mitchell than with her grandmother. Rae sat down near old Mrs Gilcrist, received her sherry from Mitchell, and was asked by Gran, 'You don't know what it's all about, do you, dear? You see, Mitchell, she doesn't know this is our wine.'

Rae sipped her drink and looked the question again. Mitchell smiled coldly down at her. 'Come now—we use an excellent advertising agency. Everyone knows Gilcrist Wines.'

Rae actually felt herself colouring. Of course she

had heard of Gilcrist Wines. It simply hadn't occurred to her to connect them with these Gilcrists. It was clear to her now why Pam had asked would she prefer ' something with a kick ' and what Mitchell had meant when he referred to the Gilcrist family. And she, Rae Lambert, had been as innocent as a babe in the wood. It had all passed over her head. If she protested her ignorance now, she was pretty sure Mitch wouldn't believe her. So she said coolly, ' Yes, of course I've heard of Gilcrist Wines.'

' Well, we make them, my dear,' said Mrs Gilcrist. ' And they're our pride as well as our livelihood. What do you think of this sherry? It comes from the Riverina. Mitchell doesn't make any fortified wines at Millunga in the Valley.'

Rae sipped again. They were all looking at her.

' It's a rather special flor,' said Pam good-humouredly, ' so you'd better like it.'

' It's very pleasant,' said Rae. She lifted her eyes and found Mitchell's blue gaze, half amused, half cynical, on her, and added, ' But I can't pretend to be a connoisseur.'

' Then we must educate you,' Mitch said. ' If you like that flor, then it's a good start. It's a little too dry for the average Australian taste.'

' Rae is English,' offered Pam. But Mitchell didn't take that up. Instead, he turned to Helen and said rather grimly, ' See if Joan's in the studio, will you, Helen? If not, we'll start dinner without her.'

Joan was not to be found, and consequently they presently went into the dining room without her, and took their places at a long narrow table lit by candles in a three-sconce silver bracket, and elegantly set with natural linen table mats and gleaming silver. Mitchell sat at one end of the table with Helen and Pam on either side of him. Mrs Gilcrist was at the other end with Rae on her left, next to Helen. Joan's chair, opposite Rae, remained empty until dinner had begun. The main course was casseroled chicken in an unusual sauce, and while Mrs McPhail served it, Mitchell poured wine, though Pam refused any. The glasses were long-stemmed and tulip-shaped, and the wine, Rae noticed from the label, was Millunga Christine Rosé. It was slightly chilled and had a fresh fruity taste and was an excellent accompaniment to the chicken.

Rather to Rae's amusement, Mrs Gilcrist held her glass to the light, sniffed the wine and tasted it with a very critical expression on her face. Then she said decidedly, ' It's not as good as my father used to make, Mitchell. I still maintain that the old handpresses and natural fermentation give the best results.'

' Rubbish, Grandmother,' said Mitchell cheerfully but equally decidedly. ' You just want an argument. My Wilmes press has innumerable advantages. Of course Great-grandfather Darvale made some admirable wines, but I maintain he'd judge this particular rosé to be well up to the old Millunga standard. It's a rather specially good one, you know. And come to think of it, I seriously doubt if a rosé was made at all at Millunga in the old days.'

' Hmph,' snorted his grandmother. ' And to what do we owe the honour of opening this very special bottle tonight?' She gave a wicked chuckle. ' Don't tell me we're celebrating the arrival of my new companion!'

Rae felt a sudden surge of colour in her cheeks, but Mitchell answered smoothly, ' I wanted to see how it had travelled. I brought a half dozen bottles down a week or two ago. Sometimes a trip of even a hundred miles can upset a wine for a few weeks, but I think in this case no harm has been done.' He turned to Rae. ' Lest you get the wrong impression, Miss Lambert, we confine our wine-drinking here—apart from an occasional glass of vin ordinaire—to the occasions when I happen to be home. Wine with dinner is the exception rather than the rule.'

'That suits me very well,' said Rae agreeably, though her cheeks were still red. 'I'm used to plain living.'

'Good.' As he spoke, a small sturdy-looking girl with thick untidy dark hair came into the room, carrying a loaded dinner plate which she set down on the table. With a mutinous look at Mitch, she pulled out her chair and sat down.

'You're late, Joan,' he said, frowning at her. 'I think you owe us an apology.'

'I'm sorry,' she said. She turned her glass upside down to indicate that she didn't want it filled.

'Naughty girl,' said Mrs Gilcrist fondly. 'Where have you been?'

'Out,' said Joan. She looked across at Rae. She had heavy brows and eyes the same blue as Mitchell's, and in an odd way she was very like him. Her sullen expression turned to a smile and she put a hand on her grandmother's arm. 'Introduce me to your new companion, Gran darling.'

Mrs Gilcrist did so, and Joan made a comic face at Rae. 'I'm awfully glad you've come, but you're going to be sorry, Rae! You don't know what you've let yourself in for, taking on my wicked little grandmother.'

'Gran's going to be very good,' said Pam. 'Aren't you, darling?'

'I'm going to be as I always am—myself,' said the old lady crossly. 'So don't talk of me—or to me—as though I were a child. I'm fully adult, and I have all my wits about me, and in fact there are times when I know better than any of you. Admit it, Mitchell. Admit that my choice of Rae here was a good one.'

'Choice?' Mitchell said good-humouredly, with a lift of his eyebrows. And then, with a cold smile in Rae's direction, 'We shall see. Miss Lambert hasn't begun work yet.' He turned to Joan. 'I want to see you after dinner, Joan, so kindly don't disappear and lock yourself in the studio.'

During the rest of the meal the conversation was more general, and when it was over, Mrs Gilcrist said she was going upstairs to watch television, and would have her coffee there. Helen went upstairs with her, and in the sitting room, Pam poured coffee.

'I must go when I've had this,' she said. She sank into a chair and sighed. 'That long drive!'

'Don't ask me for sympathy,' said Mitch. 'You could be staying here—and would if you had any sense.'

'I want to be independent,' said Pam. 'I've been looked after so well all my life. Flatting is something I just feel I must try for myself.'

'You've tried it for three months. Doesn't that satisfy you?'

'Sorry, Mitch, but no.' Pam sounded stubborn, but she smiled winningly at her brother and after a moment he smiled back. Rae thought, 'Those two understand each other—and go their own ways.'

Joan, sprawling back in a chair, set her empty coffee cup on the floor and looked directly at Mitchell. 'You said you wanted to speak to me. Well, fire away, let's get it over.'

'You might prefer to hear what I have to say in private.'

Joan flicked a glance in Rae's direction. 'I wouldn't. There's nothing I'm ashamed of—nothing I want kept secret.'

Rae wondered if she should offer to leave the company,

but decided not to. Helen came in and helped herself to coffee, then stood by the long windows looking dreamily towards the ocean. After a moment, Mitch said, 'Very well, Joan—as you wish.' He stood up too and moved over beside Helen where he stood staring hard at his youngest sister.

'Where were you this afternoon? Apart, I mean, from being *out*.'

'Connor and I went for a walk around Paddington. I made some sketches of some of the old terrace houses. Would you like to see them?'

'Never mind that. You know I don't like your friendship with Connor Birch.'

'So what?' Joan's eyes were bright and defiant. Rae uncomfortably wished she had excused herself, but it was too late now, and Pam was making little half-humorous grimaces at her across the room.

'So now I'm pointing out to you that he's nothing but a fortune-hunting layabout, and I'm asking you to see no more of him.'

'You can't stop me.'

Mitchell sighed and put a hand briefly to his eyes.

'No, I can't stop you. But I don't want to see you make a complete fool of yourself. You may discover the hard way what it is he wants from you.'

'Do you mean sex or money?' asked Joan impudently. 'Either way you're wrong. And Con knows you keep me poor.'

'I make you a very fair allowance. You must remember you're a student—by your own choice. Your sisters earn money and are consequently better off than you. That will continue while you're at art school. If you're not satisfied, then you must get yourself a job. . . . However, that's hardly the point. I don't imagine for a moment that Connor Birch assesses you on your present means.'

'I shouldn't think he assessed me on my means at all.'

'Well, I should.' Mitchell moved abruptly across the room. 'I've had more experience of the world than you have, and I assure you it's full of people who are on the make.'

Like me, thought Rae, wryly. But more painfully, she thought of Ralph too, and she wondered whether Mitchell was right about this Connor Birch. He so easily could be.

'I'll remember Alison. And I haven't forgotten poor Aunt Valerie's sad case,' said Joan flippantly. 'May I go now?' She pulled herself out of her chair and looked at him aggressively.

He said in a suddenly soft voice, 'Joanie, I just don't want you *hurt*.'

Joan's head went down and she almost ran from the room.

Helen said with a sigh, 'Why doesn't she listen to you, Mitch?'

And Pam said, 'Poor kid. I'm afraid you're right, though, Mitch.'

'I damn well know I am.' He sat down with a sigh. 'Will you play something, Helen? I could do with a little music.'

'Of course,' said Helen, turning back into the room. 'What shall it be?'

'That thing of Mozart's.' He hummed a few bars, and Helen with a smile went to the piano and began to look through her music.

Pam said, 'Excuse me. I'm going upstairs to fetch my little dilly bag and then I'll be off.' She dropped a kiss on Mitch's cheek and one on the back of Helen's neck, and gave Rae a friendly smile. 'See you later, Rae—maybe next weekend. 'Bye, all.'

When she had gone, Helen sat down at the piano and began to play, smoothly and faultlessly. Mitch said to Rae in a low tone, ' If you don't like music—or family set-tos—you don't have to stay with us, Miss Lambert.'

Did he mean here at Illalangi, or simply in this room, right now? Rae didn't know. She didn't like family arguments, but she did like music and she wanted to hear Helen play. So she gave him a cool smile, said ' Thank you,' and sat tight.

He had nothing more to say to her that night, and neither had Helen, who of the three girls was the quietest and appeared the most submissive to her brother. Rae was sorry that Pam didn't live at Illalangi; she was so friendly and lively and natural. However, she was here to do a job, not to fraternize with the Gilcrists—as no doubt Mitch would have been quick to point out if he could have read her thoughts, and the next day her work would begin in earnest.

Rae started the day early. Neatly and simply dressed, she went down to the kitchen at eight o'clock to consult Mrs McPhail, since no one else had thought to advise or instruct her.

The housekeeper was a tall dignified woman who rarely smiled. Rae was to discover that she was extremely efficient and hard to ruffle. She told Rae that Mrs Gilcrist breakfasted upstairs in her room at a little table by the window. She would want Rae to sit with her, to read various items from the morning paper, and later they would discuss plans for the day. Then she would bathe and dress.

' She'll need your help if her arthritis is troubling her, but she won't mention that—she'll pretend she wants you to talk to her,' Mrs McPhail advised. ' She likes to go out somewhere in the car most mornings, but on her bad days she'll say she feels lazy and will sit in the garden and doze or gossip. Anyway, you'll soon get the hang of it,' the housekeeper concluded. ' It's not going to be a very exciting life for you.'

' I'm not expecting excitement,' said Rae cheerfully.

Mitchell, she discovered, had left early to drive up to the Valley, some hundred miles north. Joan had gone by bus to the city, and Helen was not yet down. Rae suggested that she might get her own breakfast.

' Please yourself, Miss Lambert. I always cooked something for Miss Campbell and took it into the dining room for her. I'm not pressed for time at this hour.'

' Well, neither am I,' said Rae, after a moment's reflection. She decided it was only common sense to establish a good relationship with a fellow employee. Alison Campbell may have liked to be waited on, but Rae was used to fraternizing. She asked Mrs McPhail to call her Rae, set about making coffee and toast, and presently was sitting opposite the housekeeper at the table in the big modern kitchen.

' I don't want to seem inquisitive,' she said after a moment, ' but I would like to know a little more about the various members of the family. Joan, I understand, is an art student—'

' That's right. She's not at the Tech, she's studying under Tom Lee, who has a small art school in the city. She has classes every weekday—has to leave early as she doesn't have a car, and Mr Gilcrist won't let her go into the flat with Pam. That's at Wollstonecraft, just the north side of the harbour bridge. Mr Gilcrist doesn't like Pam flatting much, but she's always gone her own way regardless. She has a lot of good sense and he knows it. She works in the administration office in town for the Gilcrist firm.'

Rae poured some more coffee. ' And Helen?'

'She's the docile one. Doesn't think of much other than her music—and pleasing her brother.'

'She plays very well.'

'Oh, well enough,' agreed Mrs McPhail offhandedly. 'But she's no ambition. She takes a few pupils in the small sitting room in the afternoon—that's to earn a bit of pin money. Then there are occasional concerts—she's quite a good accompanist, nothing marvellous—and she has a lesson in town once a week. Mornings she spends practising. It's a sad little life, I sometimes think— empty, leading nowhere. She should be thinking of marriage at her age, but she doesn't.'

Rae thought this strange, because Helen was very pretty. But it was not her business and she had no intention of gossiping. Mrs McPhail didn't offer any further details, but said briskly, 'And Mr Gilcrist. He's always busy at Millunga. If he were like other members of his family he'd be taking it easy, but he manages his own vineyards and has quite a reputation as a wine-maker, as I suppose you know.'

'No,' said Rae, aware of the shrewd eyes watching her. 'You may not believe it, but I didn't realize until last night that these Gilcrists had anything at all to do with wine.'

Mrs McPhail allowed herself a brief smile. 'Is that a fact? Well, it's hard to believe, but no doubt true . . . This time of year he's busy spraying his vines, but he always finds time to come to Sydney every week or so to keep a check on his family. It's a big responsibility and he takes it very seriously. That's why—if you'll excuse my frankness—he was a bit put out when Mrs Gilcrist went over his head in the matter of a new com-panion.'

'I'll do my best to see there are no regrets on either side,' Rae said with a smile.

In the week that followed, she found that she certainly
had to keep her nose to the grindstone. Mrs Gilcrist was
so delighted to have such an agreeable and young companion that Rae had scarcely a moment to herself. Her
days flew by in much the way that Pam—and Mitchell
too—had decreed they would. While she had been
without a companion, Mrs Gilcrist had fallen behind with
many of her activities. Luncheon with a certain Clara
Livingstone who lived at Manly came high on the list of
priorities, and this was arranged for Wednesday. In
preparation for this there was a visit to the hairdresser
on Tuesday. The old lady had quite a vain streak in
her, Rae discovered. Mrs Livingstone had been her
friend since the early days of her marriage, and kept herself as did Mrs Gilcrist, in as near mint condition as
possible.

Rae sat in on the luncheon at Mrs Livingstone's apartment, whose windows looked directly down on to the
ocean beach, so that there was a perpetual background
murmur from the sea. They were waited on by a most
unlikely maid—'my darling factotum,' Mrs Livingstone
called her affectionately. She was a girl called Cilla, no
older than Rae, and apt to burst into giggles at all sorts
of odd moments. Yet behind the lighthearted façade
there was evidently something, for Cilla had prepared a
most delectable meal—a lamb Stroganoff, served with
lemon-flavoured rice and crisp shredded Chinese cab-
bage. This was followed by a cheesecake which Rae
for one found a little too rich. Mrs Gilcrist, who enjoyed
it so much she had two servings, suffered accordingly
that night from indigestion—or maybe plain overeating.
This meant that Rae was well and truly on duty that
night, for Mrs Gilcrist was too uncomfortable to settle
down to sleep. She sat up in her bed, sipped Alka-
Seltzer, and demanded that Rae play chess with her. As

neither of the two was a particularly astute player, the game dragged on and on, and Rae was almost falling asleep when at last her employer decided to call it a day and settle down to sleep.

Thursday found her completely recovered and clamouring for a day in town. The procedure was that Rae drove the car to Manly, parked it there, and they took the ferry to the city. Rae enjoyed the peaceful boat journey, but once they reached the shops, all peace was shattered. There was a hat and a blouse to be bought, birthday gifts for elderly friends, and a bottle of French cologne—very expensive—which, to Rae's embarrassment, turned out to be a present for her. They lunched at the Summit Restaurant in the Australia Square Tower. Far too expensive, Rae thought, uneasy and guilty at the treat rather than delighted.

'We shan't call on Pam. She'd only tell Mitchell and he'd be cross. He doesn't like me to come to town— says I can find all I want in the suburbs. But that's not true, I like to see all the new buildings, all that glittering glass, all that change. And the young people—so excitingly dressed, so free of convention.'

As was only to be expected, she was exhausted that night, and so was Rae.

'Dinner in bed,' Mrs Gilcrist decreed. 'Just a little soup and an iced dessert. And a glass of white wine.' She named the wine she wanted—one of Mitchell's lovely Traminers. It appeared that when Mitchell was not there to witness it, she had a healthy pride in his talents as a winemaker. Rae must bring her dinner upstairs and join her in a glass. Joan was not in evidence and Helen, who was playing in a concert at a private home at Palm Beach, was not interested in eating. Mrs McPhail bemoaned the waste of the chicken so carefully prepared, and Rae tried to appease her by taking a good-sized helping.

The Traminer was delicious, so gentle on the palate.
Rae didn't know the language of wine lovers, but
described it to herself thus. When she went downstairs
with the trays Helen, beautiful in a long white gown and
sapphires, was ready to leave. Rae expected to see some
handsome male escorting her, but it was a middle-aged
couple who came from the sitting room where they had
been drinking the last of the Traminer.

Rae went to bed as early as she could, and fell at once
into a deep sleep. She was wakened later by the sound
of a door being closed—Helen's—and later still heard
someone else creeping up the stairs. She wondered
sleepily if Joan had been out with the unpopular Connor
Birch again, and though it was not her business, could
not help worrying, which kept her awake. No one really
kept an eye on Joan. Rae had observed her fondness
for her grandmother and the fact that she was the apple
of the old lady's eye. But Mrs Gilcrist let the girl go
her own way, and never questioned her more than idly.
Rae thought it unsatisfactory, especially if Mitchell was
really concerned about her. But it wasn't Rae's place
to keep tabs on her, or to report on her movements. She
wished she could meet Connor Birch and assess him for
herself—which was to a degree ridiculous, considering
how completely she herself had been deceived by Ralph
Stevens.

She found it hard to sleep again and woke in the morning hollow-eyed and edgy. To her relief, Mrs Gilcrist
had decided on a day at home. Part of this was spent
sorting out the contents of a large basket containing
various bits of embroidery and knitting, most of them
unfinished. Long stories were told about each piece and
Rae began to yawn behind her hand. The postman
brought her a letter from Mrs Stacy, but she had no

chance to open it until mid-afternoon. As well as the reference she had asked for, it contained a cheerful note from Mrs Stacy with the news that all was well at Tarmaroo and that Ralph, who had been given Rae's letter —and the opal ring—had not since put in an appearance. Mrs Stacy was coping tactfully as she could with the altered arrangements and had put an advertisement in the local paper that the wedding had been cancelled ' due to unforeseen circumstances'. This amused Rae, but she was glad to be well away.

On Saturday evening Mrs Gilcrist suggested that she might like to have Thursday afternoons and Sundays free.

' It can be a flexible arrangement, shall we say? If for some particular reason you want to make a change now and again I'm sure we can accommodate you.'

Rae said it would suit her admirably, and now, with a day of rest in sight, admitted to herself that she would be glad of it.

She rose later than usual on Sunday and made herself a cup of coffee in the kitchen. Mrs McPhail advised her not to give a thought to anyone but herself.

' You've worked hard and well all the week. Now enjoy yourself. I do—when I'm off duty, I'm off duty, come what may, and they all know that and respect it.'

Rae took her coffee into the spring sunshine, which was hot rather than warm. She had scarcely given a thought to Ralph all the week, she hadn't had time, and now she found that the thought of him meant next to nothing. She was ready to enjoy life again. But there seemed to be singularly few prospects for doing that to-day. She had no friends! She decided to go down to the bungalow, and maybe take a drive somewhere.

As she went back into the house she was greeted by a very alert-looking Mrs Gilcrist, dressed literally in her

Sunday best, hatted and gloved and perfumed.

'Ah, Rae my dear, I was looking for you. I wondered if you would like to come to church. Those other naughty girls have declined and I do so love to attend the service on Sunday mornings.'

So a quarter of an hour later Rae was in the car driving to church and her plans had gone by the board. Early afternoon found her drawn into another session with the workbasket in search of a particular pair of bootees and a matching bonnet, for a chance meeting at church had reminded Mrs Gilcrist of the imminent arrival into the world of another baby.

The afternoon had half gone before Rae, weary now, had walked down to her bungalow. She was relaxing on the verandah and half asleep when Mitchell arrived. He wore cotton slacks and a casual shirt and his face looked more deeply tanned than ever, while his blue eyes regarded her sharply.

'I hoped I'd find you here, Miss Lambert,' he said from where he stood on the coarse strip of grass below the verandah. 'I've made a special trip down to see you, but I have very little time. I have to go back to the Valley tonight. May I sit down?'

'Of course.' He came up the steps and took a green-cushioned patio chair near her. 'If I'd known you were coming I'd have waited at the house.'

'Surely you did know? I told you I'd be down for a check-up. Or did you expect me yesterday?'

'I didn't give it a thought,' said Rae, not altogether truthfully.

He gave her a curious glance. 'No? However, I didn't expect you to stay at the house. From what I hear, that would have been a bad mistake—but we'll discuss that presently. Meanwhile, it appears that you've shown yourself to be efficient and agreeable and patient, and my grandmother has been very happy, very satisfied. I hope it's all been due to your nature and not to a gigantic effort to impress me. But for the time being, you can consider yourself to be employed.'

Rae thought his approval, to say the least of it, grudging. She said lightly, 'Thank you for the somewhat thin seal of approval. I assure you I would have served Mrs Gilcrist just as well even if Big Brother had not been watching.'

'I would like to think so,' he said, allowing himself a faint smile at her retort. 'At all events, your conscientiousness has done you credit, even if it has put shadows around your eyes. The pace my grandmother sets is a fast one. I'm well aware of that. She'll give you presents to make up for it (Rae thought of the cologne and flushed), but if you're wise you'll think of her gifts as bribes and refuse them. That way you won't feel guilty when you insist on the freedom that's your due. If ever you're short of cash,' he added, slowly and deliberately, 'come to me, will you, not to my grandmother.'

As if she would ever ask a favour of this man! It was laughable too to consider that she, Rae Lambert, might ever be short of cash and trying to winkle more out of an old lady. She raised her eyebrows. 'Why ever should you imagine I might be short of cash? Mrs Gilcrist is paying me a generous salary.'

He shrugged. 'I know that. But I know that girls can spend a lot on dress, and I know too how it's been with other people who have worked for Grandmother.'

'I'm not Alison Campbell,' Rae reminded him coldly. 'Have you anything else to say?'

'Yes. I want your references before I go. And I want to give you some further advice. Don't, when you're tired of my grandmother's company, persuade her to take you to Millunga for a long stay. Find some outside interests—some friends of your own, and get right away from Illalangi on your day off.'

Rae knew very well that he was warning her yet again that he did not want her chasing him, and she was a little tired of it. She said carefully, 'Mr Gilcrist, I've just left the outback to come to the city. It's not very reasonable to suggest I'd be anxious to go back to the bush again.'

'The bush?' He frowned. 'Our landscape in the Valley is rather a different proposition from—the western plains, wasn't it? Besides, was it the bush you ran away from or a broken love affair?'

'You asked me something of the kind before. I don't consider it any concern of yours.'

'It's not, of course. But you know the answer—and you know what you're looking for.'

'Do you think I'm looking for a husband?'

'Most young women are. Confine your search to the city, will you?'

'I'll do as I please,' said Rae with a pleasant smile, though she was seething. 'And I should like you to remember that *you* are not my employer.'

'I'm an interested party.' They stared at each other with hostility, and then he put his hand to his eyes and sighed. She noticed he had long, sensitive-looking fingers, and that even the backs of his hands were tanned. 'I think enough has been said on either side. If I could just have that reference—'

'I'm afraid it's up at the house.'

'Then come along and I'll drive you there.'

'No, thank you,' said Rae. 'I'd rather drive up myself. I shan't be having dinner with you at Illalangi tonight. I want to come back here.'

This time she felt she had definitely scored a point. After a second he nodded and went out to his car. Rae followed in her own and once the reference was handed over and carefully perused, she came back to the bungalow. Her opinion of Mitchell Gilcrist had been strengthened. He was conceited and domineering, and the last person she would be likely to fall in love with.

CHAPTER IV

Pam came home the following weekend, and as Mitchell too was expected on the Sunday, Rae made plans to be out of his way. The difficulty lay in having no friends, and she did not really relish the thought of going to the Art Gallery by herself, but that was what she planned to do. Then she would go to the Domain and listen to some of the soapbox orators.

However, at breakfast, which she took alone with Pam, for Joan was already in her studio and Helen upstairs with Mrs Gilcrist—her plans were altered. At the time, it seemed like a godsend, but later she was to wonder if the whole thing had been a mistake.

'This is your free day, isn't it?' Pam asked chattily over grapefruit and coffee. 'Have you anything interesting teed up?'

Rae shrugged slightly. 'Not really. My main purpose is to remove myself from the scene.'

Pam's blue eyes narrowed. 'Why don't we drive up to the Valley? You'd like to see the vineyards, wouldn't you?'

'Yes, I should,' said Rae cautiously. 'But I don't necessarily *expect* to see them.'

'Oh, you must! And I'd love to show them to you.' Pam glanced at her watch. 'If we left soon we'd be there in time for lunch.'

'Shouldn't we let anyone know we're coming?' asked Rae, still hesitating, although it seemed an ideal time to go, as Mitchell was coming to Sydney.

'Millunga doesn't belong to Aunt Valerie. And there's always loads to eat, so we've nothing to worry about.'

Reassured, convinced, Rae finished her breakfast and

hurried up to her room to tidy it and to get ready. In half an hour, she and Pam were on their way and had soon reached the Pacific Highway and were heading north. They went over the Hawkesbury River on to the new tollway. Pam was a good driver, the tollway was fast, and the morning bright and clear. Rae relaxed and enjoyed herself. It was good to be with Pam, and she looked forward to seeing Millunga, which always seemed to be cropping up in family conversation. It would give her something more to talk to Mrs Gilcrist about.

' Tell me, Rae,' Pam said somewhere along the way, ' has Joan been seeing Connor Birch again?'

' I don't know,' said Rae cagily. She believed Joan had been seeing him, but she didn't intend becoming involved in something that was outside her province.

Pam gave her a quick comical look. ' I might have known you'd say that! I don't mean to be snoopy, but I am a bit worried about Joanie. You don't know Connor! Well, I can't say I know him either, but I've *seen* him and that's enough. It's quite obvious what the attraction is. If he knew the facts though, he might cool off a bit.'

' What do you mean?'

' Connor will have a long wait to get what he wants even if he persuades Joan to run off and marry him. And I only hope she's not besotted enough to do that! She and Mitch are very alike—Gran too. They're all determined to have their own way.'

' I've noticed that,' smiled Rae. ' Your grandmother was very triumphant about putting me on the payroll. I don't know a great deal about Joan, but it had occurred to me that she and your brother are alike in perhaps more than looks.'

' Very astute of you.' Pam concentrated on a wide

curve in the road, then continued, ' Would you believe that none of us—Helen, Joan, myself—gets more from the family firm than Mitch allows us, until we marry? That was how my father arranged it in his will.'

' But when you do marry?'

' Ah, there's another trap. Mitch has to approve of the marriage. If he doesn't—then we get nothing till we're thirty. Imagine it—thirty! And Joan's only nineteen. I'd love to tell Connor how important Mitch's approval is, but of course I shan't. Anyhow, I'm sure the whole grand passion will burn itself out if Mitch handles it the right way. And there we have a problem. Mitch can be a very high-handed and tactless. But I imagine you're aware of that!'

' Yes, I am,' said Rae wryly. She was silent for some time thinking of what Pam had told her. Mr Gilcrist had probably been wise in the provisions of his will. Clearly, ne wanted to protect his daughters from fortune-hunters. However, Rae thought that she would not care to have Mitchell telling *her* whom she could or could not marry! With his worldly wisdom, he might have seen through Ralph, but she supposed she would not have taken any notice of him if he had warned her. Joan would be the same, although he was quite probably right about Connor Birch. Pam seemed to share his opinion wholeheartedly.

She said presently, ' If Connor Birch is the sort of person you all seem to believe him, then I truly hope Joan gets over him before she's hurt. But I'm afraid I can't take part in the family dispute, and I don't consider it my business to report what Joan's doing or who she's been seeing.'

' Good for you, Rae,' said Pam. ' I knew you were that kind of girl—utterly direct as well as entirely honest.'

Rae had the grace to feel faintly ashamed at this praise.

She wished she could tell Pam the truth about herself, but that would hardly be fair. Either all the Gilcrists must know, or none of them. And Rae had no hesitation in deciding that it was to be none of them. While *they* considered her just another working girl, everyone else she met would do the same. And that was what Rae wanted. It was her protection against people like Ralph and Connor Birch.

They were driving through an unattractive coal-mining district now. The houses were small and mostly of fibro or timber, and the streets were drab. Pam said cheerfully, ' Not very prepossessing, is it? But wait till we reach the Valley! It's lovely at any time of the year. But don't expect to find fabulous old chateaux, and European style wineries. Most of our wineries are silver —galvanized iron! Part of the winery at Millunga is stone, and very old. Mitch says it was built by convict labour in the first half of last century when the convicts were shipped up here from Sydney.'

' Has Millunga always belonged to your family?' Rae asked curiously.

' No. It originally belonged to Gran's people—the Darvales. But they had to pull out before the first world war. Downy mildew or something like that. Ask Gran. And in a sense it doesn't belong to our family now. It belongs to Mitch. He bought it some years ago when it was completely run down and he's poured money and hard work into it till it's a show place.'

' Then where are the other vineyards—the Gilcrist Wine vineyards?'

' In the irrigation area down south. Mitch is a fanatically keen winemaker and considers that grapes from irrigated vineyards are inferior. I don't know if he's right—there are two schools of thought. Still, it's a fact that the Valley up here produces prestige table wines,

and Millunga wines are supposed to be some of the best.
I couldn't be sure, but I don't think any fortified wines
—sherries and so on—are made here. I know Mitch
doesn't make any. Most of the vineyards here used to be
small and privately owned, but the big companies are
moving in now. Wine is quite a big thing in Australia,
though we've lost a lot of the United Kingdom market
because import duties have made our wines too expensive to compete with Europe. But we export to Canada,
and U.S.A. and the Far East.'

'You're certainly a mine of information,' said Rae
admiringly. 'But of course you work in the administrative department.'

'Yes. Besides, I think it's a fascinating industry.'

'Is Mitch—Mr Gilcrist—entirely outside the family
concern?'

'Heavens, no! He's a director of our company. He
doesn't need to work as he does up here, but he loves it.
It's his life. He knows the whole thing inside out, and
he's invaluable to the family. He worked for Father in
the Gilcrist vineyards down south and took his diploma
in wine making at Roseworthy College in South Australia. Did a stint as vineyard manager, cellar manager
and so on. Then he was managing director, and now
director. I would say—though perhaps being his sister
I'm prejudiced—but I would honestly say he has the best
brain in the family. Of course he's personally responsible for the quality of the wines bottled under the
Millunga label.' She drew a deep breath and gave Rae
a quick look from laughing blue eyes.

Rae said, ' I can see you'll have to marry a—vigneron,
is it?' and saw Pam blush. 'I'm sorry I don't know
the Millunga wines, so I'm not able to join you in your
praise of their maker.'

'I don't think you are sorry about *that*,' said Pam

shrewdly. 'You and Mitch plainly started off your relationship on the wrong foot.'

Rae didn't comment. She thought, 'We didn't start off our relationship on either the wrong or the right foot, because there's not going to be any relationship. Apart from the most distant business relationship that I can manage.'

The Valley, she dicovered soon, was very different the scent of the blossoms with which they were laden. green vines glinted in the sun from hillside and vale. Interspersed with the vineyards were green paddocks where fat cattle grazed, and there were other fields of maize and corn and wheat. To the east, after they had entered the Valley, was a bush-clad mountain range, and on the other side of the valley, gentle hills sloped down from a darkly menacing plateau. Up on the mountain slopes the soil showed red and volcanic, but in the valley it was grey or brown. Later she was to learn that the best red wines came from grapes grown on the red volcanic soil.

At last they reached the entrance to the Millunga vineyards, and Pam drove in across the cattle grid and up a winding gravel drive flanked with beautiful old mulberry trees. At either side widely spaced rows of emerald-leafed vines extended up the slopes and over the hill on one side, and down into the flats towards the river on the other. Pam said, ' It's only a small vineyard—only about a hundred acres of vines, and in the vicinity of two tons of grapes an acre. We don't plant our vines so close together as they do in France—we have more room. That's the winery you can see up there.'

Rae saw a picturesque old stone building with a high galvanized iron roof that glinted silver in the sun. In front of it was a stretch of brilliant green lawn almost surrounded by citrus trees. Rae could already smell the slight curling of his lip and the sardonic glitter in

Pam pulled up the car at one side of the drive and she and Rae went through wide doors around which grape-vines grew, into the winery. Inside it was cool and dim. The floor was earthen and at either side rows of dark varnished oak casks rested on log beams.

Pam said, ' They're mostly French and German oak. We don't have much timber that's suitable for wine casks in Australia—only she-oak and jarrah, and Francis says they're not so good.'

Rae wondered who Francis was, but was too busy looking about her to ask. She saw what she supposed were presses and a series of empty cement fermenting vats. Above, the great wooden beams of the roof soared up, and at the far end of the winery, doors opened into sunlight. All the while she was conscious of a faint and ghostly smell of wine.

As she and Pam walked past the fermenting vats, they heard the sound of voices, and two figures appeared in sunlight that fell dappled on the old stones of a court-yard. Rae saw a girl of about eighteen, wearing an apple green dress, her auburn hair tumbling glintingly over her shoulders. The young man with her wore light-coloured trousers and a dark blue and white striped cotton sweater. Pam reached the doors quickly.

' That's my cousin Christine. I didn't know she was coming home' from school this weekend. And that's Francis Rogeon with her.' The two had momentarily disappeared and Pam looked frowningly about the court-yard. There were stone buildings at either end of it—one, Rae knew later, was the office and laboratory, the other the cellars—and at the other side was a long vine-covered arbour in front of a fine old balconied two-storied house. Pam looked at Rae with a forced smile.

' They're fixing a barbecue. They must have gone in

for matches or something. Francis has a vineyard over the hill. He's French, of course.'

By now someone was coming through the arbour. But it was not Francis Rogeon or Christine who stepped out into the sunlit courtyard. It was Mitch.

Rae was shocked. It was impossible! Mitch should be at Illalangi by now! She wanted to disappear, to fade away into the cool dimness of the winery behind her. But of course he had seen the two girls and was coming forward with a grim smile on his handsome face.

One eyebrow lifted sardonically as he greeted first her, then Pam, but he said civilly enough, 'You've chosen a perfect day to honour us with a visit, Miss Lambert. Pam, you'd better tell Aunt Valerie there are two more for the barbecue. I'm on my way to the cellars to fetch some red wine.' Rae stared after him, her cheeks burning. He looked so incredibly handsome in his casual clothes.

Pam said, 'Some special wine he wants Francis to try, I suppose. It wouldn't be for Aunt Valerie or Christine. Or for us. Come on.'

In the shade of the arbour where a long table covered with a red and white checked cloth was laid, they encountered the young French vigneron, emerging from the house with a plate of steaks.

'*Alors!*' he exclaimed on seeing them. 'You are an unexpected visitor, Pamela. It is good to see you!' His eyes were unexpectedly blue, his hair, light brown, was worn longish and made a deep wave across a broad forehead. Pam introduced her and in a moment Christine had joined them. Rae thought there was a slight hostility in her clear grey eyes as she spoke to Pam.

Mitchell now reappeared with two bottles of red wine which he placed on the table. Francis and Christine went out to the barbecue in the courtyard and Pam, without a further word to Rae, followed them.

'I'm afraid you're on your own now,' Mitch said briskly. He glanced out at the trio in the courtyard, the young man in the middle, a laughing girl on either side of him. 'It's to be hoped *your* daydreams don't centre round a handsome young Frenchman.'

'They don't,' said Rae stiffly, and then, because of the slight curling of his lip and the sardonic glitter in his blue eyes, she added, 'I understood you would be at Illalangi today.'

'Did you really? I can't think why. At all events I'm at liberty to change my plans, and I had some business here this morning.'

Rae wanted to say that she would not have dreamed of coming to Millunga had she known he would be here, but it seemed to her that there was such a thing as protesting too much and she settled for silence. So too did Mitchell, and Rae was relieved when an older woman came out of the house carrying a tray of plates and cutlery.

'Aunt Valerie, this is Gran's new companion, Miss Rae Lambert. Miss Lambert—my aunt, Mrs Vance.'

She was a fragile-looking woman, rather sad, Rae felt. She warmed to her when she said with a sweet smile, 'We're very grateful to you for looking after Mother. She's not with you, I suppose?'

'No. I came with Pam, Mrs Vance.'

Mrs Vance nodded. 'Pam loves the Valley. When she's got the city out of her system, I imagine she may want to come here to live.'

'She may indeed,' agreed Mitchell dryly. 'And that could happen any day now. However, she's not in a position to leave her job without a moment's notice, even if it is with the family firm.'

Just the kind of thing he would say, thought Rae.

She offered to help Mrs Vance, and so was able to avoid further dealings with him until they all sat down to eat. By that time they had been joined by another visitor, a man called Scott Hallam. Mrs Vance had told Rae about him while they prepared the salad together. He ran the advertising agency which handled the Gilcrist and Millunga wine account. There was to be a series of television ads, and Scott and Mitch had been discussing their ideas.

'Mitchell doesn't want anything undignified, it wouldn't be good for the family.'

'Dear me, no,' thought Rae somewhat unfairly. 'The precious sacred family!'

'They worked out some sort of idea this morning,' said Mrs Vance, 'and then Mr Hallam went off to take some preliminary photographs. They're not to be of the winery or the cellar or the house or anything like that. But the Brokenback Range—the vines on the hill—shadows and clouds and leaf shapes and sunlight on water and the wind making everything move. It's all to be very artistic and oblique. Mitchell has some very clever ideas, he's a wonderful man.'

Rae said nothing. She was both irritated and touched by the older woman's praise of her nephew.

Scott Hallam turned out to be a man of about Mitchell's age—perhaps a little older. He was of medium height, slightly stocky, his face a ruddy brown. He had shrewd hazel eyes and gave Rae a searching smile when they were introduced by Mrs Vance.

'Shall I be poaching on anyone's preserves if I sit next to you? Has anyone any objections? His glance went, to Rae's embarrassment, to Mitch, and she flushed but said calmly, 'I'd better explain myself. I'm Mrs Gilcrist's companion. Pam brought me up here out of the kindness of her heart on my day off.'

That was the end of the matter. Rae enjoyed the simple meal of steak and salad and the red Hermitage wine that Mitch and Francis rolled around on their tongues and discussed briefly and seriously. Pam and Christine sat one on each side of Francis and though all three were full of good-humour, Rae was aware of the rivalry between the two girls, and was certain that he was the real reason for Pam's visit to Millunga. He was bestowing his attentions impartially and appeared to be enjoying himself heartily.

When the meal was finished and coffee had been drunk, Pam asked Francis if she might see the improvements he had made to his vineyard.

'Yes, do let's see what you've been doing, Francis,' cried Christine. She flipped her long hair behind her ears with a finger, first one side, then the other, and her candid grey eyes smiled at the Frenchman.

'Christine,' Mitch said sharply, 'you haven't been asked.'

Christine pulled a face. 'Neither has Pam. It was her idea.'

'You'll stay with your mother this afternoon,' Mitch decreed. 'She wants to see a little of you before you go back to school tonight.'

'But I've promised to stay home all next year when I leave school,' protested Christine.

There was a short silence, then Francis flung out his hands. '*Toc!* Why do we not all go?'

Mitch nodded. 'Scott, I think we've been over just about everything we can at this stage. Why don't you and Miss Lambert go along? I'm sure she'd like to see Francis's improvements.' His blue eyes mocked Rae, but Pam exclaimed eagerly, 'Yes, do come, Rae. You must see Francis's winery. Everything so simple— nothing modern—'

' Because I cannot afford it,' grimaced Francis. ' And I am not yet producing enough grapes to equip myself with new presses.'

As Rae had suspected, only she and Scott and Pam went with Francis. She was glad Mitch did not come, but wished she could have made it plain to him that this suited her admirably.

It was an interesting afternoon. Rae thought the small galvanized shed with its red earth floor, old basket type handpresses and somewhat worn oak casks quite fascinating.

' It doesn't look much,' said Pam, ' but Francis makes terrific wine. Even Mitch says so. We must come up at vintage and help pick the grapes. I adore vintage!'

' Who doesn't?' asked Scott.

Encouraged, Francis asked, ' Would you now like to see the new vines I have planted? I have an acre of cabernet sauvignon—a grape not so widely cultivated here in the Valley, but the best grape for red wine.' As he spoke they left the winery and crossed the long grass to stand looking down into the soft rounded hills where his vines were planted. Rae could see that some of the plants were old and gnarled while others were obviously young, their tendrils reaching gracefully for the wire trellises that looked like silver threads against the hillside.

' They grow so quickly,' Francis said. ' It is *extraordinaire!* Two inches between sunrise and sunset when there has been rain.' He wandered off into a dissertation on his plans for the next year's vintage. They were all walking slowly along, and gradually Pam and Francis dropped behind. When Rae looked back for them, Scott took her arm and said, ' Come and I'll show you a wonderful lookout spot.'

Rae glanced at him enquiringly. ' You know these

vineyards?'

'Yes indeed. I knew them before Francis had even left France. In fact, I once wrote a small book about the history of this valley. It was by virtue of my obvious interest, I think, that my agency landed the Gilcrist wines account and I came to know the Gilcrist family. A chain of events!' As he spoke, he led Rae farther up the hill until they were standing on a red rocky outcrop, looking down over the spreading valley with its rows of vines that made lovely graceful arcs against the background of red and green and grey. Above, in a blue, blue sky, long white clouds moved slowly.

'This valley,' said Scott, 'though you must realize you're only seeing a small part of it, was the first place in Australia to produce quality table wines. It all began with a Scot named James Busby. Most of the grapes grown in Australia today are descendants of the cuttings he brought out from Europe in 1831. Amazing, isn't it?'

'Tell me some more,' Rae said when he paused. 'Tell me about the Valley.'

He looked amused. 'It's too fair a day for lessons. I'll have to lend you my book.'

'I'd like that.'

'It's a promise, then.' He took her hand lightly in his and his hazel eyes looked into hers. 'You're English, aren't you?'

'Yes. But my mother was an Australian.'

'Really? And how long have you been out here?'

'Not much more than two years. We came to visit my mother's people, but my mother died the day we arrived in Sydney.'

'I'm sorry.' His eyes were soft. 'Did your relatives take care of you? Or how is it you're working for the Gilcrists?'

Rae tried to make up her mind what to tell him. She

was already regretting that she had told him as much as she had.

'It's best to be independent,' she said at last, and reverted to what she had told the Gilcrists. 'I worked out on the western plains before I came here, at a place called Tarmaroo.'

'Tarmaroo,' he repeated thoughtfully. 'And how did you like the west?'

'Not very much.'

Scott smiled sympathetically. 'It either gets you or it doesn't. I spent much of my youth out that way too. My father was a doctor beyond Bourke, on the Darling. I did some jackerooing for a while, and I remember Tarmaroo, though I didn't work there. Some people called Steele owned the property.'

'That's right,' nodded Rae, slightly unnerved.

Now Scott's eyes were narrowed in thought. 'There was a daughter who'd have been a few years older than I—Estelle. She ran away and married without her parents' consent. Some said it was a Frenchman, others said it was an Englishman. The old lady never talked about it.' He stopped, staring at her scarlet cheeks, and exclaimed softly, 'Your mother! Estelle Steele was your mother!'

Rae wanted to deny it, but she could say nothing.

'And they wouldn't accept you into the family? Not when your mother had died and you must have been a mere child—and alone?'

Rae shook her head. 'It wasn't like that. They were very good to me. They gave me a home—everything I wanted. But they both—my grandmother and my uncle —lost their lives in an accident this year.'

'You've had a bad time! Who got the property? There were only two children, weren't there? Estelle and Jack. Did Jack have a son?'

'No, he didn't have any children. His wife died a long time ago.'

'Then Tarmaroo—' He cocked an eyebrow at her. She was silent, but she knew perfectly well that her face gave her away. Scott said, 'You don't want to talk about it. All right, that's fair enough. I'm a stranger— I'm intruding—it's nothing to do with me.' His hazel eyes were quizzical. 'I admit I'm most curious. As I read it, Tarmaroo is yours—and if I recall correctly, it's an enormous property and was always expertly managed —yet here you are, companion to a charming but demanding old lady. I can't work it out.'

'I know it seems crazy. But please don't give me away. It's just that—I prefer to be an ordinary working girl. As far as the Gilcrists know, I'm just that.'

'Something's made you wise to the disadvantages of being an heiress, then,' guessed Scott. 'There are certainly hazards. Some men will give you a wide berth— others will rush you.'

'Yes,' said Rae briefly. Below them on the hillside Pam and Francis were making their way back to the winery. 'Will you promise me to say nothing?'

'Yes, of course I'll respect your secret. Though I don't imagine the Gilcrists would take advantage of you,' he added dryly.

'Just the same, I'd prefer them not to know.'

'I'm sorry I was so inquisitive—and that I just happen to come from roughly the same neck of the woods.' He took her arm. 'We'd better join the others. But first I'm going to ask you to pay a small price for my silence.'

'What?' Ridiculously, Rae thought he was going to ask for a kiss.

'I'd like to take you out sometimes—see something of you.'

' Thank you, I should like that. Do you know where I live?'

He laughed. ' Of course I do! I used to visit Illalangi now and again and play chess with old Mrs Gilcrist.'

' But you don't now?'

' No.' He turned his face away abruptly and began to move down the hill.

Rae, feeling faintly rebuffed, asked him presently, ' Where do you live, Scott?'

He turned and grinned at her and his face had lost its closed look. ' Wait for it! I live less than five minutes' walk away from Illalangi—down the hill a bit.'

Rae said no more, but she wondered why it was that he no longer visited Illalangi.

She had a kind of an answer to her query when she and Pam were on their way back to Sydney that evening.

' Enjoy the day?' Pam had asked. And then, before Rae could reply, she wanted to know, ' Did Scott make a pass at you?'

' No,' said Rae, surprised. ' He asked if he might take me out some time, that's all. Why?'

Pam shrugged. ' Oh, I don't know. He's a bit of a mystery. I guess I've been brought up to think there's something wicked about him. *Mitch* associates with him, but *we*'re not supposed to. Today was an exception, and I don't think Mitch was pleased when we turned up. I've always thought he must have done something absolutely frightful—Scott, I mean. I'd love to know what it was.'

' I don't imagine it's anything. He seemed a very nice person to me,' said Rae. ' Intelligent—interesting. He's promised to lend me the book he wrote, and I said I should like to go out with him.'

' Better change your mind. Mitch mightn't like it. And there must be some reason. I mean, Mitch is a good judge of people.'

Rae digested that. She reflected that Mitch did not like her! She said innocently, 'He likes Francis Rogeon, doesn't he?'

Pam reddened. 'Yes.'

'Lucky for you.'

'I'm not so lucky,' said Pam gloomily. 'I hardly ever see Francis. And soon Christine will be at Millunga all the time. I've a good mind to give up my job and go up there myself.' She switched the subject back to Rae. 'I don't think you ought to encourage Scott, Rae. It would be asking for trouble.'

'I don't agree. I like Scott,' said Rae lightly.

'I didn't mean trouble from Scott. I meant from Mitch.'

'My personal life is my own affair,' said Rae. She hoped that Scott would ask her out soon. She would go, and she would make a point of letting Mitchell Gilcrist know about it. He would soon discover that he couldn't dictate to her!

CHAPTER V

Scott invited her to a concert in the city early that week. Rae went, dressing with care and enjoyment in a long-skirted, long-sleeved dress of orange Thai silk that had been part of her trousseau.

'You're quite a beautiful young woman, Rae,' said Mrs Gilcrist approvingly when she went in to say good-bye to her, for Scott was already waiting downstairs. She added bluntly, 'Who's taking you to this concert?'

'Scott Hallam. I met him at Millunga on Sunday.'

'Goodness me! I thought Scott Hallam must have lost his heart elsewhere! He used to come here often. I always believed Helen was the attraction, though he played a game of chess with me every now and again. It must be about two years since I've seen him. I enjoyed his company. He knows a great deal about the wine country, that young man, and he always listened to what I had to say. Not like Mitchell, who I suppose has heard it all before. Ah well, you'd better run along. I shall be quite all right. Enjoy yourself!'

'Thank you. I'm sure I shall.'

Scott was waiting in the hall at the foot of the stairs and when Rae appeared he looked at her appreciatively. She found it good to be admired. He had taken her hand and she was smiling back at him when Helen came into the hall from the little sitting room. Rae observed the look of blank shock and surprise that came over her face, but she collected herself quickly, greeted Scott coolly, and continued on her way upstairs.

Rae thought, as she and Scott went out to his car, that Mitch was sure to hear from either Helen or his grandmother who had been her escort tonight. She wondered if he would bother to issue her with a warning.

On Thursday, Rae had dinner with Scott at a local Chinese restaurant, and afterwards he showed her his home. It was a modern bungalow built closer to the street than Illalangi and lacking the spectacular view exclusive to the homes high on the hill. But at the back of the house was a pleasant secluded garden, fringed with shrubs and centred round a swimming pool complete with cabanas for changing. There was a barbecue at one end of the flagging, and a jasmine-covered pergola.

'It's beautiful,' commented Rae, relaxing in a fibre-glass lounger. He had switched on two little lantern-type lamps and the garden looked very intimate and romantic. 'Do you live here alone?'

'Yes. I bought the place about three years ago, more or less on impulse. Sometimes I wish I hadn't. It's too big for me—too far from town, yet I can't persuade myself to leave. I eat out a lot, and I have a local woman come in every second day to clean.'

'You should be married,' said Rae lightly. She could not help wondering about Helen. Had he, as Mrs Gilcrist suspected, been in love with her and bought this house on her account? But Mitch had clamped down. Rae did not doubt it, but she wondered why. She simply could not believe that there was anything as unacceptable as all that in his past.

'Maybe I should be,' said Scott. 'But it's not a thing one should go into lightly. I've learned that. I was married once. Or did you already know that?'

'I didn't,' said Rae. He was sitting on the grass, one hand trailed idly in the pool, and he flicked an arc of water into the air, then turned to give her a faint smile.

'It was a long time ago. She died—another road victim. She was in a car with some idiot of a drunken driver. But I'd rather not talk about it.' He was silent for a moment, frowning. ' By the way, I think I owe it to you to add a little to what I told you the other day. I said I didn't go to Illalangi now. Well, that's because Mitchell made it fairly plain that he preferred me to remain a business acquaintance rather than a family friend. So I got out before any harm was done. Nowadays it's only by accident that I occasionally run into any of the girls—as I did last Sunday at Millunga.'

' But *why*?" Rae wanted to know.

Scott shrugged. ' Isn't it enough that that's the way it is? I'm not egotistical enough to try to force the issue. Now let's forget it . . . I wanted to offer you the use of this pool of mine at any time you care to use it whether I'm here or not. You might appreciate it on days you have a spare hour or two and neither the time nor the energy to walk down to the beach.'

' Thank you,' said Rae. ' As a matter of fact, I have a car down at the bungalow I own near the beach. I can't garage it at Illalangi.'

' Then use my car port,' Scott said instantly. ' There's room for two cars, and it won't put me out at all.'

' I don't know why you should be so kind to me.'

' Because I like you. Believe me, it's simply that.'

Rae thought about that later, and she believed it was true and that he had meant her to take it as such. It wasn't that he was in the least in love with her. He liked her—and she liked him. In a way they needed each other. And it didn't matter to him in the least that she was Rae Lambert who owned Tarmaroo sheep station.

As he had promised, he lent her the book he had written about the development of the Valley, and Rae turned first of all to the section devoted to Millunga. The Millunga vineyards had been planted on a land grant made to the family when they came out to Australia

in 1838. The homestead and the winery were built of
stone quarried by convicts, and convict labour was used
to plant the first vines. The Darvale family had worked
the Millunga vineyards until they came to grief in 1905.
Two things conspired to defeat Edward Darvale, the
last Darvale to be in charge. One was the Federation
of the six Australian colonies into the Commonwealth
of Australia in 1900. This removed trade barriers in
Australia, and there was an influx of wines into New
South Wales from South Australia. These wines were
cheaper because the South Australian government gave
a subsidy to growers while that of New South Wales did
not. As if this were not a bad enough blow—and some
of the smaller wineries were ruined at once—the entire
Millunga crop was ruined by downy mildew in one
season, and two years later Edward, despite desperate
efforts to recover, was compelled to sell the family
property as farming land. He took his family south
to the Murrumbidgee area where, later, his daughter
Margaret married into another winegrowing family, the
Gilcrists.

So Margaret Darvale was her Mrs Gilcrist, thought Rae.
with a little shock of recognition. She read on, 'A
grandson of this union, Mitchell Gilcrist, bought back
Millunga and a neighbouring property in 1961. Mitchell
is a winemaker of no small repute, and once again the
vine flourishes on Millunga's acres, and the Millunga
label is a sure sign of a high quality table wine. The
old homestead has been restored, the winery renovated
and enlarged, new cellars built and a general air of
prosperity prevails.'

' Hmm,' thought Rae, unable to help feeling approving.
She found the whole book interesting and informative,
and was amazed to learn that up until the new century,
the hundred-mile journey she and Pam had made that

Sunday morning had taken three or four days. A boat had to be taken to Maitland, and from there the journey to the vineyards was made by dray or on horseback. She finished the book one afternoon as she waited for Mrs Gilcrist at the hairdresser's. Later, in the car, seeing the book, her employer remarked, ' I can see you're determined to keep abreast of the family's absorbing interest, my dear. Very intelligent of you. Tell me— I don't recall if any disreputable facts about our family were uncovered by Mr Scott Hallam. Neither the Darvales nor the Gilcrists were ever either gamblers or drinkers, or so I am persuaded to believe.'

Rae smiled. ' I certainly read nothing to your disadvantage, Mrs Gilcrist.' She kept her eye carefully on the traffic, heavy at this time of day. ' You must have been quite young when you left Millunga.'

' I was in my late teens. I must say it's given me great joy to have it back in the family again. Yet I have no wish to live there again. One can't call back the essence of happy times past. Besides, my daughter irritates me, a dreadful thing to confess. Poor Valerie is ill and needs consideration, and '—she flung out her hands—' I'm too impatient to give it.'

' I met Mrs Vance,' said Rae. ' I thought she looked frail.'

' Yes, so she is. She was not always frail, but she was a wayward and silly girl, and it's due to her foolishness that Mitchell has so much extra responsibility now. Are you quite lost? Has no one told you the family scandal? Well then, I shall do so.'

' There's no need—' began Rae, but her protests were waved aside.

' Valerie made an impetuous marriage. Ashley Vance was a charming and persuasive man, and he deceived us all with no difficulty at all. Mitchell at that time,' she added dryly, 'was too young to be of any use as a stabilizer. Ashley appeared to be a successful importer, and it was not until he'd persuaded Valerie to sell all her shares in the family company that we became suspicious. But it was too late. He used every penny she had and somehow—don't ask me how, I was never a business woman—managed to go bankrupt as well. As if that were not bad enough he had a heart attack and died, since which time Mitchell has made himself responsible for both Valerie and Christine, and as well as that my son Charles has saddled him with his sisters. Charming girls, thank goodness, and I'm sure not in need of the strictness he metes out.'

'Is he so strict?' Rae asked. 'When he's at Millunga and they're down here—'

'He is strict,' Mrs Gilcrist said firmly. '*They* are aware of it. And perhaps I should have been stricter with Valerie. However, that's why Millunga is not for me. It irritates me that Valerie has made such a sorry mess of her life. A daughter of mine! My three sons have proved themselves more responsible. Charles—the oldest—was always my favourite. Now I've lost him, but I enjoy living with his children.'

They were home now, and Rae helped her from the car and escorted her into the house, while she continued talking.

'But I suppose you want to hear stories of Millunga in the earlier days. *My* clearest memory is of riding about the countryside—I was something of a tomboy, I suppose—jumping fences, falling in the river. I remember the sound of the grapes fermenting in the wooden vats at vintage time—that extraordinary bubbling and boiling used to fascinate and mystify me. And the smell of the wine—very nostalgic.' On the way upstairs she remembered something else. 'Eating the fruit of the prickly pear. It's a noxious weed now, but oh, the delicious red flesh! Once, even though I'd brushed the spikes off, I got one in my tongue. Father tried to pull it out with tweezers, but couldn't, and there it stayed until it dissolved away.' She gave a little chuckle. 'Mitchell sometimes says the barb's still there.'

Rae laughed too. 'Not very tactful of him! I suppose those prickly pears would be descendants of the ones James Busby planted as windbreaks back in the eighteen-thirties.'

'Yes, I daresay I can thank him for my lovely red fruit as well as the barb in my tongue.'

After dinner that night when Mrs Gilcrist went up to her room, Joan for the first time invited Rae to come out to see her studio.

'Perhaps Rae has another date with Scott,' suggested Helen, not turning from her seat at the piano.

'Not tonight,' Rae said cheerfully, wondering if there had been an acid note in that comment. 'I'd like to see where you work, Joan.' She followed the youngest Gilcrist through the garden at the back of the house to the white-painted brick outbuilding that she used as a studio. Joan took a key from the pocket of dirty blue jeans and unlocked the door. Inside she switched on strip lighting.

Rae saw at once that Mitchell must have gone to some trouble to see that she had good working space. The floor was bare except for a strip of seagrass matting, but there were long benches down the side wall, shelves above, and a large sink at one end of the room. Joan had loads of art materials—canvas, paints, clay, plaster. And Rae's eye was caught by what looked a life-size head on one of the benches. It was swathed in plastic, which Joan presently began to draw off carefully.

'This is what I'm working on at the moment. I really

think I like sculpture better than painting—I get more of a kick from something three-dimensional.' Once she had pulled away the plastic sheeting, she waited rather self-consciously for Rae's reaction. Rae saw the head of a young man with puckish eyebrows, a broad forehead and slightly tip-tilted nose. The hair had not been finished, but it looked as if it were going to be rather long and rough. Rae was surprised at the competence of the work and at the character revealed in the clay portrait. She exclaimed, ' It's terrific!'

Joan turned to her swiftly, her usually sombre little face flushed.

' Do you think so? I've been a little in love with it, but I wanted to see what somebody else would say. So often I wake up one day and what I thought good looks absolutely terrible. It's very disheartening. I expect I shall feel the same way about this.' As she spoke she had taken up a knife and now began, rather boldly it seemed to Rae, to slice at the cheek.

Rae wanted to stop her—to take the knife away.

' It's not free enough—it's too literal,' Joan said discontentedly. ' The sort of thing any competent student could do. I don't want to turn out work like that. I mean, what would you *do* with a thing like this? Who on earth would want it? You might as well have John the Baptist's head on a plate on your mantelpiece.' She looked at Rae. ' Do you know anything about art? I wish you did.'

' I'm afraid I don't know a great deal,' Rae said regretfully. She hoisted herself on to a nearby stool, looking at the cheek Joan had slashed at with new eyes. Maybe the lines had been too smooth and lovely and literal! She asked, ' Who is it? Or did you invent it?'

' I'm not idiotic enough to try to do that—not experienced enough, anyhow. It's a friend of mine.'

Connor Birch, thought Rae instantly.

' He'd hate it. Though he wouldn't exactly say so, he's not that sort of person. He'd say, That sort of literal stuff is just something you've got to get out of your system, and the sooner the better. I wish I could get over it. I wish I really believed I was capable of something better. But I have no self-confidence—nobody takes me seriously. Only—' She broke off. Only Connor Birch?

' Mitchell sends you to art school,' Rae said. ' That shows *he* takes you seriously.'

' No. At the drop of a hat he'd make me leave and send me to secretarial school or something, try to make a *nice* girl of me. And I hate the thought of being *nice*. I guess I'm a throwback or something. I just don't fit into this family. I'm a potential black sheep.' She was leaning back against the bench now, scowling, her sturdy legs astride, the thick dark hair falling across her eyes. There was a smudge of clay on her chin, and Rae noticed that a button was missing from her crumpled tie-dyed blouse.

' I hate being rich,' Joan said after a minute. ' I'd change places with you any day.'

Rae raised her eyebrows comically. ' And be a lady's companion? I shouldn't have thought that would suit your book at all.'

' I didn't mean that,' said Joan impatiently. ' I mean I'd rather be free of my family—free to be myself. Your people are in England, I suppose. Did they mind your cutting loose?'

Rae was not sure what answer she would have made to that, but she had no need to say anything, for at that moment Mitchell knocked on the half open door and came in.

He said, ' May I come in?' but he was already two

paces inside the room as he said it.

'You are in!' said Joan in the impudent tone Rae had heard her use more than once when addressing her brother. She was aware, for some reason, of a quickening of her heartbeats—as though she were guilty of something, surely. She had had no idea Mitchell was coming to Illalangi tonight. As a rule, he appeared to come at the weekend.

As if aware of the slight turmoil into which he had thrown her, he flicked her an amused glance.

'Good evening, Miss Lambert. It's good to know you're not up to your ears in my grandmother's concerns all twenty-four hours of the day. I was afraid for a while that your assiduousness was going to make a slave of you . . . Come to see what Joan's up to, have you? I hope she can depend on you for honest criticism—and good advice.'

As he said this, he saw for the first time the head which had been half hidden behind Joan as she lounged against the bench looking rebellious. Rae said lightly, 'I came to learn, not to preach,' but she knew that nobody was listening. Sparks were about to fly and in a moment the air was crackling with them.

Mitch snapped his fingers at the head and asked angrily, 'Has that layabout been here?'

Joan straightened herself and stared back at him stonily. 'I don't know any layabouts.'

'You know well enough who I mean. That's Connor Birch's head you're modelling. I want to know if he's been here.'

Rae stayed as if glued to the stool. Afterwards she wondered why she had not slipped quietly from the room. Nobody would have noticed. But she sat there listening, never quite sure whose side she was on. She bristled for both of them. How dared he speak of Joan's friends like that? And how naïve was this girl to be taken in by a man like Connor Birch? She listened to their angry voices, and they ignored her completely.

'I'm working from sketches.'

'From sketches! When and where did you make *them*? I've told you I won't have you encouraging him—'

'What do you mean, "encougaging him"? Encouraging him to do what?'

'Don't be a little idiot. To imagine he can ever mean anything in your life.'

'Perhaps he can. How would you know? Anyhow, it's none of your business.'

'It most certainly is. I'm responsible for you.' Mitch's lips were tight and his brow drawn. Rae felt thankful that he had no control over *her* personal life. He was a man who was used to his own way and expected to get it, and anyone who fought him would have to fight hard. But perhaps Joan, most of all the three Gilcrist girls, was capable of fighting hard.

Mitch went on after a second during which the two of them stared at each other unblinkingly, 'If you won't listen to me and do as you're told then you can damn well give up all this fooling about with art and put your head down and do some honest work. If you won't do typing and shorthand you can come up to Millunga and work in the vineyards. I promised you a year to see what you could make of yourself as an artist, and that year's just about ended.'

'I haven't fooled around,' Joan flashed. 'You'll see at the students' exhibition. You just don't understand the first thing about creative art—all you think about is your rotten old vineyard and the family *name* and *fortune*,' she finished with scornful emphasis.

'Part of which fortune belongs to you,' he reminded

her smoothly.

'I don't want it.'

'It's easy to talk when you've always had everything . . . Another point I want to make—did you go in to dinner tonight in that gear?'

'Yes. Why shouldn't I? This is supposed to be my home.'

'Just don't ever appear at the table looking like that when I'm in the house, because I won't tolerate it.'

Joan hoisted herself up on the bench and looked consideringly at the legs of her blue jeans, and at her shabby blue and white sneakers. Then she looked at Mitch from under her brows—a look so like his own it was almost laughable. 'On my miserable allowance—for all your talk about how I have *everything*—how do you expect me to look?'

'You get about as much as Miss Lambert here,' said Mitch. 'And she always manages to look very attractive.'

Rae was not going to be used in this battle. She said mildly, knowing as she spoke how he would interpret it, 'I came by most of my clothes while I was at Tarmaroo, Mr Gilcrist.' Her heart had begun to pound again, but she returned levelly the scrutiny he gave her. Then abruptly, he turned on his heel and went, tossing over his shoulder, 'I'll have more to say to you later, Joan.'

Joan jumped down from the bench. She said loudly and angrily, 'He doesn't even *know* Con—none of them do. They don't understand anyone who's eaten up by creative ambition. Unless it's an ambition to grow grapes and make wine—and loads of money—Mitch discounts it. I hate him!'

Rae didn't know what to say. She was of two minds regarding Connor Birch. Joan seemed the only one

who had a good word for him. She asked thoughtfully,
' You admire Connor's work very much, do you, Joan?'

' Yes, he's good. He's not recognized yet, but he will
be. Mitch hasn't even seen his stuff—he's just plain
pigheaded, and thinks he knows everything. Sometimes
I think I'm mad to stay here. I'd clear out like a shot
if Connor wanted it.' She began covering her clay with
the plastic sheet again, and Rae thought, ' So Connor
doesn't want her to clear out.' There could be two
reasons for that. Either he had a real regard for Joan
or she would not have the same attraction for him if she
dissociated herself from her family—and its fortune!
Rae began to wish she could meet Connor Birch!

When she went back into the house a little later, she
encountered Mitchell on the stairs. He gave her a hard
look and remarked, ' I hope I can count on you not to
encourage Joan in her delusions, Miss Lambert.'

Rae said distantly, ' I'm not here tò take part in family
politics, Mr Gilcrist. You made that plain to me when
I was employed. I don't know Connor Birch, and I'm
strictly neutral.'

' None the less,' he insisted, ' you paid us a visit at
Millunga. That suggests a personal interest.'

' I wanted to be able to talk more intelligently on a
subject dear to Mrs Gilcrist's heart,' said Rae not
altogether truthfully. ' And as I told you, I thought
that you would be at Illalangi on that particular day.'

' And you wanted to avoid me?'

Rae shrugged. ' I think you prefer it that way too.'

He surprised her by saying, ' I don't want to avoid
you. I see no reason why we shouldn't conduct a perfectly amicable relationship. It helps me to hear about
my grandmother from someone who is close to her.'

Rae, whose spirits had lifted unaccountably, was now
equally unaccountably disappointed. She said shortly,

'As you wish. I'm available for questioning at any time. Goodnight, Mr Gilcrist.' And she continued briskly up the stairs.

CHAPTER VI

Mitchell went by plane to a company meeting in the irrigation area the next morning, and was back at Illalangi late on Friday night. On Saturday morning when he came upstairs to see his grandmother after breakfast, Rae went down to the kitchen and made sure he was out of the way before she returned to her employer.

Joan too had been watching her brother's movements, and appeared in Mrs Gilcrist's room no more than five minutes after Rae. She skipped across to hug the old lady, who was leafing through the Saturday paper.

'Gran darling, are you in a good mood? I hope so, because I've come to cash in on it.'

Rae heard no more, for she went to prepare the bath. When she came out again, Joan was thrusting a handful of notes into the pocket of her jeans, and Mrs Gilcrist was pointing to a fashion advertisement in the *Herald*.

'How about something like this, my dear? Just the thing for an artist—Picasso prints, Toulouse-Lautrec prints—and a much more graceful length than the mini.' She smiled rather fatuously at her favourite grand-daughter.

Joan made a comical face. 'Grannie, where would I wear it? I'm a poor student! I need paints and brushes and books more than I need a fifty-dollar gown. But I'll get something, I promise you, a skirt maybe. You shall see it the minute I come home.' She blew her grandmother a kiss and danced from the room.

Mrs Gilcrist narrowed her eyes. 'I'll have to speak to Mitchell. He's too hard on that poor little girl. You can't tell me she wouldn't like to wear pretty clothes. But she's determined to prove herself at art school, and

he apparently has no idea how much art materials cost.'
She got up from her chair. ' I'll have a few words with
him after I've had my bath. Tell him he keeps too tight
a hand on the reins—his father would have wanted him
to be more tolerant. Go downstairs, will you, Rae, and
tell my grandson I'll see him on the terrace for coffee at
eleven o'clock.'

She spoke as if she were arranging a duel, and perhaps
it would be something of the sort! Rae, going in search
of Mitchell, determined that this time she would not
listen in on a family argument. She could see some home
truths being aired and did not relish the idea of being
a witness. At the back of her mind there was a suspicion
that Joan was not using her allowance—or the handouts
she received from her grandmother—entirely for her own
needs.

She found Mitchell half way down the terraced
garden, smoking a cigarette and staring out at the glittering blue of the ocean, and the hazy horizon that promised
a hot day.

' Mr Gilcrist?'

' Yes?' His eyes swept over her, her crisp yellow
dress, the neat embroidered band that kept her hair back
from her face, her white sandals.

' Mrs Gilcrist would like to see you on the terrace at
eleven. For coffee,' finished Rae, disconcerted by his
appraisal of her.

' That suits me,' he said agreeably, and added humorously, ' Are we to carry arms, or is it to be a peaceable
meeting?'

Rae smiled faintly. ' I don't think anyone would
ever catch you unarmed, Mr Gilcrist.'

' And my grandmother always has at least a knife
tucked into her garter,' he agreed, laughing. ' I hope
you'll take coffee with us, Rae.'

The unexpected invitation and his use of her name made Rae blink. He was being positively genial! But knowing what the topic of conversation was to be, she said pleasantly, ' Thank you, but there are several things I shall have to do.'

' Oh, leave them for a little. There can't be anything that won't keep. It's a very pretty day, and an hour or so in the sun will do you good. Besides which, your company will help us to keep our tempers.'

' I'll see about it, then,' said Rae, not meaning it. She went up the path, and as she reached the terrace he called after her softly, ' By the way, yellow is definitely one of your colours!'

Rae's step lightened. Relations were improving! Or was he testing her—giving her the proverbial inch? She would have to tread warily. She could hear one of Helen's pupils playing Czerny in the small sitting room, and then, when she had taken two steps up the stairs, the telephone rang. Rae, being nearest, answered it. It was Clara Livingstone.

' Is that you, Rae my dear? What are your plans for the day?'

' Coffee with Mr Gilcrist at eleven,' said Rae, knowing what she meant. ' Otherwise Mrs Gilcrist is free today.'

' Then she must come to lunch. I'm reading the most extraordinarily interesting book about the gold rushes in Victoria. There's a face in one of the old photographs that I want her to see. I shan't say·any more, but tell her I'll expect her at twelve. Or will that be impossible?'

' I'll do my best,' said Rae, amused. She knew Mrs Gilcrist would not be able to resist this bait, and wondered if the battle with Mitchell would be called off.

Mrs Gilcrist was suitably intrigued. She hurried with her dressing, and Rae was sent to tell Mitchell that she would be down to coffee immediately and could spare only twenty minutes. Mitchell raised his eyebrows.

'What's happened? Clara Livingstone's intervened, would be my guess. She has some sort of incredible information to impart.'

'Something like that,' smiled Rae.

Mitchell grinned. 'It happens so often. And frankly, I'm thankful it does. Those two have such a zest for living—they extract every ounce of enjoyment from the smallest thing. Boring for you, of course. I suggest you leave the two old dears to have their lunch and talk and come home.'

'Home?' said Rae with a little lift of her eyebrows. Then quickly, 'I'll do whatever Mrs Gilcrist wants.'

'She'll invite you to stay. But believe me, there's no need to.'

'If it will add to her enjoyment, then I'll stay,' said Rae firmly.

'You're too virtuous by far,' said Mitch. 'Why not come home?' They stared at each other. 'I'm not falling for that line,' thought Rae. No slacking! Moreover, if she came back to Illalangi, Mitchell might think she was chasing him. He might even be out, just to put her in her place. No, wherever she spent her day it would not be here. She thought all this as she escorted Mrs Gilcrist down to the terrace a few minutes later. And there, whether she wanted it or not, she was included in the party.

'Don't go away, Rae. As soon as I've said what I have to say to Mitchell, I want to be on my way.'

So they all sat over coffee, and Mrs Gilcrist had her little sparring match with her grandson.

'You're too hard on the girls, Mitchell.'

'All of them?'

'On Joan, then. And sometimes, it seems to me, on Helen. You've frozen something in that girl. She's as afraid of you as if you were a Victorian papa.'

'Rubbish,' said Mitchell, but Rae thought he looked uncomfortable. She had determined to try not to listen, yet listen she did and could not help herself. These Gilcrists fascinated her—even Mitch. Particularly Mitch?

'Of course she admires you, and loves you. But she reminds me of Elizabeth Barrett.' Mrs Gilcrist set down her cup and looked at Mitchell and then at Rae. She was a little pleased with her remark.

'And who plays the role of Robert Browning?' asked Mitchell, amused.

'Scott Hallam,' said his grandmother instantly, surprising both Rae and Mitchell. 'That young man had a passion for Helen.'

'Young? He's a couple of years older than I am. And Helen did not—and does not—return his passion.'

'I wouldn't be too sure about Helen's feelings . . . However, it was Joan I wanted to talk about. She needs money for little things to make herself pretty. I may be old, but there are times when I know better than you, Mitchell, and this is one of them. I must win sometimes —if I didn't then I shouldn't be blessed with Rae here.' She paused and Mitchell said nothing. He refilled his coffee cup and helped himself to sugar. 'You're stubborn, Mitchell, and very irritating. Saying nothing's not the way to make for understanding.'

'What would you like me to say?' asked Mitchell. 'That you're always right? You're not. That I'll increase Joan's allowance? I shan't. As for Rae here—' he smiled at Rae, a lazy smile, his blue eyes half shut—'well, perhaps you were right about Rae.'

'Heavens!' thought Rae disbelievingly. 'I'll have to watch my step after this. A little kindness, a little encouragement and I'll be forgetting my place, and that will be the finish.' She smiled innocently back at

Mitchell.

'If I had my way,' said Mrs Gilcrist, rising, 'you'd have less control over the financial affairs of the family. You're not the paragon your father assumed.'

'Perhaps I'm the best of a hopeless lot,' said Mitchell, rising too and escorting her down the steps. '*You* would have the girls ruined in no time, all of them married to blackguards and the family fortunes lost—vanished like a puff of smoke.'

His grandmother snorted. 'All I want is their happiness.'

'And I too,' he said sombrely.

Rae, who had said nothing, followed them down to the car and took the driver's seat.

'Mind how you go,' said Mitch, leaning down to the window. He smiled at her and Rae smiled back. It occurred to her that she and Mitch were doing a fair bit of smiling at each other today. It made her feel wary. She thought of her predecessor, Alison Campbell. Perhaps it had been this way with her, with Mitch smiling, approving, offering little compliments. And the next thing she had lost her heart and her head, and, finally, her job. It was unfair of Mitchell. 'It won't happen to me,' thought Rae.

She was not wanted as an audience at Mrs Livingstone's luncheon. On the way, Mrs Gilcrist said, 'You don't get much time to yourself, Rae. Do what you like while I'm at Clara's. Take the car and enjoy yourself —so long as you're back for me at four-thirty. Make your plans around that nucleus.'

'Thank you, Mrs Gilcrist. You're good to me.'

'I'm not. I put myself first, and I sometimes think it's unfair. You're at the beginning of your life, I'm at the end of mine. You're the one who should be free.'

'You've given me a job when I needed one,' said Rae.

' And a home,' she nearly added, ' and a feeling of almost belonging.' But that might reach Mitch's ears.

She delivered her passenger safely, remarked on the delicious smells coming from the kitchen where the treasured Cilla was cooking lunch, and took her departure.

It was a wonderful day of blue skies and hot sunshine and the surf called to Rae. She wished she had brought her bathing gear with her and decided to go back to Illalangi and collect it. Her main concern would be to avoid Mitchell. This she accomplished without trouble, but on her way out Mrs McPhail waylaid her.

' I thought I heard you go up, Rae. Mr Hallam's here. I left him in the little sitting room.'

Rae found Scott standing by the piano rather pensively touching the keys and playing with one finger some nostalgic tune that Rae could not place. He turned to smile at her.

' This is my lucky day! I didn't know you were free.'

Rae explained quickly what had happened and what she was doing back at the house.

Scott said, ' Actually I came to see what you were doing tonight. I'm having a few friends in and thought you might like to join us.'

' I'd love it, thank you. Though I can't promise to be there at any specific time.'

' Whenever you're able . . . But about now—why go back to Manly for your swim? What's wrong with here—and my company?'

' Nothing,' said Rae happily. ' I don't really care to swim by myself.'

' Fine,' said Scott. He closed the lid of the piano. ' Have you eaten?'

' No. But I'm not very hungry.'

' We'll find a sandwich at my place.' He glanced at

478

his watch. 'What time did you say you must be back at Manly?'

'At four-thirty.' Rae preceded him through the door and nearly collided with Helen, who said coldly, 'I thought you were with my grandmother.'

'She doesn't need me for a few hours,' said Rae. She was aware of hostility. She had had very little to do with Helen, who had not made any overtures to be friendly, although she had always been civil. Behind her, Scott spoke to Helen, saying rather awkwardly, 'You're looking well, Helen.'

Helen made no answer. She brushed past them and as they crossed the terrace they could hear her at the piano. Scott said, 'I used to enjoy listening to Helen playing. Ah well!' He sighed and took Rae's arm as they went down to the street where the two cars were parked. 'I guess I'll always have a very soft spot for Helen . . . We'll take my car, Rae, and I'll bring you back here after our swim.'

As she sat beside him during the short run to his home he said, 'How does the idea of the pool strike you? A lobster sandwich with yoghurt and horseradish dressing, a glass of white wine—Millunga, of course!—then the two of us stretching out lazily in the sun while you doze and I admire your legs and wish I were fifteen years younger.'

Rae laughed lightheartedly. She was sure that Scott was not in love with her, and she found his company both enjoyable and good for her self-esteem. Nevertheless, she said, 'I'd rather go down to the surf.' She had been alone with him once at his house, but thought it was wiser and more discreet not to repeat the performance.

'You don't trust me?'

'Of course I do. But people talk, and I was brought

up to be conventional. Besides, the surf appeals to me today.'

' Then the surf it shall be,' Scott conceded.

They combined efforts in the kitchen to produce a sketchy but delectable lunch on the lines he had proposed—but minus the wine, which Rae said would make her sleepy. They took Rae's car down to the beach as she had not used it for some time and didn't want the battery to go flat.

They both enjoyed themselves on the beach. Rae, who had left the surf sooner than Scott, fell asleep as she lay sunbaking. When she woke, the first thing she did was reach for her watch. She was already ten minutes later than she had meant to be! She looked around for Scott and found him talking to someone he had met. She called to him to hurry and was on edge as they drove back to his house. To save time she changed there while he waited in the car for her. She knew she was going to be late and felt very guilty about not keeping her word. She hoped Mrs Gilcrist would not think she had taken advantage of her kindness. At the back of her mind lurked the shadow of Mitchell, waiting to find fault. She comforted herself with the thought that there was no need for him to know anything about today's little mishap. She would explain to Mrs Gilcrist what had happened and was sure it would go no further.

But when Scott drove her to Illalangi she had a shock. The car she had left parked at the kerb was gone. Rae's heart gave a leap of fright, and Scott exclaimed, ' Good God! It's been stolen! Did you leave the keys in it?'

' Of course not.' Rae fished them out of her bag to prove it.

' Go up to the house and see what you can find out,' said Scott. ' I'll see if anyone in the neighbourhood saw anything.'

Rae raced up to the house. There she could find no one but Mrs McPhail, who knew nothing. Rae looked in the drawer of the telephone table where all the duplicate keys were kept. The keys to Mrs Gilcrist's car were missing. Then someone here had taken the car! Was it Mitch or Helen, or had Joan taken it for a jaunt? Rae looked at her watch. It was four-twenty-five and it would take at least half an hour to get to Manly. She lifted the telephone and dialled Mrs Livingstone's number. It was Cilla who answered. 'Don't worry, Helen Gilcrist is here,' she told Rae, as if she knew all about it. 'They're just about to leave.'

Rae let out a deep breath. 'I'd like to speak to Helen,' she said. While she waited she thanked heaven it had not been Mitchell who had taken the car. But what on earth had possessed Helen? She would find out soon. But finally, it was Cilla again.

'They're leaving, Rae,' Cilla said. 'Helen says it can wait. She'll be seeing you shortly.'

'Thank you, Cilla.' She hung up and turned from the telephone as Scott came in. He said at once, 'You know it was Helen? Some people over the way saw her driving off. I just don't get it.'

'Neither do I,' said Rae lightly. She was remembering her encounter with Helen before she went out with Scott. Of course Helen must have heard their conversation—though that hardly explained her behaviour. 'Well, never mind,' she told Scott. 'I shall explain to Mrs Gilcrist that I was a little later than I'd meant to be.' Though not all *that* late, she thought.

'I hope it won't cost you your job,' Scott said, and then laughed. 'I guess it won't be a tragedy if it does.'

Rae stared at him.

'Don't look at me like that. I promise you I shan't say a word. Your secret's safe with me. I'll see you tonight, shall I?'

'I hope so.'

Scott put an arm around her shoulders and hugged her lightly. 'Goodbye for now. I enjoyed this afternoon.'

'I too,' said Rae, but she was troubled. When he had gone she went upstairs and rinsed out her bathing costume. Then she sat on the balcony off Mrs Gilcrist's room and watched for the car. She remembered Mrs Gilcrist's suspicion that Scott had been interested in Helen, and her remark to Mitch that morning—'I wouldn't be too sure about Helen's feelings'. Could it possibly be that Helen was jealous of her, Rae? She sighed. There was no romantic attachment between herself and Scott . . .

At that moment she saw Mitchell's car pull up in the street, and while he had got out apparently to open the garage doors, Mrs Gilcrist's car arrived. Presently he, Helen and Mrs Gilcrist appeared on the terrace. They were talking, but not loudly, and Helen was gesturing. Mitch, behind the others, glanced up before he went under the porch. He was looking very serious and though he caught Rae's eye, this time he did not smile. In fact, he gave no sign of having seen her. With a feeling of apprehension, Rae left the balcony and went to face whatever was in store for her.

The three of them were in the hall, and they all looked towards her as she came down the stairs. Helen glanced away quickly and went into the little sitting room; Mitch glared at her with thunder in his face, and Mrs Gilcrist, who looked tired, said, 'I shall go straight to my room and have a little rest. Rae, I shall need you.'

Rae took the old lady's arm. Her heart was hammering absurdly, and all sorts of excuses buzzed about in her head. But she said nothing. Presently, when they were alone, she would apologize to her employer. It was nothing to do with Mitchell, and surely there was no reason for him to wear such a face of doom.

He said in a steely voice, ' I'll see you in the library as soon as you're free, Miss Lambert.'

' Certainly, Mr Gilcrist.' Rae tried for casualness, but somehow managed to sound pert.

' Clara and I had a lovely day,' said Mrs Gilcrist as they mounted the stairs. ' But I am exhausted. All I want is to lie on my bed with the curtains drawn and the satin comforter over my legs and a little dab of Christian Dior Cologne on my pillow. Tell Mrs McPhail I'll have a savoury omelette tonight, and you may wake me at seven-fifteen. There's a recital that I want to listen to at eight o'clock.' By now they had reached her rooms, and once the door was closed behind them, she said sharply, ' Now tell me exactly what happened, Rae.'

' What happened?' repeated Rae, frowning slightly.

' Yes. You didn't come for me. I want to hear your version of what happened.' She took off her hat and began to pull the hairpins out of her hair. Rae, automatically putting her hat, gloves and handbag away, now knelt on the floor to unfasten Mrs Gilcrist's shoes. She offered her excuses simply but humbly.

' I'm truly sorry, Mrs Gilcrist. I was swimming, and afterwards I fell asleep on the sand. When I woke up it was later than I'd meant to be, and then—the car was gone. That's all there is to say really, and of course you must be displeased with me. I can only repeat that I'm sorry.'

Mrs Gilcrist slipped her arms into the quilted dressing gown that Rae held ready for her. She sat down on the chair at the dressing table. ' Brush my hair, Rae. My head aches.'

Rae took up the silver-backed brush and began smoothly and rhythmically to brush the long silvery hair.

Mrs Gilcrist watched her in the mirror, and presently their eyes met.

' Where did you swim, Rae?'

' I'd meant to go back to Manly, but while I was here collecting my beach things Scott Hallam came in. He suggested we swim here, and so we did. We made a lobster sandwich and went down to the beach.'

' I'd have thought you'd have settled for that pool of his.'

Rae shook her head. The brush swished gently through the hair.

' Can you enjoy Scott's company as well on the beach as at his home?'

' Of course. And besides—' She met the old blue eyes in the glass and suddenly they were smiling at her.

' I believe you're an old-fashioned girl, Rae. Are you in love with Scott?'

' No.'

' I'm glad to hear that . . . My head's better now. I'll have a magazine to glance through before I go to sleep. Just cover my feet and fetch that cologne. And don't forget Mitchell wants to see you. He's probably very impatient by now.' Her eyes were definitely twinkling. ' If he should want to know if I took you to task, tell him I'm perfectly satisfied with your excuses.'

' Thank you, Mrs Gilcrist. I shouldn't have fallen asleep. I shan't slip up like that again, I promise you.'

' Still, I shan't expect you to be perfect.'

Rae's step was light as she made her way to the library. Mitchell was standing by the window and swung round as she knocked and came in.

' You've taken your time, Miss Lambert.'

' My time is not my own.'

' Hmm. I hope my grandmother made it plain to you

that we will not tolerate that kind of behaviour?'

Rae blinked. This was surely going too far! 'She was very kind—very understanding. She was perfectly satisfied with my excuses.'

'Was she really? Sit down, Miss Lambert, and let's get this straight.' He waited until Rae had seated herself, and then, not taking his eyes from her face, sat down opposite her. 'Just what *were* your excuses?'

'I don't see that I need repeat them to you.'

His eyebrows went up. 'Perhaps because I'm not so easily fooled as my grandmother.'

Rae felt angry colour in her cheeks. 'I don't want to fool anyone. I told Mrs Gilcrist the truth. It's a very simple story, and she was perfectly reasonable about it. Though I would be the first to admit *she* had a right to be displeased.'

'Displeased,' he repeated musingly. 'Is that the extent of the reaction you would expect?'

'Yes. To be late is not such a gross sin.'

He frowned and glanced down at his hands. Then he said, 'I shan't ask what made you late, but I shall repeat what I've already said once. The kind of behaviour you indulged in this afternoon will not be tolerated.'

'You mean,' said Rae, 'that if you had *your* way, I would be dismissed—for being late. Frankly, I think it was stupid of Helen to take the car without leaving a message with *anyone* that she had done so. Imagine my feelings when I found it gone!'

He smiled unpleasantly. 'Don't be so virtuously outraged, Miss Lambert. If you're known to be spending long hours alone with a man like Scott Hallam, you must expect there to be some doubt as to whether you will emerge in time to take up your duties. Unfortunately, I had no idea until today that you'd been seeing him—'

'I thought Scott Hallam was a friend of yours,' Rae interrupted.

'In a man's world. I don't encourage my sisters to mix with him socially.'

'Then I'm very glad that I'm not your sister!' snapped Rae, and for a moment she saw his face lighten as though he wanted to laugh. Then he was grim and censorious again. 'Also, I wouldn't call it spending hours alone with a man to go swimming with him on a fairly crowded beach.'

He gave her a sharp look. 'Scott's car was still in his car port. You're not going to tell me you walked down to the beach.'

Rae stared. So that was what it was all about! Helen, whose name had not been mentioned by either of them, had put her own interpretation on what she had heard and seen. And of course Mitch would listen to Helen, who never put a foot wrong. Rae was sure now that Helen was in love with Scott—that she was jealous—that she was determined Rae was not going to have him if she could not. And she could not, because it was not in her nature to go against her brother's wishes.

She stood up and when she spoke her voice was soft and kind. 'We took *my* car, Mr Gilcrist. Scott lets me keep it in his car port. It's there now, if you care to check up. We went to the beach—I fell asleep—Scott met a friend. So I was late, that's all. I told your grandmother that, and she believed me. She hasn't, fortunately, your sort of mind.'

Mitch stood up too, his blue eyes narrowed and piercing. He said slowly, 'I'd like to believe what you say.'

'Would you? Then feel free to do so.' She turned away, but he spoke again.

'Rae, you've been seeing a lot of Scott, haven't you?'

' A fair bit.' Rae looked at him levelly. ' I'm going to a small party at his home tonight.'

' Well, I would advise you not to—' He stopped abruptly.

Rae said with a cool smile, ' I don't need advice. I can manage my own affairs quite well, thank you.' ' Now,' she thought, ' now that I am so much sadder and wiser after my experience with Ralph Stevens.'

' I see . . . Then at least accept my apologies, as it appears I've misjudged you. If my grandmother is satisfied then we'll say no more.' He added, ' You're a very unusual girl, Miss Lambert.'

' Thank you,' said Rae. She had no idea whether it was meant as a compliment or not.

She went to the kitchen to see Mrs McPhail. She should have felt elated that she had defeated Mitch. Instead, she felt vaguely depressed. Moreover, she found she was not looking forward to going out tonight. Perhaps by the time Mrs Gilcrist had had her late meal, it would not be worth her while going.

Rae yawned. The afternoon on the beach, followed by the brush with Mitchell, had made her tired.

But if she didn't go to Scott's, then Mitch would think he had scored, that she was ready to be dominated by him.

CHAPTER VII

Rae was now more fully aware of Helen's attitude to her. She determined to tackle her about what she had suggested to Mitchell, but found it hard to pin her down and it was not until some days had passed that she was able to broach the subject. Which was, when it came to the point, a difficult one.

Mrs McPhail had been laid up with a cold for a couple of days, and Rae had taken over the cooking—not a very onerous task, as Joan was continually out and neither Helen nor Mrs Gilcrist had very hearty appetites. Rae thought Helen was looking very fragile these days. 'Lovelorn' was a word that came often to her mind when she saw her. Perhaps if she understood the relationship between Rae and Scott she would feel better!

It was an evening when Mrs Gilcrist, tired after a day of shopping, had decided to have her meal upstairs and go early to bed. Joan rang to say she would not be in while Helen was busy with a pupil in the little sitting room, so the table set for two took Helen by surprise when she came into the dining room later.

Rae, aware of her discomfiture, led the conversation on to the topic of music and of a certain European concert pianist who was visiting Australia, so that the first part of the meal passed pleasantly enough. Though Helen was still far from being friendly, it was a sort of armed truce. When Rae brought in the coffee she was offered a polite compliment on the dinner.

'Thank you,' Rae smiled, and then without a pause, ' By the way, did Mrs Gilcrist explain to you what really happened on Saturday afternoon?'

Helen glanced down at her cup, her fine brows drawn

together. She said coldly, 'We haven't discussed it. What you do is not my concern.'

'Really? I was under the impression you felt otherwise,' retorted Rae, stung by her tone. 'In any case, I should like you to know that Scott and I spent the afternoon on the beach, not, as you so rashly deduced, alone at his house.'

Helen flushed fiercely. She raised her blue eyes. 'So that's what you told Mitchell. And he believed you!'

'Why shouldn't he?'

Helen's shoulders lifted a fraction. 'Scott's car was in the car port. I was passing, and I saw it.'

'You were passing,' repeated Rae cryptically. 'Did you go in and knock at the door?'

'I wouldn't have expected an answer.'

Rae felt herself boiling with rage and for a few seconds she forced herself to say nothing, then, 'What you imply is intolerable—and neither just nor reasonable. We took my car. Scott lets me garage it there.'

Helen listened impassively, and when she spoke it was not to offer an apology. She sounded almost vindictive as she said, 'Really? You're supposed to be here as my grandmother's paid companion. Instead, you're doing your best to mix around with our friends. So much so that your social life appears to take precedence over your duties.'

'That,' said Rae, 'is a ridiculous statement to make and is simply not true. Also I didn't know that you counted Scott as one of your friends.'

Now the colour flared more fiercely in Helen's cheeks. She pushed back her chair. 'Neither I do. And if you knew the kind of scandal he'd been mixed up in perhaps you wouldn't be so keen to call him "friend" either. I'm surprised Mitchell hasn't put a stop to it.' Without another word, she left the room, and Rae sighed. All she had done was to worsen her relationship with Helen. She could not see that refusing to see Scott any more would improve things as far as Helen was concerned. She wished she knew what dire events had made him so undesirable a suitor for a Gilcrist.

Mitch, she reflected as she carried the dishes out to the kitchen, had too many women on his hands. It was perhaps understandable if he was inclined to be didactic and authoritarian. It could not be easy to carry so much responsibility. The vineyards at Millunga took up most of his time, and as well there was his directorship in the family firm. In his personal life, he had three sisters in his charge, an aunt and a cousin. *And* his grandmother.

'And now me,' thought Rae wryly, busy at the sink. He was certainly surrounded by women! For the first time she sympathized with him. As to herself, a girl of twenty-one could have been an absolutely hopeless proposition, and could easily have had her sights set on a future as part of the Gilcrist family. Like Alison Campbell. Well, she wasn't a hopeless proposition, she wasn't chasing after Mitchell, and she hoped he was beginning to realize it. And to appreciate it.

He didn't put in an appearance at Illalangi the following weekend. Nor did Pam, who now spent most weekends at Millunga. No doubt she had been told by Mitchell not to bring Rae there again, and perhaps because she suspected it was forbidden, Rae longed for another look at the Valley. She loved the rolling hilly country, the green of the vineyards, the dark ranges that sent their shadows across the red and grey paddocks and the rows of vines. The young green grapes would be on the vines now. Mitchell would be busy with his spray machine guarding his crops from the dreaded downy mildew. Perhaps already he would be checking his casks and vats and storage tanks in preparation for vintage in February.

She was greatly tempted when Scott, who had business with Mitchell, invited her to go with him to Millunga on Sunday. But she refused.

'Doing something better?' Scott wanted to know. It was not yet nine o'clock in the morning and Rae was in the garden enjoying the sunshine before it became too hot. Inside, Helen and Joan had indulged in a mild dispute as to who was to stay on call with Rae off duty. Rae had caught a few words of it as she came down the stairs. Joan had been protesting that she had work to prepare for the student exhibition the art school was putting on shortly. Rae didn't know how they had sorted themselves out.

She answered Scott with a shake of her head. 'I'm going to have a lazy day—go down to the beach and sunbake and read a book. I must look in at the bungalow and give it an airing too.' She asked on a sudden impulse, 'Why don't you ask Helen to go with you?'

He was momentarily taken aback, then laughed without amusement. 'What on earth made you say that? Helen would knock me back very smartly.'

'You can't be sure unless you try.' They had been wandering along and had now reached a wrought iron seat in the shade of a bougainvillea, and sat down. Rae looked at the man beside her, his ruddy healthy face, his good-humoured but firm mouth, and wondered again what it was that made him unacceptable.

'My dear girl, there's no question of trying. I've known my place for a long time.'

'But you were in love with Helen once, weren't you, Scott?' It was an impertinent question and she had no right to ask it, but Scott answered it.

'I was. And though I wouldn't admit it to anyone

else, I'm afraid I still am. Which makes me a hopeless romantic. And that's the biggest laugh of all time, because I'm supposed to be some sort of libertine.'

Rae's dark grey eyes met his candidly. 'That's what Mitchell thinks of you, isn't it? But *why*, Scott? Or shouldn't I ask?'

He sighed. 'You believe in me, don't you? Those eyes of yours are so devastatingly trusting. All right then, I'll tell you a story . . . Fifteen years ago, when I was twenty-two and had just taken my arts degree and found myself a job in advertising, I married a girl called Carol. She was not long out of drama school, and she had me dazzled, but it was no time before I discovered she was a nymphomaniac. Do you know what I mean?'

'Yes.'

'Any man was game for Carol, and my life was hell. I was very inexperienced and I had no idea how to handle the situation. As a sort of defence mechanism, I began to console myself elsewhere. The girl I chose—Gay—was a wholesome comforting creature, though only a year or two older than I, and our association was strictly platonic. Of course, I'd never have admitted that to anyone—least of all to Carol. Gay, by the way, entered a religious order a few years later.' He stared into space for a minute, his hazel eyes tender. But when he spoke again his voice was bitter. 'I was with Gay at her flat the night Carol was involved in a car crash. She was with her current lover, of course, and there was another couple in the car—people connected with a play she had a part in. As far as the newspapers were concerned, she was on her innocent way home from the theatre. And as far as the Sunday papers were concerned, her erring husband was spending the night with his mistress, and unavailable when asked to come to her deathbed.'

'Surely that was libellous!' exclaimed Rae, appalled.

'Couldn't you have taken some kind of action?'

Scott shook his head. 'It was carefully done. Gay's name was not mentioned, for which I was thankful. My father insisted that I saw a lawyer, but finally I was advised to keep my mouth shut and let the whole thing blow over. Which, to tell the truth, I was glad enough to do. People forget; and to help, I switched to another agency. After a while, it seemed to be all behind me. Then a few years later, the whole thing blew up in my face. By that time I was handling the Gilcrist account, and I'd gone with Mitchell to their Murrumbidgee estate on business. Helen and I had become friendly, I'd bought my house, and I meant to ask Mitchell for the go-ahead sign. I was aware of the terms of Charles Gilcrist's will, you understand. I take it you've been told about that?'

'Yes. I know Mitchell has to approve of the men his sisters marry.'

'Well, some member of the family had raked up the old story about me, and Mitchell let me know quite pleasantly that there was nothing doing. I think he'd have been right if the story had been true—for him, the sun shines out of Helen—and it was a little late for me to protest my innocence.'

'Why didn't you ignore him, and go ahead? Surely Helen would have believed you!'

Scott shrugged. 'I'd said nothing to Helen. I didn't even know if she had any special feelings about me. And I was hardly inclined to offer her myself in lieu of a brother whom she hero-worships, and her share in the Gilcrist fortune. She's such a fragile bloom.'

Rae privately was not so sure of that, but she agreed it was a sticky situation.

'So now you see,' said Scott, getting up from the seat, 'why I shan't invite Helen to come to Millunga with me.

Are you sure you won't change your mind and come?'

' Definitely not. It's the beach for me today,' Rae said cheerfully. They walked towards the house together. Scott said, ' You're coming down for your car, I take it. I'll wait while you fetch your things.'

When Rae was on her way out a few minutes later, Helen confronted her.

' I presume it's you Scott Hallam's waiting for?'

' Yes.'

' I'm sure you'll enjoy yourself,' said Helen coldly, and turning abruptly, almost ran away.

Rae stood frowning. She was certain Helen was in love with Scott—and jealous of her, Rae. Why didn't she speak up for herself? Why didn't she defy her brother? Rae remembered Mrs McPhail saying that hers was a ' sad little life '. She thought it was time someone gave it a push in the right direction.

Maybe she was the very one to do it.

A couple of weeks later, on a Friday, the students' exhibition for which Joan had been preparing was held. Her work in this connection was generally supposed to be the reason why so little was seen of Joan. Rae alone, it seemed, wondered about that. One would expect Joan to have a positive mountain of work to show, the amount of time she was presumed to be devoting to it. But she held her peace and tried to confine herself to what concerned her. She had not heard Connor Birch's name mentioned for some time, though for all she knew, Mitchell might have talked to Joan about him a dozen times. And since that night when she had shown her the clay head, Joan, though friendly enough, had made no specific efforts to extend their knowledge of each other. Perhaps she had been told to keep Rae at arms' length! Perhaps all the girls had!

It was a thought that had not occurred to Rae before, but now, as she finished dressing to go to the exhibition, it struck her as a distinct possibility, and she paused as she buttoned the coat of her linen suit, her grey eyes reflective. 'You are not one of the family,' Mitch had told her at their first meeting. 'You'll be at Illalangi to give service.' So had he nipped in the bud Pam's offers of friendship, Joan's friendly advances? Helen was different—she had kept her distance from the first, and now was definitely unfriendly. Rae could not honestly warm to her, but thought that she might find a happier, more fulfilled Helen more attractive.

She tied the silk scarf that held her hair back and met her own eyes in the mirror. Did she, in her heart, *want* to be considered one of the family? Did she want to be accepted—liked—by them all?

Mrs Gilcrist was resplendent in silvery mauve silk, with a coat in a deeper colour to match. She wore her pearls, and a becoming hat of white silk flowers.

'Must do the artist of the family credit,' she said. In the car as they drove to Manly, she exclaimed suddenly and dramatically, 'Stop, Rae! I've forgotten my cheque-book.'

'It's in your handbag, Mrs Gilcrist,' said Rae, taking her foot off the brake again. 'I saw to that.'

'Oh, good girl! I'm going to buy one of my granddaughter's paintings—give it to Mitchell for a Christmas present, keep it in the family. And if there's anything there that you fancy and haven't the money, then I shall lend it to you. Must encourage the young artists.'

'Thank you, Mr Gilcrist.' She smiled inwardly, recalling how Mitch had said, 'If you're ever short of cash, come to me, not to my grandmother.' Mitch would be there this afternoon. They would all be there. He was to bring Christine and her mother down from the

Valley with him.

They left the car in Manly, caught a ferry to Circular Quay, and from there took a taxi to the Tom Lee Art School. The exhibition was being held in two upstairs rooms. Rae helped Mrs Gilcrist up narrow stairs and they emerged into a big room that was full of noisy excited young people and their friends and relatives. Around the walls, against panels of natural-coloured hessian, the paintings, many of them unframed because of expense, were hung. In an adjoining room, sculpture was on display, and in both rooms there was a small side table containing roneoed catalogues of the exhibits.

Joan emerged from the crowd and came to greet her grandmother almost immediately. She looked pale and a little nervous and she wore no make-up. She was dressed in a black pant-suit, and the only colour about her was the blue of her eyes, and the flash of enamel from the necklace she wore that swung from her neck to below her waist. No one, Rae reflected, could call her by any means a pretty girl, but her face had plenty of strength and character.

'Gran! So you made it! That's marvellous! Wait here a minute and I'll bring Tom Lee to meet you, darling.'

Mrs Gilcrist was glad enough to rest for a while on the flimsy gilt chair with crushed velvet upholstery that Joan dragged from somewhere. Rae stood by her and glanced interestedly around the room. There was to be no official opening to the exhibition, no speeches, but sherry and biscuits were being offered by some of the students.

Mrs Gilcrist touched Rae's arm. 'Look about for Clara Livingstone, will you, my dear? And Lillian Traill. I don't believe you know her—a little wispy woman with red hair and rouged cheeks and a delightful sense of humour. A countrywoman. We're planning a get-together at the Menzies Hotel later on. Will that bore you too much?'

'Of course not,' smiled Rae. Joan came back with Tom Lee, a big handsome man whose thick wavy hair showed streaks of grey. His dress was a concession to two worlds: stylish buttoned up floral shirt, and immaculate charcoal trousers. He stooped attentively over Mrs Gilcrist, then helped her up and began to escort her around the room as though she were a celebrity. Rae helped herself to a catalogue and began to move in the opposite direction.

She found the students' work interesting. Much of it was bold, some was exciting, some astonishingly good. Or so Rae thought. It was some time before she found any of Joan's work—two large canvases signed Joan G. in which a certain clumsiness was combined with a startlingly penetrating beauty. They were street scenes, designated ' Terrace Houses, Darlinghurst I and II ' in the catalogue. Two other paintings were listed under Joan's name, and Rae guessed they were at the other side of the room, where Tom Lee had taken Mrs Gilcrist.

Rae looked about her but could see neither Mrs Livingstone nor any of the Gilcrist family. She made her way into the room where the sculpture was being exhibited, and immediately caught sight of Joan. She was standing in a corner of the room with a young man, and they were talking together and holding hands. Rae recognized him at once as Connor Birch. He was tallish and slight and young-looking, with a pale face and the broad forehead and slightly tip-tilted nose that she already knew. His hair, a light brown, was thick and wavy and reached well below his ears. He wore a blue cotton shirt with a polo neck and a scarf, and sandals showed below his faded jeans.

Rae's heart sank a little. He was certainly far from

the kind of man Mitch would expect his sisters to marry!
She turned away to look at the sculptures, and was studying one of Joan's—' Compressed figure, Cement Fondu '
—when Joan herself spoke to her.

' Rae, this is Connor Birch. He's not a student, he's
an artist. Con, Rae Lambert who looks after Gran.'

Connor didn't say, ' How do you do '. He said, his
grey-green eyes staring openly at Rae, ' What does it
feel like? What do you get out of running around a
rich old lady and buttering her up?'

' *Connor!* ' said Joan. ' If Rae didn't do it, then I
should have to.'

' Not you,' said Connor. ' You've got your own
work.'

' Well, someone has to do it,' Joan said. ' I mean,
old people— Anyhow, Gran's sweet. You must come
and meet her.'

' I've told you no,' Connor said shortly. ' I came here
to see you, not your bourgeois family.'

Rae offered, ' I saw two of your paintings, Joan.'

' And what did you think of them?' This was Connor.

' I thought them—clumsily beautiful,' said Rae.

' At least she didn't say they were *lovely*,' said Connor.
' Don't you think the prices ridiculous? No one will
pay all that for a student's work.'

' Gran will,' said Joan. ' And if you come and let
me introduce you, and if you behave nicely, she might
even bring some of her rich friends to *your* show.'

' No, thank you,' grimaced Connor. ' My work's
serious.'

Rae said, ' Will you excuse me? I want to have a
quick look around and then I must go back to Mrs
Gilcrist.'

' Yes, have a quick look,' agreed Connor. ' That's
about all most of this lot deserves.'

' Tell me if you see Mitch, will you, Rae? ' Joan asked quickly as Rae moved away.

Rae thought she couldn't stand much more of Connor. His rudeness and self-opinionatedness were decidedly irritating. How could Joan possibly be in love with him? She agreed wholeheartedly with Mitch: Joan should drop him. Rae hardly saw the sculpture as she thought about Connor Birch.

Presently she found Mrs Gilcrist, by now the centre of a group. Pam, Helen, Christine, Mrs Vance—all were there. But not Mitch. Rae was aware of a sharp stab of disappointment. Scott had just joined the group and spoke to Helen. To Rae's surprise, the girl turned and greeted him with a warm smile. Rae's eyes nearly fell out of her head! Could it be that Helen had decided to go into action? Rae certainly hoped so—but doubted it. She caught sight of Mrs Livingstone nearby, peering at a painting through her lorgnette.

' Where's Joan? ' Mrs Gilcrist called. ' Find her, will you, Rae? I can't think why Mitchell isn't here.'

' He has some business to do at the office while he's down, Mother,' said Mrs Vance. She looked pale and tired, and Rae thought she ought to be sitting down, but Mrs Gilcrist gave her a quick impatient look.

' It's hardly too much to ask him to take an interest in his clever little sister once a year or so, is it? ' she asked acidly.

Rae murmured that she would look for Joan, and when she found her the girl was alone.

' Connor had to go. Is Mitch here? '

' Not yet,' said Rae. Her eye was caught by a small birdlike woman in a rakish hat of cherry-coloured straw. Wisps of dyed red hair framed a face that was over-rouged, and her large painted mouth stretched in a laugh as her bright eyes darted about the walls. A little clawlike hand flapped a white glove and a creased catalogue in the direction of a particularly gay and colourful painting. Rae thought in some amusement that this must surely be Lillian Traill, Mrs Gilcrist's friend. She was about to ask Joan when she stopped, appalled. That woman with Lillian Traill—she had seen her before—out west! She felt a surge of colour flood her face and then recede, and she began hastily to push her way into the crowd, urging Joan to come along.

The woman was a Mrs Jamieson. Rae had met her more than once at the C.W.A. tea-rooms when she had gone into town with her grandmother. Her heart was pounding with fright. She did not want to be seen and recognized—particularly before the whole of the Gilcrist clan! Beside her, Joan was saying something, but Rae's head was whirling and she hardly heard. She saw Mitchell before anyone else. Mrs Gilcrist was waving her cheque-book and asking for Tom Lee. Paintings were to be bought, a donation made to the school. Mrs Gilcrist was delighted with her granddaughter's progress.

'Yours is by far the best work here, my dear,' she told Joan extravagantly. Over the heads of the others Mitchell smiled at Rae and she smiled nervously back. Her face felt completely drained of colour. At any moment she expected Lillian Traill and Mrs Jamieson to burst into the circle, and then she would be exposed —denounced.

Mrs Gilcrist was staring at her. 'Rae, you look quite ill! What is it?'

'A—a headache,' stammered Rae. It was true enough, she discovered. Her head had begun to ache dreadfully.

'You need some fresh air,' decided Mrs Gilcrist. 'It's too crowded in here. Better go outside for a while. But don't forget we're meeting at the Menzies, afterwards.

There'll be four of us now. And you. Lillian has a friend from the country.' She broke off then to give her attention to Tom Lee, and Pam said softly, 'Poor Rae! You do look off colour. Gran can't expect you to go to a hen-party after this. Go home and rest. I'll take over for you. Where's the car?'

'In Manly,' said Rae weakly. She hardly dared to turn her head for fear Mrs Jamieson was there.

'In Manly! Oh, lord. Well then, get Mitch to drive you,' Pam suggested.

'I'll ask Scott,' Rae said, thinking of him with relief. He would understand. She felt she could not escape quickly enough.

'Toddle off, then, Rae,' said Pam. 'And don't worry, I'll look after everything.' With a businesslike air, she went off in her grandmother's direction, and Rae felt someone touch her arm. It was Helen.

'Take a taxi, Rae. I'll give you the money.'

Rae began to protest as Helen opened her handbag and took out a five-dollar note, but the other girl said in a hard voice, 'You can't expect Scott to come running whenever you choose. You've imposed on him enough as it is, using his swimming pool and his car port and getting him to take you out every Sunday. This time you can manage without him. You're on your own.'

Rae opened her mouth, then closed it again. So Helen *was* taking action! Well, good luck to her. Still, she refused the money, but said meekly, 'Don't worry, Helen, I can manage.'

Then without further hesitation she made her escape. Downstairs in the street she hesitated. She felt guilty about shirking her duty, but one thing was certain— she could not take the risk of meeting Mrs Jamieson. She could only hope that if her name came up there would be no reason for Mrs Jamieson to associate her with the girl she had known as Irene out west.

Rae decided not to bother about a taxi. She would walk down to Circular Quay and take the ferry and then the bus. The fresh air would cure her headache and she would be home long before anyone else. She had gone only a few yards when a mocking voice behind her said, 'Hold on, Miss Lambert.'

A firm hand grasped her arm, blue eyes looked down into her startled face.

'Now tell me, is your headache real, or are you sulking because Scott is neglecting you?'

It was Mitchell, of course, and Rae pulled herself together and managed a bright smile.

CHAPTER VIII

'It's hardly the way to go about keeping your job, you know,' Mitchell said. 'Deserting your post in a fit of pique.'

'Pique?' Rae frowned. 'My headache's real, and Pam—who happens to regard me as a friend—has offered to take over.' She kept walking, and Mitchell, still grasping her arm, walked too. It was late afternoon, city workers were on their way home and the footpaths were crowded.

After a moment's consideration, Mitchell said, 'No, that just doesn't fit in. I'd have thought some aspirin would have set you up—a girl with your sense of duty. I'm afraid I still favour the fit of pique.'

'You would,' said Rae softly—but not too softly for him to hear.

'*I* would? What do you mean by that?'

'You've been determined to think the worst of me from the beginning.'

'Have I? You can't deny seeing a great deal of Scott.'

'I like him very much. He's been kind to me.'

'Well, I shouldn't worry about Helen if I were you. She knows better than to fall in love with him, so you don't need to be jealous.'

'Helen's more in need of your comforting words than I am,' said Rae sharply before she could stop herself. He had released her arm, but was now shepherding her into a coffee restaurant. Rae tried to edge her way back on to the pavement.

'I'm going to catch the ferry.'

'There's no hurry,' said Mitchell, effectively blocking

her way so that, short of causing a scene, she had to go
where he had decided to take her. 'You've assured me
that my grandmother's being adequately taken care of,
and as she's planned a gossip session afterwards at the
Menzies—I don't blame you for dodging *that*, believe
me—we have all the time in the world for a talk.'

'But I don't *want* to talk,' said Rae stubbornly.
Nevertheless, she sat down at one of the small tables and
watched Mitchell install himself opposite her. Without
consulting her, he ordered black coffee and aspirin from
an attentive waitress. It struck her, as it always did,
how good-looking he was, but this time she was more
aware of the strength of character in his face—in the
strong jaw, the firm but pleasant mouth, the intelligent
dark blue eyes; which at that instant were turned on
her so that she was caught out staring. 'I'm not dodging
the gossip session,' said Rae, flushing, and immediately
aware of the complete falsity of her statement.

He leaned towards her. 'My dear Rae, of course you
are! And I should like to know exactly why. You
must have a very good reason, to be so determined about
it.'

Rae, who did have a good reason, had no idea how to
answer this. Perversely, she now wished she had settled
for pique. She hoped he was not going to persist with his
interrogation, and decided that silence would be her
best defence. Neither of them spoke again until after
the coffee, the headache powder, and a glass of water
had been brought.

'Now swallow that down,' said Mitchell, and watched
her with faint amusement as she did what she was told.
Then, stirring sugar into his coffee, he asked with a
sudden return to seriousness, 'Are you in love with
Scott, Rae? And don't tell me it's none of my business.'

'It is none of your business,' said Rae. 'But I'm not in love with Scott.'

He looked puzzled. 'Then why the withdrawal? Why the handing over of duties you're paid to do? Is your head really as bad as all that?'

Rae drank some of her coffee, her eyes looking past him vaguely. 'It's bad enough. And I'm not perfect.'

'No, I'll concede you're human and fallible. You slipped up once with my grandmother, and you've answered me back more times than I can count.'

Rae coloured and switched the focus. 'All right, so you're human and fallible too.'

He took her seriously. 'Yes, you think me very arrogant and overbearing, don't you?'

Rae almost admitted it. Instead, she said moderately, 'You've a lot on your plate. You have to be positive. But since we're here for a *talk*, there's something else I'd like to say.' She thought his blue eyes looked at her coldly, and she swallowed nervously. She was going to strike a blow for Helen. 'I think—I think you're *too* positive for Helen. Perhaps you don't mean to dominate her, but you do, you know. She values your good opinion so highly that often she doesn't really think for herself.'

'*I* think,' said Mitchell after a second, 'that you're improvising—drawing a red herring across your own trail. Helen goes her own way, and she's happy.'

'Do you think so? She's always seemed a little sad to me. She seems to use her music to fulfil some need in herself that hasn't been satisfied.'

'If you mean she should be married—at twenty-four she's hardly out of the running,' he said dryly.

Rae gave him a thoughtful look. 'She may consider she is—since you sent Scott away.'

'Oh, heavens,' he exclaimed impatiently, 'you don't

want to take any notice of my grandmother.'

'I'm paid to take notice of your grandmother,' Rae couldn't resist saying.

His lips quirked. 'Very well, then. However, I didn't "send Scott away" as you so dramatically put it. He and Helen were no more than ordinarily friendly. But as I didn't—and don't—consider him a desirable husband for *any* of my sisters, I made sure he was aware of the fact.'

'Exactly! You didn't allow Helen to make up her own mind—you made it up for her well in advance.'

His eyes hardened. 'I had a good reason for my opinion.'

'Something Scott did when he was very young that *appeared* indiscreet.'

'What do you know about it?'

'A good deal more than you do,' said Rae firmly. 'Scott's life has been as blameless as yours. But because Helen is so loyal to you—and because Scott's regard for Helen is high—the poor girl is likely to finish up an embittered spinster. In her heart she may even blame you for it, eventually.'

Mitchell gave her an odd look, his blue eyes glittering. He said slowly, 'You're an impudent girl, Miss Lambert.' A minute ago it had been Rae, and the return to a formal address sent Rae's spirits down. She had made him angry. She was surprised at his next words. 'I think you're honest too—and kind-hearted. I shan't ask what Scott has told you that's made you his champion, but I'll think about the matter. And now, how is your head?'

'Much better, thank you,' said Rae, brightening. Her headache had gone. She had forgotten her fright over Mrs Jamieson and that had helped.

'Shall we join the party at the Menzies, then? I don't

think we'll be too late.'

Rae blinked. She was trapped and didn't know what to say. Mitch was smiling at her hesitation, and at last he said, ' The idea doesn't appeal to you, that's obvious. Well, we're in accord there. I suggest we have dinner together somewhere, and if your conscience troubles you, then you can put in some overtime on Sunday.'

Rae felt bewildered. She couldn't think why he was asking her to have dinner with him, and oddly the idea appealed to her very much. But would he take it out on her later? Say she had been chasing him—' doing an Alison Campbell '?

She said slowly, cautiously, her eyes on his face, ' I'd like that. But it's not necessary, you know.'

' Of course it's not necessary. But it may be very pleasant. You agree?'

' Yes, thank you.'

He excused himself and used the restaurant telephone to book a table for dinner, and they paid for their coffee and wandered down to Circular Quay. The harbour was beginning to lose its colour in the evening light, and to assume a silvery grey romantic air. They stood at the railings looking out over the water as ferry-boats came in or put out from the wharves with their burden of home-going people.

' D'you know Sydney well, Rae?' Mitchell asked, and Rae admitted that she scarcely knew it at all—' only what I've seen with Mrs Gilcrist.'

' Then we'll have to remedy that.'

Away to the left was the overseas terminal where a great liner lay, and beyond, in the arch of the harbour bridge, the lights of home-bound cars and double-decker buses flashed. To the east, off Benelong Point, Rae could see the spectacular white sails of the Opera House, not yet completed.

'It's a beautiful structure,' Mitchell said, following her gaze. 'There's been a lot of controversy about it, as you must know, and a lot of indignation about the cost, which is estimated at about eighty-five million dollars. Indignation too about the time it's taking to complete it. But great buildings need time—it covers about four and a half acres, and many of the piers have had to be sunk seventy feet or so below sea level. Do you agree that it's fantastically lovely with the light on those great curved shells with their shimmering white tiles?'

Rae turned to smile at him. 'I do agree. Until I came to Sydney I'd only read about it and listened to people arguing. Some of them get quite heated.'

'That's true. It's good to think that you and I are on common ground there.' His hand touched hers briefly, but she thought it was by accident rather than design.

All the lights of the city were beginning to shine out. Turning, Rae saw the forty-eight-storey Australian Square tower, a circular building with the revolving restaurant at the top, where she had lunched one day with Mrs Gilcrist. The sky hovered between day and night, a lovely semi-darkness against which the lighted buildings glimmered. She felt a shiver of delight run through her, and Mitch put a protective arm around her shoulders.

'Cold? We'll take a taxi to the Tavern.'

Idiotically, Rae felt cherished and immensely happy. It was a ridiculous and unfounded feeling, but she couldn't help herself. She enjoyed the hour that followed with Mitch. The Tavern was an old convict-built place, restored and decorated in keeping with its origins. The dinner—whole pig roasted on a spit—was delicious, and Mitch ordered some of his own Valley wine. They didn't stay to dance, but walked slowly through the city streets to where his car was parked. The air was soft and warm, and Rae felt oddly content.

It was not until they were driving home that they so much as mentioned the exhibition. Then, as they sped up one of the expressways on the north side of the harbour bridge, Mitchell asked seriously, 'What did you think of Joan's paintings, Rae?'

'Interesting,' said Rae promptly. 'I think she has a lot of talent.'

'Promise,' said Mitch, his voice wry. 'I had a talk to Tom Lee, and that seemed to be the operative word: Promise. I've been trying to make up my mind whether it meant anything more than that he's determined to get another year's fees out of me.'

'You must be joking!' exclaimed Rae. 'Surely you believe in Joan's ability.'

'She's my sister. Naturally I'm proud of her—and wary of my pride.'

Involuntarily, Rae thought of what Connor Birch had said to Joan—'You've got your own work.' As if *he* believed in her. But she could hardly quote Connor Birch, and Mitch would be sure to think he had an axe to grind.

'I suppose I'll leave it up to Joan,' he said presently. 'If she's willing to put up with a repetition of this year's conditions—which I'll admit I've made a little rigorous —then she can go on. If she wants it easy, I'll conclude she's only playing around, and she can stand down. Does that seem fair to you?'

Rae wondered why he had asked her opinion, but she answered lightly, 'Yes, fair enough.'

'The only thing I'm afraid of is that she'll get herself mixed up with a lot of drop-outs. She's a bit of an experimentalist, is Joan.' He sounded troubled, but he made no mention of Connor. Rae had the distinct feeling that he believed Joan had given him up. It was hardly her place to enlighten him—to say, Connor was at the show this afternoon and they were holding hands and acting like two people in love.

'I don't know why I'm unburdening myself to you like this—a girl of twenty-one or so.' Mitch flashed her a brief smile.

'I don't know why you are either,' said Rae mildly. 'I don't ask for it, you know.'

'I know you don't. You've been very self-effacing. I haven't told you how much I appreciate what you've been doing for us. You've taken a load off my mind. The last couple of years have been—problematical, as far as my grandmother was concerned. But I've been able to depend on you—to trust you.'

Rae writhed a little. What would he say if he knew she had deceived him from the very beginning—and was now hiding from him the fact that his sister was disobeying his wishes quite blatantly? She had interfered in family affairs on Helen's behalf, but was certainly not going to tell tales on Joan. She said, 'You're responsible for a lot of people. If I've helped with one of them, then I'm happy.'

'You have helped . . . My present worry is Christine. I've promised her a year at Millunga now her schooling is finished, but I'm not altogether happy about it.' He pulled up at traffic lights and leaned back in the car seat. 'She has a schoolgirl crush on Francis Rogeon, and I don't want to encourage that. But her mother is a sick woman—she has at the most another two years to live. She feels safe at Millunga and she's looking forward to having Christine with her. It leaves me no alternative really; Christine will have to stay. I foresee a horrible fracas.' The lights changed and the traffic surged on. Mitch explained, 'Because of Pamela.'

Rae said easily, 'Why don't you simply let it take its

course? It won't do any good to worry. I know a great many problems are your responsibility, but not that, surely. Francis must choose the girl he wants.'

He gave her a swift look. ' Is this a lecture? You've already taken me to task over Helen.'

' I apologize,' said Rae instantly. ' I talk too much.'

' Not you. You're a wise young girl in many ways. Something of an enigma, too. You don't talk about yourself.' He sounded thoughtful. ' I tried to draw you out over dinner—did you know? But you wouldn't be drawn. Still, I've enjoyed your company, and that, to you, sounds patronizing no doubt. But I don't mean it that way. I might as well admit that I had no intention whatsoever of taking you out to dinner. It just seemed to happen.'

' I hope you won't blame me,' said Rae, laughing a little. ' I assure you I didn't engineer it.'

' That I know. I can't fool myself that you've ever run after me.'

Suddenly they were smiling at each other in a very friendly, easy way, and though little was said during the rest of the drive home, Rae was conscious of a closeness and companionship between them.

When they reached Illalangi, Mrs Gilcrist had gone to bed. No one seemed quite sure where Helen was—she had simply not come in. Rae hoped she was with Scott. Christine and Mrs Vance were in the sitting room watching television and drinking coffee. Christine, her shoes off, sprawled in her chair looking bored.

' Fetch some more coffee for Mitchell and Rae, dear,' her mother urged, but Rae said she would do this. When she came back with fresh coffee, Christine was complaining, ' Why couldn't I have gone back to Millunga with Pam? There's nothing to do here.'

Rae handed Mitchell his cup and stood for a moment

uncertain as to whether she should go or stay, until Mitchell said pleasantly, 'Sit down with us and drink your coffee, Rae.'

Mrs Vance reasoned with Christine. 'We have shopping to do in the morning, dear. If you're going to stay in the Valley then we must stock up with a few clothes. You won't be wearing school uniform any more.'

'Oh, Mother, for goodness' sake—I know all that! But what's to stop me coming down during the week to shop, if that's all you're worrying about?'

'It's what we'd planned,' insisted her mother.

'I don't care what we'd planned. Pam might have been decent enough to take me when I asked her.'

Mitchell looked at her wearily. 'Grow up, Christine. Why would Pam cart you along when you're always at loggerheads anyhow?'

Christine tossed back her long red hair. 'Grow up? You don't give me much of a chance. You all push me around as if I were a kid—particularly Pam.'

'Well, shut up, then,' said Mitch good-humouredly. He turned to his aunt. 'How did you enjoy the show?'

She grimaced slightly. 'Not very much. Too many pictures of what you couldn't make head nor tail of. When I was a girl we had to paint realistically. And such odd people! I wonder you don't worry about Joan. I'm sure I should. She didn't introduce any of us to her young man except Rae here, and I'm not surprised. He looked like a hippy to me. I shouldn't like Christine to be involved with anyone like that.'

She babbled on and Rae saw Mitch drink his coffee down and lean across to put his empty cup on the table. He didn't look at Rae. He felt in his pocket for cigarettes and asked casually, 'Where is Joan, by the way? Gone early to bed after all the excitement?'

Mrs Vance looked blank, and Christine shrugged and

said, 'Probably out celebrating with her arty friends.
She and I hardly exchanged a word. She thinks I'm
bourgeois.'

Mitchell looked irritated. 'See if she's home, will you,
Rae?'

'Yes, of course.' Rae went to do as she was asked,
feeling, and she was sure looking, guilty. Yet she hadn't
lied to Mitch, she had simply held her peace. She knew
well enough what was troubling her. She and Mitchell
had talked with apparent frankness to each other. Now
he was wondering why she had not said she had met
Connor.

'Why should I care?' thought Rae, running up the
stairs. But she did care—she cared very much. She
wanted Mitch to think well of her. She wanted it *personally*. Something had changed drastically in the way
she thought about him . . . She knocked at Joan's door,
opened it and looked in. The room was empty. On
her way to the studio, she couldn't decide whether she
hoped Joan would be there or not. If she was, there
would be a scene. If she wasn't, then maybe there would
be a worse scene later.

The studio was in darkness and the door was locked,
and when she went inside Mitch was waiting for her.

'Not there?'

'No.'

'Do you know where she is?'

'No,' said Rae again, and didn't embellish it. His
blue eyes searched hers, and she saw doubt in them.

'You and Joan have been on pretty friendly terms, I
think. There aren't many people she'll allow into her
studio—' He paused, and Rae said calmly, 'I've been
there once. I see very little of Joan—or of any of your
sisters.'

'But she's been seeing Connor. That affair hasn't

ended.'

'Apparently not.'

'You met Connor Birch today—that suggests you're in Joan's confidence.'

'If I were, I shouldn't betray it,' said Rae. 'But I'm not.'

'You knew my wishes—my orders—about that association.'

Rae sighed. 'Yes, I knew. But I'm not in the habit of spying and making reports. That's not what I'm employed to do.'

His face softened suddenly, the tension and hostility went out of him. 'I'm sorry, I'm being autocratic. But I'm worried, and I consider I have good reason to be. I wish I could ask you to help me.'

Rae said nothing and they looked at one another for a long moment. Then he said shortly, 'It's a pity you and Joan don't see more of each other . . . Well, it will have to wait. Are you coming back to join us in the sitting room?'

'No. I think I'll go up to bed.'

'Then goodnight, Rae.' His fingers touched her arm briefly, he gave her a fleeting smile and they parted.

'And that leaves me where?' Rae wondered.

Before she reached her room she heard someone come in the front door. Voices told her it was Helen and Scott, and she longed to see what kind of a reception they were given by Mitchell. But if she went downstairs again it would be too obvious, and Helen would quite likely conclude she had come down to see Scott. There was nothing for it but to wait until morning.

She had been asleep for some time when some sound awakened her. She heard Mitchell's voice, angry and low. 'It's not to go on, do you hear? If he has any decent feelings he'll come and see me, instead of sneak-

ing around behind my back—' A door slammed, there
was a short silence, then footsteps and nothing more.

The following morning, Mrs Gilcrist was tired. She
was also in a talkative mood. Rae must have breakfast
upstairs and they would talk about the exhibition—and
the young people who had been at it.

'The young are so different these days! And Joan's
a girl who belongs heart and soul to the new generation.
They question everything—they refuse to accept what
to us has always been accepted and is unquestionable.
They want to discover everything for themselves.
They're right in many ways, you know—they see the
world with the eyes of children, everything is new. You
could see it in those paintings. Poor Valerie drove me
nearly demented with her continual "What's it meant
to be?" I pride myself that I'm more in touch with
the young than she is.'

'She'll have Christine with her now,' said Rae cheerfully. 'Then she'll be more in touch.'

'Oh, bah to that! Look at it from the girl's angle—
there's nothing in the Valley for *her*!'

'Only Francis Rogeon,' thought Rae to herself. She
suggested, 'There must be some social life—'

'But not the stimulation and excitement you find in
the city. Wouldn't you sooner be here than out on the
western plains again, Rae ? Or do you plan to go back
there one day?'

'I don't think I want to go back,' said Rae, colouring under the rather penetrating look she was receiving.
'Not—not to live.'

'Hmm. Didn't you tell me you nearly married some
young man out there?'

Rae was not sure if she had told her or not, but she
said, 'Yes, I was engaged.'

'You never did say what ended it all.'

'No.' She gave a rueful smile. 'I'd rather not talk about it, if you don't mind.'

'I can't insist, can I?' Mrs Gilcrist said humorously. 'But if ever you do want to talk about it, you'll find I have a very sympathetic ear, my dear . . . By the way, I was sorry you weren't with us at the Menzies yesterday.'

Rae felt a quick alarm. 'I hope you enjoyed yourself. But I had such a headache—'

'You certainly looked ill. I don't remember if you met Lillian Traill and her friend Mrs Jamieson?'

'No, I didn't,' said Rae faintly. 'But I think I saw Mrs Traill. I recognized her from your description.'

'Did you indeed? Very interesting! You'd have liked her—and Mrs Jamieson.'

Rae gave her a quick look, but she was innocently buttering toast and in another moment there was a tap at the door and Mitchell came in.

'Good morning, Grandmother. Good morning, Rae.' He was looking strained and tired. 'How are you both this morning?'

'Oh, I'm in fine fettle,' said the old lady, though she had told Rae she was ready for a lazy idle day. 'As for Rae, she seems to have recovered from her headache sufficiently to help me conduct a post-mortem on yesterday's events . . . Sit down, Mitchell. I want to talk to you.'

He took the small straight-backed chair at the opposite side of the table and gave her a wry smile. 'What have I done this time? You'll have to tell me quickly—I have a meeting to attend in the city this morning.'

'Then you shall have it straight from the shoulder . . . Yesterday Joan asked me to lend her a hundred dollars. No, don't go, Rae, there's nothing that's not fit for your ears.' She glared at her grandson. 'Now I don't mind advancing it—though as a gift, not a loan, for I'm not a penny-pincher. What I don't like is that the girl should find herself in such a position. What if I were not here? What if I were an old skinflint like you?' She screwed up her mouth and waited for his retort.

He said calmly, 'I'm not spoiling for a fight even if you are, Grandmother. If you like to call me a skinflint, then go ahead. But just tell me this: Did Joan tell you why she needed a hundred dollars? Or why she chose to go to you for it instead of to me?'

'For goodness' sake, the girl's human! Pinching and scraping are not her nature. You leave her no room to manœuvre. Every cent is accounted for before it's spent. She came to me because she knew I'd understand, and she didn't want a fight on her hands.'

Mitchell thought for a moment. Rae began to stack the breakfast dishes on a tray. She wondered if Joan had given that hundred dollars to Connor yesterday and she knew Mitch was wondering too.

'Tell me, Gran, just what do you think I allow Joan per month?' Rae didn't hear the answer, but she heard Mitchell's dry, 'Multiply that by five and you have something like the truth. And that's why I insist she keeps strictly within it.' He got up. 'I'll look into this when Joan comes home. She was out of the house before I came down this morning. I'll find out what the devil she's doing with her money.' His blue eyes were narrowed and he had no smile for Rae as he crossed to the door, and said, 'If you see my young sister today, Miss Lambert, tell her she'll see me before I go back to the Valley or she'll regret it. That gives her until tonight. Will you do that for me?'

'Yes, of course,' said Rae quietly. She felt troubled and aware of his many responsibilities, and began to think he had had more than one reason for wanting a middle-aged woman as companion to his grandmother. Such a woman would have co-operated with him in controlling his sisters! She, Rae, refused—and was in any case far too young. As the door shut behind him, Mrs Gilcrist said, 'Now I've upset the applecart! Maybe the girl's had a little flutter on the horses.'

Mitchell, Rae discovered later in the day, had no such delusions, but shared her own ideas. It was sunset, and Mrs Gilcrist was resting before dinner. Joan had not come home, and all the others were out visiting friends. Rae looked out on the terrace, but seeing Mitchell there was about to withdraw when he called her back.

'Don't go, Rae. Or were you looking for someone?'

Rae stepped outside again. 'No. Mrs Gilcrist's having a nap and I thought I'd get a breath of air.'

'Come and join me, then.' There was a jug of ice and some fresh orange juice on the table beside him, and two glasses, one of them used. Rae hesitated.

'You're expecting someone.'

'I was hoping you might come out,' he said with a smile. Her heart lifted and she dared not look at him. She dared not think about her own feelings, either. She sat down and allowed him to pour her a drink. She kept her eyes on the fading blue of the ocean, and on a ship out on the horizon moving slowly north. Massed clouds reflected the brilliance of the sunset and moved slowly as if they would cover the sky.

'Relax,' said Mitchell. 'I'm sure you've earned a rest.'

'I've done nothing all day.'

'Except listen? That can be tiring. And I'll guarantee you've gone up and down the stairs more times than you can count. One of these days I'm going to install a little elevator in this house. Gran's next companion may not be so young and fleet of foot as you are.'

Rae said, ' You talk as if I were leaving.'

'I don't expect you will stay for ever . . . I saw Joan last night when she came in. I told her I wanted to see Connor Birch. Has it occurred to you that she wanted that money for him? For of course she did.'

' You can't know that,' protested Rae.

' You've met him. What do you think? Or are you going to refuse to offer an opinion on the grounds that it may incriminate you?' He was half joking and Rae was not sure how to take his remark. He said seriously, ' Rae, I'd like to know your impression. As a personal favour, shall we say.'

' We only exchanged a few words.'

' Go on.'

' He was—abrupt. Yet I don't know—maybe he was just natural—honest. One becomes so used to the conventional lie, the polite remark. Connor Birch didn't seem to care if he offended anyone.'

' That's not a virtue, in my book.'

' It's not exactly a major fault either, is it?'

Mitchell gave her a sharp look.

' Whose side are you on?'

' Nobody's side,' said Rae unhappily. She was surprised at herself. Yesterday she had thought Mitchell was right, she had disliked Connor, and thought Joan crazy. Nothing had happened to make her change her mind, yet here she was, refusing to side with Mitchell. She could only think that Connor must have made some impact on her subconscious mind, on the part of her that didn't think, and didn't measure by rational known standards. She added lamely, ' I don't know him, Mitchell.'

' His looks are against him for sure,' said Mitch. He was thoughtful, then he said, ' I thought you'd agree with me in this. I don't like the fellow at all. I don't think he's a good influence on Joan, and I suspect his motives. What I'd planned to do was to buy him off— and let Joan know it. A hateful undertaking, you'll agree, but—definitive.'

Rae was shocked. ' No, don't, Mitch,' she exclaimed, sounding distressed. ' It would be too humiliating for Joan—whether he accepted the offer or not.'

' Oh, he'd accept it.'

' Not necessarily.'

Mitch's mouth quirked. ' You think he may love her. You're young enough to believe in pure romantic love. But believe me, my dear, there are men who will do anything for money.'

' I know that,' said Rae quietly.

' Do you?' He didn't sound as if he believed her. ' Well, what's the alternative? I can't sit back and see my sister walking blindly into disaster.'

' No. But I think,' said Rae slowly, feeling her way, ' I think he should be given a chance to prove himself. For Joan's sake.'

' If he were to get out and work at some decent job it might prove something,' said Mitch. ' If he knew that Joan was going to be dependent on him rather than he on her then we might discover just how deep this attachment is. You have a point there, Rae! I shall ask him to prove himself.'

He sounded as if he had no doubt what the outcome of such a demand would be. Rae was not so sure.

It was almost dark now, and the clouds were swarming across the sky. Rae felt sorry for Joan, but she knew that Mitch could not in this case sit back and let matters take their own course—especially if that hundred dollars had been for Connor. Joan was an inexperienced nineteen and she needed protection.

At that moment there was the sound of voices and two people emerged from the near dark of the garden and stepped up on to the terrace. They were Joan and Connor and they were hand in hand.

CHAPTER IX

Rae would have risen, but Mitch's hand held her back.

'Don't go. I want you here.'

She would still sooner have gone, but by now Joan was saying in a cheerfully defiant way, 'Hello, Rae, hello, Mitch. Connor's come to see you.'

'Fine,' said Mitch. He nodded to Connor, but that was as much of a greeting as he gave him. 'Switch on the end light, will you, Joan. I don't think it's too chilly to talk out here, and we shan't be long. Sit down, both of you.'

Connor chose a fibre-glass chair and sat down before Joan did, leaning back and staring through half-closed eyes at the view from the hill. He curled his fists and looked through his fingers, using them as binoculars. Joan slanted a glance at her brother.

'What?'

'What did you want a hundred dollars for?'

Joan scowled. 'Who told you?'

'Grandmother, of course. She has the idea that I'm forcing you to live on next to nothing. Now you know and I know that this is not so. For that reason, I should like to hear why you needed a hundred dollars.'

'I don't have to tell you!'

'You're going to do so just the same.'

'But I'm not,' insisted Joan. 'It was a loan and it's between Gran and me.'

'Not any more it isn't,' said Mitch relentlessly. 'Now come along, Joan, let's have it.'

Joan said not a word and stared him in the eye.

Connor stopped squinting at the dark sea and the cloudy sky and said unexpectedly, 'Oh, come on,

Joanie, what's wrong with the truth?' Then to Mitchell, a little smile on his lips, 'You're right, the money was for me. I needed it rather badly.'

'Really?' said Mitch coldly. 'And you had no qualms about taking it from my sister?'

'I don't think of her as your sister. She's the girl I love. Hence I had no qualms at all.'

'Very convenient for you,' said Mitchell dryly.

'He'd have been thrown out of his flat if he hadn't had it,' Joan blurted out.

Mitch turned to Connor. 'How old are you?'

'Twenty-two.'

'Isn't it time you were earning a living?'

'I'm an artist.'

'So I've been told. But artist or not, my sister is not in future going to pay your rent. If you want the right to say you love her then you must be able to support her. Her family is not going to stand the party, and that's final. If you're still interested, then find yourself a job. If you're not, then that's fine with me. Do I make myself clear?'

'Yes, very clear.' Connor spoke lazily, almost insolently. 'But just don't try to push me around. I'm damn well not going to tug my forelock and toddle off to a nine-to-five job. I'm an artist whether you like it or not, and whether or not Joan goes along with me is up to her.'

'Joan,' said Mitchell icily, 'will be going to Millunga. She'll be ready to see you again when you've started earning a decent living—not when you're next in need of a hand-out.'

'I'm *not* going to Millunga,' said Joan. 'And I'm not staying here either—not another day!'

'Joanie,' Connor said mildly, 'we haven't talked it over yet, have we? This is serious. Your brother means what he says. Come and we'll take a walk and talk about it.' He looked at Mitch and said gravely, ' Is that allowed? Before you ship her off to Millunga, wherever that might be?'

' By all means have your talk. But just remember what I've said.'

' How could I forget?' Connor smiled mockingly, then with Joan's hand in his disappeared once more into the garden.

Mitchell sighed and looked at Rae. ' Well, that's that. I think the result of their talk is a foregone conclusion. Connor's no fool. Frankly, I hope to God we never see him again . . . You were very quiet. Were you impressed by his little speech?'

To tell the truth, Rae had been a little impressed. There had been a certain force in his assertion that he was an artist—even a certain rough dignity. She was inclined to think that if he had shown Mitchell some respect, and if he had come decently dressed instead of in a crumpled skivvy, jeans and thongs, he might have won a hearing for himself. But of course, that would not have been Connor, and Connor as he was Mitch found insupportable.

She said, ' You must admit he has character.'

' Then it's not the kind of character I admire.'

' I rather wish I hadn't stayed.'

' I wanted you to know the status quo. I have to go back to the Valley in the morning. Joan can come with me.'

' I wish you'd give her a day's grace,' Rae said slowly. ' It would be less humiliating for her. After all, she's not a child.'

' I rather wish she were. She'd be easier to handle . . . All right then, you've won her the dignity of a day's grace. It may be Tuesday before I can come and fetch her. Meanwhile, I'll have a word in Grandmother's ear and tell her there are to be absolutely no more loans. I don't think I need mention the man in the case. We'll gloss over all that. It would quite likely start a feud —she'd take Joan's part on principle and forget there were people like Ashley Vance.'

Rae went inside and helped Mrs Gilcrist dress for dinner. By the time they came downstairs, Helen, Christine and Mrs Vance had come in. Joan was with them, though not of them, in the sitting room, lolling in a chair saying nothing, her eyes cloudy and mutinous. Rae had only a minute alone with Mitchell that night. He took the opportunity to tell her the outcome of the ' talk '. ' Joan's going to Millunga. He's coming back when he has something to offer.'

Rae widened her eyes. ' Connor's going to get a job?'

Mitch shrugged. ' What do you think? I don't expect to hear any more of him. At least it will give Joan a chance to cool off and come to her senses, away from his influence.'

The next day was her day off, and Rae left the house early. Mitchell, with Mrs Vance and Christine, had set off for the Valley even earlier. Rae took her bathing things and went down the hill to Scott's house. There she collected her car and drove down to the bungalow. It was a relief to be by herself for a little while, away from family problems and turmoils. She made herself a pot of coffee, changed into shorts and a sun-top, and stretched out with a book on a lounger on the verandah that faced the beach.

Soon she found she was not reading, but thinking of Mitch. She could picture his face very clearly, hear his voice calling her Rae; could visualize the blueness of his eyes as they sought her own. She found such

pleasure in this daydream that she became a little uneasy. Surely she was not mad enough to have fallen in
love with him! Just because they had been getting on so
amicably lately, and he had taken her into his confidence.
Rae told herself sternly to remember Alison Campbell,
and returned to her book.

When she heard a car pull up outside the gate, her
heart gave a leap before she remembered that Mitch had
gone back to the Valley.

It was Scott who came across the coarse grass and on
to the verandah.

' Hello, Rae.' He dropped a kiss on her forehead and
sat down on the end of the lounger. ' I hoped I'd find
you here. You look all set for a day of ease.'

' I am,' said Rae. ' Away from it all.'

' Is it getting you down? At least you don't have to
go on if it's too much for you.'

' No,' said Rae, ' it's not getting me down at all. I'm
really, in most ways, very contented. I even feel I'm
doing a good job in looking after Mrs Gilcrist. Mitchell
has so much to contend with—at least I'm saving him
some worry.'

Scott looked at her thoughtfully. ' Don't get too soft,
Rae. It doesn't pay off.'

' Alison Campbell?' Rae said with a wry smile and a
little twist at her heart.

' I don't quite get the connection. I simply meant
don't let them ask too much of you, that's all,' said
Scott, sounding puzzled and surprised.

' Oh,' said Rae lamely. She changed the subject. ' I
had a letter from Mrs Stacy this week. She says that
Frank Warner—he was a friend of Uncle Jack's—is
interested in buying Tarmaroo. It may be only an idea.
My solicitor—Mr Belrose—hasn't been in touch about it.'

' Would you sell?'

'I've been thinking about it. I suppose I might. It doesn't seem sensible to own a property if you don't take a personal interest in it. And I don't think I could ever take a personal interest in Tarmaroo. I don't care for that semi-desert country.'

'What about the fellow you were engaged to? I suppose you don't particularly want to encounter him again?'

'No. Mrs Stacy says he's been offered a managership in south-west Queensland, and will be quitting the district at the end of the year.'

'Then at least you'll be free to make up your mind whether or not to go back when you've finished with this job.' He hesitated, then caught her eye and said apologetically, 'Rae, do you mind if we don't see as much of each other in the future?'

'Of course not,' said Rae, smiling. 'Helen?' she guessed.

'Yes.' He looked relieved, then frowned. 'I'm not quite sure yet how Mitchell will take it.'

Rae raised her eyebrows. 'Does it matter that much?'

'To Helen it does. And therefore to me.'

'Then you must straighten things out. Tell Mitch what you told me.'

'He's not as easily persuaded as you are. Besides, I don't feel inclined to rake over the past. I'd like Helen to have the facts right. I don't think she's ever actually heard the story—just has the idea I was mixed up in some frightful scandal. It's an odd turn for events to have taken after all this time. On Friday we began talking about a concert we'd both been to and suddenly we seemed to be back where we used to be. Somehow or other—I don't quite know how it happened—I asked her out to dinner. Or did she ask me?' he grinned. 'At all events, we had a night out.'

'I'm glad. I heard you come in when you brought her home.' Rae couldn't resist asking, 'What sort of a reception did you get?'

'From Mitchell? Oh, a conventionally affable one. You'd have thought it was nothing new for me to be taking Helen out. But of course, Christine and Mrs Vance were present. And I didn't stay.'

'You should have,' said Rae with an impish grin.

'You're rather a young chick to be giving advice to a mature man like me, aren't you?' he teased.

'Perhaps. My next advice is not to waste your time here chatting me up. Besides, I want to go down on the beach. Why don't you go and pay a call on Mrs Gilcrist? I'm sure she'd appreciate a game of chess.'

'I might do that,' said Scott. 'Sorry to desert you, honey.'

'No ill feelings,' said Rae airily. 'I'm still your friend.'

'And I yours,' said Scott.

Rae was delighted with what he had told her. She thought all the signs pointed to a modification of his attitude by Mitch, and Helen seemed to have decided to come out into the open rather than see Rae run away with the man she loved. It looked like a happy ending to that story, Rae reflected as she closed the bungalow and made for the beach.

Now that it was summer, the beach was fairly crowded. She enjoyed for a while the challenge of the surf, then came out to lie with the sun on her back. She recalled that day not so very long ago when she had listened to two girls talking about their grandmother—and about someone called Mitch. Her life had changed completely since then. Now she was deeply involved with all those people—more deeply involved than she had any right to be. It was almost as if she belonged with them . . .

Some time later a pair of sturdy brown legs came into her sight and she looked up to see Joan standing there in her swimsuit.

'D'you mind if I dump myself here? I'm feeling kind of blue.'

Rae sat up and leaned back on her hands as Joan threw herself down on the sand. She said awkwardly, 'I suppose you are,' and felt she should apologize for having been present when Mitch took his younger sister and her lover to task.

Joan looked amused. 'You think Con and I are washed up? We're not. It's just that we're not going to see each other for a while. We talked over what Mitch had said and Connor said he could see his angle—Mitch is just so conventional he thinks everyone should have a good steady job and all that sort of stuff, you know. It's all right for *him*—he's doing the thing he likes, and it happens to be very lucrative. The funny part is that in a way Connor is the same—he's doing the thing *he* likes. Only just at the moment it's far from lucrative. Well, Mitch will come round once Con's show opens.'

'Con's show?' queried Rae, who had been listening attentively and with interest. Joan made Con sound quite a reasonable young man!

'Yes. He's having his first one-man exhibition soon. It takes a while to get enough paintings together to make a decent show, and Con's very self-critical. He's worked hard—he's only twenty-two, you know. It's going to be fearfully exciting.' She looked at Rae earnestly with eyes that were very like her brother's. 'I didn't want to go to Millunga. I said I'd leave home and get a job. But Con said no, he'll manage somehow and I'm to stay on good terms with my family.'

'He didn't help much last evening, did he?' said Rae mildly.

Joan made a face. ' No. Well, that's Con. He says what he thinks. But he says my family are basically nice people—not like his, who were always squabbling, mostly over him. He says the Gilcrists are nice even if they're bourgeois. Considering how awful Mitch was, I think that's big of him, don't you?' She giggled. ' It's funny too—they'd hate to be called bourgeois, particularly dear old Gran. She'd like Connor. Well, that will have to wait.' She rolled on to her side and put on her sunglasses, and Rae could no longer see her eyes when she said, ' I'm going to put you in a spot, Rae.'

' What do you mean?'

' Well, you heard the whole thing—and I've explained what Con thinks—are you on our side?'

' I'm not taking sides.'

' Oh.' She thought for a moment, then said determinedly, ' Well, look, I'm afraid Con will get himself into a mess again. He does part-time jobs, you see—he needs money to live—but he gets so involved with his work that sooner or later he forgets to turn up for a day or two. Then he gets the sack. When you're working as a car-washer or a window-cleaner it's pretty easy to be replaced. And Con has a lot of extra expense just now—getting his pictures framed for the show. He falls behind with the rent, and where he lives that can be big trouble.'

' All right,' said Rae. ' What's the spot you're going to put me in?'

' Please, Rae, if he needs money, get a loan from Gran. We'll pay it back—though it's not as if she'd ever miss it. Tell her you want to send money to England, or buy a new dress or something.'

' I couldn't possibly—' began Rae, but Joan broke in, ' I've told Con you would. There has to be *some-*

body on our side. He won't want to ask you—he may not have to. But it would make me happier if I knew you were there.' She stopped, then said hopelessly, ' Do I have to tell him when I see him tomorrow that it's all off—you won't be in it?'

Rae sighed. She knew that she would not have to go to Mrs Gilcrist, she had money of her own. ' I can't very well refuse, I suppose.'

Joan was all smiles. ' I knew you wouldn't mind, Rae!'

' I do mind, really,' said Rae. ' I mind very much . . . When does Con's show open?'

' In the middle of January.' She took a handful of the fine white sand and let it run through her fingers. ' I wonder what Mitch told Gran? I don't want her to have a wrong impression of Con. He's not a bit like Ashley Vance—our money doesn't count with him at all.'

Rae let that pass without comment. ' I'm sure Mitch will have handled the matter tactfully.'

' Maybe he will have. He's not completely horrible. He's given me a day's grace to get ready for Millunga and I'm actually allowed one more meeting with Connor. It's a wonder he trusts us as far as that.'

Rae smiled and reached for her towel. ' I'm glad you're not too blue. I'm going up to the bungalow now. Would you like to come in for a coffee later, or do you have to go home?'

Joan raised her head and took off her glasses. Her blue eyes were wide. ' No—Helen's there. Scott too, playing chess with Gran. But *what* bungalow?'

' I thought everyone knew about my bungalow.' Rae waved a hand. ' The little squat one on the corner behind all those masses of grass and sand. It was left me by—by someone.'

'*I* didn't know,' said Joan. ' I thought you were just a penniless working girl.' She grinned a little maliciously. ' You want to watch out someone doesn't start pursuing you on account of it.'

' I'll watch out,' said Rae equably. ' I'll see you later, then, Joan.'

Rae didn't see Mitchell when he came for Joan on Tuesday. She had taken Mrs Gilcrist to Manly for a morning's shopping, and when they came back to Illa-langi in time for lunch Joan had already gone. Rae was more disappointed than she cared to admit. She had counted on seeing Mitch. Their relationship had altered radically and she was eager to test it out. Was Mitch perhaps not so eager, that he hadn't stayed to lunch? She wondered if he had been having second thoughts; if he regretted having taken her into his confidence and made of her far more than a paid companion to his grandmother. At least no blame rested with her; the first moves most definitely had been his.

There was a note from Joan beside Mrs Gilcrist's place at the lunch table which they had to themselves. The old lady read it, then passed it to Rae.

' Dear Gran,' Rae read, ' Sorry not to say goodbye. We haven't had a chat and I wanted to explain to you— Mitch thinks I am getting mixed up with a lot of drop-outs, but they are only students and artists. He thinks a spell at Millunga will do something spectacular to my metabolism! But it won't—artists are my kind of people. Still, I'm hardy enough to put in a few weeks in the Valley. I'm going to do lots and lots of drawings like I used to do when I was supposed to be doing home-work, remember? I'll see you at Christmas, darling. And in January—wow! Wait and see! Love, Joan.'

Rae looked up with a smile, though under the circumstances she found the letter a little touching.

'So that's what's behind all Mitchell's talk of Joan needing a holiday in the country! Pity he ever went to that exhibition. I could have told you he wouldn't like those young people—wouldn't understand them. Personally I thought them delightful, and if they're at all like Joan, then there's no harm in them in spite of their fancy dress.' She looked at Rae shrewdly. 'I suppose there's a man in the case somewhere.'

Rae decided to look blank and say nothing.

'Joan's not a fool, like Valerie,' Mrs Gilcrist said, beginning to attack her salad. 'I must remind Mitchell of that fact. She has style, my little granddaughter. She's pioneer stuff—rough and determined and honest. She'll win through . . . I remember those drawings and how Mitchell used to say she was wasting her time. It's a blessing he was at least reasonable enough to send her to art school.'

Joan certainly had a champion here, Rae reflected. She thought it quite likely that the old lady would even take to Connor. She wondered very much what kind of an artist he was and wished she could see some of his work before January. Joan was surely setting great store by his show. Yet the chances were it would go almost unnoticed. There were so many artists' exhibitions in Sydney—Rae had seen them advertised in the Saturday paper.

The weeks before Christmas passed quietly. Helen's pupils were on holiday now, but Rae saw very little of Helen—and still less of Pam and Mitch. Scott came frequently to Illalangi in the evenings. Sometimes he played chess with Mrs Gilcrist, sometimes he and Helen listened to music in the little sitting room, or she played the piano. Rae effaced herself as much as possible.

She was kept busy helping Mrs Gilcrist with her Christmas cards—she sent literally hundreds of them—and working with her over her list of Christmas gifts. They made several visits to the city shopping for these.

' You'll spend Christmas with us, won't you, dear?' the old lady asked her on one of these days. They were having another extravagant luncheon in the revolving restaurant at the top of the Australia Square tower, and Rae was fascinated anew by the slowly changing view from this highest of all Sydney's buildings.

' Thank you, I should very much like to,' she assented with a smile. ' So long as I'm not intruding on a family celebration.'

' Oh, you're quite one of the family,' Mrs Gilcrist said airily. ' Besides, it won't be all family. Francis is to join us, and Mitchell is sure to invite Scott since he and Helen have become so friendly again.' She preened herself. ' I feel I can take some of the credit for *that* . . . And now I'm going to top up with a deliciously rich dessert. What about you, Rae?'

' I'd like a gelato,' Rae said, after studying the menu. ' Mango flavour. If I may. I love tropical fruits. But we still have lots of shopping to do, and if I eat too much I shan't feel like making the effort in this heat.'

' We'll take a taxi to David Jones,' Mrs Gilcrist decided. ' I'll be able to get everything else on my list there. And we must allow some time for your gifts too. I expect you have friends in the country you'll want to remember.'

Rae coloured a little under her gaze. ' Yes, there are one or two people. Mrs Stacy at Tarmaroo—'

' Do you hear from her at all?' Mrs Gilcrist broke off as the waitress came with their sweets, but as soon as she had gone she turned enquiringly to Rae.

' I hear occasionally.'

' That reminds me—what a memory I have! Clara

Livingstone had a thank-you letter from Mrs Jamieson the other day. You'd have been interested in what she had to say—she comes from your part of the world.'

Rae felt the blood drain from her cheeks.

' What—what did she have to say?'

' Why, she told Clara that Tarmaroo had been left to a granddaughter, Irene, but that the girl evidently had no interest in the place and she thought it was to be sold.'

' Oh,' said Rae faintly. She was reassured by that name, Irene with three syllables. Mrs Gilcrist couldn't possibly connect it with her, Rae, and she had never told her that her name was Irène. She recovered enough to say, ' Yes, Mrs Stacy wrote me there was somebody interested in buying Tarmaroo—a man who had been a friend of—of Mr Steele's.'

' You certainly are up to date,' said Mrs Gilcrist dryly. ' And here was I thinking I had news for you . . . How is your gelato?'

' Delicious,' said Rae. And to her relief, the subject of Tarmaroo and Mrs Jamieson was dropped.

CHAPTER X

Christmas Eve came and Rae, somewhat to her relief, had heard nothing of Connor. Mitchell came down to Illalangi to drive them to the Valley. Pam had started her annual vacation, and as she was to spend it at Millunga, she was taking her own car, with Helen as passenger. Rae and Mrs Gilcrist—who elected to sit in the back seat —travelled with Mitch, and Scott was to drive up on Christmas morning.

It was almost eleven o'clock and a brilliant moonlit night when they reached the Valley. Pam's car was not far behind as they drove up the long avenue of mulberry trees to the elegant old two-storeyed house on the hill. The tall peaked roof of the winery stood out against the starry sky, the sloping lawns were smooth and moon-washed, tree shadows long and black. The vineyards stretched out on either side up and over the hill, down and into the valley. The grapes were ripening now, the vines heavy with great bloomy bunches of hermitage, semillon, cabernet sauvignon, traminer. The names rang in Rae's mind like bells, she felt she shared Mitch's pride, his hopes and fears—for at this time of year there was always the chance of a heavy summer storm that could ruin much of the crop. He spoke of this now, and as if dividing her interest, told her which grapes grew in the various paddocks. Rae knew a sense of intimacy which was very sweet.

At Millunga homestead, Mrs Vance and Joan had already gone to bed and it was Christine who welcomed them.

'Mother's not feeling well, Gran,' she said as she kissed her grandmother. 'She said to apologize for not being here to greet you.'

'Oh, I don't expect her to wait up for me,' said the old lady caustically. But Rae saw the concern in her eyes and knew that she cared for her daughter even if she claimed impatience with her. Mitchell had taken the luggage upstairs and rejoined them as Pam and Helen came in.

'Hello,' said Christine casually. 'There's coffee if you'd like it, and anyone who's hungry is welcome to use the kitchen. Mrs Grant's finished here till after Boxing Day.'

'I shall dispense with coffee,' said Mrs Gilcrist. 'It will only keep me awake. I presume I am to have my old room, Christine?'

'Yes, Granny. And Helen and Pam the pink room. Rae, would you like to sleep on the verandah with Joan and me? And you can take your pick of our rooms to dress in.'

'Thank you,' said Rae. 'I like sleeping on verandahs.' She took Mrs Gilcrist's arm to escort her up the stairs, and Mitchell said softly, 'Come down again, won't you, Rae?'

She nodded and her heart leapt at his tone.

'I lived here as a child,' said Mrs Gilcrist as they made their way up the stairs. 'It always brings back memories to sleep here again. Funny the things that stay with you the longest . . . I remember my Uncle William carrying me up the stairs on his back. I was holding a candle in a white enamel candlestick—one of those yellow tallow candles—and the wax ran over on to his neck and he all but dropped me. Thought I'd done it on purpose, too.' She chuckled and Rae laughed. 'This is my room, Rae. I know you're anxious to go downstairs again to Mitchell, but I'd appreciate a little help.' She yawned. 'I'm tired and lazy—a lazy old woman.'

'Of course you're not lazy. And I'm here to help you,' Rae said. She began to prepare her night things, to set out brushes and comb, to turn down the bed, and in one corner of her mind she was wondering about that remark—I know you're anxious to go downstairs to Mitchell. So she was, but she had not imagined anyone had guessed it.

A quarter of an hour later she joined the others in the high-ceilinged sitting room, with its old-fashioned wall-paper and sturdy colonial type furniture. There was a tall coffee pot on the cedar sideboard, all the luggage had been brought in and the two Gilcrist girls were busily stacking Christmas gifts under a small ornamental tree that stood in front of the fireplace. Christine, her long red hair falling across her cheeks, sat in an armchair watching them and drinking coffee. Mostly she watched Pam, and her eyes were not altogether friendly.

'Gran tucked in?' asked Mitchell, coming to meet Rae. 'I'll pour you some coffee, shall I? And then you might like to have a look at the vineyards by moon-light.'

Rae felt a shock of pleasure. Her eyes met his and she was sure she could not mistake the expression in them.

'I'd love that,' she said. A little disturbed, she glanced about for her small handcase, discovered it and turned back to him. 'May I put my gifts with the others?'

'Of course. But I hope you haven't been over-generous. We don't expect it of you, you know.'

'You're giving me my Christmas,' said Rae, smiling.

'And glad to,' he said. He went to fetch her coffee, and Rae, her heart full of happiness, took the small gaily wrapped gifts from her case and put them under the tree. She had bought Mitch a book on the vineyards of

Europe. It was only recently published and she felt pretty certain he would not have read it, and she felt it was personal, yet not too personal.

She drank her coffee, chatting lightly with the other girls. Christmas Day was bound to be hot, dinner was to be a cold picnic style affair. All the cooking had been done by Mrs Grant ('With my help,' said Christine perkily) who was now free to spend Christmas with her husband and children in their cottage on the Millunga estate.

'Get up when you feel like it,' said Christine. 'It's each man for himself at breakfast.'

'My dear girl,' said Pam, busy at the sideboard, her back turned to her cousin, 'we're not guests, we're family. We know all this. You seem to forget we've been having Christmas here far longer than you. We don't need you to act as hostess and to order us about.'

Christine looked nettled. 'I said it for Rae's benefit. And I have just as much right as you to act as hostess. More if anything. This is my home now, and Mother's not well. So until Mitch gets married, I guess it's up to me to act as hostess.'

'Then just don't forget it entails duties as well as proprietorial airs,' flashed Pam. 'If we're to be guests don't expect all the help you would like.'

Mitch had crossed the room and now put a hand firmly on her arm. 'That's enough, Pam. We'll have no squabbling over Christmas.'

She met his eyes and blinked angrily, then somehow managed a smile and said quickly, 'I'm sorry, Chris. I was being childish.'

'That's better. If you're going to be difficult we shan't let you stay for your holiday.'

'We?' repeated Pam, aggressive again.

'Aunt Valerie and I,' said Mitch calmly. He looked

across at Rae. 'Finished your coffee? Come and I'll show you around. It will be too hot tomorrow, and besides, we shan't have an opportunity.'

'Rae's seen around, surely,' said Helen, who up till now had had little to say. 'This is not her first visit to Millunga.'

'That was different,' said Mitch blandly. He took Rae's arm. 'Goodnight,' he said to the others. 'Don't stay up quarrelling.'

He still had hold of her arm as they went out into the moonlit night and across the courtyard.

'These old stones we're treading on are from the original Millunga cellars. They were built into the hillside, half underground—and still here when Gran was a girl. I had new cellars built when I bought the place back, and I've gradually had the old house modernized. Gran sniffs and criticizes, but it's given her a great kick to have Millunga back in the family again, even if we're Gilcrists and not Darvales.'

'You're good to your family,' said Rae.

'I try to be. But I'm impatient and impulsive— worse than my sisters, worse than Joanie—and I make mistakes. Sometimes bad ones, as no doubt you've noticed. I was wrong about Scott, and sadly lacking in understanding of Helen. They're to announce their engagement tomorrow, by the way.'

'I'm glad,' said Rae. 'I think Helen will feel a lot more secure. She finds it hard to forgive me for having had Scott's friendship.'

'No doubt she suspects it was more than friendship. You're a very charming girl you know, Rae.'

'Thank you,' said Rae colouring faintly. 'And Joan, Mitch—is she happy?'

'I wouldn't say she was marvellously happy, but she's all right. Not sulking, though I'm certain she hasn't heard from Connor. Give her long enough away from him and she'll come to her senses. She's been sketching a lot and chipping away at an old bit of rock up on the hill. Even taking some interest in the crop in between times too. Could be she'll stay here at Millunga next year instead of going back to art school.' They were standing in the courtyard in the shadow of the winery, and his face was no more than a blur. After a moment he went on abruptly, ' Illalangi's going to be all but empty next year—Helen marrying, Pam coming to the Valley—she's to work in the office here instead of in Sydney, did she tell you?'

' No. But I can imagine she'd want to.'

' Yes. And I suppose it's only fair . . . So what I was about to say was that I might close Illalangi up. Gran can come up here to us.'

' And you won't need me,' thought Rae with a sense of shock. He didn't say it, but it surely must be what he meant.

' Well, we'll talk about that later. I brought you out here to show you my domain, not to talk about domestic affairs.'

Rae found it hard to give her whole mind to their sightseeing tour after that. It had lost some of its savour. He showed her the eerie cellars with their great oaken casks and racks of bottles; the winery with its presses and concrete fermenting vats and intricate cooling system; the office where Pam would work next year, the laboratory where he carried out various scientific tests on grape and wine; the bottling plant. Everywhere there was the lingering smell of wine until outside in the summer night again it was gone. Then, instead of going back to the house, they went over the lawns to a seat in a vine-wreathed arbour where they sat looking down towards the vineyards.

' It's beautiful,' said Rae softly after a full minute's
silence. Her eyes were full of tears. Was this her last
visit to Millunga? How soon after Christmas would
she have to go?

Mitch, unaware of her mood, said, ' Yes, these vineyards are my life. They're the earth—the mystery of
life and growth; and through them I gain a sense of
personal achievement in creating good wines. I'd be
happy here even if I didn't have the family firm behind
me. That's a burden I sometimes feel I could do without, to tell the truth. But I have a responsibility to
the family. Wealth, it may be fortunately, entails worry
and a lot of hard work.' He sighed and turned towards
her, and in the moonlight she could see the glint of his
eyes as he looked at her. She could see his mouth, its
hard line softened, and her heart seemed to melt within
her. His voice was softened too as he went on, ' There's
something else I want to say to you tonight, Rae. I want
to take back everything offensive I said to you before
you came to live at Illalangi. I think perhaps there
were some things that are pretty well unforgivable. Will
you try to forgive? And accept my apology?'

' Yes, of course. I was angry then—and rude too—
and I've since come to realize that you were only protecting your grandmother.'

' And myself,' said Mitch. He was smiling, his gaze
fixed on her face. ' A great many things have changed
since then. We understand each other a great deal better.
Do you agree?'

' Yes.'

' And have you been happy with us?'

' Yes,' said Rae again.

They looked at each other for a moment longer. For
some reason, Rae had the crazy idea that he was going
to kiss her, but he didn't. He sighed again and said, ' I

mustn't keep you up,' and then they were walking slowly
back to the house.

Joan came in to wish her grandmother a happy Christmas at breakfast time the following morning. She had
brought some of her drawings with her too, and perched
on the edge of the bed displaying them. She seemed
cheerful and not in the least moody and Rae stayed for
a little to see her work. She had several pen and ink
drawings, done on large sheets of board, and they were
very detailed and very intricate. They must have
occupied many hours of her time, Rae reflected, looking
fascinated at the insects, leaves, tendrils, roots, birds
interweaving and overlapping. She left them to talk
and went out to the verandah to strip off her bed. They
were going back to Illalangi tonight, for Mrs Gilcrist
always spent Boxing Day with Clara Livingstone.

While she was there, Joan came out and finding her
alone, asked instantly,

' Have you seen Connor?'

' No,' said Rae.

' I didn't think you would. He doesn't want to use
Gran—he's determined to play fair. We're not going to
see each other or communicate till the show opens, then
Con says Mitch will see once and for all that he has
something to offer, and isn't a drop-out. I'm trying to
think of it as a kind of game—otherwise I don't think I
could bear it. But Con says he's not going to be the
cause of a family bust-up—not unless the worst comes
to the worst.'

As Christine came out then, nothing more was said.
Rae was beginning to wonder how this affair would end.
Somehow she could not imagine Connor being taken to
the family bosom . . .

The whole family went to church a little later, even

Mrs Vance, who was feeling better after a good night's sleep. When they came back, Scott and Francis were there, gifts and greetings were exchanged, and Rae went to help set out the meal. She was not sure where she stood now. Mitch had sat next to her at church, and she was wearing the silver bracelet he had given her. It was very simple, very elegant, and teamed well with her sleeveless blue silk jersey. On the greeting card he had written, ' I hope you will wear this.' Rae couldn't feel it was strictly impersonal—perhaps because she wanted to think that it was not.

Dinner was a kind of elaborate picnic. It was set out in the courtyard in the shade of the vines on a long trestle table covered in a white damask cloth. It was a pleasant relaxed meal, everyone was affable, Christine and Pam seemed to have called a truce and sat one on either side of Francis enjoying his company, which he seemed agile enough to dispense without favouritism. Mitch, helping his grandmother to salad from a large wooden bowl, followed her fascinated gaze and found her watching the threesome. With a quirk of his mouth he murmured, ' Both of them at it! What must Francis think?'

' That two silly young girls are in love with him,' said Mrs Gilcrist crisply. ' I'm pleased to see Rae's not making a fool of herself. Aren't you, Mitchell?'

' I am indeed,' said Mitchell, meeting Rae's eyes with such a steady stare that she felt herself blushing, and thought that she could very easily make a complete and utter fool of herself.

When dinner was nearly over, Mitchell announced Scott's and Helen's engagement, and there was a fresh round of kisses and, this time, congratulations. Mrs Gilcrist told Scott, ' I hope you're not going to let that granddaughter of mine keep you waiting too long. Insist on a simple wedding without fuss. There's no point in these grand affairs that take months of preparation and have everyone exhausted before the great day arrives.'

'We're going to set a date some time in February,' said Scott. 'And I think Helen hopes to have the wedding here in the Valley.'

'Very nice,' approved the old lady, but Mitch said with raised eyebrows, 'February? Then the earlier the better, for we shan't be able to cope with vintage and a wedding at one and the same time. And you'll have to confer with Pam and Christine, Helen, I'm not going to have Aunt Valerie implicated.'

'Don't *fuss*, Mitch,' said Pam gaily. 'We girls can cope. When are you going to realize that we're not children any more?'

'I realize it now,' said Mitch a trifle grimly.

'Poor Mitch! Have we been such a trial to you?' asked Pam.

'Of course you have,' said their grandmother. 'And it's high time you all settled down or went abroad and left your brother some time for his own personal life.' She spoke sharply enough to sober them all a little, and there was a tiny silence. It was broken by Mrs Gilcrist announcing firmly, 'Now I'm going upstairs to rest, so that I at least shall be out of the way.'

The afternoon was far from peaceful. There was a steady stream of callers at Millunga—wine-growers, cattle men from the river flats, families from the horse studs further inland. Rae was kept constantly busy replenishing the supplies of savouries and cool drinks. Joan, wearing a wide-brimmed cotton hat, had gone off with her sketch pad, Christine and Pam were each intent upon seeing that the other was not left alone with Francis, Helen and Scott were wrapped up in each other. Mrs Vance was looking tired, her blue eyes ringed with fatigue and that left only Rae to help Mitch. Though she enjoyed being able to do this, she had not a single moment alone with him.

Late in the afternoon when she went upstairs to see if Mrs Gilcrist was ready to come down again, she thought ruefully, 'If he had wanted to see me alone, he'd have managed it. But he doesn't want to, and the sooner I accept the fact the better for me.'

Mrs Gilcrist was standing by her window looking out beyond the cellar roof to the vine-covered hillside. She turned as Rae came in and said, ' No, I'm afraid I can't do it.'

' Can't do what?'

' Hasn't Mitchell spoken to you about it yet? He has plans to transplant me here next year. I'm to be incarcerated in his vineyard; to leave my city haunts and my city friends and grow really and truly old in the Valley. Full circle. Back to my origins. But I shan't do it.' She gave Rae a sharp look. ' For another thing, I refuse to be used.'

' To be used?' repeated Rae, puzzled.

' Yes. Only too authoritarian and positive when it concerns others, he's over-cautious where his own feelings are concerned. Quite plainly—to my way of thinking—he wants to see *you* against the background of his vines.'

Rae was staring at her. ' You mean I would come to Millunga too? But I thought—I understood I wouldn't be wanted—'

' Oh, *you*'d be wanted,' said her employer acidly. ' I, on the other hand, would be no more than an excuse to have you here. Well, he will have to sort out his feelings for you some other way, for I am not prepared to live here.'

' His—feelings for me?' repeated Rae faintly.

' Yes. You're attracted to each other, aren't you?'
asked the old lady bluntly.

' There's been a better understanding between us,
but—'

' But he's not in a hurry to show his hand. Will you
be put out, my dear, if I don't fall in with his plans?
For I'm not going to, you know.'

' Of course I shan't be put out,' said Rae. She was
mad enough to wonder if Mrs Gilcrist were right—if
Mitch really was attracted to her—if he did want her to
come to Millunga. But she was clutching at straws, she
must steady down.

Mrs Gilcrist had left the window. ' It's time I dressed
and went downstairs . . . You like my grandson, don't
you, Rae?'

'.Yes,' said Rae, her grey eyes unwavering although
her cheeks were stained red.

' I thought as much. Well, you have my full approval.'

' But truly, Mrs Gilcrist,' said Rae, ' nothing's happened except that Mitchell's changed his initial opinion
of me, that's all.'

' If it is all, then he's a bigger fool than I think. And
it may be a very good thing if he finds he can't have you
here for consideration after all.'

They returned to Sydney that night as planned—
Helen, Mrs Gilcrist and Rae. They went in Scott's car
to Rae's disappointment, for she had been foolish
enough to hope that Mitch would drive them. She had
no idea whether Mrs Gilcrist was right or wrong about
his intentions for next year. He came out to the car
with the others to see them off, and told Rae only, ' I'll
be down to see you soon.' Which meant exactly nothing,
for of course he would have to see her if the household
at Illalangi were to be reorganized.

Rae felt restless and unsettled. She knew that she was

in love with Mitch and she was finding that it did not make her very happy. The best thing to do would be to forget him and concentrate on other things. It was a blessing that Mrs Gilcrist was such an active old lady, for that meant Rae was kept busy during the following days. One night after a particularly hot and hectic day during which she had driven her employer on a round of visits, Rae went out to the terrace for a breath of air. The old lady had gone to bed and was already asleep and Helen was not yet home. The night was warm and Rae wandered a little way down the garden hoping to catch a cooling sea breeze. She was startled suddenly to encounter a man coming up the path towards her.

It was Connor Birch.

He stopped within three feet of her and exclaimed in relief, ' It's you! I'm lucky. I didn't know whether to ring or write or call, and finally decided on the personal approach.'

' What do you want?' Rae asked. She felt herself stiffening.

' You sound hostile. I thought Joanie said you were amiably disposed. I want money, of course.'

' Are you behind with the rent again?' Rae asked cautiously. She didn't want to be used by Connor, and she didn't know whether she was amiably disposed to him or not. She wished very much that Joan had not put her in this position.

' I'm behind with everything,' he said.

Rae sighed. He was certainly a hopeless young man. No-one could blame Mitch for being so set against his association with Joan. She said flatly, ' Connor, why don't you get yourself a regular job? It takes money for one to live, and more for two.'

' D'you think I don't know that? But I'm an artist.'

' One grows a little tired of hearing you harping on

that string,' said Rae impatiently. 'What would you do if you couldn't come here for money?'

'Frankly, at this stage of the game, I don't know what I'd do.' He stood, arms folded, unmoving in the pathway. 'I've gone without sleep doing office cleaning at night and washing cars by day. My show's due to open shortly, I've pictures still to be framed and others not paid for. And of course there's the rent. And now my money's been stolen. I wouldn't have come here but for that. As things stand, it doesn't appeal to me to have to ask for help from Joan's family.'

'You're not asking for help from Joan's family,' Rae pointed out. 'You're asking me to deceive Joan's grandmother—to get money from her under false pretences. If you don't return it I'm the one who'll be embarrassed. I might even lose my job.'

'I wouldn't let that happen under any circumstances,' said Connor. 'But I've simply no one else to ask. I can only promise you that the money will be returned.'

'When your show is a big success?' Rae asked cynically, and saw his mouth tighten.

He said shortly, 'I haven't lost either of my jobs. I'll pay you what I earn as I earn it. How will that do? And before you sneer at my work, I suggest you take a look at it.'

'I should certainly like to do that before I hand over any money,' said Rae, feeling inwardly a little ashamed.

'How will tonight do? I have a couple of hours before I start work.'

'Very well,' said Rae, taken by surprise. 'Wait here for a minute while I fetch my handbag.'

Inside the house she gathered handbag and car keys, checked that Mrs Gilcrist was still sleeping, then went to Mrs McPhail's quarters to tell her she was going out. As she reached the front door it opened and Helen came in. Rae had only a second to wonder in dismay if she had seen Connor, for she said with a look of censure on her lovely face, ' I saw Connor Birch in the garden. He said he was waiting for you.'

' Yes,' said Rae inadequately.

Helen frowned. ' Mitch has forbidden us to have anything to do with him.'

' He hasn't forbidden me,' said Rae. ' I'm not one of his womenfolk.'

' And he's not to have any more money from my grandmother,' said Helen more sharply.

' I know that,' said Rae. Her face had whitened. ' Just don't worry, Helen . . . Goodnight.'

As she crossed the terrace she wondered if Helen would report this to Mitch. And she wondered too what construction he would put on it.

CHAPTER XI

Connor lived in a fifteen-foot-wide two-storey terrace house in Darlinghurst.

Rae left her car at the kerb and they climbed three worn stone steps to a door opening on to a balcony so narrow that it was almost on to the street. It was a stone house and had recently been scrubbed clean, so that, with the cast-iron lace on the narrow balconies, it had a certain charm. Rae saw a date set in the stone above the door —1862—as she followed Connor into a tiny hall from which stairs led to the upstairs flat—Connor's.

She glanced quickly about the room in which she found herself a minute later. It was a living room and contained a divan bed as well. It was sparely and frugally furnished, but the walls were fresh and white, and there was seagrass matting on the floor and several paintings had been hung. There was a bit of clutter—clothes and books, and on a small round table some unwashed dishes.

Connor said, ' I don't have much time for refinements. Joan used to tidy up and do a bit of cleaning now and again . . . I work in the front room—it's supposed to be the bedroom, but has the best light. As you see, we're a bit short on windows. Come through, will you?'

His paintings, as she stepped into the next room, surprised her. Shocked her almost. They were so huge— so extraordinary. Scenes and yet not scenes. People and yet not people. Somehow frightening, yet beautiful as well. One, in a vibrant greenish grey with streaks of black and white and here and there a spark of vermilion like blood, fascinated her. She couldn't keep her eyes away from it. Was it a terrible city? Was it a waste land strewn with the trunks and tortured branches of dead trees? Strewn with corpses? Rae didn't know. She was confounded. She looked about her helplessly and she had no idea whether Connor's paintings were magnificent or whether they were abortive attempts at magnificence.

She turned towards him, but he was not watching her. His strange greenish eyes were narrowed and he was staring at one of the unframed paintings. He didn't seem aware of her at all. She was reminded of that evening at Illalangi when he had looked through his curled fingers at the ocean as though nothing else mattered.

Suddenly she saw him differently. Here, in this room with its litter of paints and rags and brushes and pictures, with its bare paint-spattered wooden floor, Connor was at home. He was in his element. Rae knew with certainty that she would let him have what money he needed. There was no longer any doubt in her mind about that. She asked abruptly, ' Do you want cash?'

' What?' It took him a second to collect his senses. ' Oh, the money. Yes—cash, of course.'

' Tomorrow night? I don't think I can get away earlier.'

' Right. I'll come and collect it, shall I? It's the least I can do.'

' Very well. But I'd rather you didn't come to the house.' She took a pencil from a table that held jars of brushes and scribbled the address of her bungalow on the edge of a piece of paper. ' Tell me how much you want.'

He screwed up his puckish face and considered.

' I don't want to make it too difficult for you. Could you possibly explain fifty dollars? I might get by on that for a while.'

' But you need more,' said Rae shrewdly. ' How much was stolen?' She had not been sure before whether or not to believe that story, now for some reason she did.

'A hundred and thirty,' said Connor. 'And don't remind me there are such things as banks. I don't use them.'

Rae decided she would replace just as much as he had lost. That way, she wouldn't feel she was being soft. Of course, it could turn out that as an artist he counted for nothing, though Rae didn't think so. Her eye was drawn to another of those paintings. She thought, 'That would look well in the high-ceilinged sitting room at Millunga.' Which was odd, because everything at Millunga was so old. 'What are your prices, Connor? That, for instance—'

'That? I've put two hundred dollars on that one. They're give-away prices.' There was a gleam in his eye and she was not sure if he was serious or joking, and decided to make no comment. 'Want me to keep it for you?'

Rae said, 'Yes,' and left him to make what he could of that!

The following morning she had a letter from Mr Belrose regarding the sale of Tarmaroo. She had written to him earlier to say that she was prepared to sell, and now it appeared the sale was almost through. He had enclosed documents that required her signature, and drew her attention to the fact that Frank Warner wished to take possession as soon as possible. 'You have done a wise thing, Miss Lambert,' the solicitor wrote. 'I shall be glad to advise you at any time in the future on the investment of your capital, which will be, as you must appreciate, considerable. I should like to recommend that you get in touch with Mrs Stacy and make some arrangement with her as to the disposal of any personal property remaining in the homestead.'

Rae signed the papers and wondered vaguely what she would do with all that money when she had it. She would certainly need someone to advise her! Later in the morning when she was out with Mrs Gilcrist, she posted her letter and went to the bank where she withdrew the money for Connor.

Connor was not at the bungalow when she arrived there some time after dinner. Rae thought she had better ring Mrs Stacy, then decided to wait until Connor had been and gone. She sat out on the verandah with the intention of thinking about her business affairs, but very soon found she was thinking of Mitch instead. She longed to see him again, longed to know if he wanted her at Millunga or not; and whether he would give in to his grandmother and allow her to stay on at Illalangi. She reflected that some time she might have to tell him the truth about herself, though she wanted to delay that for as long as possible. She hardly dared to contemplate the fact that she might soon no longer be needed by the Gilcrists, or to wonder what she would do in that case. What was there to do when you were alone in the world?

Connor came then, and she got up and went into the house with him and gave him the envelope containing the hundred and thirty dollars.

' Did you have any trouble about this? Believe it or not, but I feel bad about making things awkward for you—'

' Don't worry.' She hesitated. ' As a matter of fact, I didn't go to Mrs Gilcrist. I happen to have some money in the bank myself and I thought it would be better all round if I used that.'

' Oh, lord!' Connor actually appeared embarrassed. ' Are you sure you can spare it?'

' Quite sure . . . Have you time for some coffee or must you go?'

'What's the time?'

She told him and he said, 'I'd better not wait. I can't afford to get the sack. If you're in touch with Joan, send her my love, will you?'

'Yes,' said Rae. She asked curiously, 'You're very serious about Joan, aren't you?'

'Yes. I mean to marry her. I'd rather it was with her family's approval, but if it's not it can't be helped. It's my bad luck they're so stinking rich and suspicious. I'd far rather she were an ordinary sort of working girl like yourself. I'm not interested in money.'

Rae thought he genuinely meant it. She said impulsively, 'I wish you luck, Connor.'

'Thank you. But you're still not quite sure about me, are you—in any way?' He didn't wait for her to answer, but went on, 'Look, that painting you asked about—I'd like you to have that. Not instead of the money I owe you, but in addition to it.'

Rae shook her head, smiling. 'I'll buy it.'

'You're crazy,' he said. 'But—a friend?'

'Yes,' said Rae. She thought of Mitch. What would he make of this conversation? Undoubtedly he would think she was crazy too. She didn't think she would find it as easy to persuade him that Connor was a good fellow as it had been to reconcile him to the idea of Scott as a brother-in-law!

'You'll come to the show, won't you?' asked Connor. 'I'll get the gallery to send you an invitation. I'll see you there.'

'Thank you.' She put out her hand and he took it, then pulled her towards him and kissed her.

'I like you, Rae. You can come to our wedding.'

Her hand was still in his and she looked up at him and laughed. 'I might do that. Provided you get your hair cut for the occasion.'

' Well, I shan't. I'm afraid I can't see that it matters.'

Rae sighed. ' Of course it doesn't. But most of us are so used to certain conventions—when they're broken, even if they are senseless, pointless—it makes a barrier.'

' You mean between me and Joan's brother, for instance?'

' Yes, I do mean that.'

' I'm not going to change to please him. I am as I am, and he can take it or leave it. He strikes me as being a little too dictatorial.'

' He is as he is too, and he's not going to change for you!'

' I suppose not. Well, he can go to hell if he can't be reasonable. Joanie and I don't need him.'

' *You* don't need him. But he's Joan's brother, and he's looked after her for a long time. He's only trying to protect her when you think he's being dictatorial.'

Connor looked at her thoughtfully. ' Are you by any chance in love with him? Heaven help you if you are! And while you're running me down, you might remember that I've made one concession to try to appease him. It's not because I *want* it that Joan and I are separated now. Well, I must go. See you at the show. Goodnight.'

She watched him go, thinking that he had his good points, then came inside and went to the telephone.

She could not get through to Tarmaroo. There was a delay on the line. She said she would wait and went back to the verandah to sit in the dark thinking about Connor and Joan. She knew more about Connor now and was inclined to think that he and Joan would suit one another very well. But Mitch would not see it that way. He would not think Connor good enough for his little sister, and Rae doubted whether he would give his consent to their marriage. In which case she thought ruefully they were probably unconventional enough to do without it. Her thoughts had drifted to Mitch and the vague and unsatisfactory state of their relationship. She for one was not content that it should stay the way it was. Alternate waves of hope and despair washed over her, and she was in the midst of a daydream in which everything had come right when the telephone rang.

She went in and answered it and in another minute was through to Tarmaroo Station and talking to Mrs Stacy. She told her that she had signed the papers for the transfer of the property and that Frank Warner wanted to take over as soon as possible.

' Well, that's fine, but you sound anxious, Irène,' said Mrs Stacy. ' What's worrying you? You've done the right thing—you were never really happy out here, were you—not like me.'

' I am a little worried. About you,' said Rae.

' Then you needn't be. I've talked to Frank Warner. He and his wife want me to stay on. They're nice people and I'll be very happy to work for them. One thing though—I wish you'd come home for a few days and go through the house with me. The Warners will have a lot of furniture of their own and there are things here— family things—that should be given some thought.'

' I'll see what I can arrange and let you know,' Rae assured her, and when Mrs Stacy asked ' How are you making out now, Irène?' she answered brightly that everything was fine.

' Why don't you give up that job and take a trip? I dare say there are people back in England you'd like to see again.'

' It's a thought,' said Rae.

' Unless,' said Mrs Stacey, ' you have other plans?' She waited and then added, ' Marriage-wise.'

' I don't think so,' said Rae. The pips sounded. ' I'll

let you know what I can fix about coming up. Goodbye for now, Mrs Stacy.'

She put the receiver back on its cradle, closed up the bungalow and drove up the hill. Scott's house was in darkness when she left her car there and walked on up to Illalangi, enjoying the cool night air. Up at the top of the hill she could see the outline of Illalangi with its tall dark trees behind it, and she thought that she had been happy there. Not the least contributing factor had been Mitchell, and Rae was inclined to think that even in the first stormy days of their relationship she must have been attracted to him. She had certainly never been indifferent to him!

He was still in her mind as she climbed through the garden and came out upon the terrace, and it was like a continuation of her thoughts when he rose from a chair and stood waiting for her.

' Mitchell!' she exclaimed, her pulses racing, her heart filled with sudden delight.

' Miss Lambert,' he said unsmilingly, ' I want to talk to you.'

Miss Lambert! Rae felt as if icy water had been dashed in her face.

' Sit down.' He indicated a chair and, struck into silence, Rae took it. A single lamp burning in the sitting room cast a soft light on the far end of the terrace, and she could see his face only indistinctly, but she knew that it was grim and unsmiling.

He said, ' I've been waiting for you. You've been a long time.'

' I've been at the bungalow,' said Rae.

' I know that. I wanted to talk to you and thought I might find you there.' His voice was harsh. ' Sure enough I did. But you had a visitor.'

' Yes,' said Rae. ' It was Connor Birch.' He made

her feel like a disobedient teenager and automatically she reacted with forthrightness.

' You appeared to be on very friendly terms with my sister's erstwhile admirer.'

' What do you mean?'

' Simply that I saw him embracing you. Anyone could have seen it from the road. If I'd thought you were an unwilling victim I'd have gone to your assistance, but obviously you were more than amenable.'

Rae thought for a moment. She didn't see why she should allow a false construction to be put on that kiss. She said carefully, ' You're mistaken in what you think.'

' Am I? I haven't yet told you what I do think. And that is that Connor Birch is trying to get at my grandmother through you.'

' That, as it happens, is absurd,' began Rae, but he interrupted her.

' I haven't finished. You're a very pretty girl, you have a great deal of charm and a very persuasive tongue —as I know from personal experience. But those things are of secondary importance to a man like Connor Birch. The main thing is that you're a possible means of tapping a nice source of money.'

' You must think me very stupid indeed,' said Rae, nettled. ' I have my eyes wide open and I know exactly what I'm doing.'

' I'm afraid I do think you stupid,' he said coldly. ' I've been sitting here waiting for you for a good hour and a half. It amazes me, though perhaps it shouldn't, that you should be so indiscreet.'

Rae stood up. ' What are you implying?'

Mitch stood up too. ' You know well enough what I'm implying. And this time you needn't try to explain it away with some plausible story about being down at the coffee bar or with a crowd of people somewhere or other.'

' I'm not obliged to make any explanation at all,' said Rae, furious and shaken. ' My personal life is my own, and what I do or don't do with it is my concern entirely.'

' We'll extend that statement.' Mitch was icily cold. ' As from now, your entire life is your own. In plain words, your employment by my grandmother is terminated. You haven't approached her for money yet —I checked that when Helen told me you'd been fraternizing with Birch. And I'm going to see you have no further opportunity to do so in future.'

They were standing facing each other, and Rae was breathing quickly. She felt she hated him—and didn't care if she never saw him again.

' How dare you suggest I'd take money from Mrs Gilcrist! Any money Connor Birch happens to need I'll lend him myself!'

'Don't tell me that the son of your former employer left you a bank account as well as a bungalow and a car,' Mitch said hatefully.

Rae stared at him. It was on the tip of her tongue to tell him the truth, but why should she? She turned away and made for the door, and his hand shot out and seized her roughly by the wrist and she was swung back to face him. At his touch the fight and fire went out of her. She loved him. She might hate him now, but she loved him as well. He was hot-tempered, hasty, unjust —and she was insane enough to adore him.

She said in a low voice, ' I'd like to stay. For a little while. Till you've cooled down and will listen to reason.'

Mitch let go of her wrist abruptly.

' Listen to reason? No—I've had enough of you and your wiles. It was a mistake in the first place to let you come here—a girl we knew nothing about. I'll take my grandmother to Millunga as soon as I can arrange it. You can pack your things and go tomorrow.'

'But—but what have I done?' stammered Rae, shaken and upset.

'What have you done?' He actually sounded incredulous. 'You can ask me that after your extraordinary behaviour of tonight? You know perfectly well what I think of Connor Birch, yet the moment my back is turned you're sneaking off to meet him. Not only tonight—but last night, and on goodness knows how many other occasions. You can have no part in my life, and I should have realized it long ago. You're what is called a stirrer. I'll simply tell my grandmother that you're going. I'll leave it to you to explain why. I'm sure you'll be able to think up some story that will save your face.'

Rae felt too stunned to answer. She wanted to weep and she wished with all her heart that she could hate Mitch simply and completely without the added complication of loving him as well. As she turned from him and went into the house she held her head high so that the tears would not spill over.

CHAPTER XII

' Mitchell tells me you have to leave us,' said Mrs Gilcrist over breakfast the following morning. He had come in earlier on to see her before he went back to the Valley, and Rae had left them together while he broke the news. He had had nothing to say to Rae. He had given her a long unreadable look from his blue eyes before she left the room, but he had not even answered her ' Good morning.'

And now Rae thought Mrs Gilcrist seemed singularly unperturbed. She was enjoying her breakfast and instead of taking an interest in the morning paper she was now prepared to discuss the new turn events had taken.

Her old eyes watched Rae shrewdly as she asked, ' What is it, Rae? The old life calling you back? I found Mitchell singularly uncommunicative and moody.'

Rae had not thought of any way to explain her sudden departure. She was not as adept as Mitch seemed to imagine at fabricating lies.

She said uncertainly, ' No, it's not the old life calling me back, though I may return to Tarmaroo for a while. It's being sold, as you know, and I'm sure Mrs Stacy could do with some help in turning the homestead out.'

' Then exactly why are you leaving me?'

Rae made a hopeless gesture and turned away, for tears were close. ' There's—there's no future for me here,' she began, but could say no more.

Mrs Gilcrist considered this. ' Was it your idea or my grandson's that you should go?' she asked bluntly.

' Mitchell's,' Rae answered, her voice low.

' And I thought you and he were getting on so well

together!'

'I thought so too,' said Rae. 'But—but after all, he didn't want me to come in the first place . . . I'm sorry. I hope you'll find someone else.' Her voice was husky.

'Of course I shall. You needn't worry about me. I certainly never imagined you'd stay for ever. I shall be agreeable about being bundled off to Millunga for a week or two, but I shan't stay any longer than I can help. And I really think, my dear, that on the whole this change may be for the best. You may be upset just now, but a positive step—even in the wrong direction—can solve a lot of problems.'

It hardly made sense to Rae. And she knew that for her this change was not going to be easy. She had got over Ralph in record time, but this was different. She thought it would take her a lifetime to get over Mitch.

She packed for Mrs Gilcrist during the morning, for Helen had been deputed to drive her to the Valley in the afternoon and to return the following day.

'I don't care what you pack,' said Mrs Gilcrist. 'Don't bother consulting me—I'm not greatly interested. There's nothing much for an old woman like me to do up there but sit and watch the grapes ripen. This is my home and my friends are here, and I'll come back just as soon as ever I can.'

She sat down in the shade on the terrace writing letters while Rae did her packing. Helen came in, her eyes curious, and Rae wondered what Mitch had told her. Helen didn't volunteer any information and Rae didn't ask for it. She didn't think Helen cared greatly that she was going; there had never been the camaraderie or the sense of equality between them that there had been between Rae and Pam—or even, to some extent, between Rae and Joan. Helen was Rae's least favourite among Mitch's three sisters.

Helen watched her folding clothes and wrapping shoes for some minutes and presently said, 'Don't make too arduous a task of it. We'll be able to fetch anything extra Gran needs.' Then after another pause, 'What an upheaval! Oh well, it always seems to happen when Gran's companions leave.' Rae fancied there was a faint note of satisfaction in her tone and suspected she might have touched up her tale of Rae and Connor.

Before she left for Millunga, Mrs Gilcrist made Rae a gift. It was a pearl and ruby pendant on a fine gold chain, and Rae knew that it was old and probably valuable and that it should have been given to one of the girls. She looked at the old lady wordlessly. She was deeply touched.

'I don't think you'd have much use for a cheque, my dear, but I want you to have this. It belonged to my mother. Now don't open your mouth to thank me, for I can see that if you do you'll burst into tears, and we must avoid that.' She patted Rae's cheek, and they went down to the hall where Helen was waiting. There the old lady turned to Rae again.

'What will you do when your work at Tarmaroo is finished?'

Rae managed a smile. 'Something will turn up.'

'I'm sure it will, my dear. Now kiss me goodbye, and believe me when I say I most sincerely hope we haven't seen the last of you.'

'Thank you,' said Rae. Her eyes filled with tears. 'I've loved it here, and want to thank you too.'

'For what? For being a demanding, selfish, egotistical old woman who never gave you time to lead a life of your own?'

Rae shook her head, and kissed the old cheek she was offered.

When they had gone she stood in the empty silent hall

and asked herself if this could really be happening. Her whole world so suddenly crumbling away. Mrs McPhail had said, ' Oh, I knew this was in the air—the house to be closed up, the family centre shifted to Millunga. I just didn't expect it so soon—not till after the wedding. Well, I shall be surprised if the old lady's not back before the month's out. I'm not going to bother my head about finding another position yet.'

It was all very well for Mrs McPhail, but it was different for Rae. She had been given her marching orders. By Mitch.

She went upstairs and packed her things. She wouldn't stay here tonight. She would go to the bungalow where she could weep if she wanted to. She would let Mrs Stacy know she was coming and she would set off very early in the morning. By late tomorrow night she would be back at Tarmaroo Station.

When she walked down for her car, Scott was not yet back from the city. Rae drove to Illalangi for her luggage, and then on to the bungalow. Politeness demanded that she should see Scott before she left, to thank him for garaging her car, and apart from politeness she wanted to say goodbye to him. She liked Scott—rather more than she liked the girl he was going to marry— and she hoped he would be home that night. He was, and he was surprised to see Rae when he came to the door.

' Why, hello ! I was just about to go up to see Helen.'

' Helen had to go to Millunga. May I come in ?'

' By all means,' said Scott, looking rather mystified. He took her through to the small garden by the swimming pool, saw her seated and went to fetch drinks. When he came back he asked her at once, ' Now tell me what's happened. For I know from your face that something's afoot. And you've been crying.'

'Only a little,' said Rae, trying to smile. 'It's nothing dreadful. Just that Mitch had Helen take Mrs Gilcrist to Millunga and I've been told to leave.'

Scott's eyebrows shot up. 'Good lord! Why? Isn't the old lady happy with you?'

'Mitchell asked me to go. He's—he's had enough of me. He thinks I'm too interfering and he suspects my morals.'

'*Your* morals? Why, that's damned ridiculous! Surely you can straighten it out?'

'It appears not. *You* should know, Scott, how difficult it is to budge him once Mitch has made up his mind about something.'

'Well, yes. But I had the impression you had some influence with him. And when it comes to morals, what on earth does he imagine you've been up to?'

'I'd really rather not talk about it. I came in to say goodbye and thank you.'

'You mean to say you're giving in—just like that? That's not like you, Rae. Why not stay and fight it out?'

'There'd be no point.' There were those tears again, and she shook them away determinedly.

Scott said slowly, 'Are you a little in love with Mitch? Is that the trouble? I've never met the woman yet who could get past that barrier Mitch puts up—as if he were some sort of heathen untouchable god.'

Rae laughed a little. 'Scott, what an image!'

'It's not a bad one though.' His eyes narrowed. 'I suppose he suspects your motives too. Why don't you tell him who you are, Rae? He might look at things differently then.'

'No,' said Rae definitely. 'At any rate, my being in love with him has nothing to do with it. He doesn't know anything about that. Just take my word for it,

Scott, that I have to go,' she finished forlornly.

' Very well,' he agreed reluctantly. ' What do you plan to do?'

' Tarmaroo is being sold. I'll go there for a while and help Mrs Stacy get the homestead ready. Then— I don't know—perhaps I'll take a trip to Japan or Indonesia.'

' I'm sorry you're going,' said Scott. ' Maybe when Helen and I are married you'll come and stay with us.'

Rae laughed, and he laughed too, but a little awkwardly. Even he knew that Helen would hardly take kindly to such a suggestion!

Late the following night, Rae was back at Tarmaroo; back on the red, never-ending plains of the west; sleeping on the verandah as she had done for two springs and two summers of her life, but too tired to lie awake and watch the moonlight move across the garden and on to her bed.

It was a hot summer. Every day the temperature soared above the century mark. Rae and Mrs Stacy started work early, then later in the morning sat on the verandah on the coolest side of the house, drinking iced tea and lemon and talking. Rae, trying not to think of herself and her unhappiness, caught up on all the local gossip. Ralph Stevens was engaged again—already! —to a girl whose father grew cotton. His sister Peggy had gone over to the coast where Mrs Stacy believed she was helping run a motel at Surfers' Paradise. Elspeth Jamieson had been to Sydney and come back with a rumour that Irène Lambert was going to marry someone in the wine industry. Mrs Stacy looked at Rae questioningly and waited.

' Not true,' said Rae lightly, though her heart ached. ' I can't think where she got such an idea.' She remem-

bered the party at the Menzies that she—and Mitch—
hadn't joined, and he began to wonder if Mrs Jamieson
had caught a glimpse of her after all; or if she and Mrs
Gilcrist had put their heads together and come up with
the right answer, that Rae Lambert was Irène Lambert.
Was it possible that Mrs Gilcrist had known the truth
for some time and had played the innocent? Rae
thought it was not beyond her. But she hoped she
would not tell Mitch. She didn't want him to know,
and for it to make a difference in the way he felt about
her. And then—could it have been with Mrs Gilcrist
that the rumour Mrs Jamieson had brought home had
originated? It all seemed very odd to Rae. She could
not fathom it.

Late in the afternoons, Rae and Mrs Stacy returned
to their clearing and sorting. There were old family
things like silver and china ware—a tea service that had
been brought out from Scotland by the Steeles long ago.
There were paintings, old books, letters. All these Mrs
Stacy said Rae must keep. There were two chairs, a
hall bench and a sideboard made of cedar by some
pioneering member of the Steele family well over a
hundred years ago. They would have to get the packers
in and send them away to be stored.

'Then when you think of marrying, Irène,' said Mrs
Stacy, 'you'll be glad of them.'

It was odd to think these things belonged to her family.
Rae had never thought of them that way before. Now,
perhaps because she had no family—had no one—she
did think that way, and it was an odd sort of a comfort
to her.

One morning Rae read in a Sydney paper which was
two days old a review of Connor Birch's exhibition. His
work was highly praised, and the critic ventured to
suggest that the name of Connor Birch was one that

would rank with those of Arthur Boyd and Sydney Nolan
in the not too distant future. A final note added that he
had been awarded a scholarship recently that would take
him to Europe for two years.

Rae was pleased and excited. She could not resist
telling Mrs Stacy that Connor was a close friend of Joan
Gilcrist's.

' You've never said much about these Gilcrists, Irène.
Of course I know they're the wine people, but that's
about all. So you can excuse me if I thought there might
be something in what Elspeth Jamieson said.'

' There's not,' said Rae firmly. She couldn't talk
about Mitch. She was almost frightened even to think
about him, it could cause her to lose a night's sleep
any time. And now, though she would have liked to
write to Joan, she knew it was wiser not to. She had
heard nothing from any of the Gilcrists, and she was
foolish enough to feel a little hurt. She had thought at
least that Mrs Gilcrist might write . . .

That night, after their evening meal, she and Mrs
Stacy went back to work. The Warners wanted to move
in in a few days, and Rae was anxious to have everything
settled. Frank Warner had written to say she was
welcome to stay on as a guest as long as it suited her,
but Rae didn't want to drag things out. She must make
a definite move. She had already written to a travel
agency and received enticing brochures on travel in
South-East Asia.

Shortly after nine o'clock Rae went on to the front
verandah and leaned on the rail to watch the moon come
up over the plains and make long dark shadows on
earth that was red in the daytime and became a
mysterious blue by moonlight. At the near end of the
home paddock was a group of big gum-trees, their long
silvery grey leaves glittering in the moonlight, their great

smooth trunks mottled as though splashed with paint. There was a frenzied rustling there, and Rae went swiftly and silently across the lawn by the orange trees to see if it was a brush-tailed possum, maybe even the very possum she used to feed last year. She stood in the shadow of the trees staring up and was reminded irresistibly of that night when she had ridden over to Greentrees and heard a conversation that had made her flee to Sydney and to a happiness that had not lasted.

A night for possums. Moonlight. The air as soft to-night as it had been then, in early spring. Rae sighed and found she was staring into the eyes of the inquisitive possum that had come down to see what she had, and was now scrutinizing her. She reached out a hand to-wards him and in a flash he had turned and scrambled back to the safety of a higher branch. Rae smiled and began to walk back to the homestead, meaning to fetch some bread or a piece of fruit to try to tempt him to make friends. She had nearly reached the house when the headlights of a car swept across the lawn. Rae turned around, wondering who it was coming to Tarmaroo at this time of night.

The man who climbed out of the car presently and came swiftly towards her was Mitch!

Her mind for a moment was blank with shock and disbelief. It was all she could do not to run to him and cry out his name.

She did say his name, but she said it so calmly she could hardly believe it was her own voice.

' Mitch! '

' Rae! ' He came forward and stood looking down at her. She was conscious of her limp cotton frock, the strands of hair that had fallen loose from the knot she had made high on her head for coolness, of her dusty hands. ' Are you free? Can we talk? '

'Yes. We've been clearing up. I was having a breather,' said Rae. She led him on to the verandah. Her heart had begun to beat wildly. He had called her 'Rae' and the ice had gone out of his voice.

There were chairs, but they stood and looked at each other in the semi-darkness.

'You know why I've come, of course,' he said finally. Rae shook her head. She was taking no chances.

'No? Then I must tell you . . . First, to ask your forgiveness—for all I said, for all I implied. For treating you so badly. For being jealous and ungenerous and distrustful. For hurting us both.'

Rae could only shake her head slowly, conscious of tears behind her eyes.

'You wanted to wait until I'd cooled down and would listen to reason, and I refused. I've never done things that way. I've been a law unto myself. It's late to apologize, but—' He spread his hands. Rae couldn't take her eyes from his face. She loved the very sound of his voice, the knowledge that his eyes were on her, that he was actually standing here, near her, in the summer night. For this moment she was utterly and completely happy.

'Am I forgiven?'

'Of course. For everything—for everything.' She almost sighed it. 'Mitch, how did you know where to find me?'

'My grandmother told me.' He put a hand in his pocket. 'I have something here for you from Connor Birch—some money you lent him. He wanted to know where to find you too, and I was ready to knock his head off. But the story he told me was convincing—and that young sister of mine, Joan, was at the back of it all, as I might have guessed.' He smiled slightly. 'Gran took the opportunity to tell me a few home truths about myself as well as several things about you. And here I am.'

'Several things about me?' A little chill came into Rae's heart. There was one thing she'd rather he didn't know yet. Had Mrs Gilcrist told him that?—and had it influenced him to come here, knowing she was not just a nobody?

'Yes, several things,' he repeated. 'A certain Mrs Jamieson told her all the things we didn't know about you, and some of which we might have guessed. How good you'd been to the old lady here, the high regard in which you were held in this district. The rather mysterious ending to your engagement to a neighbouring property manager.' He paused for a second. 'I want to know about that.'

Rae hesitated. 'Not just now, Mitch—please.' She was still not certain how much he knew. He had said 'the old lady here'—not 'your grandmother' . . .

'Just one thing, then,' Mitch conceded. 'Is it over? You haven't—picked up the threads again?'

'Definitely not,' said Rae. 'Didn't Mrs Gilcrist tell you why I came to Tarmaroo?' she prompted.

'Yes. The place has been sold and you're helping the housekeeper put it in order.' He touched her disordered hair. 'I can see you're being kept busy—even at night!'

'Yes. It's cooler working at night,' said Rae gaily. She almost laughed with pleasure. He *didn't* know! She would tell him later, but not yet.

Mitch took her gently by the shoulders and pulled her a little towards him. 'The other reason why I came here was to ask you to marry me. I love you, Rae —too much for my peace of mind.'

Rae had been holding her breath. Now she let it out slowly. Very softly, at the back of her mind, she could hear the words of the old ballad—' '' He does not love me for my birth, Nor for my lands so broad and fair.

He loves me for my own true worth, And that is well,"
said Lady Claire.'

Mitch had drawn her gently against him and they
stood there, half in moonlight, half in shadow.

'Will you marry me, Rae?'

'Yes, Mitch. Oh—yes!'

She raised her face and he held her close and kissed
her. Then at last he put her away and looked down at
her smilingly. 'How long must you stay here, Rae? I
suppose being you, you'll insist on finishing what you've
contracted to do.'

'It needn't be long,' said Rae. 'Now tell me about
Joan and Connor, Mitch. I saw the review of his
exhibition—and that he had won a scholarship. You
must know now that he has a future as an artist—that
he's not just a drop-out. And he loves Joan—I'm
absolutely certain of it.'

'All right,' said Mitch dryly. 'I acknowledge that
he appears to have a great deal of promise, and perhaps
he loves Joan.'

'He does. I know it.'

'Well, we shall see . . . At least I tuned him up. He
earned that money to pay you back, Rae—by the sweat
of his brow. There's some good in him, I suppose. And
Joan has informed me that she's going to marry him
with or without my consent. She's a very stubborn
girl.'

Rae laughed. 'Of course you'll give it! I think you
should.'

'Then I suppose I must—as *you* are in favour of it.
But I'm damned if she's going to get her money yet.
She can wait for that.'

'Mitch! Not till she's thirty?'

'Why not?' He sounded as stubborn as he claimed
his sister to be, but Rae had an idea he might relent long

before Joan turned thirty. 'One other thing,' she said quickly, as he reached for her again. 'Pam and Francis—?'

'And Christine,' said Mitch ruefully. 'It's still a threesome there. I can't provide a happy ending to *all* the love stories, and to tell the truth I have no idea which way the cat's going to jump in that triangle. I intend to keep well out of it. Pam can continue to work at Millunga, but the rest is up to them.'

'Yes, of course. And Mrs Gilcrist?'

'Oh, Gran's become too sophisticated for country life. It's back to Illalangi for her, and another new companion.'

'Middle-aged?'

He grinned. 'What do you think?' He kissed her then, and they had barely drawn apart when Mrs Stacy came on to the verandah.

'Oh, excuse me, I thought it would be Mr and Mrs Warner.'

'This is Mr Mitchell Gilcrist,' Rae said. 'Mrs Stacy, Mitch.'

Mrs Stacy, Rae knew, was immediately burning with curiosity, but she contained herself and said what she had come out to say. 'I found two copper candlesticks in that old box of junk in the sewing room, Irène. They'd have belonged to your great-grandmother, I should imagine, and I think you ought to keep them. They should polish up beautifully.'

Rae glanced at Mitchell, who was staring at the housekeeper in some bewilderment.

'I'm sure they will, Mrs Stacy.'

'And your Uncle Jack's rock crystal inkstand. He put that away years ago, and it somehow got into that junkheap. He used to prize that, and would want you to have it.' She looked at Mitchell. 'They're only little things, but they have a sentimental value. And they're family.'

'Yes indeed,' agreed Mitchell smoothly. 'I'll come out with—*Irène*—in a moment to inspect them.'

Mrs Stacy, who was no fool, took this for a tactful dismissal and went back into the house. Mitch turned to Rae and put his two hands around her waist.

'So besides everything else, you're an heiress, are you?' he asked wryly. 'It will take me some time to digest *that*.'

He took her in his arms again, and everything looked very beautiful to Rae—the red sandy plains that were blue in the moonlight, the great flat paddocks, the old gum-trees whose leaves were shaken by the possums. But she was glad she was leaving it all—to go with Mitch to the rolling hills and the old two-storied house and the green, green vineyards of Millunga.